# SAVAGE KISS

"It's me."

The voice made Samantha jump. Hawk slipped out of the shadows, moving as silently as his namesake.

"You just about scared the very life out of me."

"Sorry. I didn't mean to."

Samantha watched as he approached. He moved, she thought, like a night predator, at home in the shadows. "My heart's pounding," she said, giving him a cross look as he moved even closer. "I can hardly catch my breath."

His stark facial features became even more pronounced in the moonlight. He was, she decided then, much more beautiful than he had any right to be.

Hawk stood close, raising his hands to rest lightly upon her shoulders. "Scaring a beautiful woman seems an entirely inappropriate way of making her heart race and leaving her breathless."

Hawk raised his right hand to lightly cup Samantha's face in his palm. Tenderly, he pressed the pad of his thumb back and forth over her lips. "Have you ever been . . . breathless before, Samantha?" he asked, his eyes as dark as midnight, shiny as diamonds boring into hers. "I'm inclined to think not, though I couldn't really say with any certainty. At least, not until I've kissed you . . ."

Books by Robin Gideon

SHADOW PASSION
OUTLAW ECSTASY
PASSION'S TENDER EMBRACE
ECSTASY'S PRINCESS
PIRATE'S PASSIONATE SLAVE
WILD CARESS
ROYAL ECSTASY
VIKING ECSTASY
PASSION'S BANDIT
CHEYENNE DESIRE
ROYAL RAPTURE

Published by Zebra Books

# LOVING SAMANTHA

# ROBIN GIDEON

**ZEBRA BOOKS**
**KENSINGTON PUBLISHING CORP.**

*To Jennifewr and Hannah;*

*and to Don Pendleton,*
*friend and mentor.*
—R. G.

ZEBRA BOOKS are published by

Kensington Publishing Corp.
850 Third Avenue
New York, NY 10022

First Printing: April, 1996
10 9 8 7 6 5 4 3 2 1

Printed in the United States of America

# One

Samantha Sanders looked at the three dead men, an overwhelming sense of relief sweeping over her. They were dead, thank God; they could no longer touch her, could no longer hurt her, could no longer force her to bend to their will.

The nightmare had lasted not much more than a minute. Samantha had been returning through the Badlands after looking at some prize horses her brother was considering buying when three Indians appeared out of nowhere. They'd said nothing when they'd blocked her path. Samantha had smiled, her internal warning signals not yet registering danger. Then the Indians attacked, swiftly and silently, pulling her from her horse, tearing at her clothes—her familiar cotton man-cut shirt and new Levi's. With the buttons of her shirt popping off when the men attacked, she fought and screamed, managing to kick one of her attackers in the groin so hard that he fell to his knees and abandoned his assault upon her.

But the other two hadn't. Grim-faced, as silent as death itself, they'd moved in relentlessly, separating Samantha from her horse, making sure she had no avenue of escape.

Suddenly her rescuers rode in, guns blazing. And though both cowboys were badly in need of shaves, baths, and a clean change of clothes, they seemed heaven-sent to Samantha. They swiftly and surely cut her attackers down with a barrage of gunfire as deadly as it was quick.

"Thank y-you," Samantha stammered, getting to her feet.

She pulled her shirt closed, covering her chemise, badly torn during the assault.

If Samantha's warning signals had been slow initially, they intensified when her "heroes" dismounted. The nearest one— the one who had wielded the shotgun with lethal efficiency and great pleasure against her Indian attackers—grinned wide to show stained, rotting, and missing teeth. He spit a long stream of tobacco juice into the ground in the general direction of the corpses. Then, with his free hand, he rubbed his crotch as he walked slowly toward Samantha, his eyes devouring her as a wolf's eyes might devour a young fawn moments before he moves in for the kill.

"Killin' redskins is what I do second best in the whole world," the man said with a twisted glint in his eyes. "An' 'cause I'm such a nice fella, I'm gonna show you what I do best."

Samantha stepped backward, nearly stumbling, unable to believe at first that the men who had saved her were no better than those who had first attacked her. And perhaps, judging from the filthy appearance of these two white men, they were even worse!

"D-don't do this," Samantha said, the breathy rush of words little more than a whisper, hating the weakness her voice betrayed.

The man chuckled, then spit another stream of tobacco juice into the ground. "You're not being very social, 'specially after what me an' my partner here jus' saved you from."

Samantha turned her attention away from the leader. The other man was grinning, hungrily assessing her as he moved to the side. All Samantha had to do was look into the man's eyes to know that he would obey any orders given to him. Samantha would find no sympathy in his heart.

"Make it easy on yerself," the leader said, slowly walking forward, still fondling himself. "It ain't a matter of *if* we're gonna do it, only on how mad you make me 'fore we start."

The sound of pounding hooves made all three turn to see a tall, lean Indian riding through the trees into the clearing. The

Indian leaped from his horse at a gallop, lunging for the man closest to Samantha, moving with astonishing speed and precision, not giving the man time to raise his shotgun. Together they went spinning and tumbling to the ground.

Samantha watched the Indian react like an agile, powerful mountain lion. After knocking the white man to the ground he moved quickly to his knees. Samantha trembled, awestruck with what she saw, as the Indian drew a revolver from the holster at his hip and fired with speed and deadly accuracy.

The shotgun-wielding white man, the first to demand Samantha's sexual favors, had recovered and was raising his weapon to cut the Indian down.

"Look out!" Samantha shouted instinctively, lunging at the shotgun and knocking it aside a second before it roared with a lethal charge of buckshot.

Samantha fell facedown in the grass at the crack of a firearm a moment after the shotgun blast. She heard the startled gasp of the white man but felt no sympathy for him at all as she looked up to see him fall heavily to the ground.

"Was it just those two?" the Indian asked, the revolver still in his big right hand.

Samantha got quickly to her feet, clutching at her chemise and shirt to pull it even more tightly around her. She looked at the Indian suspiciously, unwilling to trust any man after what had happened to her during the past ten minutes.

"Was it just those two?" the Indian asked again, a hint of anger in his tone. He was obviously concerned that the danger was not over. He looked first at the two white men whom he'd killed, then at the three Indians they'd shot. Finally, he holstered his weapon and approached Samantha slowly, his hands out in front of him, his palms pointed upward, as though to show he would not harm her. "It's over now. There's nothing more to fear."

Samantha backed away from the man. She would not trust him. She had trusted too many men already, and it had very nearly gotten her raped. She refused to trust this one, even if he was looking at her with compassion and sympathy in his dark eyes instead of lust and savagery.

"Don't come any closer," Samantha said, biting the words off sharply, sounding considerably more forceful and in control of herself and her emotions than she really felt.

"I won't hurt you," the tall Indian said, the timbre of his voice resonating with Samantha's need to trust him. "I promise, I won't hurt you. And these men can't hurt you any more."

Ten feet separated them. Samantha looked straight into his eyes and he did not look away, as she'd expected him to. Her surprise made her remember that the eyes were the window to the soul, and that a liar instinctively knew this. If he was lying to her, telling her the words she wanted to hear just so she would let down her guard, she would see the mendacity reflected in his eyes. But he wasn't trying to hide anything at all . . . or did it just seem that way?

"My name is Hawk Two Feather," he said. When he gave her a half smile a dimple formed in his gaunt cheek. "I'm telling you the truth. I'm not going to hurt you."

Samantha's blue eyes narrowed in momentary suspicion. "You speak English very well."

"And you'll hold that against me?" Hawk replied, cocking a brow over eyes that feigned offense.

"No, I guess not. My name's Samantha."

"Samantha . . . ?"

Instantly, all her protective walls went up once more, and she took a step away from Hawk. She wouldn't give her last name.

"Just Samantha," she said quietly.

For several seconds they stood there, eyeing each other, passing silent questions back and forth. Still, Samantha didn't speak. The Sanders name was well known throughout the territory, and the Circle S horse ranch was famous for the quality of its riding stock. She did not want to tempt Hawk with the possibility of getting a ransom for her safe return. So far, he'd shown himself to be a gentleman, but she'd assumed the two grizzled men who'd killed her original attackers to be honorable men too. It had been too late by the time she'd discovered she was wrong.

Hawk looked around for his horse, a tall painted stallion with plenty of heart and courage. The horse was nowhere nearby, but he knew the animal hadn't run far. Samantha's horse, too, had run off, frightened by the chaos of gunfire, by the smell of blood, and by the innate fear of instant death.

"Where are you from?" Samantha asked, breaking the silence with a question.

Hawk looked at her and gave her the first truly honest smile. "I'm a Sioux," he said. "I was hunting elk near the creek fork and I heard your screams."

Samantha tucked her chemise into her Levi's, then pulled her shirt tighter and tucked that in too. It was difficult maintaining modesty when the chemise had been rent in half, and all the buttons from her shirt were missing. Even though she was suitably covered, there was something in Hawk's eyes that made her feel just a little bit exposed, almost as though her breasts were naked to his gaze. But strangely, he wasn't leering at her, nor ogling her like the men who had attacked her. He was just looking at her, nothing more than that, and yet there was an intensity to his dark, fathomless gaze that touched Samantha and made tiny shivers run up her spine.

As Hawk inspected the area where the fighting had occurred and paid a second look at the corpses that moments earlier had been would-be rapists, Samantha was given the chance to look at the enigmatic man more closely. He was tall, particularly for a Sioux, standing at least an inch or two over six feet. His shoulders were broad, swathed in a leather shirt that laced in the front. His waist narrowed nicely, and he had lean hips. His thighs were thickly muscled, telling Samantha that he was a man who'd spent his life on horseback, though she'd already guessed as much, having been witness to his riding skill.

"Are you going to bury them?" Samantha asked softly,

though she didn't care if these contemptible men received a
burial, or not.

"We'd better not take the time," Hawk replied, having finished his inspection. "This is Cheyenne territory. Or maybe
it's Crow. Either way, I'm not welcome here, and neither will
you be. We'd better just get our horses and . . ."

His words trailed off and his expression went blank, as
though he was listening to some mysterious voice in his head.
And then, several seconds after Hawk heard the approaching
riders, Samantha did, too.

"Come on," Hawk said, reaching out his hand for Samantha
as he rushed toward her.

Samantha hesitated for only a moment before taking Hawk's
hand. Hearing the approaching riders, she decided there was
absolutely no telling whether the newcomers would be a
greater or lesser threat to her than Hawk himself. Samantha
had already been "rescued" once, only to find herself needing
to be saved from her rescuers.

Hawk's fingers were long and strong, Samantha noticed
when she placed her small, pale hand in his much darker one.
Yanking her hand, he took off like a shot, half-dragging her
through the trees behind him. In the hilly, wooded area Hawk
moved with the instinctive grace of a natural-born hunter and,
in just a few seconds, the forest had swallowed them up.

"Where are we going?" Samantha asked, almost breathless.
Keeping up the pace Hawk had set had been difficult, especially since he was pulling her left arm and she was using her
right hand to hold her shirt closed.

"Quiet!" Hawk snapped, looking over his shoulder at
Samantha for just an instant.

As they ran in a wide circle, Samantha quickly discovered
what the Sioux warrior had in mind. They again approached
the clearing, only this time coming upon it from a different
direction. Samantha was gasping from the exertion of the run;
Hawk was hardly breathing faster than he had been when he'd
first started running. Though she'd always considered herself

physically fit, Samantha was nowhere near the athlete Hawk was.

He still held her hand as he crouched down on the balls of his moccasin-shod feet. Twisting, he faced Samantha and put a finger to his lips, indicating silence.

Who were they running from? she wondered.

Behind a thick bush that concealed their presence, they looked at the clearing from a southerly angle. Samantha wanted to pull her hand from Hawk's grasp, but when she tugged he only tightened his fingers around hers. Studying his profile up close, Samantha was startled by the starkness of his features. His cheekbones were high and clearly defined, and his cheeks were slightly hollowed, in keeping with the gauntness of his physique. His hair was dark black, pushed away from his forehead to sweep almost straight back and coming down over the neck of his buckskin shirt. His nose was prominent and hawkish, rather slender, and his eyes moderately deepset. He was, even upon close inspection, a strikingly handsome man.

*Don't start thinking that way!* Samantha thought. This man had just killed two men in the blink of an eye!

Three riders approached the clearing, moving slowly, cautiously, speaking in a language she did not understand. They were Indians, though Samantha had no idea from which tribe. It was clear that they weren't Sioux—at least not from the band that Hawk belonged to—and they weren't from the same tribe as the three men who had originally attacked her, since they didn't show the slightest remorse over the deaths.

Samantha's heart began beating faster. She'd already been witness to more violence and bloodshed than she cared to remember, and she didn't want to see any more.

She tugged at Hawk's hand, wanting to draw his attention away from the clearing so that she could whisper to him. But, his attention fixed, he refused to look away. More forcefully, Samantha pulled at Hawk's hand, and when he turned the full force of his deep brown eyes upon her, she knew instantly that he was not pleased that she had broken his concentration.

"I don't want—" she began, only to be silenced by Hawk's broad palm over her mouth.

Angry, Samantha twisted her face, trying to get the hand off her mouth. Hawk pulled her against him, his strength like a steel band around her. Her struggling stopped, Samantha found herself eye-to-eye with Hawk, their foreheads nearly touching, his hand still clamped tightly over her mouth.

"Are you trying to get both of us killed?" he whispered furiously, his dark eyes cutting into Samantha. "There are a dozen men out there who'd love to cut my throat! And what they'd do to you *before* they cut your throat is something you don't want to think about."

She felt his arm loosen around her and his hand soften its grip over her mouth. Slowly, tentatively, Samantha looked into the clearing again. This time, after searching for the men she'd been told were there, she found them. A dozen or so were combing the brush on the far side of the clearing, apparently following the tracks left by the horses who'd run off in panic.

"Come on," Hawk said, backing away from the clearing.

For the first time Samantha experienced a fear that terrified her. When the three Indians had first attacked her, everything had happened so swiftly that she was hardly aware, even, of their intention. And when the unwashed white men had arrived on the scene, they, like the Indians, had attacked swiftly and without provocation. Again, there hadn't been time to think or feel fear.

But now there was time, and she knew what it was she dreaded, knew the beast that lurked in the shadows of her consciousness. As she ran alongside Hawk, she prayed for the strength and stamina to keep up with him. She cursed her riding boots, perfect for stirrups but terrible for running. Hawk, with his long legs and his moccasins, ran with effortless ease. But looking at his profile, Samantha could see that he was not the cold, invincible warrior she had first thought him to be.

He wanted no fight with a dozen enemies if he could avoid it. This realization surprised Samantha, and in some ways she rather appreciated knowing that Hawk was not immune to fear.

They ran for nearly a half mile without stopping. Spotting a game trail that led through the woods, Hawk stopped to look closely at the gasping Samantha.

"I'm sorry this happened to you," Hawk said quietly, looking down at Samantha as she caught her breath. They were both leaning against the same tree at the edge of the game trail. "This shouldn't happen to anyone. I don't know exactly what happened back there in the clearing, but I can guess much of it from the signs and . . ."

His words trailed away and, though he tried to keep his gaze centered only upon Samantha's face, he couldn't prevent himself from glancing down at her open shirt and torn chemise, which allowed a hint of pale bosom to show. He looked away quickly, guiltily, his lips pursing into a thin line of self-anger.

Samantha noticed all, however, even Hawk's anger at himself. She was pleased to discover that he was a man of desire and passion, like other men, but one who *governed* his passion, controlling it and himself. She now knew he was a man with high expectations of himself; apparently, taking advantage of a young woman who'd already had a horrifying experience with men was not what he considered acceptable behavior.

In the distance to the south they heard an Indian brave shouting in victory. In that direction lay a grassy valley, but it was also the direction in which the danger would be the greatest. Hawk and Samantha looked questioningly at each other.

"We might as well," Samantha said after a moment. How eerie it was that she and Hawk could communicate so well without words! How could this be, when they came from two entirely different worlds and knew almost nothing about each other?

"Yes, we might as well," Hawk responded after a long doubting pause.

Cautiously, they moved to the edge of the treeline, to the

point where the upper rim of the valley began. Looking down into the valley, they saw two braves doing a victory dance around the stallion Hawk had ridden into the clearing. Hawk cursed under his breath in a language that Samantha did not understand, with an unmistakably obscene and angry meaning.

"Now they know who they're after," Hawk whispered, shaking his head slowly.

Samantha looked at him critically, wishing he wasn't so handsome. In her society, Hawk would never be considered one of *us,* only one of *them,* and that meant that if Samantha was to follow propriety, she would never think of Hawk as handsome. She'd never before wondered what it would be like to be kissed by one of *them.*

Hawk, no longer holding her hand, began to move away from the edge of the valley, once again heading deeper into the cover of the trees. When she did not immediately follow him he stopped to look at her, his dark eyes expressing annoyance, though only part of his ill-humor was directed at her.

"How will they know they're following you?" Samantha asked, pulling once again at her blouse to close it tightly around her, then tucking the tails into her Levi's.

"From the markings on my horse." Every Sioux brave painted his own marking on the rump of his horse, as distinctive to the various tribes as the brand was to the white man.

"Are you somebody I should know?" Samantha asked, at last moving in step with Hawk.

He looked at her for several seconds. Was she taunting him, or did she generally ask bold and insulting questions without thinking about them first? He finally replied, "The Sioux and the Cheyenne have been fighting for many years. The little wars go back generations. The Cheyenne warrior who kills me will gain favor with his tribe."

Samantha was shocked. How could anyone live with the knowledge that his death would bring status to the person who killed him? A little voice inside her warned her that she would be safer if she wasn't with Hawk, but what could she do? She was on foot, unarmed, and pursued by an enemy of at least a dozen men she knew nothing about. She needed someone to help her if she was to survive, and that someone had appeared in the form of Hawk Two Feather.

"You've done something to the Cheyenne, haven't you?" Samantha accused without meaning to.

Hawk looked sideways at Samantha. A grin, at once boyish and devilish, pulled at the right side of his mouth, prompting the reemergence of his dimple. He reached out to tuck a lock of honey blond hair behind Samantha's ear. Looking at him then, she would have sworn he was a young man in his teens who'd been caught being naughty.

"Let's just say that whenever there's a raid being organized by the Sioux to steal Cheyenne horses, it's safe to assume I'll be there."

"You're a horse thief?" Samantha exclaimed.

Hawk's smile broadened, his dazzling, straight white teeth on display. "The Cheyenne would call me a horse thief; the Sioux call me a warrior. Viewpoint, as you can see, is everything. Among the Sioux and the Cheyenne, stealing horses from each other's tribe is a rite of manhood, something that must be done if a young man is to be considered a true warrior."

Samantha shook her head. She didn't understand the logic, but then, there was much about the Sioux that she found absolutely unfathomable. She was certain that she was in a great deal of danger, and that at least a dozen men were chasing her and the man she was with.

"Let's go," Hawk said, reaching out once again for Samantha's hand. "They're not going to give up easily."

Samantha cautiously placed her hand in Hawk's and muttered, "I know I'm going to regret this."

# Two

"Do . . . do you . . ." Samantha gasped, finding speaking almost as impossible as breathing. Hawk, his hands on his hips, looked at her. He, too, was breathing harder.

"Catch your breath first, then ask me," Hawk suggested, placing his large hand gently, comfortingly, upon Samantha's shoulder. "I'll keep an eye out behind us."

Samantha simply nodded her head. Bent over, her hands on her knees, she gulped in air. Seeing that Hawk was going to allow her a minute or two to rest, she crouched, then lay flat upon the ground on her back, her arms stretched high above her head.

How much time had passed since she'd first set eyes on Hawk? How many miles had she run since the Cheyenne had found Hawk's horse, as well as her own? Many times during her life Samantha had been forced to reach deep into her inner reserves of strength to face a challenge, but she could never remember needing to physically push herself so hard for so long.

She looked at the Dakota sky overhead. It was a beautiful day, with thick white clouds drifting lazily by. A beautiful day for a picnic, or in which to train a new horse, or maybe even get into a race with her brother around the homestead. A perfect day for almost anything other than running for her life while relying on an Indian brave who spoke flawless English and provoked many more questions than he supplied answers.

Samantha closed her eyes and forced herself to calm her

breathing. Every second counted, she knew, so it was critical that she regain as much strength and stamina as possible in what little time was allotted to her by Hawk.

Not far away, Hawk was down on one knee, studying the trail they'd been following for the past hour. He knew the Cheyenne were back there somewhere. Twice he'd lost them, using tricks he'd learned during his wars with the enemy of his people, but his evasive tactics couldn't succeed in completely stopping his enemies, only in fooling them momentarily. They were at least an hour behind, he figured, maybe even more than that. But they were still following. Like himself, they were tenacious.

Every time Hawk thought about his stallion being ridden by a Cheyenne warrior he grit his teeth in rage. The value of a good horse to the Sioux was almost incalculable, and Hawk had trained that particular stallion from a colt. When he returned to his tribe the elders would ask him what had happened to the stallion, and Hawk would have to tell the truth. . . . He could already hear the laughter the other braves would try to hide. And some would not try to hide their derision. Hawk had been borne a bastard, and there were those who would never let him forget it.

Hawk knew that he was not liked by the entire tribe. His mother's white blood flowed in his veins, and there were those among the Sioux who felt he could not be trusted because of it. Also, some braves resented Hawk's considerable charms with the squaws. More often than not, the women had thrown themselves at him and, though he tried to be temperate in his life where women were concerned, Hawk was a man with a prodigious sexual appetite that occasionally bordered on the unquenchable, even the insatiable.

Satisfied that the Cheyenne would not be upon them in the immediate future, Hawk turned away from the trail to see how Samantha was faring. He took one step toward her, then froze in his tracks at what he saw.

On her back with her arms flat on the ground above her

head, Samantha was a vision of beauty. Since the attack she had been struggling to maintain her modesty, fighting with her now buttonless cotton shirt and a chemise that had been torn very nearly in half. So far, Hawk had tried to keep his eyes averted, and to some extent he had succeeded. But from this angle, with Samantha breathing deeply and slowly, he was given a stunning view of her cleavage, of skin that glistened with fresh perspiration, of firm flesh that was smooth and pale and absolutely forbidden to him.

For an instant Hawk wondered whether Samantha had intentionally positioned herself to have just this effect upon him. He immediately dismissed this notion. She was too frightened and exhausted to have seduction on her mind. Besides, something about her suggested that, though her life had been spent with men, her sexual experience with them was limited—if she had any experience at all.

"We'd better keep a move on . . . if you can," Hawk said quietly, his eyes gently caressing the inner swells of her undulating bosom. He needed to be on the run again if he was to get his mind off Samantha, and away from the attraction— the *forbidden* attraction—that she represented.

"Yes, of course," Samantha sighed.

He watched as she rolled over, curling her knees beneath her. He witnessed the heavy sway of her breasts when she moved, though her seductive display, he now believed, was completely accidental. No woman could appear *that* innocently seductive without being truly innocent. He looked away as she again pulled the shirt tightly around herself, causing the tails to overlap at her stomach again as she tightly tucked them into the waistband of her Levi's.

"Can you keep going?" Hawk asked, moving closer.

Samantha was sitting on the backs of her heels, still kneeling on the ground. Tendrils of honey blond hair curled softly against her cheeks, having come loose from the ribbon. As Hawk extended a hand to help her to her feet, he tried to tell himself that she really wasn't as beautiful as she appeared, that her allure was as much powered by the fact that he had spent days searching for game, away from his tribe and consequently had been celibate for over a fortnight. Naturally, his separation from the squaws, his quiet and discreet lovers, would account for Samantha's intoxicating beauty, he tried to tell himself.

*I don't even come close to believing that,* Hawk realized as he pulled Samantha to her feet.

"You don't have to worry about me," Samantha replied, sweeping grass from her knees with her hands. "I'm tougher than I look. Just ask my brother, if you don't believe me."

"When I get you home perhaps I will," Hawk said, a smile again tickling his mouth.

Samantha straightened suddenly, looking up into Hawk's dark eyes. "Do you mean it?" she asked in a hushed whisper. "Will you really take me home?"

"Yes," he said. Hawk was pleased to see happiness shine in Samantha's blue eyes. Then, as the reality of the situation insinuated itself into his thoughts, he added, "Just as soon as I can."

He looked away, pretending to be checking the trail they had followed, though it was just that he couldn't bear to look into her eyes a moment longer. She trusted him in a way that made Hawk uncomfortable. Typically, women trusted him not to hurt them; they trusted him to be discreet about the passion they shared with him; they trusted him to see that they were satisfied in every way possible; but they did not look at him as a man who could right whatever wrongs life had thrust upon them— and that was the look Samantha was giving him now.

"Come on," Hawk said. The suddenly gruff tone of his voice surprised Samantha. "We can talk more about getting you home as soon as we're sure you're not going to be the main reason for a Cheyenne victory dance."

The water was cool and clean and felt exquisite to Samantha—just the elixir for rejuvenating her aching body. She glanced once more at Hawk, who was kneeling some distance away with his back to her. He had not once turned around to look at her, and for that she was thankful.

Her opinion of Hawk had gone from one extreme to the other and now was settled somewhere in between. She had at first seen him as a devil, then as an angel. Now he was a man. Just a man. But, oh! What a man! His word, it seemed, was a contract that he did not violate, and that was something that she could not say with absolute certainty about any other man.

She had made him promise he would not try to look at her while she bathed in the cool artesian pond bubbling up naturally from the ground. As she stripped out of her shirt and then out of her chemise, she kept her eyes upon him, expecting to catch him turning to look. But he never did, not once. Not during the entire time that she had been completely naked less than thirty feet from him.

But he did like looking at her, Samantha knew, because she'd seen the way he tried to keep his eyes from her bosom and couldn't. That was enough to let her know she was not without physical charms.

She thought of all the boys with whom she had danced at weddings and other celebrations, and how they had ogled her and how tightly they'd held her. Samantha had been disdainful of their interest in her, scornful of their boyish desires for her. To her, they were just boys: occasionally pleasant companions but nothing more than that.

She had yet to reconcile herself to what her feelings were at Hawk's interest, but she *did* know that she felt differently about him than she had about any other man ever to enter her life.

Sinking into the pool to rinse herself again, she considered his background. Though not as brown as most Indians she'd seen, he was certainly too dark to be considered a white man. He was, she realized, a mixture of the two races.

Would a Sioux brave kiss the same way as a cultured white man?

The thought brought a smile to Samantha's lips, immediately followed by a self-deprecating frown. That was *not* a line of thinking appropriate for a well-bred young woman, especially not when she was completely naked in the company of the man whose kisses she was pondering.

She rose uncertainly out of the pool, her eyes never leaving Hawk, expecting his gentlemanly behavior to end any second. It didn't. She was able to shake the water from her legs, then shimmy into her pantalets. Within seconds she had her Levi's on. Her chemise, torn as it was, was useless. After a moment of contemplation she used the remains of the undergarment to dry herself, then tossed it aside. She put her shirt on, pulling it tightly around herself, then tucked the tails into her Levi's again, feeling vaguely scandalous for not wearing anything beneath the shirt. Still, she had no choice in the matter and should therefore be blameless.

"I'm done," Samantha said, sitting on the ground to pull on her thick white cotton socks. "You can turn around now."

Hawk turned slowly and looked at Samantha, his expression unreadable, his eyes veiled. He would not let whatever pleasure he received in looking at Samantha show in his eyes.

Samantha felt refreshed and considerably more confident now that she had bathed in the cool pond. Even though her shirt was still damp from a wash and clinging to her skin, it was at least clean. For that she was grateful. She would no longer take clean clothes for granted.

"Now what?" Samantha asked, holding her boots in one hand as Hawk approached her. "Do we keep moving on?"

"It's going to get dark soon." Hawk came over and sat on the ground beside Samantha. His gaze looked distant, unfocused, Samantha decided. She waited for him to say more, not wanting to disturb his thoughts. "The Cheyenne will be making camp as well." Hawk nibbled on his lower lip for a moment. This unconscious gesture drew Samantha's attention to his mouth. "That was a good stallion. He had the heart of a true warrior."

Samantha could sympathize with his loss; she'd been around high-quality horses her entire life. "What was his name?"

"Didn't have a name," Hawk said quietly, pulling absent-mindedly at the grass near his moccasins. "The Sioux don't give their horses names. Just respect."

Samantha thought about the way she'd seen horses treated by so-called civilized white men, then replied, "More often than not, the opposite is the case where I come from." She watched as Hawk nibbled on his lip, and an idea came to her. At first she struggled against it, not wanting to put it into words, but finally she had to set the thought free. "If you didn't have me with you, what course of action would you take?"

Hawk grinned then, glancing at Samantha. For a moment he said nothing, just smiled with that devilish twinkle in his eyes. Then he shook his head and made a passing motion with his hand, as though to dismiss the question without comment.

"Please, I want to know," Samantha prodded. She placed her hand lightly on his arm. Even through the soft buckskin of his shirt she could feel that his biceps was as solid as iron. "Be honest with me."

"If I didn't have to worry about you, I'd be working to double back on the Cheyenne. That stallion's too valuable to walk away from so easily."

Samantha was visibly shocked. "You mean you'd attack them, even though they outnumber you?"

"Of course I would. They're the enemy. They've stolen my horse—and yours as well, I might add. Why shouldn't I try to take back what is rightly mine? Besides, they'd never expect me to do that, which is what would probably enable me to succeed."

"You are a bold man, Mr. Hawk Two Feather," Samantha said softly, shaking her head in amazement.

His eyebrows did a little dance and he grinned. Samantha was just barely able to keep from asking him how he had learned to speak English so well. Several hours earlier she had

alluded to his grasp of the language and she hadn't gotten
another word out of him for a long time. Though asking personal questions was a mistake she didn't want to repeat, her
curiosity was burning.

"It would be foolish of me to try it now, though. I will wait
until later; then I will go on the attack again, and take back
what is mine." He ran his fingers through his shoulder-length
ebony hair. "You will find that we Sioux are a very patient
people . . . with very long memories. We don't forget what is
ours, or who our enemies are."

Samantha shook her head, as though fighting against ideas
too forceful to be denied. "Let's do it," she heard herself say.
The words were tumbling from her lips, with Samantha hearing
them at the same time Hawk did. "Let's steal our horses back!
They'd never expect it from us! You said so yourself."

"Not with you," Hawk replied, the smile fading from his
lips. "It would be too dangerous."

"No, it wouldn't!" Samantha continued, rising swiftly to her
feet, youthful energy making it impossible for her to remain
still. "We could do it! I know we could! And you don't have
to worry about me, I've been playing these sorts of games
with my brother my whole life! I've kept up with you today,
haven't I?"

Hawk watched her moving, pacing nervously like a young
colt. He watched the scissoring motion of her legs as she
walked, and the way the Levi's molded to her behind. Her legs
were strong, and she was nimble on her feet; he'd been witness
to that many times during their flight from the Cheyenne.
When she turned to pace past him again he watched the rise
and fall of her full breasts beneath the cotton shirt. With the
tattered chemise gone now, her breasts moved even more
freely, and their swaying motion brought an immediately and
entirely unwelcome awakening in Hawk's lower regions.

"The difference is that when this particular game is over
men will probably be dead," Hawk said in an icy voice, trying
to turn his thoughts away from the direction they were headed.

He'd fought too many battles, been in too many wars and skir-mishes, to have any romantic notion of warfare.

His words brought Samantha to a standstill. She looked at him silently, allowing the full weight and impact of his words to sink in.

"You're right, of course," she said softly, "but I still think it's what we should do. How long do you think we can elude them? They're on horseback—*our* horses, as frustrating as that is to admit—and we're on foot."

Hawk had to look away from Samantha. Her frantic pacing had caused her shirt to open again, showing the inner swells of her pale breasts. The vitality and energy she exuded forced Hawk to wonder if she would be as energetic on a warrior's buffalo mat. Thinking such thoughts heightened his anger even further. He began doing mental calculations of how far from his tribe's encampment they currently were, and how long it would take him to return on horseback. He didn't like the guesses he came to.

"Where do you live?" he asked.

Samantha wondered if she had anything to fear in letting Hawk know exactly who she was. He had shown his code of honor many times in the short time they had been together. Her heart said he wouldn't demand a ransom for her return. Just the same, she replied ambiguously, "I live on a ranch outside of Deadwood."

Hawk's eyes narrowed. "You're a long way from home," he said softly, with a trace of annoyance. Her presence in his life wasn't something he had been counting on. "What do your parents think of a girl traveling so far from home all alone?"

Samantha shot Hawk an angry glare. "My parents are dead. And before you make any snide comments about my brother and sister not raising me right, let me put that thought com-pletely out of your head. I'll have you know that I was raised to be independent, to be able to look after myself."

She would have liked to explain to Hawk that her family counted on her judgment of horseflesh, which was the reason she was so far from home. Samantha indisputably had the best eye for foals of any of the Sanders, a skill she'd developed from a very early age, and Sonny and Vanessa knew it.

"And I'm a woman, not a girl, I'll have you know," she concluded, immediately wishing she hadn't finished her diatribe against Hawk that way. It was difficult enough being taken seriously without sounding petty and childish.

With sarcasm not even thinly disguised, Hawk replied, "I would not dream of impugning your family name in any way . . . even if I knew what it was."

Samantha tried to keep a smile from her face but just couldn't. Not while observing Hawk's battle to keep from smiling, too. All right; she had to admit that she'd been less than forthcoming with a man who'd put himself in considerable jeopardy to help her.

"My name is Samantha Anne, and I absolutely hate being called a girl," she said, putting her hands on her hips, conveniently forgetting to give her last name.

Unfortunately, the movement of her arms caused her shirt to open another inch. Luckily, Hawk looked away in time, hiding his unruly thoughts from her, trying to ignore his awakening phallus.

With his back to her, he thought about the options he could take. Deadwood was days away. His own encampment was a full day away, maybe more . . . and all in terms of travel on horseback. On foot it would take twice the time, especially if the Cheyenne continued to follow them. Avoiding them would take time.

"Do you think you're up to it?" Hawk asked.

Samantha dropped down to her knees beside Hawk, her light blue eyes shimmering brilliantly. A smile played on her moist, glistening lips that made Hawk want to taste them. Though her shirt had opened with her movements, she was oblivious to it, and Hawk kept his eyes trained upon her face.

"I've trusted you; now you've got to trust me," Samantha said, confidence ringing in every word she spoke.

\* \* \*

The moon was a crescent overhead, so eerily close that Samantha believed she could reach out and touch it. She stood with her back against a tree that had died from a lightning strike years earlier. Only a twisted, charred trunk remained, its silhouette distinctive on the midnight horizon.

Hawk had been gone for at least an hour. Samantha tried to remind herself that he'd warned her it might take that long, or even longer, for him to gather the information he needed. While alone, Samantha took time to truly ponder the events that the day had brought her. Oddly, no matter how she looked at it, she couldn't tell if it was the most exciting day of her life or the most hideous one. The attack still made her shiver whenever she thought about it. Samantha had no doubt at all that it would be a long, long time before the nightmares would stop altogether.

But there was Hawk to consider. He had behaved as a cultured gentleman of honor, even if he did wear buckskin trousers and shirt. Not only had he treated her with every possible respect, but when she'd wanted to be a part of the two-person raiding party to steal back their horses, he eventually had relented. Though it was clear he didn't think much of a woman participating in such matters, Samantha considered it a good sign that he was capable of changing his mind, of listening to reason.

"It's me."

The voice made Samantha jump, her heart racing. Hawk slipped out of the shadows, moving as silently as his namesake. Samantha at last saw his tall, broad-shouldered silhouette as she slumped against the tree trunk, a hand over her heart.

"You about scared the very life out of me!"

"Sorry. I didn't mean to."

Samantha watched as he approached, stepping with his typical long-legged, athletic gait. He moved, she thought, like a night predator, at home in the shadows, the moon his friend. There was no trepidation in his step despite the darkness.

"My heart's pounding," Samantha said, giving Hawk a cross look as he moved even closer. "I can hardly catch my breath."

His stark facial features became even more pronounced in the moonlight. He was, she decided then, much more beautiful than he had any right to be.

Hawk stood close, raising his hands to rest lightly on Samantha's shoulders. "Scaring a beautiful woman seems an entirely inappropriate way of making her heart race and leaving her breathless."

At that very moment, looking up into Hawk's face, Samantha couldn't say whether her heart was racing, or if it had stopped altogether. All she knew was that in her life she had been kissed four times by two different men—or boys, more precisely. In each instance, Samantha had found the first kiss distasteful, but had been willing to receive a second, in hopes that somehow the second wouldn't be as bad as the first. But, after two bad kisses, she'd decided that men, kissing, and everything else kissing led up to, simply weren't worth the effort.

Hawk raised his right hand to lightly cup Samantha's face in his huge palm. Tenderly, he passed the pad of his thumb back and forth over her lips.

"Have you ever been . . . breathless before, Samantha?" Hawk asked, his eyes dark as midnight, shiny as diamonds boring into hers. "I'm inclined to think not, though I couldn't really say with any certainty. At least, not until I've kissed you. Then I'd know if you've ever been breathless."

As he began to bend down, his face coming closer and closer to Samantha's, he asked, "Are your lips really as delicious as they look?"

# Three

Samantha, watching his face coming closer, moved away, feeling herself spinning from between the tree trunk and Hawk. Unconsciously moistening her lips in preparation warned her that she was about to make a mistake. Hadn't her better judgment warned her from the very beginning that Hawk was a dangerous man, and that she would regret following him?

"W-what did you find out?" Samantha asked, continuing to retreat from Hawk.

Her heart hammered against her ribs, and when she tried to smooth the tangle of her hair into place she noticed that her hands were shaking. Was this the kind of reaction from her that Hawk had wanted? To her irritation, Hawk appeared entirely composed and not at all angry that she'd successfully avoided his kiss.

She wanted to be angry with him for wanting to kiss her, but how could she be angry when she'd *wanted* him to kiss her—and still wanted him to! For reasons even she herself did not fully understand, she could not let herself enjoy the pleasure that his lips silently promised.

"The Cheyenne are closer to us than I'd thought," Hawk continued, his face utterly devoid of expression.

Samantha still had no clue how he felt about the fact that she had eluded his kiss.

Hawk continued, "I found the place where they made camp. It's not really that far from here."

Samantha was brought back to reality. "Did you see the horses? Do they have Daisy?"

"Daisy? You named your horse Daisy?" Hawk smiled.

"Why not? It's a perfectly fine name."

"Daisy is the name of a flower!"

"And hawk is the name of a bird!"

Hawk looked at Samantha for a moment; then his grin spread slowly across his face. "Touché," he said softly.

"Where did you learn to speak like that?"

The words were out of Samantha's mouth before she had thought them through. When she heard them she winced, not wanting Hawk to freeze up on her again. He looked straight at her, weighing the importance of her question, then shrugged his broad shoulders beneath the buckskin shirt.

"From many places, I suppose. I didn't want to be at any of them; but then, nobody was asking what I wanted." They were old and not entirely comfortable memories for Hawk.

"You've learned well," Samantha said softly, well aware that she had been given a glimpse into Hawk that he usually kept hidden.

"I've learned many things," Hawk replied quietly, his gaze once more taking on a distant quality. "Some of them a man is better off not knowing; some things a man must know if he is to be any kind of man at all. Either way, I've learned many, many lessons in my life, Samantha, and I've learned most of them the hard way." His gaze quite suddenly became as sharp and precise as the blade of a straight razor as he said, "If we're going to get our horses back, we'll need to hurry. I've got a plan, but the only way it will work is if you help me."

His abrupt switch from man of seduction to deadly warrior left Samantha feeling disoriented.

The more Hawk thought about it, the more amazed he felt that he was allowing Samantha to go with him on the Cheyenne raid. This lack of solid judgment on his part, he decided,

was simply due to lust, infuriating lust! Samantha, the beautiful
young woman who'd tempted him, had successfully avoided
his kiss. It was for this reason, he tried to tell himself, that he
had allowed her to come with him.

For a man who'd prided himself on clear thinking under all
circumstances, taking Samantha was damning proof that he
wasn't immune to stupidity. He'd counted thirteen Cheyenne
in the raiding party. That was as many as Hawk had seen moving about the camp, anyway, their guard up and alert for danger. They had camped in a copse of trees in a hilly area,
keeping themselves well hidden, and this rather surprised
Hawk.

Were these braves renegades? That could be a reason they
were behaving so cautiously. They wouldn't be the first group
of young warriors who had decided to split off from their tribe
and try their luck on their own.

Renegades, Hawk knew, were always dangerous. They
tended to make raids on the white man's wealth. And the white
man, rather than blaming the individual Indian or Indians responsible for thefts or murders, invariably blamed all Indians.
Many people suffered because of events set into motion by
renegades.

"What's wrong?" Samantha asked, kneeling beside Hawk
in the darkness.

Together they'd been watching the activity near the campfire
in the distance. She placed her fingertips lightly on his shoulder, enjoying the rough-smooth texture of his buckskin shirt.

Hawk temporarily ignored Samantha's question. Now he understood his original plan for stealing the horses would not
work. The Cheyenne were not as content with their victory as
he had at first thought; it wouldn't work to have him divert
their attention while Samantha stole the horses.

"Tell me," Samantha prodded, whispering just a little louder.
Her fingers unconsciously kneaded the solid muscles of
Hawk's shoulder. Though she was unaware of it, she was
touching him more often.

Hawk shook his head. He was angry that the Cheyenne were too alert for him to retrieve his prized stallion; angry that Samantha had gone with him on the raid; angry that the only way he could prevent Samantha from being on the raid with him was to break his word, something no true Sioux warrior would ever do lightly.

He looked over at her; in the thin moonlight filtering through the trees she was almost supernaturally beautiful. The shimmering luxury of her blond hair, still pulled back and tied loosely at the back of her neck with a ribbon, caught the moonlight, reflecting a golden hue. Her lips, full and moist, glistened invitingly.

He thought it might be possible to convince her not to follow him on the raid. If she *agreed* not to be a part of it, then it wouldn't really be quite as if he had broken his word.

"What's wrong?" Samantha whispered, her face very close to Hawk's. "Please, we're in this together. I want to know."

*What's wrong is that you're much too beautiful,* Hawk thought. He said, "I'll explain it later. We can't go for the horses tonight. They're expecting trouble. We'd never get away with it."

"Keep your voice down," Hawk warned. "We're not that far from their camp."

Samantha was doing everything she could to keep from pacing. She simply couldn't understand why Hawk wouldn't at least *try* to steal their horses back, especially after all the trouble they'd gone through to find the Cheyenne camp. At one time they'd been within thirty feet of the Cheyenne sentries!

"Why not at least *try?*" Samantha pressed.

She sensed that she was getting into dangerous ground with Hawk, but she didn't care if he did get angry with her. Samantha had discovered within herself a surprisingly strong desire for revenge. The Cheyenne had stolen her horse and she wanted Daisy back. It was as simple as that.

"Because to try now would—"

The words stopped in Hawk's mouth so quickly that it frightened Samantha. He raised his hand palm outward to her, indicating the need for silence. Then, a second later, he bolted to his feet, grabbing Samantha's hand in the process, and pulled her away from the small, grassy clearing that they had intended to use as their camp for the night.

The experiences of the past hours had taught Samantha that sometimes it was better to keep all her questions to herself and just do whatever Hawk indicated he wanted. So she followed him, ducking her head beneath a low-hanging tree limb, moving swiftly without actually breaking into a noisy run through the underbrush. Hawk moved in a semicircle, as he had before, so that he could look back into the camp. Only this time, near the edge of the clearing, he leaped high to catch a tree limb, pulled himself up with startling swiftness, then reached down for Samantha.

She looked first up at him, then at the hand he reached down for her. It had been years since she'd climbed a tree and, though she did not quite understand why it was so necessary now, she leaped to catch Hawk's wrist. Instantly, his fingers curled around her wrist, and he easily hoisted her up to where she could kick her booted foot around the tree limb. As she did this, her buttonless shirt pulled free from her Levi's once more. A warm flush of embarrassment colored her cheeks as she hauled herself onto the thick, horizontal limb, gaining a secure position before her cotton shirt came completely free.

Quietly, Hawk led the way higher in the tree, all his movements quick, silent, and economical, indicating a menace in the shadows that Samantha could not see. After taking the time to tuck her shirttails in once more—and drawing a frown from Hawk for her delay—she followed him, having difficulty seeing in the near total darkness as she worked her way higher into the thick foliage.

When they were far up the tree Hawk sat on a substantial limb and pulled Samantha to sit between him and the trunk of the tree. They were, she now realized, safely ensconced between two different limbs of almost the same thickness and level on the trunk, and a third one behind her that she could reach to use as a support.

She looked at Hawk, who sat so close beside her that she could feel his strength and heat emanating into herself. Smiling, he gave her a quick wink, which rather worried Samantha because it was a jaunty gesture meant to buck up her confidence. Samantha knew it meant they were in greater danger than Hawk wanted her to realize. It was, ironically, the kind of thing her brother would do when a situation was looking bleak.

Hawk took her hand and squeezed it, then placed the tip of his finger against Samantha's lips. Silence, he was indicating without words, was absolutely necessary.

Samantha soon found that on this limb she was reasonably well balanced, with the trunk of the tree against her shoulder, a limb in front of her to put a foot on, and a limb behind her on which to place a steadying hand. Just when she started to relax, since it appeared the wait might take a while, she heard voices directly below her, and the meaning of all that Hawk had done now became clear to her.

Below were at least three Cheyenne braves, as far as Samantha could tell, though she was afraid to move much for fear of drawing attention to herself. Hearing a whistle of some sort, sounding like something an owl would make, she guessed that there were more Cheyenne communicating in the shadows.

Hawk looked at Samantha again, reaching out to touch his fingertips lightly to her chin to raise it, so that she was forced to look at him rather than at the danger below. He smiled at her, as though to say, *The danger is all down there. We're safe up here. That's nothing to fear as long as I'm with you.*

With all her courage, Samantha forced herself to smile back at Hawk, though it was a tight, strained smile. He was trying

to ease her fears, and even though his efforts were only mar-
ginally successful, she was thankful for his concern, and her
estimation of him as a man rose because of the effort.

Samantha waited, making the supreme effort to remain silent. Below, the braves moved about, inspecting the area where
she and Hawk had been sitting, taking note of the cushion of
grass they'd gathered and constructed for sleeping. Gratefully,
she realized that if Hawk had not heard the Cheyenne's approach, she most assuredly would now be a captive of the men
below. A shiver ran up her spine.

As time passed, Samantha heard other sounds, other voices,
and then it was clear to her why Hawk had climbed the tree
rather than run. The Cheyenne were all around them and would
certainly discover anyone on foot.

Hawk leaned over, and Samantha angled her head to the
side, offering her ear to him. "It won't take long," he whispered, so softly that Samantha had to strain to hear him.
"They'll look around, find nothing, then go back to their
camp."

When Samantha shifted so that she could whisper into
Hawk's ear the tips of her breasts brushed against the thickly
muscled surface of his biceps, and warm, unintended tingles
went through her instantaneously. The force of the feeling was
so shocking that Samantha could not at first speak, so she
sucked in her breath and held it until the feeling passed and
she was once more in control.

"How did they know about us? Where to look?" she whispered.

Her lips brushed against Hawk's ear as she spoke, and she
wondered what it would be like to explore the shell-like cir-
cumference of his ear with the tip of her tongue. It was a
naughty thought, she knew, but she dismissed it as an irrational
response to Hawk's beauty and the other circumstances that
were entirely beyond her control.

Additional conversation was difficult, since both Hawk and
Samantha had to shift positions slightly to speak directly into

the other's ear. When Samantha shifted positions again to offer
her ear to Hawk her breasts again brushed against his arm.

Was he aware of the contact? she wondered. Was he just as
aware of it as she was? To Samantha, though she wore a shirt
of cotton and Hawk one of buckskin, the contact was such
that it felt as though it had been skin to skin.

"You stepped on a twig that broke when we were walking
away from their camp," Hawk explained. "I thought one of
them might have heard it. They probably found your boot-
prints."

A chill went through Samantha as she realized she was dealing with men who lived in a world so vastly different from
her own that she could not truly conceive of it. Though she
had always been a tomboy, and thought that she was aware of
the world around her, she had been completely oblivious of
the twig—even if Hawk hadn't.

Samantha wanted to ask Hawk more questions, but she did
not because she knew that moving again would cause her to
again brush against him, and that in its own and tempting way
could be more dangerous than facing the Cheyenne who were
searching for her on the ground below.

Her body felt sensitized in a way that it never had before,
as though in Hawk's presence she was heightened to the possibilities of touch. Samantha wondered if the nearness of danger made her skin tingle, her flesh feel alive, and what it would
be like if she allowed Hawk to *intentionally* touch her.

Hawk looked down, but he could not see any of the Cheyenne who had trailed them to this spot. The leaves and
branches were too thick, and the only way that they'd be spotted at all was if one of the Cheyenne stood at the base of the
tree and looked straight up. The possibility of that happening
didn't seem likely.

At last Hawk felt that he could relax, at least slightly, and
he breathed a soft sigh of relief. When he'd heard the approaching footsteps he hadn't at first been sure that it was the Cheyenne. The sound could have come from one of the many night

creatures that walk and stalk these grounds. But he had been cautious, which had proven to be a lifesaver.

And now Hawk Two Feather was enormously pleased with the spirits, feeling that they were guiding him. Never before had he ever climbed up a tree to avoid an enemy, or even thought of doing such a thing. The advice had come from the spirits. It was their wisdom that he had to thank, not his own intelligence, Hawk suspected.

He could hear the Cheyenne speaking in hushed tones and, though he could not hear all that was said, the topic and tone were clear to him. Where had Hawk and the white woman gone? the Cheyenne wanted to know. How could they have disappeared into the night like shadows?

Hawk smiled. His legend might grow because of the events of this night. And though a flattering notion to him, it also meant that among the Cheyenne, his death would provide great rewards and coups for the warrior who killed him.

He looked at Samantha's profile. She had impressed him enormously in the little time they had spent together, especially with her actions of the past half hour. Following his direction without comment or protest, they'd managed to baffle the Cheyenne, with not a drop of blood shed by anyone.

He would have liked to speak more words of reassurance, but he didn't dare to. Each time she swiveled her shoulders to whisper into his ear, he felt the soft fullness of her breasts slide lightly across his arms and, though there was danger everywhere, his body was once more responding in a most disquieting way to Samantha's lush, subtle sensuality.

On the ground below, Hawk could hear the Cheyenne slowly expanding the circle of their search. They were completely at a loss as to where the Sioux and the woman had gone. Hawk thanked the spirit guides that climbing a tree had never occurred to them. Now all Hawk had to do was wait quietly until the danger finally walked away.

He began thinking of Samantha, of the tender flesh that he'd seen when he pulled her up onto the lowest of the tree limbs, the gentle curve of pale bosom so near to him yet so untouchable.

*Stop thinking that way!* Hawk warned himself as he felt a tightening beneath his buckskin trousers.

He fought against the impulses of his burgeoning manhood. This was *not* what he needed at a time like this. He did not need to embarrass himself with an unwanted and unwarranted response to a woman who had refused to even kiss him, much less allow him a caress or the release of his desires.

But the problem was that logic held no sway over his passions. And now the buckskin was restricting his continued expansion, which wasn't at all comfortable. Hawk tried to concentrate on the Cheyenne, tried to consider the threat that they represented, so that his body would not react to Samantha. Surprisingly, the danger of the Cheyenne was nothing compared to the allure of the young woman beside him.

For a man who could go days without eating, ignoring his own hunger, a warrior who could withstand the cold in the winter and the heat in the summer without complaint, a Sioux whose code of honor and greatest personal pride was derived from his willpower being stronger than the weaknesses of his physical self . . . being drawn in by Samantha's allure was slow torture.

His unruly manhood continued expanding, responding to the young woman's nearness, and there was nothing Hawk could do to stop it. Though he was uncomfortable, the tenting of his buckskins was an embarrassingly blatant testimony to the direction of his thoughts.

Careful to remain silent, Hawk leaned forward, placing his foot on the branch in front of them. Then, cautiously, he stood and twisted so that he was standing on the branch beneath the one Samantha was sitting on. He swiveled his hips and surreptitiously adjusted his irrational manhood to a more comfortable position, then fidgeted with his holster, hoping that Samantha would be unaware of the real reason he'd needed to change positions.

His back was to her when he felt Samantha's small, soft
hand upon his shoulder. Hoping that she would remain oblivious to his condition, he turned toward her, carefully reposi-
tioning his moccasined foot on the thick branch to remain
balanced, then dipped his head down so that she could whisper
into his ear.

"What's wrong?" Samantha breathed.

Her right hand curled lightly around Hawk's neck, her fingers touching beneath the ebony silk of his shoulder-length
hair. The anxiety she tried hard to conceal could be heard in
the softness of her voice. She was putting on a courageous
front for Hawk, and he felt a pang of guilt for his libidinous
thoughts when her primary emotion was fear.

"Nothing," Hawk lied. Absolutely everything was wrong because he wasn't in control of his own thoughts and emotions,
which left him feeling set adrift and starkly vulnerable.

He tried to stand upright once more, to put some distance
between himself and Samantha. He turned to look directly at
Samantha, and this was his undoing. Stunningly beautiful to
him then, her face glowed pale and flawless in the shadows.
Her honey blond hair was radiant with vitality and, in the back
of his mind, Hawk wondered whether he was enthralled with
Samantha because she looked so different from the women he
usually pleasured himself with, or whether in some mysterious
way she had bewitched him with tricks an evil shaman might
use.

*I should stay far from her,* Hawk considered, feeling himself
being irrepressibly drawn in by Samantha's gentle strength, by
her beauty, and by the mystery surrounding her.

With Hawk now standing, Samantha did not dare to speak,
afraid that the Cheyenne below might hear her, so she simply
mouthed the words, *What's wrong?* Hawk shook his head, as
though he did not understand, so Samantha reached up for him
with her right hand, indicating that she wanted him to bend
down toward her. When he did she slid her fingers beneath

his thick, ebony hair and pulled him so close to her that her lips brushed against his ear when she spoke.

"What's wrong?" she repeated. "You look . . . I don't know what the word for it is. . . . You seem . . ."

She pulled back just enough so that she could look into his eyes, and when she did it was as though for a moment she could glimpse into his unguarded soul. Now she saw his anxiety was not caused by the danger the Cheyenne represented, but caused by her. . . .

Should she feel proud or ashamed of the reaction she had drawn from the powerful Sioux warrior? she wondered.

As he'd done before, Hawk bent his head toward Samantha, only this time she could not escape. There was no spinning away from him this time. This time, she closed her eyes and waited for the touch of his lips against her own.

# Four

He kissed her softly, his lips warm and moist, just barely touching her mouth. Samantha heard a throaty sigh that shocked her as she realized that the sound had come from herself. This sound, she thought, should have come from someone else, some woman far more experienced in the glories of passion than she.

Her heart was beating strong and fast, pounding against her ribs. Samantha was confused about what was expected of her, of what exactly she should do, though this fear was short-lived because a little voice inside her head whispered confidently that whatever she needed to know, Hawk could teach her.

Softly, from one side of her mouth to the other, Hawk kissed her lightly, occasionally trailing his tongue along the sensitive surface to moisten her lips. Samantha trembled softly, simultaneously confused and enthralled at what was happening, shocked at the pleasure coursing through her.

In a distant corner of her mind a single logical thought whispered that it really shouldn't feel so good to be kissing Hawk. The kisses were light, and their impact upon her senses couldn't possibly be as powerful as it seemed, she reasoned.

Samantha quickly concluded that logic held no sway over her body when she was kissing Hawk. Her head was spinning, and she worried about falling off the limb. She leaned just a little more firmly against the trunk of the tree for support, and ʰ·⁺ᵉᵈ her arm a bit more securely around Hawk's neck.

⁺ʰᵃ was mystified at her own reaction to Hawk's

kisses, he was equally confused at his need to taste her sweet lips. He was no stranger to passion, to kisses from a beautiful and willing woman. He was also well aware of the danger that the Cheyenne represented. So why, he wondered, considering his experience with women and the Cheyenne, was he feeling the blood need to kiss the frightened young blond woman until she trembled with desire and begged for more? Why did it please him so to kiss her when, as she kissed him back, he could tell that she had not kissed often in her life?

Hawk, still standing on a limb beneath Samantha's, moved to the right, nudging her knee to the side. Then he leaned forward fractionally, sliding his leather-clad hips between Samantha's knees. He felt her try to close her legs, the pressure of her knees on either side of him, and a powerful rush of delicious images made him sigh softly into Samantha's mouth as he kissed her. What would it feel like to feel her knees parting for him, to feel the strength and velvety softness of her thighs surrounding him as he plunged deeply inside her?

He felt her hand at the nape of his neck, slowly winding his long hair around her fingers. Then she slid her hand once more across his shoulders, touching him through his buckskin shirt, holding on to him tightly as they kissed. Hawk kissed her more firmly then, wanting the tension between them to heighten and deepen the feelings they shared. But Samantha only tilted backward upon the tree limb to lessen the pressure, and the instant she did, she lost her balance and her feet shot out. Her legs now surrounded Hawk's lean waist. He instantly whipped his one free arm around her waist to pull her toward him, once again securely positioning her.

"W-wait . . . Hawk," Samantha stammered.

When Hawk move to kiss her again she turned her face to the side, avoiding the warrior's lips. Undeterred, Hawk kissed Samantha's cheek, then bent lower to kiss her jaw, her throat. The sensations that seeped into Samantha's body when she felt his warm, tantalizing lips touching her neck were much dif-

ferent than when he had been kissing her mouth, though no
less stimulating.

"I c-can't breathe," she whispered, wanting Hawk to stop
his passionate assault upon her better judgment but lacking
the conviction to push him away.

A stern denial of her own passion and an insistence that
Hawk no longer kiss her would put an end to it all, Samantha
knew. Hawk had the ability to control himself, even if she did
not. She'd seen him exercise his self-control earlier in the day.
But now she needed him to stop of his own accord because
she could not insist upon it herself with anything other than
a halfhearted plea, spoken through a breathy sigh of pleasure
that whispered its own honesty.

She angled her head to the side, tilting her chin slightly
upward to allow Hawk easier access to her sensitive throat.
His teeth were sharp against her flesh, nipping at the skin,
drawing a short, high gasp of surprise.

The dizzying kisses continued, much to Samantha's mixed
feelings of ecstasy and dismay. To steady herself, she lightly
hooked her heels around the backs of Hawk's knees. In a corner of her mind she was thankful that she had never worn
spurs, or she surely would have stabbed him!

"That's right," Hawk whispered, the timbre of his voice
richly sensual. He edged just a little closer to Samantha, forcing her legs wider apart, his lean hips tight between her thighs,
the straining front of his buckskins so close to Samantha now
that she could feel its strength and heat.

The words rang in Samantha's ears. *No!* she wanted to
scream, *I didn't do it to make you happy! I was afraid of losing
my balance again!*

She squirmed as she sat on the tree limb, trying to move
so that she no longer had Hawk's hips between her thighs. But
her perch on the limb was not terribly solid, and when she
once again nearly fell backward her booted feet hooked around
Hawk's legs to hold on to him tightly, almost as though they
were making love.

She felt his mouth against her collar and another soft cry of desire escaped her parted lips. Every place his lips touched her, every time he kissed her, a new part of her body blazed in passionate reception to pleasure.

Samantha had not dreamed that she could feel anything so intensely. Every sensation passing through her was unprecedented, mysterious in its scope. She wondered how she had failed to realize how capable she was of feeling passion until this moment, until Hawk entered her life and saved her from the evil men who meant her harm.

"Kiss me," Hawk whispered, standing straight, his ebony hair framing his starkly masculine face. The command in his voice suggested he had made similar demands before and was accustomed to compliance.

Samantha looked at Hawk for a moment, wanting to resist him, her natural feistiness coming to the fore. She did not accept orders from *anyone,* and most certainly not an order of *that* nature, under these circumstances.

"I shouldn't," she whispered. It wasn't much of a refusal, but it was all she could manage.

Samantha looked at Hawk's mouth. How had she drawn so much pleasure, her body become so heated, so impassioned, just from his kisses? He was so completely different from any other man who'd ever shared any part of her life that there was no possible correlation between him and anyone else. But why couldn't she resist his kisses when she'd adamantly resisted, refused, and hotly denied nearly all the other men a taste of her lips?

"You're wrong," Hawk replied, bending low, powerful, irresistible, his masculine presence hovering about him, ready to engulf and surround Samantha.

She closed her eyes, tilted her face up to him, and slid her arm more tightly around his powerful shoulders. And as she began to taste Hawk's lips against her own, she feared she'd never again resist the temptation of his kisses.

As the kiss grew deeper, more commanding and forceful,

Samantha shivered, melting into Hawk. Samantha nearly swooned, kissing Hawk passionately.

Was it possible to be completely consumed with passion? she wondered. Was this Hawk's own way of kissing, or did everyone, except the two boys she'd previously kissed, kiss like this? She didn't care right now; all that mattered was that Hawk was kissing her and, with each passing second, the heat within her intensified.

She felt Hawk's hand against her hip, sliding slowly up her side, his broad palm warming her skin through the denim of her trousers. His warmth now touched her shirt.

*He's going to touch my breast.* Samantha flinched, though she did not stop kissing Hawk.

Then, as Hawk caught her lower lip between his teeth and bit softly, she breathed surprise and passion into his mouth. In the near total darkness she felt him smile, and wondered what she could have done that he found amusing. Was it that he could make her body feel on fire? Or did he find her passionate confusion a source of humor?

Hawk leaned back then, pulling partially away from her and into a space of moonlight. She looked up into his shadowed face, into those dark, fathomless eyes glowing with vitality. He smiled again, a soft, wry half smile, she saw this time, one that tugged at the corner of his mouth, making his dimple appear. Despite her confusion, she smiled back.

"This is madness," Samantha heard herself whisper.

Her lips tingled; so did her scalp. She felt all jittery inside. Though she'd led an active, athletic life, her balance now was so poor that, without the tree or Hawk to hold on to, she would not have been able to remain sitting on the thick limb.

Suddenly Hawk's mouth was an inch from Samantha, whispering, "Divine madness, perhaps."

He seemed to know exactly how long to kiss her, and when to pull away so that she could breathe again. He was, she realized instinctively and a bit peevishly, truly experienced in these matters.

*Don't be competitive,* Samantha thought, recalling the refrain her older sister had used so many times. *It isn't ladylike.*

From the branch below, Hawk stood upright again, looking down into the pale face of the young woman he'd saved hours earlier. By allowing her to accompany him on the raid he'd gotten her into this situation with the Cheyenne. She was his weakness, he thought then, and it was an unsettling revelation for him, since he was not a man who accepted weaknesses in others, or tolerated them in himself.

Slowly, he raised his hand to her face, needing to touch her, to see his fingers against the smoothness of her cheek. Could this beautiful weakness be merely some illusion created within the confines of his own mind?

"Lovely," he whispered, his fingertips brushing lightly over Samantha's cheek.

She said nothing in reply. Rather, she simply looked up at him, her clear blue eyes reflecting the moonlight and showing the confusion she felt.

Hawk brushed the pad of his thumb lightly across the moist fullness of her lips, watching as she made only the slightest move to kiss his thumb. Her gesture was a sign of passionate acceptance that his masculine senses—honed to precision to just such responses from women—picked up on instantly. The blood surged through his veins, and only superior self-restraint kept Hawk from pulling her into his arms.

"The Chey-Cheyenne . . ." Samantha whispered.

She tried to concentrate on the Cheyenne warriors walking in darkness beneath her, to think about the danger that those men represented to her, but she couldn't dwell on such a subject when Hawk's fingertips were trailing slowly, tantalizingly down her throat. Unconsciously, she tilted her chin upward, making her throat taut and available to Hawk's caresses. Though Samantha suspected she shouldn't make this seduction easier for him—her surrender appeared too easily won as it was—she couldn't force herself away from those fingertips.

"The Cheyenne are my enemy," Hawk whispered, his voice a breathy sigh.

As his fingertips trailed back and forth along the line of Samantha's collarbone, he saw the rise and fall of her breasts, rapid and uneven, proof of her agitation. When his gaze at last moved up to her face he saw that she had closed her eyes. Was she concentrating on the feelings going through her? That was a pleasant notion for Hawk. Or was she doing all she could to ignore him? For only an instant a hardness of purpose creased Hawk's mouth, turning it into a thin line.

"You shouldn't be thinking of my enemy now."

Samantha tried to say something in response, but she could not. This madness had to come to an end! But how could she protest when her throat felt tight and breathing was nearly impossible with Hawk's strong, long-fingered hand slowly and casually brushing the lapels of her shirt aside, opening it even farther, exposing more of her breasts?

*Open your eyes, glare hatefully at him, and slap his hand away!* she thought, recalling how successfully that had worked on another night with another man.

But knowing what should be done and doing it were two entirely different things. Hawk's kisses had intoxicated her, had stripped away her judgment. No wonder she couldn't tear Hawk apart with a glare and a few sharply chosen words, as she'd done with any man who dared taunt her in any way.

Now his fingers slid down the front of her body, brushing lightly against the inner swells of her breasts to push the cotton shirt open even more. Samantha's nipples, erect and aching, throbbed with tension. When she opened her eyes she watched as the long, bronze fingers moved slowly, tantalizingly, brushing right and left to very nearly touch the tips of her breasts.

Why wasn't he going farther? wondered Samantha in passion-fogged confusion. She didn't want him to touch her, she tried to tell herself, but as long as he was going to touch her anyway, he might just as well caress her nipples.

It was that thought, that acceptance of a passion she'd never before considered, let alone desired, that warned Samantha she was going too far.

With a trembling hand, Samantha took Hawk by the wrist and pulled his hand from her body. A faint smile putting a curl to her mouth and a gleam in her pale blue eyes, she looked up at him, gaining some semblance of control at last. Several weighty seconds passed, with Samantha staring up into Hawk's shadowed face. During those intervening moments she was able to calm her racing heart and recover the sound common sense she'd always felt she possessed.

About to speak, to whisper that Hawk must never again kiss her, she heard the sudden sharp, high cry of a Cheyenne warrior, standing almost directly beneath her. The warrior's scream rumbled through the trees, luckily masking Samantha's own startled gasp. Pushing herself against the tree, the bark's rough texture harsh against her shoulder, her eyes grew wide and round as she stared at Hawk, hoping that he would know what to do.

Hawk was almost thankful for the diversion, allowing him time to think about his foolish behavior of late, and to remember exactly who and what he was . . . and, perhaps even more importantly, who and what *Samantha* was.

Below them, a Cheyenne was talking. One of the party had taken Samantha's discarded chemise, tied it around himself, and was cavorting about in a lewd pantomime. But the Cheyenne hadn't discovered anything of importance, hadn't a clue that the quarry they pursued was so close at hand.

Realizing he wasn't in any immediate danger of being discovered gave Hawk time to think about Samantha, and precisely what it was he had been doing with her. She was forbidden, of course. Hawk knew there were many braves in his tribe who coveted white women, who lusted after them even more than after Sioux maidens. Hawk's own mother was white. He'd seen the tribe's subtle bigotry against him because of the white blood running through his veins, just as he'd ex-

perienced raw hatred in the white man's villages he'd visited
with his mother.

Who hated half-breeds more? he often wondered. The white
man or the Sioux?

It didn't really matter. Hatred was hatred, pure and simple.
Hawk wasn't going to get caught up in it. He was going to
find a lovely Sioux maiden when the time was right, and take
her to his tepee. His child would have only a trace of white
blood flowing in his veins. His child would not know the confusion, the sense of dislocation, that Hawk had known as a
child, that he had struggled with when he was young, and on
occasion still fought.

So Samantha was out of the question. Definitely out of the
question, with her long blond hair and her pale white skin.
She might well have been the fantasy woman for another man,
but not for Hawk.

Added to her race was the fact that she'd already had enough
trouble with men, hadn't she? She'd tossed away her chemise
because it had been destroyed by callused hands, and her shirt
was missing its buttons because of other vicious men. Did
Hawk really want to put himself in league with men like that?

"What's wrong?" Samantha whispered.

Hawk had angled himself away from Samantha. He looked
over at her, startled. How deeply he had sunk into himself and
his thoughts! With the laughter of the Cheyenne moving away
now, the danger was receding. He realized then, as he looked
at her pulling her shirt more tightly around herself, that he
had to remove her from here—put her some place safe where
she would be out of danger from the Cheyenne and no longer
a lure to his senses.

But first he needed to steal back their horses. Once that was
accomplished he could ride with her until she was once again
in a white man's village, where *she* belonged, and he could
ride away, back to his own Sioux camp, where *he* belonged.

"Nothing is wrong," Hawk said gruffly. "I'll help you down.
We can't stay here all night."

Samantha was confused once again by Hawk's change of mood. Had she done something terribly wrong to make him unhappy with her? One moment he was confident, passionate, lusty, and seductive; the next he was quiet and brooding, angry about something she didn't understand.

Saying nothing, promising herself that in the future she would try to keep more distance between herself and the handsome warrior, she followed him back down the tree.

# Five

"Brandy?" Sonny Sanders asked.

Vanessa Sanders nodded, then accepted a snifter from her brother. Her thoughts, even as she sipped the fine Napoleon brandy, were on her sister Samantha. Another day had passed without a telegram. Sonny, the eldest child in the family, had wanted to take charge of the situation, sending a telegram of concern and hiring men to ride to Fort Keogh to investigate the matter. That was Sonny's way—take charge, take immediate action. It was left to Vanessa to be the voice of moderation, to be the one to let reason and logic prevail.

"She can be damned annoying," Sonny said, throwing himself onto the library sofa.

"Samantha can be more than just annoying," Vanessa replied, "and we both know it. We also know this is neither the first, nor the second, nor even the third time that we've sent her off to look at horses and she's gotten so involved in her work that she has neglected to telegram us on how she's progressing."

"I ought to put her over my knee," Sonny mumbled.

Vanessa laughed softly. She could imagine the ensuing battle between her headstrong older brother and her equally willful younger sister if he tried to spank her like a child.

"I know you're angry with her," Vanessa continued. "I'm angry, too. But if we take a moment to think about it, we'll realize that Samantha is not like other women her age. She can take care of herself."

"Woman?" Sonny made a sound of derision in his throat. "She's just a girl!"

"A mere child, you'll say next, right?" Vanessa smiled to herself. "If that's so, then why do several of the girls she grew up with now have husbands and children?"

Sonny shot his sister a fierce look. It was always difficult arguing with her. As a lawyer, Vanessa's skills in debating issues such as this one were greater than his own and he knew it, though he didn't much like it.

"Are you intentionally trying to get on my nerves?" he asked sharply.

"No, I'm trying to tell the truth. It's the truth that's getting on your nerves."

She smiled at Sonny, raising her brandy snifter in a silent toast and, even though he was angry, he smiled back. His tension evaporated quickly. Sonny shook his head, mumbling about how much easier his life would be if he'd been blessed with younger brothers instead of sisters. Vanessa heard the love behind the criticism and let her brother calm down at his own pace.

"When will you be leaving for Fargo?" Sonny asked.

"I'm not certain, actually," Vanessa replied, pleased at the change in subject. Though she was, in fact, a little worried about Samantha's welfare herself, her sister had neglected to inform them about her activities or whereabouts more times than she could remember.

Vanessa turned her thoughts to the right-of-way water dispute that required her to go to Fargo to file the necessary legal documents at territorial court.

"I'd guess in a day or two," she answered at last. "I can't wait too long, but there's no great hurry. These cases tend to move at a snail's pace."

Sonny huffed, shaking his head in disgust. He had no patience for such slow-moving problem-solving, though he was eternally grateful that his sister did. She was his eyes and ears

in the courts, and he counted on her to fight the legal battles
that he could not fight himself.

"Don't worry so much," Vanessa said as she finished her
brandy, rising to her feet to go to bed. "I'm certain Samantha's
sleeping like a baby, having worked herself to exhaustion for
days now. And when we finally do get word from her she'll
be asking for much more money to be sent to her, claiming
it is the only way we'll get the bloodlines the Circle S needs."

Sonny grinned, nodding his head. Whenever Samantha
didn't keep in close touch it meant more money spent on fine
riding stock.

As he finished his own brandy and headed off to bed, Sonny
was finally content to worry about how much money Samantha
was spending rather than whether she was safe.


Samantha wondered what time it was. Typical of people in
the ranching business, she was accustomed to going to bed
early and rising at dawn. It had to be close to three in the
morning by now, she decided.

Sitting on the ground with her back to a tree trunk, she
watched Hawk complete his circuit of the area. He'd already
told her that there were no Cheyenne around, but he went to
check anyway.

Hawk moved like some giant cat stalking an unseen prey.
Though a big man, he was silent, light and quick on his feet.
The loose-limbed grace of his body when he walked, climbed
a tree, did almost anything, reminded Samantha again of a
lazy cat. Except there didn't seem to be anything at all lazy
about Hawk. He almost quivered with energy and vitality even
when he was perfectly motionless.

*Such a man!* Samantha thought with amazement as she
watched him approaching her, at last finished with his inves-
tigation of the surrounding area. When he knelt beside her in
the grass her heart fluttered a bit.

"Try to get some sleep," he said, keeping his voice low. "A couple of hours will do wonders for recovering your energy."

"I *am* exhausted," Samantha admitted. "Are you going to sleep, too?"

Hawk shook his head, his raven black hair swirling. "I'll stay awake for a while. Someone has to keep an eye out. Maybe I'll sleep some later."

"You can't go on forever without sleeping," Samantha reminded him softly. She reached out to lightly touch the buckskin sleeve of Hawk's shirt. "Even *you* have your limits."

Hawk grinned and took his distance from her. Then he motioned for Samantha to lie down, which she did, rolling onto her stomach and cradling her head in her arms. She liked it when Hawk smiled. He didn't do it often enough, she decided; not nearly often enough.

Samantha looked at Hawk one last time, then closed her eyes and was asleep before she knew it.

Samantha watched Hawk kneeling at the stream, splashing cool water on his face. He hadn't gotten much sleep, but at least he'd gotten some, she had awakened to notice. With four hours' sleep, not her usual seven, Samantha felt fine, though a little stiff from sleeping on the ground.

Arching her spine, she threw her head back and raised her arms skyward, stretching out all the stiffness.

Hawk pivoted on his knees to watch Samantha. With her face tilted upward, her arms raised high, and her eyes closed to the morning sun, she looked as if she was worshipping the sun. A wry smile curled Hawk's lips. No, Samantha wouldn't worship the sun, but a Sioux maiden would, he thought. And though he wasn't sure what Samantha's spiritual life was like, he was certain it wasn't at all like his.

As she turned and stretched, working loose the muscles in her back, her shirt loosened somewhat, and once again he was given a glimpse of pale bosom. He turned away immediately.

The allure that Samantha represented was much too great to be toyed with. He'd demonstrated his weakness the previous night; he didn't need to prove it once again.

He would have given Samantha something to eat but all the provisions he'd brought with him on the hunt were in his pack, with his stallion.

At the thought of his horse, Hawk grit his teeth. The Cheyenne had his stallion, and they were probably still gloating over their victory. It galled him to realize that enemy warriors would be speaking of Hawk Two Feather with derision, telling exaggerated stories of the way they'd stolen his stallion.

He turned his attention back to Samantha, who was tucking the tails of her cotton shirt back into her Levi's. Why did she wear trousers like a man? Hawk wondered.

"How do you feel?" he asked quietly.

Smiling, Samantha rose and walked over to kneel beside Hawk. "Fine. I'm ready to go after the Cheyenne just as soon as you are."

"I'm afraid not. Last night proved to me that it's going to be much too dangerous to have you along."

"According to you," Samantha said softly, her eyes promising anger.

"Yes, according to me."

"But not according to me, and my opinion doesn't count, right?"

"That isn't what I said."

Samantha bolted to her feet. For an instant she had a height advantage to Hawk, which she wanted. "You didn't have to."

Hawk rose swiftly; then, edging closer, he looked down at Samantha from his much greater height. "Do you always attack men when they disagree with you?"

Samantha refused to be intimidated by Hawk's size and strength. "No, only when they're wrong. Most times, it's men who attack me!"

The words were out of Samantha's mouth before the full significance of them hit her. Suddenly she turned away from

Hawk. The pleasure of kissing Hawk, and the frustration of dealing with his stubbornness, had made her forget—at least momentarily—the horror of the multiple attacks she'd suffered, along with the trauma of seeing the violence Hawk had dealt to her attackers.

Samantha wasn't sorry that the men who had attacked her had died; not at all. But just the same, the ugliness of violence was something she would not soon forget, no matter how desperately she tried to.

She took several steps, needing to put some distance between herself and Hawk, if only for a moment. Then, slowly, she turned toward him again, and when she did there was fiery defiance blazing in the depths of her blue eyes.

"Do what you want to do," she said quietly. *"I'm* going to get my horse back."

"Alone?"

"If necessary."

"You're crazy."

"Quite likely, but I'm still going to get my horse back. At least I'm going to try."

Hawk stared at Samantha, unable to fully comprehend her intractability. In his culture the wars were fought by the men and the tepees were managed by the women. One gender did not presume to encroach on the other's territory. But this trouser-wearing young blond with the fiery blue eyes wasn't guided by those same unwritten rules. Quite frankly, Hawk didn't have a clue as to how he was supposed to argue with a woman. He'd never done it before and had never known any man who had.

Samantha waited for Hawk to continue to resist her or to relent and at last accept that she had a legitimate right to fight the Cheyenne. Instead, he simply stood there, tall and imposing, impressive in his fringed buckskins, an uncomprehending expression in his ebony eyes.

"Fine; be stubborn then!" Samantha said, stomping her booted foot on the ground.

She turned and started walking strong and fast, without the slightest knowledge of exactly where she was headed. A moment later, just as she had hoped, she felt Hawk's strong fingers encircling her elbow, stopping her and spinning her around so that she faced him.

"You can't be serious," Hawk said incredulously.

"You don't know me very well, Mr. Two Feather," Samantha replied. Saying his last name formally sounded strange in her ears, so different from his first name, which fell wonderfully upon her tongue . . . almost as wonderful as his kisses had, though that was something she was trying hard to forget.

Several seconds passed. Hawk and Samantha looked at each other, angry, suspecting that their lives would have been safer but infinitely less enjoyable if they had never met.

"You're a little fool," Hawk whispered, but Samantha could hardly take offense at the remark.

She nodded, a smile spreading slowly across the lips that the previous evening Hawk had found so enjoyable to kiss.

"A little fool, indeed," she said proudly, "but this little fool isn't going to have her horse stolen from her without making at least a very serious attempt at getting that horse back. Besides, Daisy would be heartbroken if I didn't try to rescue her."

Hawk rolled his eyes skyward, turning away from Samantha. "I'm risking my neck for a horse named after a flower," he muttered softly, sarcastically, wondering why on earth he was making exceptions for Samantha when he wouldn't make them for anyone else in the world.


They'd gotten close enough to hear the Cheyenne talking now. Samantha was certain her heart was pounding so hard that she would alert the enemy braves. She glanced over at Hawk, and he made a brief motion with his hand that she was to remain in place.

*Calm down,* she told herself. *You've done everything right so far. Don't make a stupid mistake now, when the Cheyenne are so close.*

The day had been difficult. After convincing Hawk to take her along on the raid, Samantha had run endless miles, pushing herself to the limit of her endurance. The Cheyenne braves, on horseback, were moving in no particular hurry, but being on horseback gave them an enormous advantage.

"Don't worry," Hawk had said at least a dozen times that day already. "We'll get them. They're moving without a set destination and, if my guess is correct, they're no longer worried about being followed. Remember how in the morning they checked to see if they were being followed? Now they're checking to see if they are riding into a trap. That tells you where they think the next danger will come from."

Once this had been explained to her Samantha had paid attention to the Cheyenne warriors as they rode along, leading the stolen horses. Again and again, she saw that everything Hawk had said was correct.

A Sioux warrior like Hawk Two Feather was never to be destined for her, Samantha thought. Despite this, she questioned whether he might be the only one man enough to interest her where the other men traipsing through her life had not. And there had been many men. From the time she was sixteen the men had begun lining up, all of them wanting to walk with her, to hold her hand, to impress her with the things they owned, the things they had done, the things they could say.

A quirky smile tugged at the corner of Samantha's mouth. She had never once been impressed with the tales she'd heard. She recognized bragging when she heard it, and it didn't matter to Samantha if a man had more money than her family, or less. What mattered most was that *he* thought she would be impressed, when in fact Samantha's reaction to hyperbolic tales of business acumen simply bored her. And when she wasn't bored she was disgusted.

So many men had paraded through Samantha's life, each

trying to get her to trade in her Levi's for a formal gown! And
what was the appropriate number of dresses a well-bred
woman was to wear in a day? Six? Bosh! Samantha was much
too busy to worry about that kind of nonsense. She wasn't
going to change from one dress into another just to go from
lunch to tea.

And it wasn't just that Hawk was monumentally different
from any of the men Samantha had ever known. It was also
that she felt different when she was with him. She had responded to his kisses, expanded in ways she'd never dreamed
possible. The few times she'd been kissed she'd either pretended to swoon or hadn't bothered to pretend to feel any emotion at all. Either way, Samantha had never felt passion—not
the raw-nerve kind of passion she'd known in Hawk's arms.

That was the key to it, she thought. Her body was telling
her something that her upbringing could not tolerate. Samantha
had responded physically—her *body* responded without any
prompting from her mind—to a man who, by standards with
which she'd been imprinted since birth, was unequivocally unacceptable. Why, she was an heir to the second-largest private
fortune and largest cattle and horse empire in the burgeoning
Dakota territory! There were expectations for Samantha to
marry within the small, elite society she represented!

As she knelt in the grass, assuring herself again that the
Cheyenne could not see her, Samantha closed her eyes and
tried to see inside herself. Perhaps the truth was there, hidden
deep within her own heart; the answer to the questions that
tormented her.

Was Hawk a good man or simply a seductive one? Samantha
had seen enough of her female friends fall under the spell of
what they had thought was simply a naughty or misunderstood
boy. In time they learned he was an immature and selfish
young man, quick with a smile and even quicker to run away
from responsibility of any kind.

Samantha shivered, recalling the mistakes some of her
friends had made. Not all of them, of course; there were some

good men in the territory. But she did know young women who had made horrendous decisions about the men with whom they wanted to spend the rest of their lives. Shortly after marriage—and certainly instantly after they'd given birth—these women discovered that they'd made the mistake of a lifetime. The women, wanting desperately to make love last, too often refused to believe their husbands were at fault. Ignoring warnings from their friends, they'd found themselves alone, living with unfaithful and bitter men who felt children were a woman's responsibility.

Samantha opened her eyes with a start. *No, not me,* she thought then. *It'll never be like that for me!*

She turned her eyes toward Hawk at precisely the same moment that he looked at her. When he saw the concern in her blue eyes he offered her a confident smile and extended his hand toward her, palm upward. Though she couldn't possibly reach his hand, Samantha understood the gesture. He was letting her know that there was nothing to fear, that as long as he was there, she needn't worry. Even though logic dictated that this couldn't possibly be true, Samantha felt her heart constricting; Hawk had done what he could to ease her fears and comfort her, silently and without moving from his sentry position.

Samantha smiled at Hawk. Though not much of a smile, it kept him from moving from his position to investigate why she'd had that worried look on her face.

She closed her eyes, shutting out everything in order to recall their kisses of the night before, high up in the tree. Was there any other man who could kiss like Hawk? Any "civilized" white man who could make her ache for his caresses? Her breasts had felt so tight and full from the desultory, almost casual way Hawk had touched them. He'd teased her by coming so very close to caressing her nipples without ever quite touching them, making her long to beg him to touch the risen crests. But she'd controlled herself, as a "civilized" woman should.

A slow, creeping smile curled the lush contours of Saman-

tha's mouth. She'd enjoyed Hawk's kisses, thrilled in his caresses, and then been able to insist that he stop.

She opened her eyes then and saw Hawk, more beautiful
than any man had a right to be. More charming and intelligent
as well.

Feeling guilty, Samantha turned her face away. Hawk
shouldn't see the way she was looking at him, shouldn't look
into her blue eyes and see the passion she could feel rising
warmly within her.

Really, what was the harm in flirting with Hawk? she wondered impishly. He was a man who would not act the barbarian;
he'd already proven that many times over. So where was the
harm in some innocent fun?

Samantha moistened her lips with the tip of her tongue.
Would it be so naughty to taste his kisses just once more?
Once more, before she returned to her life at the Circle S, and
again was required on most Saturday nights to sit on the porch
swing with this rancher's son or that banker's son, pretending
to find the conversation entertaining?

Hawk had returned to Samantha and was kneeling beside
her. He'd move so silently that he'd startled her at first, seeming
to appearing right before her eyes.

"We'll wait until dark, and when they're asleep we'll take
the horses," Hawk said. "They're not a bit worried that they're
being followed, and that's going to make all the difference. I
hope you don't mind waiting another night before going home."

"My pleasure," Samantha replied cryptically, only a part of
her thoughts on getting Daisy back.

Only one man—a sleepy Cheyenne brave with the lowest
rank of the band—had been assigned to watch over the horses.
During the day the Cheyenne had stolen four more horses.

Hawk moved like smoke through the shadows, and though
his natural inclination was to take permanent measures to in-
capacitate his enemy, for Samantha's benefit he only struck

the sentry hard on the back of the head with his gun, knocking him unconscious. The sentry, who had been sitting cross-legged on the ground, slumped to the side without uttering so much as a gasp.

Hawk motioned for Samantha to circle around the horses. They would each locate a horse.

The horses weren't hobbled, though two long ropes had been fastened around a group of trees to form a makeshift corral. Most of the horses had bridles on them. Some had brands, others Cheyenne paint marks. It didn't take long for Hawk to find his powerful stallion, who nuzzled his chest in greeting.

Leaping on the stallion's back, Hawk took the reins in his left hand, keeping his revolver in his right. The horses were making more noise now, and he knew that soon someone from the sleeping camp would come to investigate.

He looked for Samantha. She still wasn't astride her mare. Hawk grit his teeth. What was taking her so long?

Hawk heard a male voice from the camp call out but he couldn't make out the words. Certain that the first stages of a band-wide warning had sounded, Hawk hissed through clenched teeth, "Hurry!"

The moon, obscured by clouds, allowed him little light. Where was Samantha? The horses were spreading out, no longer restricted by the rope, which he had cut.

Two things happened simultaneously: Samantha found Daisy and leaped on her, allowing Hawk to finally see her, and a Cheyenne warrior spotted a horse walking nervously through the camp. The Cheyenne, realizing the corral had been breached, let out a high warning cry. The horses, already spooked, reacted to the sound; turning in a single, chaotic unit, they ran off into the night.

Hawk kicked his heels to his stallion's flanks and the powerful animal took off like a shot, instinctively sensing the importance of speed. Moments later, futile gunshots rang out in the night, but Hawk was smiling; he knew the bullets had been

fired blindly and that he and Samantha had accomplished all
they'd set out to do.

They pushed the horses through the trees and into the grass-
land, where they could keep them moving more quickly as a
herd. Three times Hawk counted the stolen band, counting
twenty-three horses. Not including Samantha's Daisy, he'd be
able to return to his tribe with a veritable fortune in horses.

For her part, Samantha had needed time to get her heart to
settle down. Even though she'd been riding Daisy at an easy
canter for almost an hour, she continued to look over her shoulder, convinced that somehow the Cheyenne were still following
them. Logic told her they couldn't possibly keep to such a
pace on foot, but the gunshots she'd heard had put a fear to
her that went to the marrow of her bones.

When they reached a small stream Hawk pulled his stallion
to a halt. "Let's let them drink," he said. His teeth gleamed
brilliantly in the moonlight. "We're safe now." He tossed a
long buckskin-clad leg over his stallion and jumped to the
ground. He closed the distance separating them and reached
out to assist Samantha to the ground. "I don't suppose you're
used to riding bareback."

Samantha twisted on Daisy and kicked a foot over the mare's
head. As she slipped off the mare's back, Hawk caught her by
the waist, his powerful hands warm and strong around her,
slowing her descent. In all the activity and riding, Samantha's
shirt had once again pulled free of her Levi's, this time revealing the entire front of her body to the stomach, as well as the
pale swells of her breasts. As she felt the ground against her
feet, she looked up into Hawk's face and saw that he was
looking at her open shirtfront.

"That was," Samantha said in a whisper, "the second most
exciting thing I've ever done in my life."

The quirky half smile so characteristic of Hawk's charming
ways brought the dimple to his cheek. "Would you like to
enlighten me on your most exciting experience?"

His hands were still at her waist, warming her skin through

the fabric of her shirt. Samantha knew she should step away from him, take his hands from her so that she could turn her back, tuck her shirt once more into her pants, and then talk to him in a civilized manner. She knew what she *should* do. What she was less certain of was exactly what she *wanted* to do.

"Are you going to tell me?" Hawk asked, inching just a little closer to Samantha and looming over her. Beginning to bend down, his eyes focused on the tempting mouth that had so beguiled him. "Or am I going to have to guess?"

# Six

"You're a very dangerous man, Hawk," Samantha whispered a moment before his mouth slanted down over hers. She felt him claiming her lips in a breathtaking kiss that demanded a response.

Samantha couldn't help leaning into Hawk. Her head was still spinning from the dizzying excitement of stealing horses from murderous men; from a whirlwind ride through the night; from being so near a man as courageous, seductive, and unmistakably dangerous as Hawk Two Feather. When his mouth covered hers, Samantha could do nothing but give in to the carnal cravings that had tugged at her consciousness since that first kiss she'd shared with Hawk.

His arms wound around her, pulling her in tight. Samantha moaned softly at the soft, pleasing tingles emanating from her peaked nipples and spreading slowly throughout her body.

*I'm only kissing,* Samantha thought. But she was creating an illusion, and she knew it. She enjoyed the warmth of Hawk's magnificent body against her breasts, and she could not deny this because she had done nothing to pull her shirt more securely and modestly around herself. Even now, as she angled her head a bit to the side to silently invite Hawk to pleasure her throat with his tantalizing kisses, she wondered if she'd ever be able to deny herself Hawk's more intimate caresses. She wanted them, but what would she think of herself afterward? Could she control Hawk's passion after she'd let him go too far?

She felt his teeth at her throat, nipping softly against her neck. Samantha issued a startled gasp and her knees trembled even more. When she wrapped her arms around Hawk's middle the texture of his buckskin shirt against her fingertips pleased her.

Bent backward, Samantha allowed Hawk to kiss her throat. Without his secure hold on her she would have fallen backward. Feeling disoriented, she opened her eyes to see the crescent moon and a few stars overhead.

"Hawk," she whispered, for no other reason than that she liked the sound of his name.

He kissed her neck, his tongue tasting her flesh. Samantha turned in his arms, directing his kisses across her collar and the front of her throat to the other side of her neck. Suddenly he was down on one knee before her, and she placed her hands lightly on his shoulders.

Where was her resistance? she wondered. Samantha had behaved as bravely as she could, facing dangers that evening that no woman she'd ever known had ever encountered. And now, kissing Hawk, feeling his powerful body so close to her own, was just one more excursion into new, exotic, and perilous territory.

Kissing Samantha's collarbone, he slowly began working his way down the front of her body. When she pushed her fingers into his long, dark hair he tilted his head back, to look up at her looking down at him.

For several seconds neither of them spoke, uncertain of what would happen next. Then, giving in to curiosity and burgeoning passion, Samantha simply closed her eyes and tilted her head back. Turning her face up to the stars, she decided to let whatever would happen next happen of its own accord.

Then his lips pressed against her stomach, kissing her, his strong teeth nipping at her. Samantha's heart raced, pounding against her ribs. How could she remain standing . . . motionless? Not with the giddy feel of his shoulder-length hair against her fingers! Not with his moist lips kissing her stomach!

*Where has my sanity gone?* Samantha thought.

She nearly fainted at the slick caress of Hawk's tongue against her navel. She trembled at the surprising caress but made no effort to move away. And when she felt his large hands reach around her hips to cup her buttocks she still didn't try to get away, despite all the whispered warnings that had sounded in her brain, which were now panicked screams to escape while it was still possible.

"Hawk . . . oh, Hawk!" Samantha whispered, weaving slightly as he kissed her stomach, his tongue circling her navel. His hands against her buttocks kneaded her taut flesh through the denim trousers. Hawk's caresses had ignited a fire down low, where she felt moist, as though her insides were melting.

His kisses ended, and for a moment Samantha stood waiting impatiently for them to continue. Then she opened her eyes and looked down to see that he was once again gazing up at her.

"Have I done something wrong?" she asked softly.

Hawk shook his head, and Samantha entwined her fingers a bit more securely into his ebony hair. She loved the silken feel of it as much as she enjoyed the sensation that his hands on her body elicited.

He smiled at her lazily, and as he kissed her stomach, his chin nudged her shirt open just a little bit more. How intoxicating it was to have such a large and powerful man kneeling before her! Could this be an act of supplication from a man as forceful as Hawk, who never would have to beg for anything, certainly not for attention from a woman? Not with his abundance of seductive charm and devastating looks!

"I've never . . ." Samantha began but didn't know what to say. She'd never felt more lost. Hawk, she had noticed, was infinitely more knowledgeable in these matters. Could he give her some hint of what was expected of her? "Hawk, I don't know . . ."

He turned his fiery, magnetic gaze on her, straightening his spine so that his face was level with her breasts. His hands never left her buttocks, nor did his dark eyes ever release

Samantha's frightened blue gaze. Slowly, seductively, he kissed the tip of her left breast, the warmth of his mouth passing through her cotton shirt to make her nipple throb so powerfully, it was almost painful.

The sensation of heated moisture against the sensitive tip of her breast startled Samantha with its intensity. A gasp caught in her throat and her entire body quivered responsively, though she neither tried to get away from Hawk nor did she prevent his deliciously passionate quest.

For a moment Samantha concentrated on what she was feeling, on the intense sensations charging through her body.

This moment was too good to be true, Samantha decided—having a handsome warrior like Hawk Two Feather kissing her breast through her cotton shirt. Her mind told her that Hawk was probably not the right man for her future, but emotion said that for the here and now Hawk was perfect.

Samantha opened her eyes to look down, needing the visual confirmation of his magnificence. But the moment she looked down Hawk pulled away from her, leaning back slightly, a smile still twinkling in his dark eyes, though no longer on his seductive lips.

Once again they exchanged glances, though neither spoke. And once more Samantha was filled with an overwhelming sense of insecurity, with the awareness that Hawk knew exactly what was happening and what was expected—perhaps entirely too well for her own good—but Samantha did not.

She looked at him, confused and shaken. Then she looked down at her own breast, concealed by her shirt, and saw the round, darkened area that had been moistened by his kiss. Her nipples were erect, making prominent dents in the cotton fabric, an undeniable indication of the excitement her body was experiencing.

Then, very slowly, Samantha reached up with her left hand, sliding her palm along her side and across her body so that she very nearly cupped her own breast. She twisted her right hand a bit more securely into the hair at the back of Hawk's neck. Trembling softly, not at all sure she was doing what she should—but absolutely convinced she was doing what she was compelled to do by desires unprecedented and irrepressible—she pulled her shirt aside. Her breast was full and round, the areola surrounding the passion-peaked nipple a soft pink.

When she heard Hawk's sudden, sharp intake of breath, a hint of a smile, softly confident in its nature, curled the fullness of Samantha's mouth. She knew Hawk enjoyed looking at her and, searching his eyes, Samantha realized that he wasn't nearly as aloof and casual as he had seemed.

"Kiss me," Samantha whispered, pulling Hawk to her exposed breast.

The intensity of the feeling was infinitely stronger without a barrier between Hawk's lips and tongue and the sensitive crest of her breast. A cry of ecstasy was ripped from her throat, and her knees sagged briefly.

"K-Kiss me," Samantha begged.

The initial intensity of the pleasure had been transformed from a searing heat spreading through her flesh to a warmth of passion going deeper, into her bones. The warmth passed through her fingertips, her toes, and even the top of her head. Urgently, she exposed her other breast, and Hawk quickly showered it with kisses.

Time stood still as she guided Hawk, turning her shoulders, her breasts, to appreciate the warrior's sensual skills. Hawk's great, bronzed hands were caressing her—from the backs of her knees to her buttocks, his long fingers sliding around her thighs, pressing to feel the heat of her excitement even through her Levi's and pantalets.

Samantha trembled, her hips slowly undulating from side to side. Hawk's hands had ignited a fire within her, quickly burning away the last vestiges of the untouchable tomboy who loved horses more than men. His powerful fingers were at once commanding and gentle. Samantha moaned incoherently, her eyes pinched shut as a strange pressure began to build inside her, as though a mainspring was being wound tighter and tighter inside her.

A little voice in the back of Samantha's mind whispered a warning that at first she did not recognize and then, when she did, would not heed.

*Too far, too fast,* the tiny voice repeated.

Samantha didn't want to believe that she was out of control, that the passion now erupting within her was beyond her comprehension or influence. Thus far, she'd proudly lived her life without the usual constraints holding women back, the tomboy in Levi's, rather than anyone's "little lady." She wasn't going to be just like the other simpering ladies of her social milieu. She wasn't going to attend teas and gossip about inconsequential things; she was going to live her life as she wanted to, in charge every step of the way.

But now she wasn't in charge—not even a little bit. The strange, powerful, dangerous, absurdly handsome half-breed Sioux warrior named Hawk Two Feather was in control, and if Samantha tried to tell herself that she was holding the reins, she was only deluding herself . . . and the worst thing of all was that she knew it.

Hawk's hand between her legs touched with strength and forcefulness, demanding that she respond to his caresses even though two layers of clothing separated hand from responsive flesh.

*It's wrong,* Samantha's brain warned again. *Don't let him touch you there!*

Yet she found herself spreading her feet a little wider, further availing herself of the enigmatic warrior's powerful caresses, shivering as he kissed her breast and used his teeth against the aroused nipple; trembling while his hand worked with increasing urgency between her thighs.

The pressure was growing on itself, making it difficult for her to breathe evenly. She gulped air, trying to relax, feeling the muscles in her stomach tighten with each revolution of

Hawk's hand, with each devilish swipe of his tongue against her nipple.

*Stop it! Stop it now . . . before you can't stop him at all!*

The pressure within her was almost painful, and this in part helped Samantha regain control. She opened her eyes and watched as Hawk's tantalizing lips pressed kisses along the slopes of her breasts, moving from one crest to the other. Her fingers still entwined in his ebony hair, she suddenly pushed him backward, using such force that Hawk was knocked off balance. She twisted sharply, turning her back to him, disentangling herself from his arm, which was still wrapped tightly around her hips.

Samantha took three steps, staggering slightly, then took another three. Distance from Hawk would help her regain her composure.

"D-Don't!"

The single word warbled in the night air. She stopped, her back toward Hawk, gathering her shirttails and tucking them into the waistband of her Levi's. Her breath came in deep, uneven gulps. Samantha believed that she'd just experienced something close to intoxication, or else some temporary madness that no one ever spoke of. All she knew was that her behavior had not been characteristic of the young woman she'd always thought herself to be. And even now, even after Hawk's kisses and caresses had ended, her body still tingled, her heart still pounded, her breasts and other sensitive places remained even more desirous of his touch.

"What's wrong?" Hawk demanded, getting to his feet to follow Samantha. He was clearly angry with her abrupt change of mood.

"Everything! Everything! Please, just leave me alone! Please . . . at least for a little while! I need to think!"


Red Wolf sat in front of the campfire, his belly full and his spirits at ease. Several tribal elders had joined him around the fire, as well as Aja, Hawk Two Feather's younger sister.

Red Wolf prepared to say the well-rehearsed words, pretending that they were spontaneous. Speaking to the distinguished and powerful Sioux elders, Red Wolf would not actually have to present his "suspicions" to them formally.

"I do not understand why Hawk Two Feather is not here." Red Wolf shrugged his naked shoulders, as though the matter really did not mean much to him. "After all, is not Hawk the one who says we must plan for the next season today? He is the one who says we must all work together if we are to do the most good for the tribe. And where is he now? He is off hunting on his own. He said he would be gone for two days, maybe three. He has been gone five days now."

Aja, hearing the veiled insults toward her brother, commented, "Maybe he is busy. You do not know him as I do. Maybe he has been hurt. What if he needs your help instead of your insults?"

"Needs my help? Been hurt?" Red Wolf asked, leaning away from Aja, as though shocked by the questions. "More likely he has found a squaw, and he will not return to us until he has had his fill of her. For that he does not need my help!"

Red Wolf laughed then and, though Hawk was respected by the elders, many of them laughed as well, knowing Hawk's weakness was his fondness for squaws.

Aja, hearing the laughter at her brother's expense, quickly rose to her feet and stomped off, her teeth clenched in rage. Why did Red Wolf always insult and demean Hawk the most savagely whenever he was away from the tribe but have nothing to say to Hawk when they were face-to-face? Then he had nothing but compliments for the Sioux warrior! Aja loathed Red Wolf and couldn't understand why so many of the elders listened to him.

Watching her retreat into the darkness, Red Wolf managed to keep the smile of victory from his lips. Aja was furious with him and he knew it, just as he knew that some of the tribal elders did not appreciate his talking about Hawk when he wasn't there to defend himself. But Red Wolf also knew

that he had planted the seed of doubt in every mind—even in
the minds of the men who did not approve of what he said.

Red Wolf could have said more regarding Hawk, but he did
not. To be too negative might jeopardize the victory he had
gained, and he'd lived too long with the dream of destroying
Hawk Two Feather to let impatience get in his way now.

# Seven

Wishing she could sleep longer, Samantha awoke slowly, sleepily, blinking her eyes. Her body, pushed long and hard, had needed the rest.

Suddenly she remembered that she wasn't at home, recovering from a hard day in the breaking corral, but was sleeping outside. She sat bolt upright and was completely awake in an instant. She looked around the small campsite, sensing that something was wrong.

The horses they'd taken from the Cheyenne were still grazing on the thick grass near the bank of the stream, a little more than twenty-five yards to her left. They seemed at ease, and that was a good sign. If the Cheyenne were approaching, the horses might be spooked.

Hawk. Where was Hawk?

Samantha whipped her head to the right and left, looking for the tall warrior with the bold smile. Until that very instant she hadn't realized how completely she counted on him to keep her safe.

"Hawk?" She spoke in a conversational tone. She wanted Hawk with her. Only then would she feel safe. "Hawk, where are you?" she repeated, louder this time. "Hawk! Hawk, where are you?"

Rising to her feet, Samantha searched the thick trees, hoping to see the Sioux warrior leaning nonchalantly against a pine. He'd be there, a smile on his wide, sensual mouth, his arms crossed over his broad chest, taking naughty delight in Samantha's anxiety. She began looking up into the trees, hoping to find him sitting on a limb, perhaps looking into the distance for the Cheyenne. She looked, and looked again.

Hawk was nowhere to be found.

"He wouldn't leave me," Samantha said aloud, trying to reassure herself as she combed her fingers through her tousled blond hair. She'd unconsciously hoped that the sound of her own voice would give her confidence, but it didn't. She could detect in her tone the rising panic she was pretending didn't exist.

She looked at the horses again. Some were looking at her now, their senses instantly picking up on her fear, watching her as she moved slowly, uncertainly, around the campsite.

Memories flooded through Samantha as she adjusted her shirt, tucking the tails into the waistband of her Levi's. In her mind's eye she saw herself in Hawk's arms, kissing him passionately, her heart racing with excitement as his practiced sensuality melted her resistance. She recalled that *she* had been the one to pull open her shirt to expose her breasts, that *she* had guided Hawk's kisses to receive them wherever she most wanted them.

Samantha shuddered, recalling the way she had pushed Hawk away, staggering away from him on legs weakened with passion. Frightened of her own ecstasy, she'd walked into the shadows, where she'd remained, alone, until her hands had finally stopped trembling and good judgment was once more guiding her actions.

A tentative truce had been called between Hawk and Samantha, so that when he'd suggested they get some sleep she'd been only too happy to find a grassy place—at least ten yards from Hawk—to stretch out and close her eyes. Samantha had expected a sleepless night, with her mind spinning in circles, but exhaustion had overtaken her and, before she knew it, she was sleeping soundly under the stars.

Soundly . . . until she woke to find she was alone; the Sioux warrior who was her protector had abandoned her.

Samantha went to the roped-off area where the stolen horses grazed. Munching on grass, Daisy walked forward and tossed her head up and down in greeting.

"Hey, girl," Samantha whispered, rubbing the horse's powerful neck. "At least you didn't leave me, did you?"

Hawk's big stallion wasn't there, which didn't surprise Samantha. If he was going to abandon her while she slept, he'd certainly take the stallion he'd risked his neck to retrieve from the Cheyenne.

Samantha shook her head in disgust. Men were such fools! She knew that Hawk had left her because she had turned him away, stopping his seduction before she'd lost her honor and dignity. Fool! Samantha realized now that it didn't matter if a man's heritage was European or Indian. In the end, the common factor was that they were all fools; simpleminded, stubborn, lusty fools, every one of them!

"At least he left you here to take me home," Samantha said aloud, still rubbing Daisy's neck. "He could have left me on foot, I suppose."

Samantha's slender eyebrows pushed together at a troubling thought. Why would Hawk leave behind the horses he'd risked his life to steal?

Samantha could understand him leaving her, even for a very stupid reason. What made no sense at all, no matter how angry Hawk was with her, was his abandonment of the stolen horses. He'd been overjoyed when they'd recaptured them the previous night, calling it a personal victory over his enemy, the Cheyenne. The exuberance and triumph she'd witnessed in his eyes had led to that first kiss, which had led immediately to the second kiss, which had led to a near-complete seduction.

Turning away from Daisy, Samantha closed her eyes and rubbed her temples lightly with her fingertips. Where was Hawk, and what was he doing?

She began to inspect the grass around the horses, hoping to find a clue to Hawk's disappearance. Though she'd been around horses her entire life, she'd never developed tracking

skills. Why should she? The Sanders family had never needed
to track their stock.

"Now what do I do?" Samantha mumbled, looking at the
ground and trying to decipher what the stallion's hoofprints
meant.

Should she wait around for Hawk to return, or should she
get on Daisy and ride away? Though she wasn't certain of her
location, it wouldn't be long before she would find some tree,
some valley, some geographical marker that would help her
find her way back through the Dakota territory. And then it
would just be a matter of time before she was home again.

Was she safer with Hawk or without him? Safer? What were
the real dangers? The Cheyenne, or Hawk himself?

When she was with him she certainly behaved in ways dia-
metrically opposed to the way she behaved without him. But
what about the Cheyenne? She had no idea where they were
now. If they had traveled throughout the night, the Cheyenne
could be stalking her, perhaps even—

*Stop thinking that way!* Samantha was angry with herself
for letting in fear.

But stopping the questions from going through her thoughts
was not as easy as she had hoped. She *did* know why Hawk
frightened her so. He'd made her feel things she had dreamed
of on so many nights. She had for several years had passionate
dreams that made her toss and turn in her bed as she slept,
tormented by the dream-caresses of a faceless stranger who
made her tremble with desire. In the morning when she would
awaken from her restless sleep, she would recall fragments of
her dreams and feel embarrassed and frightened by her own
mind.

It hadn't mattered to Samantha that the dreams were just
that—dreams she could not direct or guide in any way. She
was still embarrassed by their ungovernable passion, especially
because in her dreams she was ecstatically happy, erotically
aroused to a point where she'd tingled from head to toe.

She cautiously asked several friends whether they'd ever had such dreams. "Never! Have you?" came a typical response, with eyes large and round with shock. Samantha knew then that she had to keep the nature of her dreams a secret from everyone. Otherwise she would surely suffer social censure the likes of which would make the scorn she received for being a tomboy appear as nothing more than the mildest teasing.

As she had done since childhood, Samantha sat down with her legs folded beneath her and tried to force everything from her mind. She must think clearly! What should she do now? Worrying about her erotic dreams—or were they nightmares?—was not of immediate concern. Later, when she was in the safety of her own home, she could contemplate those naughty dreams and ponder their meaning. Now, this instant, she had to consider the Cheyenne and her possession of their stolen horses. And what would happen if the white men who'd attacked her—the ones Hawk had dispatched with such startling swiftness and finality—had friends or family looking for her?

She opened her eyes, then, and smiled. What a ridiculous notion—that her would-be rapists would have family who would hunt her down!

She was on her feet an instant later, walking purposefully toward Daisy. How much better, she thought, to take control of her own life, even at the risk of making a mistake, than to wait, doing nothing, hoping that someone else would show up to make all her troubles disappear.

"Girl, we're getting out of here," Samantha said to Daisy, just about to step over the rope surrounding the horses.

"Without me?"

Samantha wheeled around, her heart in her throat, to find Hawk standing directly behind her, his great stallion at his side. The smirking half smile on his face that Samantha had hoped to see had appeared, but now she was furious. There could be no doubt that Hawk had intentionally sneaked up behind her to scare her.

"Someday somebody's going to punch you in the nose!"

Samantha warned, thinking that her brother Sonny probably
wouldn't mind doing it. "And if you ever scare me like that
again, *I'm* going to be that somebody!" She hit his steely arm
with her fist.

Hawk laughed softly, not at all put off by Samantha's attack.
"Did you think I'd left you?" he asked.

Samantha scowled, wishing there was something she could
do to wipe the smile from his lips. "Of course I thought that!
What else could I possibly think when I wake up to find you
gone?"

"Only temporarily," Hawk replied, the timbre of his voice
suggesting added meaning that sent a shiver up Samantha's
spine. "There were things that I had to do, and I didn't want
to put you in danger. Also, you needed your sleep."

Finally Samantha noticed the packhorse Hawk had been
leading. Piled high on the horse were the possessions he'd
taken from the Cheyenne—and Samantha's saddle.

"You got my saddle back!" she exclaimed, rushing to examine the saddle she'd used for six years. It had been a gift
from Sonny, so she was emotionally attached to it, as well as
being appreciative for its quality and craftsmanship. "How did
you get it?"

Hawk's dark eyes met Samantha's, but he didn't answer; he
simply stared at her. For Samantha the message that, in Hawk's
world, a woman did not ask such questions of a man came
through loud and clear. The battles were fought by the men,
and though they might brag of their exploits, they did not care
to be questioned about them.

After a moment Samantha nodded. Perhaps she shouldn't
know what had transpired during the retrieval of her saddle,
she decided. It could well be a bloody, violent tale, one she
wouldn't want to hear.

"I have food." Hawk began to unstrap Samantha's saddle
from the packhorse. "I hope you don't mind eating while we
ride. The Cheyenne were angry before, when we stole their
horses; now they're murderously mad that I've stolen most of

their belongings." A smile crossed his lips as he ran the tips of his fingers down a hickory bow. "And I've got my bow and arrows back." He spoke of his weapon as one might speak of a loved one.

"Let's not spend time standing around talking," Samantha said, much more nervous about the Cheyenne than Hawk was. "I'd rather not have to explain to the Cheyenne that I wasn't the one who decided to steal their horses."

Hawk was settled easily in his saddle, letting his stallion pick a leisurely pace. The Cheyenne had to be miles behind them at this point, and it was highly unlikely that they would have followed Hawk's tracks very far. They'd lost their horses and then been thoroughly disgraced when he'd returned to get the saddles. The Cheyenne wouldn't forget their enemy, Hawk Two Feather, but they wouldn't be foolish enough to jeopardize themselves by following him on foot.

With the Cheyenne now far behind him, Hawk could again dwell on more entertaining questions . . . like why Samantha wore trousers like a man, instead of dresses, like a woman? What would she look like in an Indian maiden's dress? The thought made him smile, and he glanced over at Samantha. Out of the corner of his eye he saw her twist in the saddle to check for the thousandth time to see whether they were being followed. Noticing that her shirt had opened slightly, she pulled it tight again.

*It'll make it easier for me when she wears something besides that shirt,* Hawk thought.

He didn't like being so continuously tempted by her. It didn't matter to him that, in many ways, she was one of the bravest people he'd ever met, and certainly the bravest woman. It didn't matter that she had a hidden, passionate nature that, he suspected, would be thrilling to help her set free. What mattered—and Hawk had to always keep this in mind—was that as a white woman, Samantha could never be the woman for him.

He wasn't going to make the same mistake his mother had. His children wouldn't know the same humiliation he'd occasionally encountered as a child.

"What's wrong?" Samantha asked.

He looked at her, his eyes as sharp as flint. "Nothing," he answered. "I was thinking; that's all."

"Oh?" Samantha had come to learn that Hawk spent a great deal of time with his own thoughts, thoughts he was seldom willing to share.

"We'll go to my camp first," Hawk said quietly. He would not tell her of the horror he had known as a child, once he'd been able to truly see his mother for what she really was. "That will give us the chance to leave the horses there, rest awhile, and get plenty to eat. After that I'll escort you home."

"That sounds fine," Samantha replied. She doubted this plan was what he had been thinking of with that scowl on his face, but she wasn't going to say so. "It won't cause any problems bringing me to your tribe?"

"No," Hawk lied, certain that riding into camp with Samantha at his side would bring trouble into his life. "The Sioux are gracious hosts. You'll be welcome."

They continued to ride, and Samantha now welcomed the silence, which gave her some uninterrupted time to put in order her feelings for Hawk.

Should she tell him that she was wealthy? Hawk Two Feather deserved a reward of some sort for rescuing her from the rapists, and for protecting her afterward. If she talked about money, would she offend him? Could the reward money help purchase items needed by the tribe?

Hawk had a fine Colt revolver and a holster strapped around his lean hips, so he clearly had used the white man's currency before, and understood the value of money. But would he look at her differently—would he behave differently—if he knew her family was one of the wealthiest in the territory?

After long and hard consideration Samantha decided to reward Hawk for saving her life—but *after* she'd been safely
returned to her home. Only then would he discover her last
name was Sanders, that her share of the family fortune was
considerable, and that the combined strength of the Sanders
name and finances made a force to be reckoned with.

She looked up at the sky. The sun sat on the horizon; they
could ride for perhaps another hour before making camp. After
spending a long day in the saddle, Samantha's feelings about
Hawk and her own behavior had mellowed. She hadn't gone
too far, had she? Was allowing a kiss and a caress such an
unforgivable thing?

Hawk was unmistakably masculine and alluring and, though
she couldn't precisely pinpoint his seductive mystery, her body
and her senses knew it was there. In the wickedly sensual
dreams that had plagued her sleep since she was sixteen
Samantha's dream man had been faceless. Now, after experiencing the passion rising from a kiss from Hawk, she wondered whether he was, in flesh and blood, the man she'd
dreamed about.

If she allowed Hawk to kiss her again, who would ever know
about it?

Samantha pushed the thought away, but not before she felt
heat rising slowly upward, coloring her neck and cheeks. *That*
line of thinking *had* to be avoided!

Realizing she needed a diversion to get her mind off the
ecstasy of Hawk's skilled embrace, she twisted in the saddle
and asked him, "Will you show me how to shoot your bow?
I've never shot one before, and I want to learn."

"No! Never!" Hawk snapped, his eyes narrowing in stunned
disbelief at the audacity of the question.

Samantha was shocked. But the vehemence of the response
served to remind her once again how little she actually knew
about Hawk and the world he called his own.

"I'm sorry for asking," she muttered, wondering why he

could be so generous with both his time and his possessions
at one moment, and then selfishly aloof in the next.

In the silence that ensued, Hawk had to remind himself that
Samantha's foolish questions were driven by ignorance of the
Sioux culture, not a callous disregard for it. She simply didn't
understand that, to a warrior, his weapons were sacred objects,
and that no one else was allowed to use them, to even touch
them.

Even now, though he was thankful that he'd been able to
recover his bow, quiver, and arrows, he needed to purify them
because they'd been touched by his enemy, the Cheyenne.
When he had time he would perform the purification ceremony
privately so that his bow and arrows would again be unsullied,
and would protect him from harm, feed himself and his family,
and not allow himself or his name to be dishonored.

But since his bow, quiver, and arrows *already* needed to be
purified . . .

"We'll make camp early," Hawk said quietly. "Then I'll
show you how to use the bow."

Samantha's face broke into an enormous smile as she almost
shouted; "You will?" Several horses flinched at the exuberance
of her response.

"Only on the condition that you never tell anyone about it,"
Hawk said.

Samantha was confused by the requirement but agreed to
it. Every time she learned something new about Hawk, she
was also just a little bit more perplexed with the man and his
culture.

The horses had been taken care of, the campfire was crackling to life, at least thirty minutes of acceptable sunlight remained . . . and Hawk was shaking his head in amazement at
the things he agreed to when Samantha was near.

"It can't be that bad," Samantha teased, seeing Hawk's dis-

comfort as he walked off twenty paces from a long-dead tree
that was to be Samantha's practice target.

"What I am about to do goes against many time-honored
laws my people believe in," Hawk said. "A warrior's weapons . . . women are not to touch that which is made for war."

Unable to find the right words to express his feelings, Hawk
was astonished that, for all his discomfort, he couldn't tell
Samantha that she wasn't allowed to use his bow. He didn't
want to see the disappointment in her eyes, eyes so beautifully
bright and blue when he had first agreed to teach her.

Samantha herself nearly confessed to Hawk that the things
she'd done with him—in his arms as she feasted on his breathtaking kisses—were against the beliefs of *her* people. Though
she bit her lip to silence the words, a smile still tugged at the
corners of her mouth. The Cheyenne now seemed far, far away,
and Samantha felt truly safe for the first time since she'd first
been attacked.

"There are two ways to grip the arrow," Hawk explained.
"One way is like this." He notched an arrow on the string. Then
he curled his right index finger tightly and pinched the notched
end of the arrow between his curled finger and his thumb. He
pulled the taut string back slightly to demonstrate how it was
done. "The other way is like this," he continued. He shifted his
grip so that the arrow was between his first and second fingers.
Then, curling just the tips of his fingers around the string, he
pulled the arrow back a bit. "See how that works?"

Samantha was eager to try. When Hawk handed her the bow,
with the arrow already notched on the string, she couldn't hide
the smile that blossomed on her lips. Even though she suspected that he had shared his passion with many women, she
knew that this was something Hawk had never done with or
for another woman. It added a special dimension to the experience for her.

At first she pinched the end of the arrow, but when she
tried to draw the arrow back, to bend the bow tightly as Hawk
had done, she could hardly move it more than a few inches

before the end of the arrow slipped from her grasp. The arrow shot weakly from the bow, missing the tree by four feet.

"Oops. I didn't mean to shoot that," Samantha said with a sheepish grin.

"Don't be embarrassed. This is difficult. A warrior starts by learning to make his own bow and arrows when he is very young. By the time he is ready to hunt he has had a bow in his hands for years." Hawk handed Samantha another arrow, standing beside her and to the back. "Try the other grip that I showed you."

He saw the determination on Samantha's face when she notched the arrow, then turned her hand so that her fingertips curled around the string. Instead of just using two or three fingers to grip the string, she used all four. Hawk smiled, knowing he'd made the bow for himself, a tall man much stronger than average, not for a woman half his size.

Samantha's jaw was clenched as she strained against the bow, pulling back on the string. Her left arm quivered as her right pulled the line more and more taut, drawing back the arrow. She squinted her left eye closed and tried to sight down the arrow at the tree stump. The strain made it impossible for her to keep her left arm steady, and her biceps were beginning to burn with fatigue, even though she'd only been tugging at the bow for a few seconds.

"Release, Samantha!" Hawk commanded.

She relaxed her fingers just a fraction and in an instant the arrow shot away. The burn of the line sliding across the sensitive tips of her fingers caused Samantha to grimace, but the arrowhead hit the tree with a resounding *thunk!* and Samantha let out a shout of joy.

"I hit it! Did you see that?"

"Maybe you've got Sioux blood in you," Hawk said through a smile.

Samantha laughed at the absurdity of such an idea, considering her ivory skin, her blue eyes, and her honey blond hair.

But once the initial burst of enthusiasm for her small victory subsided, she felt the stinging in her fingertips once again.

"Let me see," Hawk said, noting Samantha's discomfort.

When she pretended she wasn't in pain, he took her by the wrist, pulling her hand toward him and turning it palm up so he could inspect her fingertips. They were pink from the bowstring.

"There's something we can do to help prevent this," Hawk offered, quickly releasing Samantha's hand.

Touching her hand had conjured up memories of touching her elsewhere, and seeing her pink fingertips made him want to kiss them, one at a time, to make them feel better. All these thoughts, he didn't need to remind himself, were moving in a direction he'd already traveled, and had regretted.

Samantha sensed a change in Hawk, though she was not entirely certain what had caused it. As he went to his pack of belongings, she quickly adjusted her shirt, which had pulled open more than she'd liked during the archery practice. Most troubling of all was that she'd been wearing the nearly ruined shirt for so long that she'd almost grown oblivious to its condition—no longer always aware when it had opened.

Hawk returned with a small, flat piece of leather, oddly shaped. Samantha quickly discovered the shape was designed so that she could pull back on the bow with the leather cushioning her fingertips from the string.

Samantha then shot four more arrows, some hitting the tree stump and others missing. During the next set of shots, Hawk taught her how to keep both eyes open as she aimed, and Samantha was able to hit the tree the next five times.

"This bow is too much for me, though," Samantha said, when the arrows had been retrieved. "I can't get the line all the way back."

"Perhaps . . ." Hawk said, then silenced himself.

When Samantha looked at him quizzically he was thankful that she did not pursue what he had been about to say. He'd almost said that someday he could make a bow for her that would suit her strength, just as warriors do for their young sons. To make a bow for a squaw was unthinkable . . . except Hawk knew in his heart that he'd been thinking such things, and that Samantha's vitality was making him question for the first time a hundred ironclad rules.

"Will you help me?" Samantha asked, notching up another arrow, turning her back to Hawk to face the target tree once more.

Hawk stepped close behind Samantha and very carefully extended his arms, his left hand wrapping around her left wrist so he could help her steady the bow, his right hand sliding around to grip the bowstring just above her hand.

"Keep both eyes open and, instead of thinking about the arrow, think about the target," Hawk instructed, helping Samantha to pull back the bowstring.

Samantha's request for help had been issued innocently enough, but now her thoughts had nothing to do with the target. She could feel Hawk's chest touching her back, and even though he wore buckskin, she could feel his heart pounding fast . . . or was that just her own heart hammering? Why did her heart do that whenever Hawk was so near she could catch the scent of him, so subtle and indefinably masculine?

"Aim, then release," Hawk said, trying to concentrate on the task at hand.

Hawk loosened his grip on the bowstring, and the force it exerted against Samantha's fingers was much greater than she could withstand. The bowstring snapped from her fingertips, and the arrow sailed off, shooting high and well off the mark, disappearing into the distance.

"You missed," Hawk said, his voice a husky whisper as he looked over Samantha's shoulder and down at her body. Her shirt had opened, and the creamy swells of her bosom drew his attention again. His chest still against her back, he knew he should immediately step away from the enticing woman with the honey blond hair. Not even Hawk's great willpower was sufficient to do successful battle against Samantha's un-intended and yet irresistibly seductive charms, and he knew it.

Samantha lowered the bow and turned slowly, never com-pletely easing the contact of her body against Hawk's until she faced him. She tilted her head far back to look directly into his dark eyes and saw his gaze go from her own eyes down to her bosom, and then quickly back up again.

*He doesn't want to look at me,* Samantha guessed. At first she felt inadequate in the face of this suggestion that perhaps she wasn't beautiful enough, not feminine enough to hold his interest. But this fear was short-lived; in her heart she knew he found her attractive. He wasn't like the white men of Dead-wood who thought her Levi's and cotton shirt would be best left for men to wear.

She thought, *Hawk likes to look at me, but he doesn't like to like it.*

"Want to try again?" Hawk asked.

Her mouth dry, Samantha felt the tension between them. She wanted very much to tell Hawk, in plain, simple language, that what she really wanted was to have his kisses begin once again. His kisses had awakened in her a passion that she'd believed existed only in her dream world, a passion she had been afraid to experiment with in real life. Earlier, his ruggedly masculine bearing had released her constraints; now she wanted to free that passionate woman within herself once more.

*Do it, Samantha! Tell him to kiss you!*

Though the inner voice of her passionate self cried out, Samantha could not make her lips form the words that needed to be spoken. However outspoken she'd always been in the past, Samantha now found herself mute.

"It's getting late," Hawk said then, stepping backward, pull-ing his gaze away from Samantha and obviously having a dif-ficult time doing it. "Maybe we should make camp."

"Yes, of course. Camp."

The words sounded wooden in Samantha's mouth. She felt

eerily disoriented as she watched him walking away to retrieve the arrows. Make camp? They'd already made camp. Samantha realized, with some amount of relief, that Hawk was as confused by the chaotic emotions that ricocheted back and forth between them as she was.

Why couldn't he allow himself the pleasure of looking at her? she wondered. In Deadwood the men usually made no effort to hide their comments and their ogling. But Hawk was resisting that which other men had sought. Why?

A shiver ran through Samantha, working its way from her toes all the way up her spine. She felt jittery inside, knowing with absolute certainty that she wanted Hawk, wanted him with every fiber in her body. She needed him in ways that she did not entirely understand. She knew at that moment that she had wanted him from the first instant they had kissed. At least her *body* had wanted him, had known this instinctively, and had heeded the unconscious whispers that had been directing so many of her actions recently. Her mind, and all the inhibitions foisted on her by others, as well as the self-imposed guilt she felt because of the erotic nature of her dreams, had made her think that she was wrong to accept the pleasures of the deeply arousing kisses that the powerful Sioux warrior had bestowed on her.

Watching as Hawk searched for the missing arrow, Samantha felt a tingling anxiety within herself. To understand now that she had unconsciously wanted Hawk for a long, long time, thrilled her to the core. Now she knew that all the time she had spent in Hawk's presence, even when it seemed thoroughly innocent, had actually been the seduction of her. Even if he hadn't deliberately enchanted her senses, his presence, little by little, had stripped away the hindrances and barriers preventing her from accepting this pleasure.

Samantha turned her back to Hawk and quickly tucked the tails of her damnable shirt into her Levi's once more.

Then the contrary thought entered her mind: Somehow, she had to stay away from Hawk. She wanted his kisses too much.

Clearly, the next time she kissed Hawk, the next time she wound her arms around his neck and held him close, her body would not be satisfied with just his kisses. The next time in his arms she would take the next step, and Samantha knew exactly what the next step was . . . the step she couldn't allow herself to take. Her body was intemperate, she realized, and accordingly could not moderate the passion she shared with Hawk. It was all or nothing, and since she could not allow herself to have all, she would have to have nothing.

She walked to her bedroll and hoped to get some sleep, though she doubted she would.

# Eight

A gaiety passed between Samantha and Hawk throughout the morning. Samantha was delighted to be with Hawk. When he was happy he was infinitely more enjoyable to be near than when he was quiet and brooding. She didn't understand the change in him, though she suspected that his high spirits were a facade to hide an even more troubling frame of mind.

"There isn't really anything you have to know when we get there," Hawk told her.

His gaze was on the hills to the east. Sentries were positioned to protect the tribe from surprise attacks; the fact that he couldn't spot them didn't surprise him. What Sioux would allow himself to be spotted until he was ready to be seen?

"I think you'll like my sister. She'll talk your ear off and ask you a hundred questions."

"You have a sister?" Samantha asked, surprised.

"You make it sound so unusual," Hawk replied.

"I just didn't picture you with a brother or sister, that's all. No disrespect intended."

Samantha almost added that if Hawk were more open about himself and his life, she wouldn't be so surprised when she discovered something as mundane as a sister. However, Hawk was not a man she could tease about such issues.

"Actually, she and I share only our mother. We had different fathers," Hawk explained, though his tone changed considerably. As memories of his mother came to him, he shook them away, forcing himself to think only of Aja, and the pleasure his sister brought him by being in his life. "Aja—that's my sister's name—is the most spirited woman I've ever known."

"Even more spirited than I am?" Samantha asked, her coquettish tone surprising her. Hawk's easy smiles were working seductive magic on her senses, even though she was doing all she could to inure herself against them.

Hawk looked at her, his eyes narrowed and his lips pursed, as though in deep thought. "That's a difficult question to answer so quickly. I'm confident in saying that Aja has probably made as many men furious with her as you have, but in regard to pure spirit—"

"Are you saying I'm difficult to get along with?" Samantha shot back, turning Daisy to the side so that she rode so close to Hawk that their knees nearly touched. "Be honest, now; am I really difficult to get along with?"

Hawk shrugged, then shook his head slowly, his smile boyish. Samantha wanted to kiss him. She wanted to leap right out of her saddle and tackle him to the ground, and shower his face with kisses. Then she intended to kiss him on the mouth: a long, slow, unending kiss that would bring little tremors of satisfaction along the surface of her skin.

Samantha was almost thankful for her apprehension about riding into the Sioux camp. It provided a diversion to the romantic thoughts running through her mind.

"You're sure they won't mind?" Samantha asked softly.

"How many times have I told you that you'll be welcome?" Hawk asked.

"A few."

"A few dozen is more like it!"

Samantha had heard stories of Indian massacres, of unspeakable atrocities too horrifying for a woman's ears. But the women were always told eventually, and the men who spread the stories were always there to put comforting arms around the frightened ladies, and to offer promises to protect them from the redskin savages. Samantha knew that most of the stories she'd heard were lies, but she also knew that some of the stories—stories of rape and murder—were probably true. She'd been attacked by Indians herself only a few days earlier.

And saved by an Indian as well, she reminded herself.

They rode slowly over the crest of a hill, driving the horses they had taken from the Cheyenne. And then, in front of them in the valley, unfolded the Sioux camp, nearly eighty tepees grouped in the valley. Children ran everywhere excitedly.

"They know we're coming?" Samantha asked, shocked that though a considerable distance separated them from the outskirts of the camp, everyone apparently had been forewarned of their arrival.

"They've known for at least the last mile," Hawk answered, recalling his own youthful days when he'd been a sentry, with the responsibility of warning the camp of approaching danger. "We Sioux don't like surprises."

Children ran forward to greet them, their faces open and guileless. Many of them shouted out Hawk's name, and he had to raise his hand for silence so the horses would not get spooked and run. Samantha was pleased to see the children's smiling faces, but along with them came a handful of braves on horseback, armed with bows and a few rifles. These men looked on Samantha with open scorn.

A dangerous-looking brave rode alongside Hawk, speaking to him in a short, clipped fashion. Samantha didn't have to be told that there was no love lost between the man and Hawk.

"I captured the horses from the Cheyenne," Hawk said, speaking English, "but you can see that for yourself, Red Wolf. Speak the truth now . . . are you angry that I have returned late, that I have returned with such a bounty, or just angry that I have returned at all?"

Red Wolf didn't reply. He kicked his horse into a gallop and returned to the camp quickly and, in his haste, frightened two of the horses. Hawk had to retrieve them, chasing them back to the small herd before he and Samantha could ride into camp.

\* \* \*

After two hours in the Sioux camp Samantha finally relaxed enough so that she didn't jump at every sound. As Hawk had predicted, Aja had instantly stepped to the fore and volunteered to stay with Samantha while Hawk spoke to the tribal elders and chiefs.

Samantha sat cross-legged on the buffalo mat as Aja had indicated, while the younger woman rummaged in a cavernous canvas bag. Samantha guessed her age to be sixteen, but perhaps a little younger. She had all the energy Hawk had indicated, but none of the wary seriousness of her older brother. From the time they'd met Aja had stopped talking only long enough for Samantha to answer a few questions.

"Here it is," Aja said, her constant smile growing wider as she pulled a deerskin dress from the canvas bag. "Why don't you try this on?"

Samantha almost refused the offer. She didn't want to make herself a burden to anyone, but the look on Aja's face—the look of someone who wanted nothing more than to be of assistance to another young woman far from home—convinced her that to refuse would be a mistake.

"You're sure?" Samantha asked.

Aja dropped down to kneel beside Samantha, then thrust the dress into her lap. "Please. It would make me happy."

Samantha undressed quickly, leaving on only her drawers, which Aja found fascinating. She pulled the deerskin garment over her head and smoothed it down over her body. Sleeveless and somewhat snug-fitting, the dress came down to her knees in a straight line. The garment was practically shapeless without a belt. Tight across the bosom and at the hips, Samantha could tell that it was made for Aja's more youthful, less curvaceous figure.

"Try these on," Aja said excitedly, extracting moccasins from the canvas bag. She practically forced them into Samantha's hands.

Samantha glanced at her boots. Reluctant to give up this loving gift from her brother, she worried how the boots would look with a dress. The question brought a smile to her lips as she began putting on the moccasins. What difference could it possibly make how she looked? In a day or two she would be leaving the Sioux camp, and once she did she would never again see any of these people. She could paint herself red and green if she wanted to, and nobody back in Deadwood would ever know about it!

The moccasins fit perfectly, lacing up to her ankles for a pleasantly snug fit. Samantha stood up and took a few tentative steps inside the tepee. She decided she liked the feel of the moccasins. They reminded her of the kidskin slippers she'd worn in the past, the dancing slippers fashionable young ladies wore—the ones Samantha had almost never been seen in and hadn't worn in over a year.

"Do you like them?" Aja asked. Too excited to remain seated on the buffalo mat, she'd risen to her feet and was pacing along with Samantha.

"Yes, the moccasins feel wonderful," Samantha answered. Then, seeing the unhappiness flash across Aja's face, she added quickly, "And so does the dress. It's beautiful!"

Aja laughed, knowing the dress wasn't beautiful at all—just a common dress a Sioux maiden would wear on an everyday basis—but she appreciated Samantha's comment nevertheless.

"Come now," Aja said, taking Samantha's hand to tug her toward the flap of the tepee. "Hawk has to see how you look in this dress!"

Not all of the elders were as happy with Hawk's success in capturing the horses from the hostile Northern Cheyenne as Hawk had hoped. He sensed immediately that Red Wolf had been speaking badly of him to the elders, and even if Red Wolf's claims bore only a grain of truth, that would be enough to plant a seed of doubt in the minds of some of the men.

"We are all thankful for the horses that Hawk Two Feather has brought to us," Red Wolf said, turning slowly to address the collection of elderly men who represented the governance of the tribe. "But I think we must also remember that Hawk was not here when we needed him during our last hunt. Where was he then? Threatening the peace by attacking the Cheyenne? Who knows? Who can say?"

Hawk grit his teeth, but that was the only outward sign of anger he displayed. He wouldn't be able to fight Red Wolf's accusations and win without shedding a little blood of his own. The way Red Wolf had framed his accusations, Hawk was guilty of either inciting the Cheyenne or neglecting the tribe. Either way, at least some of the council elders—whether they were more or less inclined to military action—would be unhappy with Hawk's absence from the tribe.

"And he has brought an outsider to us," Red Wolf continued. "I understand she has yellow hair and eyes the color of the sky. Some might say she is beautiful, and I have nothing against beauty. What I do question is why Hawk should have involved himself in this woman's battle with the Cheyenne. The fight is hers, not ours. From what Hawk has told us, white men were killed as well in his rescue of this young woman. Hawk, it seems, has made many enemies who might now be searching for him . . . and he's made them without gain for the tribe. That makes me wonder whether he has brought his enemies, and the enemies of this woman, to us. Are they massing now, just beyond our vision, waiting for the best time to attack? Do we need the white men to hate us more than they already do? Do we need to give them another reason to hunt us?"

It took all of Hawk's discipline to keep from interrupting Red Wolf's diatribe. But to interrupt Red Wolf would only make himself look bad, so he held his tongue, waiting for his turn to speak.

Pulling his gaze away from Red Wolf's, he studied the stony, unreadable expressions of the council elders. Some of them, he guessed, would be impressed with Red Wolf's fiery speech, with his defiant rhetoric, with the subtle way he reminded everyone of half-breed Hawk's status within the tribe. But there were others of the elders who would be put off by Red Wolf's attack, who would see that it had been motivated by hatred for Hawk and not a desire to assure what was best for the tribe. Surely, none of the elders could be ignorant of the hatred that had blossomed between Hawk and Red Wolf from the time they were young men.

At last, after nearly forty minutes of innuendo and rhetoric, Red Wolf sat down. The council of elders, saying nothing, turned in unison toward Hawk, awaiting his response.

"Red Wolf talks a great deal," Hawk began, "but, unfortunately, even when he has nothing to say, he insists on saying it."

A snicker passed among the elders. Hawk did not look in Red Wolf's direction, but he felt he'd scored a telling blow. Then, with a calm confidence that belied the anger he'd been hiding, he gave his version, once again, of what he'd done since riding away from camp. The elders listened to Hawk's words and one by one they were swayed by them. Success couldn't be argued with, and there was almost nothing that was more highly prized among the Sioux than healthy, well-trained horses. Though Hawk had not returned with a bounty of food, the horses he'd taken—and, better still, taken from the Northern Cheyenne—would benefit all in the tribe by making it easier for them to hunt.

"And as for the woman with the yellow hair," Hawk continued, "she is a maiden, and will remain a maiden until she leaves our camp. A fight with the white man because of what I have done? I killed white men who were trying to rape her. Do the white men value their white rapists? I think not. So you see, the words that Red Wolf speaks are filled with zeal, filled with emotion . . . but they are not filled with knowledge or wisdom, and they certainly are not filled with the truth."

Hawk sat down after that, keeping his face thoroughly impassive. He did not want any of the elders to see into his heart, but he believed that his defense had not only been articulate but had also successfully beaten down the challenge to his reputation. Now Red Wolf looked like the warrior who would irresponsibly cast aspersions against another warrior, and do so for the unacceptable motive of trying to make himself appear superior.

"Hawk, before you go very far, can I talk with you?"

Hawk had just stepped out of the tepee in which he'd explained his actions to the tribal elders when the deep voice stopped him in his tracks. He turned sharply to his left and smiled broadly, as he did at the sight of only one man.

"Crow!" he shouted.

The two men embraced excitedly, drawing the attention of other braves standing nearby. Such open displays of affection between men were not common, though Hawk and Crow seemed oblivious to the attention they attracted.

Hawk and Crow walked toward the outskirts of the camp, discussing inconsequential matters, each aware of how many people were listening to them. Once they were alone Crow stopped walking and turned to face Hawk.

"I think we're going to have some trouble," he said, shaking his head slowly. He fished into the pocket of his cotton jacket for his tobacco pouch and cigarette papers. His attire consisted of a bizarre mixture of leather loincloth, leggings, moccasins, and a blue cotton jacket. He wore no shirt. "I've been going through some documents in Fargo."

Crow finished rolling the second cigarette. He handed one to Hawk; then they both lit up. Hawk inhaled the first cigarette he'd had in a fortnight. It tasted wonderful.

"What do you want to do?" Hawk asked.

"That's why I needed to talk to you. I'd like to go to Fargo and sit in on the trial, maybe get involved if I can. This silly young fool on trial doesn't have the slightest idea of how much trouble he's really in, and I'd like to sit in to make sure he gets as fair a trial as possible."

Crow took a second puff from the cigarette and then tossed

it aside. He'd been spending too much time in the city lately, and consequently smoking too many cigarettes in the course of a day. Crow at Dawn believed that intemperance of any sort was a mistake.

"When would you like to leave?"

"As soon as possible, but I've just returned from there."

"Ah, now I'm beginning to see," Hawk replied with a grin.

The tribal elders had profound suspicions of Crow at Dawn, even though the attorney had, on more than one occasion, protected the tribe by forcing the territorial government—and once the federal government—to make good on treaties made with the Sioux, insisting that they be fulfilled. He had also successfully defended a young brave on charges of theft, proving beyond any doubt that the charges were false. His arguments for the defense were so compelling that the all-white jury even criticized the town marshal of Kanton for bringing forward such a preposterous charge.

Crow spent considerable time in the white man's cities, wearing the white man's clothing, speaking the white man's English . . . which made the elders fearful that he would *become* a white man and turn against his own tribe unless they were ever-vigilant. Crow needed to go to Fargo, but if he asked for permission from the elders, they'd want to discuss the issue at length, and consider the matter for several days. Crow was much too impatient for that kind of delay.

"Can you help?" Crow asked.

"Leave during the night," Hawk responded. "I'll explain it to the elders. They'll be angry, and they'll be suspicious, but they'll get over it. They always do."

"Thanks. And now can I give you a little free advice?"

Hawk felt his heart sink. Crow had never truly approved of Hawk's romantic adventures with the women of the camp, though before he'd always pretty much kept his opinion to himself. Hawk wasn't in the mood for a lecture about Samantha.

"Just say the word," Crow added, when Hawk didn't answer,

"and I'll keep my mouth shut. A good attorney knows when to stay quiet."

Hawk grinned. If he couldn't take advice from his best friend, from whom could he take advice? "Go ahead; tell me what's on your mind."

"Get the girl away from here as quickly as possible, and make sure she makes it home safely," Crow said, the tone of his voice somber. "I had the chance to see her walking through the camp with Aja. Red Wolf was following her—discreetly, of course, from a distance. But he was following her nevertheless. *Stalking her* would probably be more accurate. We both know what Red Wolf is like. If that girl leaves here without an escort, Red Wolf will devour her. And nobody will ever find the body."

"Yes, I know all too well what he's like," Hawk replied quietly.

"And can I ask you something else? Again, you have the right not to answer if you don't want to."

Hawk looked at his old friend and tried to smile but couldn't. He'd been close to Crow for too long to cheapen the friendship with half truths or outright lies.

"Have you taken her as a lover?" Crow asked.

"How like an attorney of you to ask the difficult questions so bluntly," Hawk replied. He wanted to be annoyed at Crow for being so bold, but he wasn't. In his heart he knew that Crow had only his best interests in mind, was concerned only with what was best for the tribe. If Crow caused a few tempers to wear thin now and then, that seemed a small price to pay for all the good he did.

"Someone has to," Crow commented. He reached for his tobacco, then stopped himself. "Now answer the question: Are you and the white girl lovers?"

"No. Not really."

"What exactly does that mean?"

"I'm sure you can guess," Hawk snapped, not wanting to get into the specifics of his transgressions with Samantha. He didn't want to appear to be one of those repellent men who seduced women and then bragged about it afterward to his friends.

"Yes, I can guess, but I'm a lawyer, and that means I like the facts more than speculation. What's happened between you two?"

In stumbling sentences Hawk told of their time together, his and Samantha's. He did not leave out anything, but neither did he embellish the essential facts.

"Do you want to be her lover?" Crow asked when Hawk had concluded what he felt was a rather damning confession.

"What? Of course I do!" Hawk exclaimed. "But I can't! You've got to see that! I can't! I don't want to be like . . ."

"Like what?"

Hawk shot him a fierce look, and this time there was no need to feign annoyance. The anger in Hawk's heart was real enough.

"I'd rather not get into that," Hawk said quietly, his words frozen by emotions he did not wish to explore.

Crow sensed his friend's unease, but he also knew that until Hawk confronted the questions of his past he could never go on to a peaceful future. "Is it that you don't want to be like Red Wolf? Or is it that you don't want to be like your mother?"

Crow watched Hawk's pent-up rage escalate. Only their life-long friendship could protect him against Hawk's pride and temper. Crow alone, among all the Sioux, dared to force Hawk to confront his own hidden enemies.

"I . . . I really don't know," Hawk answered at last. "Samantha is beautiful. All you have to do is look at her to see that. But she's much more than that. I can't begin to tell you how much more."

"Then why aren't you lovers?" Crow could not imagine a situation where Hawk would want to sleep with a woman and not eventually succeed. In such pursuits, Hawk appeared invincible.

"I don't want to be another Red Wolf. He sleeps with our

women only when he can't find a white woman to spread her legs for him." Hawk spit on the ground, as though the truth of his words left a foul taste in his mouth. "I don't want her just because she has pale skin, blue eyes, and blond hair."

"Then want her for more than that."

"Are you trying to annoy me?"

"No, I'm trying to make you see that you're as much white as you are Sioux. Sleeping with a white woman doesn't mean you'll end up like your mother." Crow put a hand on Hawk's shoulder. "Do whatever you must. I know you as well as any man—better than any man, I'd say—and yet there are times when I'm convinced I hardly know you at all. I only want to see you happy."

"And what about you? Are you happy?"

"I'm an Indian and a lawyer. It's against the law for me to be happy."

# Nine

Samantha tried to keep her eyes and attention focused solely on Aja, but she couldn't. No matter how hard she tried, she found herself searching the camp, looking for Hawk. She hadn't seen him since the previous afternoon, when he'd left her to speak to others in the tribe.

"It's a beautiful day," Samantha murmured absently, sitting on a blanket. "So peaceful."

Aja smiled to herself as she continued working to soften an elk hide. She wasn't fooled a bit by Samantha's earlier denial about looking for Hawk, just as she hadn't been fooled when Hawk had asked her to always stay close to Samantha, adding that this white woman really meant nothing to him. Gentle-hearted and always in favor of love, Aja wanted to see her brother happy. She doubted that he really was, spending as much time as he did in the arms of many different women.

"When will you be going back to your home?" Aja asked. Her hands worked the elk hide without any conscious thought. She'd been doing this kind of work since she was a very young girl.

"I don't know," Samantha answered without opening her eyes. She kicked out her feet in front of herself, crossing them at the ankle. She tugged at the hem of the deerskin dress—finding it ironic that earlier she had worn a shirt she was forever fumbling with, and now she'd been given a dress that exposed more of herself than she liked—and then leaned back

with her hands behind her in the grass. "Hawk said there were
things he had to do, and then he would take me back."

"How far from here do you live?"

"Outside of Deadwood. On a ranch."

Samantha thought of saying more, but she stopped herself.
She genuinely liked Aja, enjoying the Sioux girl's enthusiasm
for life, but she did not want to put all her faith and trust in
the girl. Money had a way of turning decent people into cre-
tins, transforming honest people into criminals. So far, the
Sioux had treated her graciously, but Samantha saw no particular reason to inform them of her wealth. Later, when she
was home once again, she would buy gifts for everyone, and
something special for the entire tribe to thank them for all
they'd done to assist her.

A grin tickled Samantha's lips as she began thinking about
what gift Aja would enjoy receiving most, and what would
give Hawk the greatest pleasure.

"What . . . what was Hawk like when he was younger?"
Samantha asked, trying to make the question sound innocuous.

"Hawk was never young!" Aja laughed. "There was always
a streak in him, something that made him run. It is part of
the reason he hunts alone, I suppose."

"Part of the reason?"

"Hawk and I . . . our mother . . . she came from a very
wealthy family," Aja began. Her hands stopped kneading the
elk hide and her eyes took on an unfocused, distant quality.
"She wasn't very particular with whom she shared her body,
so long as it was an Indian brave. It wasn't that she loved the
Sioux so much—quite the opposite, actually. I think she hated
us. But she hated her own family more, and she figured she
could hurt her father most by sleeping with Indians. Hawk and
I don't have the same father. In fact, I don't even know who
my father is."

She shook her head, dismissing unpleasantness and her natural high spirits returned, at least partially.

"Sometimes there are those within the tribe who think less

of Hawk and me because of who our mother was," Aja continued. "I think that's why he's always been so serious when it comes to providing meat for the tribe." Aja removed her headband, smoothed her long, straight black hair, and then returned the headband. "Hawk and I have each other, though, and that's enough of a family, I think."

Samantha could not imagine her life without her family. Even when they infuriated her, all the Sanderses—brothers and sisters, aunts, uncle, and cousins—made up a family, and they stuck together. An attack upon one of them was an attack upon them all, and this knowledge provided the underpinning which had given her the confidence to follow the guidance of her heart, rather than being just another pampered debutante, giving teas and attending socials.

As Aja looked at Samantha, a mischievous glow lit her eyes. "I wonder what you'd see in a vision quest," she said, her voice lowering, as though in discussion of something dangerous or naughty.

"A vision quest? What's that?"

"Maybe I'll be able to show you," Aja said, leaning closer, her voice dropping to a whisper, even though Samantha saw no one near enough to hear. "Father Lefevre, the priest who taught Hawk, Crow, and I to read, said that the vision quest is the work of the devil, but we never believed him. They're exhausting, but once you've had one—once you've really seen the vision—you'll never think of yourself in quite the same way again. Hmmm. I wonder if it is even possible for a woman with no Sioux blood in her at all to have a vision . . ."

"I'm sure I can!" Samantha said quickly, not wanting to be left out just because of the color of her skin. It sounded like an adventure, and Samantha was ready for one. "Let's do try!"

"All right, but you mustn't tell anyone."

Enough of an audience had gathered for Red Wolf to make his move. He'd been thinking about what he was going to say and do ever since he heard that Crow at Dawn had once again left camp, this time very early in the morning and without asking permission from the elders.

"It shows disrespect," Red Wolf said, shaking his head slowly, as though amazed that any Sioux brave would even dream of doing such a thing. "To leave just like that without a word of explanation?"

Hawk, who had been busy inspecting arrows that some of the very young braves had made, turned to face Red Wolf. "I explained to the elders why he had to leave, Red Wolf, and you know that."

"I know that you have spoken for him," Red Wolf replied, "but that is not the same as saying he actually had a reason, is it?"

"What kind of accusation are you making?" Hawk's voice was low, threatening. He was in no mood to listen to a man like Red Wolf slander the name of his best friend.

"I make no accusation," Red Wolf said, feigning innocence. He was aware that many braves and squaws, and the elders themselves, were moving closer, listening more carefully to what he was saying. "I only speak the truth when I say that Crow was here and now he is gone, leaving without permission or explanation. He has not spent much time with his people lately, has he? Instead, he wears the clothes of the white man, speaks the tongue of the white man . . . and probably thinks like the white man."

For a second Hawk closed his eyes, forcing himself to remain calm. If he lost his temper, he would be playing right into Red Wolf's hands. It was bad enough to allow a man like Red Wolf to make him angry; it would be doubly bad if he actually let others in the tribe see his anger, witness his lack of self-control against a man he held in such low esteem.

"You are hardly one to talk of respect," Hawk said softly, his eyes cold and hard on Red Wolf. "Is there anything you respect? Anyone? The way you behave sometimes, it is clear you have no respect for yourself."

"I have plenty of respect for myself," Red Wolf replied softly, venomously. "But respect for you . . . ? Why haven't you taken a wife to your tepee yet, Hawk? You talk so much about what is and is not good for the tribe, but do I see you with even a single wife? No! Unless it is not a Sioux wife you want, but a woman with yellow hair and pale skin, like the one you brought to us to feed and clothe! Why did you put yourself in jeopardy, risking your life for a white stranger? What possible good can that be to us?"

"You would not understand," Hawk said, turning slowly, about to walk away. Red Wolf was looking for a fight, and Hawk wasn't going to give him one. "It has to do with understanding what a Sioux brave really is."

"And holding another brave as if he is a woman? Is that what you think a brave should be?"

Hawk turned to face Red Wolf, at first confused by what he'd said. There was an insult there, but it made no sense to him. And then it dawned on him that Red Wolf was accusing him and Crow of inappropriate affection.

"You maggot!" Hawk hissed through teeth clenched in rage. He took a step toward Red Wolf, but then a highly respected elder, Dull Knife, stepped between them.

"We have so many enemies," the old man said in his characteristic, slow manner of speaking, "why must two young men make war among themselves? Is it death you want? There are many outside our camp who will be thought heroes if they kill you. So why help your enemies by hating yourselves? Do you not see that we cannot fight among ourselves and survive?"

Hawk, instantly contrite, replied, "Yes, you are right."

Red Wolf apologized for letting his "sense of pride in the tribe" get the best of him, but the undercurrent of scorn he felt for Hawk never completely left his voice. Dull Knife walked away slowly, and Hawk turned his back on Red Wolf, promising himself that he would never again allow himself to be taken in like that again. He had behaved exactly as Red

Wolf had wanted him to, and he'd lost some of Dull Knife's respect in the process.

Hawk was furious with himself.


Samantha had never felt such heat in her life. It seeped into her pores, squeezing her body as though it was a physical thing. Sometimes, when she tried to relax, she would breathe in deeply, and when she did she felt the moist heat of the sweat lodge go down her lungs. It only made her feel all that much hotter.

"You're fighting it," Aja noted softly, her voice barely rising above the hissing of the steam coming off the rocks. She'd just poured a fresh cup of water onto the heated rocks, and the steam and heat was once again swirling with renewed energy in the small, confined tepee. "The whole point of this preparation is to release. Release everything that is within you so that you're empty inside. Only by releasing everything will you be able to receive your vision."

"You make it sound so easy," Samantha murmured.

Stretching out her legs, she leaned back onto her elbows. It was too hot to have any part of her body touching any other part. Perspiration ran down her naked body, and even though she occasionally wiped it away, an instant later she was wet again.

"I never said it was easy," Aja replied. "But it's worth the effort. If you—" She stopped herself, then began again. "*When* you receive your vision you'll know that any sacrifice needed will have been worth it. A vision will change your life, change the way you look at yourself and your world."

"Let's hope so," Samantha replied, laying on her back and placing her hands lightly on the soft buffalo hide beneath her.

*Let it go,* she thought. *Don't think about the heat. Don't think about anything at all. That's the trick.*

When the image of Hawk, smiling devilishly, entered her mind, she pushed it away quickly. If she let him into her thoughts now, she knew she'd never get him out, and she would never be receptive enough to receive her vision.

Time passed, and another thought entered Samantha's consciousness. This thought concerned only her awareness that she had, for several minutes, thought of nothing at all. Now, whenever errant thoughts came to her, she could chase them away more easily than she had in the past.

Samantha kept her eyes closed and was soon within herself, thinking of nothing at all.

Hawk's rage had not yet cooled when he was told that Aja had taken the white woman to the sweat lodge. Jumping on his stallion, Hawk rode hard out of camp. Needing to feel the wind against his face, in his hair, to feel the comforting rhythm of the horse beneath him, he needed action.

His tribe held higher expectations of him—more than for any other Sioux warrior—and he knew it. Hawk had always been tested harder, needed to prove that his white blood had not made him soft, had not made his loyalties expedient. He was *expected*—much more than any other brave, with the possible exception of Crow—to take a Sioux wife, and to have children. Only then would the white blood that ran in his own veins be diluted.

With this destiny continually taunting him, to have his sister bring a blond-haired vixen to the sweat lodge was infuriating. Was Aja trying to turn Samantha into a Sioux? Of course, the idea could have come from Samantha, Hawk mused. It could have been her idea from the very beginning, to tempt him even more as a Dakota maiden . . .

No, it couldn't have been her idea, he decided a moment later. Samantha didn't know enough about his world to have suggested it on her own. She would have followed Aja's offer willingly, though.

Women!

Hawk reined in his stallion. It wouldn't do to push the animal into a protracted gallop just to get away from camp for a while.

He looked back at the camp and shook his head slowly. Perhaps Red Wolf had been correct when he accused Hawk of carelessly becoming involved in a battle with whites and the Cheyenne. Perhaps Hawk simply should have ridden in the other direction when he'd heard Samantha's frightened screams.

No, that wouldn't have been right. No matter what Red Wolf or anyone else in the tribe thought, leaving Samantha to defend herself would not have been proper. Just as it wasn't proper now for Hawk to recall with absolute clarity the sweetness of her kisses, the warmth of her smooth skin, the trembling touch of her hands as passion burned hotter and hotter within them both.

Under his breath, Hawk uttered a single foul word. He was angry with himself for always thinking about Samantha and disappointed with himself for not having resisted the temptation that she represented. Even if he had to take Samantha kicking and screaming by the hair, he was going to get her back to her family as soon as possible. It was the only way he'd ever regain the peace in his mind and soul that had been his before she'd entered his life.

Samantha felt weak. Very weak. Her legs had so little strength that it was difficult to ascend the sloping hill, not far from camp. The sweat lodge had sapped more of her strength than she knew existed. Aja had warned her that weakness might occur, so Samantha wasn't worried. Just the same, she hoped that her efforts so far would result in a successful vision quest.

"Later, after the vision quest, we will know what your natural name is," Aja said as they reached the treeline. "Perhaps it will come to you instantly, but it is more likely that we will need to interpret your name."

"Natural name?"

"And we must find your *Wotawe*. That is important."

*"Wotawe?"* Samantha was struggling with the Sioux language, though in the time she'd spent with Aja, she'd learned a number of words.

Aja smiled over her shoulder at Samantha. She was pleased with how quickly her new friend was learning the ways of her people. "A *Wotawe* is your personal charm. It's a personal stone. It helps to keep and contain your power and to remind you always of who and what you are."

"There's so much to learn." Samantha looked over her shoulder. The camp could no longer be seen in the valley. She wondered how far up the hills into the trees Aja intended to take her. "What was that about a name?"

"A natural name. There are names that we give ourselves, and names that the spirit world gives us. When my brother went on his vision quest the spirits returned him with a hawk's feather in each hand. That is why he is Hawk Two Feather."

"I see," Samantha replied, though she wasn't entirely certain she did.

Spirits returned Hawk? Where had they taken him? The skeptical part of Samantha's nature wormed its way into her thoughts, but she quickly banished it. One could not be open to new experiences and cynical at the same time.

They followed a deer trail farther up the hill, where it eventually led to a small clearing. To Samantha, this was an idyllic place, secluded and confined by all the trees. The clearing could have been made by man, but Samantha suspected it had occurred naturally.

"This is where I had my first vision quest," Aja explained. She walked to the center of the clearing, then turned around slowly, a faint smile on her lips and in her eyes. Her memories of this place and the vision quest were obviously happy ones. "Hawk had his here also. There are good spirits here. *Ida Maka* treats us kindly here." She smiled at Samantha. *"Ida Maka* means Mother Earth."

"There's just so much to learn about your ways," Samantha said, disheartened.

"Don't think about what you don't know; think about what you do know. Only then can you keep going forward and not dwell in the past." Aja spread out the small square of elk hide on the grass in the center of the clearing. "Give me your dress and moccasins. I'll return for you tomorrow afternoon."

A heated flush instantly went through Samantha. "You're going to leave me here naked?" she exclaimed.

Aja's eyes narrowed in confusion. "You don't need to hide yourself before the spirits, and *Ida Maka* loves you as you are."

Aja made it sound so natural to be naked outdoors, but Samantha could not blithely dismiss the teachings of a lifetime. "What difference could it make?" Samantha conceded softly, after some hesitation. "Only Mother Earth will see me here, right?" She pulled the dress over her head and handed it to Aja, then removed her moccasins. Aja took the three items and placed them in the grass some yards away, as though to ensure that the garments would not interfere with the ceremony. Samantha was relieved to discover that she would not be left without any clothes.

"Now empty your mind and heart and wait for the voice of the spirits to whisper. Shortly after they do a vision will appear," Aja instructed her. "Become comfortable however you choose. To see the vision, you must look within yourself."

Samantha felt uneasy, being outdoors without any clothes on, but she did as Aja suggested. As she sat on the elk hide blanket, she found it at first impossible to get comfortable, especially with Aja still there. Then, after a murmured, "I'll be back for you tomorrow," Aja left without another sound.

The minutes ticked by, and finally Samantha was able to relax enough to allow herself to stop feeling so self-conscious.

*I am alone with Ida Maka on a sacred vision quest,* Samantha thought at last, finally regaining the self-confidence that was so much a part of her personality. *Nothing bad can happen to me when I am with Mother Earth.*

Samantha stretched out on the elk hide, slowly spreading her arms and legs, as though to catch the afternoon sunlight with as much of herself as possible, as a spring flower does the sunshine with its petals.

*I was not born Sioux, but I can learn to think like one . . . feel like one.*

Within moments she felt the tension leaving her body, gently slipping away, without regret, and she knew it was best this way. Without a care or any concern for time, or even the world around her, Samantha moved slowly deeper and deeper into herself, though she was not aware of it.

# Ten

Hawk was distinctly aware of the fact that he probably should not be doing what he was. He was also aware that he probably would regret his actions, and that the fight that would surely ensue between himself, his sister, and Samantha, would be a most regrettable one.

Even though he knew all of this, Hawk was determined to go forward. The women of the tribe were buzzing with the gossip that Aja had taken the yellow-haired woman to the sweat lodge, and then, from the lodge, Aja had escorted her out of camp. Immediately Hawk concluded that Aja was instructing Samantha on a vision quest. And if she was doing that, then more likely than not they were up on the hillside, in the small clearing in the trees Hawk had discovered so many years earlier.

The only person he'd ever told of his *Hocoka* was Aja, and it rather perplexed him that his sister had chosen to break that silence with Samantha. Why her? Aja's easygoing, loving nature had made her many friends in the tribe, in spite of her embarrassing parentage. She had many friends to confide in, yet she had chosen Samantha over all them.

Why?

"I'll go crazy trying to understand women," Hawk muttered.

Though several summers had passed since Hawk had visited the clearing, he knew it wasn't far ahead. His first vision quest had changed the way he looked at himself and his life. Even blindfolded, he would have been able to find his way back to such a momentous place in his life.

Unconsciously, he began paying more attention to his footsteps, reducing what little sound his moccasins made against the ground to virtual silence. The Sioux were trained to hunt on foot as well as on horseback, and from a very early age young braves developed the habit of silent stealth.

When he reached the clearing he broke his silence. In fact, the sound of his own breath suddenly sucked in would have drawn Samantha's attention had she not been so focused on her vision quest.

She was stretched out on an elk hide blanket with her eyes closed against the last of the sunlight making its way through the trees. Naked, her body caught in light and shadow, she was even more beautiful than Hawk had dreamed she could be.

*This is wrong.*

The reality of the impropriety of his conduct struck Hawk hard. He was a man who lived by hard rules, not malleable notions abandoned the instant they became inconvenient. Hawk *believed* in his self-made laws for living.

So why was he rooted in one place, unable to tear his eyes from the stunning young woman not thirty feet away when he knew—both emotionally and logically—that looking at her during her vision quest, when she didn't know he was there, was wrong? Why couldn't he turn his back to her and walk away?

Her beauty gripped him like an invisible hand. Her ripely curvaceous body, splendidly naked, was displayed to him in almost perfect profile, so that he might see the slow rise and fall of her pink-tipped breasts, the line of her rib cage, and the curve of her hips. But it was also something more than that: the added thrill of looking illicitly at Samantha when she was unaware of his presence heightened the eroticism of the moment. Had Samantha looked him casually in the eye and simply cast aside her clothes, he undoubtedly would have been struck by the splendor of her form. Struck, yes . . . but not dumbfounded, frozen in place as though he'd never before seen a woman's body, or understood the pleasures of the flesh.

*Ida Maka would not approve,* Hawk knew.

The invocation of the all-seeing eye of Mother Earth forced Hawk to behave as he knew he should. Turning slowly and silently away from the clearing, he headed back for camp. The things that needed to be said he would say to Samantha there, where her compelling allure would be muted by clothes, by the nearness of members of the tribe, by Hawk's own belief that the only acceptable females for him were Sioux-born.

For Samantha, the world did not exist—at least not the physical world that, had her eyes been open, she would have seen with her eyes and touched with her fingertips. Inside her mind a world had suddenly and miraculously been revealed to her, and she was utterly fascinated with it.

*It's so beautiful,* she kept thinking, *this world of Ida Maka.*

The animals nearby seemed to have no fear of her. Several rabbits munching on clover not ten yards away, ever-vigilant yet not in the least bit concerned with her presence, had caught her attention.

Deep within her mind, Samantha could not actually *see* the rabbits eating the sweet clover. Yet somehow this discrepancy—this distinction between what she knew to be true with her heart with what she knew could not be true with her mind—didn't bother her in the least. Such mundane matters of whether her eyes were open or closed should bear little significance, she realized, on whether she could see.

A doe stepped into the clearing, lightfooted, with its tail twitching nervously. Seeing Samantha, the doe gave no outward sign of alarm.

*I won't hurt you,* Samantha thought. *You needn't be afraid of me.*

*I know you won't,* the young doe replied. *But there are many others who are not like you.*

The sound of a slender tree limb snapping caused Samantha to look sharply to her left in her mind's eye. She could not see what had caused the sound, but she sensed that danger— not for her so much as for the doe—was present, lurking in the brush, hidden from her view.

Samantha turned back to the place where the doe had been, but there was no need to warn the gentle creature. The animal had already disappeared, and though Samantha was saddened at losing the company of the doe, she felt blessed for the short time they'd spent together.

Sonny Sanders was frowning, trying to convince himself that there was no reason to worry. There was still no word from Samantha, and she hadn't picked up his telegram to her. To complicate matters, he couldn't go chasing after Samantha because Vanessa had left for Fargo, and Sonny thought he might need to get the boys together to protect her. If ever there was a woman more adept than Samantha at finding trouble and embroiling herself in it, that woman had to be Vanessa.

*Sisters! They'll drive me to drink!* Sonny thought anxiously.

Sitting in the leather swivel chair in the ranch house office, Sonny decided to send one of his men after Samantha. She'd be furious with him for it, but he didn't have a moment's doubt about his action. At least then he'd know she was safe.

Sonny pushed himself out of the chair and took a last sip of coffee. The sun was just coming up in the valley, and it looked like it was going to be another beautiful day.

Samantha sat upright on the elk hide rug. She blinked her eyes several times to clear her vision, then ran her fingers through her long blond hair to put it into some semblance of order. She rolled her head back on her shoulders and winced as muscles that had not been used in hours protested.

Overhead, the sun was high in the sky, though dropping

toward the western horizon. By Samantha's calculations, it had to be several hours past noon. She'd been at the clearing more than twenty-four hours now.

As full consciousness returned to Samantha, she was aware of her nudity. She crossed her arms over her bosom and looked around the clearing guiltily. Then a soft smile pulled at her mouth, and she relaxed. She was alone with Mother Earth, and hadn't Aja explained that there was no reason for her to hide?

Samantha rose to her feet, stretching her arms and legs, twisting her back and neck until her body once more felt supple and limber. Her clothes—the soft leather dress and moccasins provided by Aja—were nearby, and though Samantha's first instincts were to go to them, she resisted the impulse.

Another smile pulled at her mouth, this one hinting at a self-satisfaction that had never been there before.

She was beginning to think like a Sioux. Samantha realized that she was only in the initial stages of the transformation, but she'd begun the journey. Of this there could be no denying, and when the awareness filled her senses she started to skip and dance naked in the clearing, unashamed of the present and unfettered by the past.

When Aja arrived an hour later Samantha was anxious to tell her friend all that she'd seen and discovered during her vision quest, but Aja put a hand up to silence the avalanche of words.

"Tell me tomorrow," Aja instructed, handing Samantha her dress, indicating that it was time to return to the camp. "Let the memories of your vision quest stay within you. If you speak of them now, while they are still so fresh within you, they may escape, and then you will lose them forever."

Keeping the experience to herself, not speaking of the wondrous new sensations, was very nearly the most difficult thing Samantha had ever done, but as she walked slowly back to camp, she began to fully grasp the wisdom of Aja's advice. By not speaking of her experiences, her memories of them remained clearer, more precise and defined. Suddenly Samantha understood that her memories of the vision quest would be as accurate and unchanging in twenty years as they were at this moment.


Hawk had heard that his sister and Samantha had returned to the camp, but he couldn't see them immediately. He was much too busy talking with Dull Knife, defending Crow's honor, integrity, and loyalty to the tribe.

"The white man trained Crow," Hawk explained for the third time. "Crow understands the laws of the white man, and that is why he is not with us now. He is needed in the white man's courts. Crow's knowledge can protect us even better than a rifle."

Dull Knife remained silent, listening carefully to everything the young warrior had to say. In his heart, Dull Knife harbored sympathy for both Hawk Two Feather and Crow at Dawn for the hardships they'd endured for being born bastards and of mixed parentage. But Dull Knife could not allow his tender feelings to make him weak, or to lose sight of what was best for the tribe. The simple truth was that both Crow and Hawk were too clever, too charming, too handsome and quick with a disarming smile for their own good. This was the reason neither had taken even a single wife, though everyone knew that both men had spent a considerable number of nights in the arms of willing women.

"If Crow knows the law so well," Dull Knife said quietly, "then why must you be here now, giving me excuses for what he has done? He knows that he must receive permission from the council before he is allowed to leave the tribe."

*Because time was critical, and the old men of the council make their decisions very slowly,* Hawk thought in wild frustration. He said, "It was necessary. Hasn't Crow worked hard to protect us from the white man, to make the white man live up to his agreements with us? I cannot tell you why it was necessary for Crow to leave so suddenly. I only know that he said it was so, and because Crow is a man of his word I believe him."

Dull Knife looked away, and Hawk knew that it was going to take a while longer to mollify the proud, stubborn elder whose wisdom had helped guide the Dakota for so long.


Hawk was furious, but Samantha couldn't focus on his anger. Not when he was wearing only a deerskin loincloth and leggings, and when his bronzed chest was naked for her eyes to caress, all the raw power he possessed there on display. Hawk was arguing quietly with Aja at the entrance to her tepee, angry that she had helped Samantha experience some of the more spiritual elements of Sioux life. Though they kept their voices low, Samantha noticed more than a few squaws and braves keeping a surreptitious eye on Hawk and Aja.

*I don't care if Hawk thinks it was wrong of me to try for a vision quest,* Samantha thought. *It opened my eyes to a new world, to a new way of thinking, and that's what's really important.*

But even as she thought this, she knew it wasn't entirely true. She *did* care what Hawk thought, because more than ever before she didn't want him to be angry and brooding. She wanted him to help her celebrate her vision quest, even though it had been only partially successful.

She noticed Hawk glance in her direction, then look quickly back at his sister. He turned, and now she saw him in profile. Samantha's mouth went dry. From the side, the loincloth covered very little of his legs, so she was able to see his thighs and the tautness of his buttocks. He possessed such power! All bronzed and beautiful, sculpted like a statue . . .

Samantha forced herself to look away, concerned with the sinful pleasure of looking at the body of a man. But, oh! What a man he was!

She couldn't help herself. She had to look at him, her eyes drinking in his arms and chest, his broad shoulders, the thick muscles in his calves and thighs . . . and, most of all, his deliciously curved buttocks.

She wondered how the squaws could control themselves and their emotions when the braves wore loincloths. Samantha decided that it was possible other women weren't the way she was. Perhaps the sensuality of looking at a beautiful man was something that only she experienced. She'd never before heard her friends say anything about wanting to look at a man's naked body, though she'd always known that men enjoyed looking at women.

Samantha went into Aja's tepee, sat down, and tried to relax. Suddenly she rose to her feet again. Too restless to remain seated, she paced the cramped confines of the tepee, trying to force the image of Hawk's tempting body from her thoughts. Samantha soon realized that nothing made her think of Hawk more than attempting not to think of him at all.

At that moment the tepee flap was thrown open and Hawk, bending low, entered. His expression was intimidating: his features granite hard, his lips tightly pursed, his eyes glittering with angry fire. Crossing his arms over his chest, he stared down at Samantha, intentionally trying to frighten her. But rather than making her afraid, his stance heightened the definition of the muscles in his arms and chest, and Samantha desired him even more.

"You're leaving for home," he said, his tone brooking no rebuttal. "If not immediately, then tomorrow morning at the latest."

"No."

Samantha understood Hawk's display of size and strength. But what he didn't understand was Samantha's lifelong experience in the company of big, strapping men. True, Hawk might be infinitely more desirable than any man she'd ever set eyes upon, but he wasn't the only powerfully built male she'd ever been face-to-face with. Ranch hands were generally big, burly men, and though Samantha had never regarded them with any real interest, she had looked on them as men just the same.

So Samantha Sanders was not without experience when it came to standing up to an angry man.

"Yes." Hawk moved closer, forcing Samantha to look straight up into his eyes. "That's final. There's to be no argument."

"Because you have so decreed," Samantha replied, a mocking eyebrow cocked high above an insolent blue eye.

"If that's the way you want to look at it, I suppose your conclusion isn't all that far from correct."

Samantha's mouth quirked into a half smile, mimicking Hawk's. Uncomfortable, he stared at her, knowing that she wasn't going to let the argument pass easily. He braced himself for the vociferous fight he had no doubt brought upon himself.

But her refusal to follow his order never quite came—at least, not the way Hawk had expected it would. Instead of putting her nose close to his and screaming, as Hawk could have anticipated, Samantha moved several steps back and appraised him coolly, allowing her eyes to appreciatively roam up and down over the length and breadth of him. Making no effort to hide the direction or intention of her gaze, neither did she attempt to conceal her deep interest in what stood before her.

"If I must leave," Samantha countered softly, slowly, enunciating the words carefully, "then the least you can do is kiss me good-bye."

Samantha saw a different fire ignite in Hawk's eyes, but she didn't have a clue whether she'd incited his fury or his passion or elements of both. When he moved toward her Samantha wanted to run away, but her mind couldn't make her feet obey.

# Eleven

"You just try to make me angry, don't you?" Hawk said as he pulled Samantha into his arms, crushing her trembling body against the hard surface of his chest.

Samantha didn't have time to answer because the instant she moistened her lips to speak he slanted his mouth down hard over hers, his tongue forcing her lips apart as it explored deeply.

Shocked at the force Hawk used, Samantha felt her breasts, already confined within the deerskin dress that was just a little too small for her voluptuous figure, crushed against his chest. She was pleasantly aware of how her nipples had elongated with excitement, becoming tight and sensitive as they were forced to rub hard against the soft inner surface of the leather dress. Samantha hesitated only a moment before she wrapped her arms around Hawk's neck and leaned into him as his mouth devoured hers.

"Why must you always fight me," Hawk asked, his lips moist from Samantha's, still touching hers even as he spoke, "in everything I try to do?"

"I'm not fighting you now," Samantha said between kisses, with guileless honesty. She could feel the fury bubbling within Hawk, but she accurately sensed that his anger was only partially directed at her refusal to follow his commands.

Hawk wanted to answer, but words were the most ineffective way for him to express himself. Instead, he kissed Samantha again, a bit less forcefully this time, as he felt her responding, her body writhing blissfully in his arms, rubbing against him, the response to his passion both instant and undeniable.

Samantha raised herself up on her tiptoes, reducing the height difference between them, and opened her mouth wider. She felt his hands slide from the small of her back down to her buttocks, forcing her tighter against him, and she loved the heat of his powerful thighs against her own legs.

"Oh, Hawk," she whispered, turning her face away, struggling to catch her breath, hoping to contain the wildfire emotions racing through her.

Raising her knee, she slid it up Hawk's leg. She was not at all surprised to feel the heat of his naked skin, nor the strength of his body, though she was shocked by the reaction of her own body. His skin to her skin, Samantha felt Hawk's vitality, his fiery outlook on life, passing right through the pores of his skin and into hers. An instant later she was shocked when he pulled her leather dress higher and cupped her naked buttocks in his large, strong hands, pinning her even tighter against him, forcing her to feel the rapidly burgeoning excitement racing through him.

All the warnings Samantha had heard before were very insistent now, clamoring for her to run, to escape from the seductive influence of this Sioux warrior whose kisses tasted like nectar and whose caresses were pure carnal indulgence. Would she listen to the warnings? Not this time. Hawk's hands, so powerful and commanding, squeezed her tightly, touched her intimately, forced her to rub against a thigh that was solid as stone from countless hours on horseback.

"I haven't been able to stop thinking about you," Hawk whispered, the words forced from his soul. He kissed Samantha again as he pulled her hips toward him so that she had no choice but to feel the length, breadth, and heat of his desire for her.

Samantha couldn't help herself. Though she'd dealt with the sin of letting Hawk touch her, it had to be even more wrong for her to touch him. She was aware of this, yet she could not

resist the temptation to bring her hands down Hawk's body,
then slide them beneath his loincloth to cup the hard contours
of his buttocks. When he sighed, his hips moving slowly,
Samantha, shocking herself, pulled him toward her so the hard
column of his arousal was pressed tightly against her stomach.
The front flap of Hawk's loincloth and her deerskin dress remained the only barriers between them.

Still on her tiptoes while Hawk kissed her, Samantha knew
the intensity of Hawk's emotions were escalating rapidly. Suddenly Samantha felt herself tumbling backward, with Hawk
following her onto the buffalo mat near the edge of the tepee.
Then Hawk pulled Samantha by the ankle, forcing her to sit
the way he wanted her to, with her legs extended in front of
herself instead of tucked beneath her. But when he kissed her
again she tumbled onto her back and pulled Hawk with her,
his weight crushing down on her, his powerful body pressed
against the full length of hers.

Nothing had ever felt quite so right, quite so satisfying, as
the weight of Hawk's powerful, warrior's body pressing on
hers. Samantha wrapped her arms tightly around Hawk's middle, sliding her hand beneath his vest to touch his naked flesh.

When he stopped kissing her Samantha raised her head, her
soft sigh protesting the interruption. Then Hawk kissed her
again, his lips firmly pressing down over hers, stealing her
breath and heightening her passion.

Unconsciously, she raised her knees, her thighs forming a
satiny valley for Hawk's lean hips. When he moved, his hips
sliding from side to side as they kissed, she realized that the
leather dress had ridden up high, bunching at her waist, and
she could finally feel the naked heat of Hawk's arousal pressed
against her abdomen.

The honeyed essence of her excitement flowed freely, and
only an inner whisper of warning said she mustn't be too bold.
But passivity had never been a part of Samantha's nature, neither in Hawk's arms nor out of them. She placed her hands

on his chest and pushed hard until he raised himself, breaking their kiss.

"Love me," she whispered hotly. Looking up at Hawk, she was astonished once again at his handsome, chiseled features, framed by his long, raven-black hair. "I'm scared . . . but love me."

"You mustn't be scared," Hawk said, easing his upper body down once again on the cushion of her breasts.

"Kiss me, and I won't be," Samantha replied.

He kissed her, running the tip of his tongue along her lower lip; then he kissed her cheek, and her neck. He moved his hips from side to side, feeling Samantha shivering, feeling her naked thighs trembling as they squeezed him.

Samantha was scared. She couldn't help it. Now she'd spoken words that she could never deny, igniting a fire within the lusty warrior who'd kissed her so sweetly. How that fire was burning her now, pressed against her stomach, throbbing with a desire so powerful she could feel it!

Hawk slipped his left arm under her neck so that her head rested on his forearm. Then, with his right hand, he reached between their bodies, and a moment later removed the leather loincloth. Samantha felt him move between her legs, the heated length of his staff pressed tightly against her moist opening. She gasped, her spine arching.

Hawk kissed her, recognizing her trepidation as well as her excitement. He'd waited so long for this moment, this final capitulation to passion. Now that Samantha was his for the taking, he wanted this moment to be special for her. He wanted to take his time so that she felt all the pleasure of which she was capable . . . and this meant he must control the clamorous desire, primal and urgent, urging him to thrust himself primitively into Samantha's depths, experiencing immediately that which had been denied him for so long.

He reached again between their bodies to cup her breast, squeezing the firm mound through the tight leather dress. Though Samantha moaned, Hawk knew that if her responsive body was to reach the heights, the dress had to be removed. He tried moving away from her, but Samantha's arms wound even more tightly around him, and he felt her fingernails against his shoulders.

"Don't!" she gasped, pulling at Hawk, her lips moist and parted as she sought yet another kiss.

"Your dress," Hawk said, reaching down to grab the bottom of it, wanting to pull it up and over Samantha's head.

"Hurry!" she replied, understanding what he wanted but not wanting the delay.

He saw fear in her blue eyes, and finally understood precisely why the young woman was so urgent. True, passion spurred on her haste, but fear also played a part in Samantha's fervent demand. Clearly, she did not know how long her courage would hold and, if Hawk did not act immediately, her passion would evaporate, replaced with the apprehension and inhibition that had plagued all their previous romantic moments.

Hawk, his heart pumping red-hot blood through his veins, raised his hips and reached between their bodies. He touched her softly, feeling the heated moisture of her readiness, hearing her breath sucked in . . . and held.

*So passionate, and yet so frightened,* he thought, finding her twin emotions simultaneously baffling and exciting.

Samantha squirmed beneath him, arching her back once more. He wanted to remind her to breathe, but he didn't. If he hadn't known her so well, if this had, instead, been the first time he'd ever felt her responding to his seduction, he would have thought that she was responding falsely, giving a theatrical performance for some reason.

Samantha had squeezed her eyes tightly shut, and it wasn't until she felt the burning in her lungs that she realized she was holding her breath. The touch of Hawk's fingertips, moving slowly and expertly, touching and probing, finding the most sensitive areas, was rapidly bringing her to new heights of ecstasy. But along with the ecstasy came the awareness that

there were people everywhere around, separated from her only
by the thin buffalo hides of the tepee.

Could they hear her? Samantha wondered. Would the entire
tribe talk about her wanton, intemperate behavior the instant
this encounter was over? She could picture herself surrounded
by a circle of elderly Sioux women, all looking on her with
scorn in their eyes.

"Are you all right?" Hawk asked, raising himself, pulling
away from Samantha. He'd felt a sudden change in her and,
however much he hungered to feel himself joined with her, he
would not force himself on her.

Samantha's eyes flew open and she reached up, cupping
Hawk's gaunt, handsome face in her hands. "Don't stop!
Hurry! Hurry, my darling!"

Hawk guided himself to her, then bore down, slowly and
with controlled force. He felt Samantha opening to him, felt
the slick nectar of her excitement, tight and stimulating, surrounding him. A low groan of excitement rumbled from his
chest as he pressed deeper and deeper, withdrawing and then
advancing once again. Discovering the barrier of her inexpe-
rience, he paused, then pressed on, and only the soft, short
exclamation of sound that Samantha emitted warned him that
she'd felt temporary pain.

Then, blissfully, at long last, he was completely engulfed
within Samantha, their bodies joined tightly, and Hawk rested
in the valley of her thighs, giving Samantha time to adjust, to
relax if possible. He kissed her and was surprised when
Samantha thrust her tongue between his lips, kissing ardently,
forcefully, not at all the kiss of a woman who moments earlier
had been frightened by the prospect of making love for the
first time.

He began to move, slowly and with a steady rhythm, and
Samantha's worry about what the tribe would say about her
vanished. Every idea disappeared from her mind except those
pertaining to the pleasure she was feeling now. Nothing could
have prepared her for the sensuous reality of having Hawk's

passion inside her, moving deeply, slowly, a slick friction from each measured stroke of his hips staggering her senses and melting her bones. She held him close, her fingernails digging into his solid back muscles, and she never wanted the kiss to end . . . at least not while they were joined so intimately, so deliciously.

Even without previous experience, Samantha felt Hawk keeping himself in check, reining in his passion so he would not hurt her. With his big, powerful body tensed, the muscles coiled like a mountain lion's before a charge, Samantha sensed that there weren't many men, if any, who would show such consideration to their young, inexperienced lover. She loved him, then, in a peculiar way, almost grateful for whatever influences had helped to shape Hawk into the man he had become.

Samantha had spent too much time in and around bunk houses and near the rough-talking, hard-living ranch hands for her to have romantically naive notions of the perceptual difference in how men and women view the act of sex. Men, she knew, could be rutting beasts.

Was this just sex, or was she making love? Samantha wasn't sure, and she didn't want to think about it. Not now, anyway. There would be plenty of time later, when she was back at the Circle S ranch and Hawk was still with his tribe, for her to dwell on regrets and wallow in self-recrimination and doubt.

She kicked a leg around Hawk's and discovered that by doing so she'd shifted her hips, changing the angle at which he entered her. Samantha kicked her other leg around him, gripping him now, their legs entwined as Hawk moved slowly and steadily, and Samantha was able at last to feel the full weight of him on her.

"Does it . . ." she began, keeping her eyes closed as she spoke. Passion cut the sentence off short, but she was determined to get her answer, so she moistened her lips and began again. "Does it always feel this wonderful?"

"No," Hawk replied. "I promise you, it always gets better."

He kissed her, needing to silence her questions as the desire to plunge hard and fast escalated. *Steady, steady,* he thought, the logical part of his mind remembering that he was a large man, and that Samantha was both small and inexperienced. He felt hard as stone as the fire in his loins raged.

For a man of Hawk's experience, it seemed as though they'd only just begun making love, but already he could feel himself losing control, feel the rushing tide of passion carrying him along. He turned his face away from Samantha, his expression displaying the strain of his futile attempt to control his excitement. *Too soon!* he thought trying to deny that he was being carried along by desires that were irrefutable.

Samantha, however, was oblivious to Hawk's inner turmoil and struggle for control. Unable to think of anything but the feelings shivering through her, the intoxicating sense of oneness with Hawk, she could feel his great heart pounding furiously close to hers, feel his manhood filling her, stripping away the doubts and turmoil that had troubled her for so much of her young life.

He groaned without changing his tempo. As he hesitated for several seconds, teetering on the brink of ecstasy, Samantha held him close. Then, with a deep growl of desire, Hawk thrust himself hard and fast into her, his willpower and self-control abandoning him as his release erupted, shuddering through him in waves of passion.

"Yes," Samantha whispered, stroking Hawk's ebony hair.

When Hawk started to move away Samantha tightened her hold on him, squeezing her eyes shut again, afraid—for one of the very few times in her life—that the tears would begin to flow, and Hawk would see them.

"Don't move," she whispered. "Not yet. Just give me a minute . . . then I promise I'll be brave."

"Don't worry," Hawk replied huskily. "Whatever you want is yours."

At that moment he believed he'd move heaven and earth to suit Samantha's wishes.

But Aja's voice, just moments later, shattered whatever tenderness Samantha had hoped for. "Samantha, are you all right in there? Dull Knife is looking for Hawk."

Hawk hissed something through his teeth, and Samantha was thankful that she could not understand the single word. He rolled away, reaching for his loincloth, apparently practiced at the art of a quick escape after a romantic interlude.

"Don't worry," Hawk said again, on his knees beside Samantha as she smoothed down the leather dress over her thighs. "Everything will be all right. I'll see you as soon as I can."

Then he was gone from the tepee, leaving Samantha alone with her thoughts, alone with her doubts and worries. She knelt without a single distraction from the recriminations ricocheting in her mind, echoing like church bells through the streets of a deserted city.

## Twelve

Three hours later, Hawk finally freed himself from his other obligations and returned to Samantha. When he at last found her she was on the outskirts of the encampment, carrying a basket made of woven reeds.

"Where are you going?" Hawk asked, though it was apparent that she was going into the mountains to pick berries.

He got off his stallion, wanting very much to take Samantha into his arms to stroke her hair softly, soothingly. Having to leave her so quickly after the culmination of their passion was, he felt, a barbaric thing to do, even though in his heart he had known he had no choice in the matter.

"I'm helping Aja," Samantha replied. There was a sleepy smile on her lips as she looked at Hawk. "She needed to pick berries, and she also needed to work on a piece of elk hide or was it buffalo hide? Either way, I thought I'd help out where I could. I don't know how to cure leather."

Hawk stepped closer. He didn't particularly care for Samantha's behavior. Was she simply hiding more turbulent emotions? He suspected so. And though he knew it wasn't very flattering to him, he preferred Samantha hiding any tumultuous emotions to not having them at all. Though not an egotistical man, Hawk could not bear the thought of being the first man to make love to a woman as beautiful and unique as Samantha and not have her thinking about it afterward. Whether for good or bad, Hawk wanted to be on her mind, in her thoughts.

"Do you need some help?" he asked quietly. Quite suddenly

he felt very young, as he had when his experience with young squaws was just beginning, and he was learning that his smile, his looks, the way he walked and moved, affected women in a powerful way.

"I would appreciate that very much," Samantha replied, her voice very soft. She looked to the western hills. "How much light do you think we have left?"

Hawk looked at the sun, calculating the time in measurements that Samantha would understand. "Two hours. Maybe three, if the clouds stay away."

Samantha's smile grew fractionally broader, and a soft but unmistakable light came into her blue eyes. "That should give us enough time, I suppose . . . but then, you know more about these things than I do."

Hawk felt a tiny release of pressure within his heart. He still couldn't guess what her feelings were, but she wasn't overwrought, and that was a good sign. The twinkle in her eyes freed Hawk from the worries plaguing him since he had left Samantha alone in Aja's tepee that afternoon.


Billy didn't like the look of it at all, not even a little bit. When his boss, Sonny Sanders, had asked him to do him a "personal favor," Billy had been overjoyed. The chance to go to the city and kick up his heels was something he just couldn't turn down. Especially when he found out that all that was expected of him was to track down Samantha and shoo her behind back to the ranch.

Billy had known Samantha for years, and when he had been told that she hadn't been sending the telegrams she'd promised, he wasn't terribly concerned. As far as Billy could tell, Samantha not doing what her older brother had specifically instructed her to do was pretty much the way it always went with her. Billy figured he'd find her at some out-of-the-way ranch, looking at horses that everyone else had either given up on, or had judged to be of inferior quality. Nobody had an eye for horseflesh like Samantha. She could spot traits, such as intelligence and temperament, better than anyone Billy had ever known. She had a knack for buying a lot of horse for a little money.

Billy had ridden off thinking he had nothing to worry about and would have a paid vacation, to boot, since Sonny had given him fifty dollars in folding money to spend however he wanted.

When the clerk at the hotel said that Samantha had been gone for several days Billy got an empty feeling in his stomach. He had better saddle up and ride off, but first Billy checked around town, talking to the various horse traders, which naturally would have drawn Samantha's attention.

Everywhere he went, he was told that she had been there, but not in several days. Samantha, it seemed, had been everywhere . . . but not recently. That worried Billy right down to his boots. And what would Sonny Sanders do if Samantha wasn't found? Would he hold Billy responsible?

With rapidly escalating unease, Billy rode to the telegraph office and sent: SAMANTHA HAS BEEN EVERYWHERE STOP STILL TRYING TO TRACK HER DOWN STOP WILL REPORT TOMORROW STOP BILLY END.

He hoped it would buy him enough time to find Samantha. Otherwise, Billy wasn't entirely certain what he would do, though he had no desire at all to find out just exactly how protective Sonny Sanders was of his kid sister.


It had been difficult for Samantha in the immediate period following Hawk's abrupt departure from the tcpcc. Aja had entered shortly thereafter, preventing Samantha from having a quiet time for reflection. Aja, spirited as ever, wanted to know just exactly how angry Hawk had been, and when he planned to take Samantha back to her home in Deadwood. Though Samantha felt guilty about her lies, she told one after another, concocting a story of the "argument" she and Hawk had had.

When finally Samantha saw the chance to spend some time

by herself—by picking berries for Aja—she leaped at the opportunity. She had intended to spend the time alone, to sort
out her feelings about Hawk's lovemaking, and of her partially
successful vision quest.

But the moment she saw Hawk astride his stallion, broad-
shouldered and regally commanding, with his head held high,
Samantha knew that she did not really want to be alone. There
would be plenty of time later, after she returned to Deadwood,
to reminisce about her brief journey into Sioux spirituality,
and remember the dark-skinned, mysterious man who'd taught
her that sensuality wasn't just in dreams and fantasies.

Now, she sat behind Hawk on his stallion as the big animal
easily carried them both higher into the hillside, where the
berries grew thick and sweet on the vines. The soft leather
dress she'd borrowed from Aja, Samantha discovered, was not
made for riding—at least, not for riding astride a horse, which
was the only way Samantha knew how to ride, the side saddle
having been noticeably absent from her education. The dress
was forced high and tight across her thighs and Hawk's hand
was resting lightly on her bare knee.

"How was your day after . . . after I left?" Hawk asked,
hoping the question sounded more casual than he felt.

"I like your sister, but she talks an awful lot," Samantha
said softly. She held the basket in one hand, the other resting
lightly on Hawk's stomach. "Sometimes it's hard to believe
the two of you are related; you can be so different."

Hawk laughed softly. "I talk," he said. "At least occasionally."

"You talk only as long as you can guide the conversation,
and make sure that it doesn't go anywhere you don't want it
to," Samantha replied, playfully slapping Hawk. "But the moment someone else starts asking questions—"

"—someone like you," Hawk cut in teasingly.

"Yes, someone like me!" She slapped him again, harder this
time. "The moment I start asking questions, you conveniently
have to ride off to tend to something vitally important, or get

so cold a woman could freeze her fingers to the bone just by touching you."

Ahead, Hawk saw bushes thick with dark red berries. Taking his hand from her knee, he pointed them out to Samantha. "Even *Ida Maka* is on my side. There's the patch we're looking for."

Samantha made a huffing sound of indignation. He had made his usual evasive reply. This time she decided to let the issue pass, having no desire to provoke a fight while they were alone together for a little while.

"Let me help you down," Hawk said, kicking his right leg over the stallion's head and sliding gracefully to the ground.

Samantha's first inclination was to leap off the stallion without waiting for Hawk's help. Too many times in the past, men—ranch hands, some well-meaning and others simply condescending—had suggested helping her into a saddle; or worse, suggested she travel via carriage. Either way, the implication was clear that the men felt riding spirited horses was too challenging an activity for a young woman. But when she looked down at Hawk she didn't see a smug you-need-my-help expression in his eyes. Samantha didn't mind accepting his help down from the long-legged stallion.

Hawk placed his hands on Samantha's narrow waist. When she slid out of the saddle he held her suspended for a moment before setting her slowly to the ground. Samantha turned until she faced him, feeling the familiar quickening of her pulse. For a moment their eyes met, but Samantha broke the contact, twisting away from Hawk and then walking toward the berry bush.

"It's been . . . it's been quite a day," Samantha observed, not looking at Hawk. A cool, gentle breeze played across her bare arms and legs and fluffed her long golden hair. "First a vision quest, then . . . then you. That's quite a day by any standards."

She sensed his presence close behind her, though he said nothing. When she walked she was suddenly aware of the gentle scissoring of her thighs, of being naked beneath the deerskin dress, and of a slight tenderness from the loving they'd shared earlier. She was a little sore, but this kind of discomfort did not bother Samantha. In fact, it brought back passionate memories only hours' old that made her shiver just to think of them.

"Are you cold?" Hawk asked.

A creeping smile tugged at the corners of Samantha's mouth. *No, Hawk,* she thought, *I'm not cold. In fact, my skin feels so hot, I might just take off my dress.* She moistened her lips, realizing that some response was required of her, but she couldn't think of a thing to say. She thought about making love to Hawk again and was aware of the extent of her ignorance about such matters. Was he even able to try so soon again?

What a sign of wantonness to even *think* about making love a second time in one day! But hadn't she already lost her virginity—or given it away, Samantha realized—to Hawk? Was it a greater or lesser offense, she wondered, to commit the same transgression with the same man a second time? And hadn't Hawk promised that the next time would be even better than the first?

It was a promise, she suspected, that he was infinitely capable of fulfilling.

She was about to turn to confront Hawk, to demand answers about the normalcy of the feelings going through her. Hawk Two Feather knew the answers. All this—the lush sensuality, the wanton surrender to pleasures of the flesh—was well within his realm of experience. He could tell her if all women responded to him this powerfully, or if she'd been weak, the erotic dreams that had plagued her sleep finally intruding into her waking world.

Before she could ask him, his hands were on her shoulders. Her eyes closed instinctively. His thumbs slid beneath her hair, then began moving in a circular motion at the base of her skull. Her scalp began to tingle, and it was only with a conscious effort that she was able to keep from moaning.

"Samantha, sweet Samantha," Hawk whispered, standing directly behind her.

Slowly and gently, he pulled her hair so that it left the left side of her neck bare. He bent low and kissed her ear, then followed the outline of it with the tip of his tongue.

She felt his hands move over her shoulders and then down her arms, and his touch elicited another moan that Samantha did not try to silence this time. His hands on her gave her pleasure, so why pretend otherwise?

When she felt his sharp teeth at her earlobe, biting her with enough pressure to hint at pain, Samantha cried out in surprise, leaning toward Hawk so that her back was against his chest.

"You're all I've been able to think about," Hawk said, the timbre of his voice already showing the hoarseness of sexual tension. "I couldn't wait to get back to you, to see you again, to kiss you again, to touch you again!"

Samantha turned her face away from Hawk, offering her neck for his kisses. His teeth caught her tender flesh, his hands pressing her breasts through the deerskin dress that brought out an incongruous beauty in this pale-skinned, blue-eyed blonde.

The touch of the dress was suddenly repellent to Hawk. He wanted no barrier between himself and Samantha. In the afternoon, Hawk hadn't removed Samantha's dress, merely pushing it up in his haste. A hurried, passionate encounter, it hadn't been the way Hawk would have wished. This time Hawk would accept nothing less than perfection—a sterling perfection that would be everything and more than their first loving had been.

Taking Samantha by the shoulders, Hawk turned her to face him. He stood motionless, looking at her, marveling at her flawless beauty, wondering why the Great Spirit had been so generous as to thrust her into his life.

He looked inside himself for words, wanting to tell Samantha that she was different from the other women who had passed briefly through his life. But words—honest ones, not the glib, romantic, facile ones with which he was so practiced—were something he'd never before had cause to summon, and he couldn't find them now when he wanted to.

Slowly, silently, he untied the slender leather cord at the

neck of Samantha's dress, loosening it sufficiently so that the garment could be pulled over her head. Samantha stood motionless, neither helping nor hindering Hawk. She was shivering, then shuddering as she looked up at him. He placed his hands firmly on her shoulders, then bent to kiss her mouth. His kiss was firm and commanding, displaying strength and a dominating confidence. Even as they kissed, Hawk's hand found the hem of the dress and raised it. As Samantha brought her arms over her head, Hawk removed the dress completely and tossed it aside.

When Hawk turned to study her, Samantha crossed her arms over her body. She felt she was being scrutinized, and it wasn't a feeling she cared for.

"You always do that, but you shouldn't." Hawk's voice was husky, seductive. "You are so beautiful, Samantha. Don't deprive me of the pleasure of looking at you."

Samantha wanted to say that she doubted Hawk had ever been deprived of much in his life—especially by women—but she remained silent.

Taking Samantha's hands by the wrists and uncrossing her arms, Hawk revealed her breasts with their soft pink areolas and bud-hard nipples.

"Too beautiful," Hawk whispered, bending his knees. "I cannot resist you, even when I try."

"Then don't try." Samantha sighed, pushing her fingers into the satiny abundance of Hawk's hair, guiding his hot, moist mouth to her breast. When she felt him capture her nipple between his lips she tossed her head back on her shoulders, giving herself over to the feeling.

"I must have you!" Samantha whispered. "Oh, Hawk, I don't care if it's wrong, I must have you!"

# Thirteen

Samantha hugged Hawk's face to her breast, reveling in the heat and moisture of his mouth against her sensitive nipple. Her eyes shut, her legs trembling, she had no intention of going anywhere, of doing anything other than experiencing the magnificence of Hawk's intimate kisses.

She ran a hand down his back and over his leather vest. The feel of the elk hide disappointed her. While continuing to twine his raven-black hair around her fingers to hold his head securely, she used her other hand to push his vest off his shoulders. The breadth of his shoulders, and the flawlessness of his bronzed flesh, must not be denied her, Samantha decided in the entirely selfish manner of a young woman aware that her lover was not merely an extraordinary man but a unique one, one desired by many. And Samantha, whether she realized it fully or not, had no intention of sharing Hawk with anyone.

Now this man's hands were upon her, touching her legs, her thighs, adding to the incredible sensations aroused by his moist kisses. And when he touched the moist, pink petals of her femininity Samantha made a soft, purring sound.

"Lie back," Hawk instructed, kneeling in the grass before Samantha.

She complied, too aroused, too needy, to do anything else. Hawk moved toward her, about to kiss her on the mouth, when she put a hand to his chest to stop him. "No!" she said firmly. "I want you to stand now. Stand . . . so that I can look at you."

A slow half smile made the dimple form in Hawk's gaunt cheek. He rose swiftly, bronzed and beautiful in the sunlight, and looked down at Samantha.

"I've never really . . . really looked at you," Samantha whispered, though there was no need to keep her voice down; they were far from anyone but *Ida Maka*. Impatient to once again receive Hawk's experienced attentions, she felt bold, daring, and infinitely curious. "Let me see, Hawk. Let me look at you the way you've looked at me."

She had expected Hawk to remove his loincloth first, but instead he, aware of the influence his beauty had on women, balanced on one foot and removed first one moccasin and then the other. The muscles in his forearms and biceps bulged with suppressed power as he removed his footwear.

When he finally stood erect again Samantha's eyes caressed his naked chest. His pectorals in particular drew her attention: hard, smooth muscles that were clearly defined beneath cinnamon skin. Then her gaze slid lower, to the rippled surface of his stomach, which led, inevitably, down to his loincloth.

"Hurry," Samantha urged in a husky voice. As she leaned back on one elbow, she realized the little game she had started was taking more time than her impatience could tolerate.

But Hawk didn't hurry. He knew the value of delay, of heightened anticipation, to increase the pleasure of the final moment of satisfaction. Rather than removing his loincloth, he took his own time in removing his leggings, first one and then the other, until at last he stood over Samantha wearing only the loincloth, which bulged over his swollen manhood.

"This, too?" he teased, touching just the corner of the loincloth with his fingertip.

Samantha nodded. Her eyes, crystal blue and glittering with excitement, were barely open, though she was intensely aware of what Hawk was doing. She nibbled on her lower lip in nervous anticipation.

The loincloth was tied at the hip. Hawk pulled loose the

knotted leather cord, but the material did not fall completely free of him. It was caught on the prominence of his manhood.

"Hawk," Samantha whispered.

Hawk slowly stepped forward, his eyes burrowing into Samantha's. Without a word he moved closer, his arousal on prominent display beneath the loincloth. Samantha tore her gaze away from Hawk's to examine his body. With a hand that trembled, she reached out and took the edge of the loincloth in her fingertips and slowly pulled it until Hawk was exposed to her greedy gaze.

The awesome sight of him, fully aroused, took Samantha's breath away. She'd never really looked at him before. Now she saw he was intimidating in size, and a shiver worked its way up her spine.

When she reached for him she saw that her hand was shaking. It stopped short of its mark.

"Touch me," Hawk said softly.

*I shouldn't,* she thought. There were many good reasons for her not to, not the least of which was that she did not like following anyone's command—and certainly not the commands of a lusty savage like Hawk.

But in her heart Samantha knew that there was a secret part of herself who *did* like following his commands. She wasn't surprised when, a moment later, she saw her hand come into view, her slender, pale fingers reaching out to curl slowly and sensually around the solid shaft of Hawk's manhood.

She felt him throb against her palm and the heat of his blood made him even larger and more rigid. As Samantha touched him, she stared at her own hand as though it belonged to someone else. Could this person be Samantha Sanders, an heiress to the largest cattle empire in the Dakota Territory, caressing a Sioux warrior—and loving every moment of it?

Samantha tried to push all thoughts of their social, cultural, and financial differences out of her mind. What good did thinking do anyone, anyway? Thoughts only got in the way of

feelings, and tactile stimulation was what was most important
now, wasn't it?

Hawk's throaty groan of pleasure drew Samantha's attention.
She looked up at his face. Seeing the pleasure reflected in his
eyes, she felt more powerful than ever before in her life. Hawk
moved his hips, forcing himself through the firm encirclement
of her fingers. Then it was Samantha's turn to sigh.

"I don't really know what you want—expect—of me,"
Samantha said softly. The instant the words were out, she regretted having said anything.

"I'll want everything from you, expect everything of you,"
Hawk said. He reached down and captured Samantha's free
hand by the wrist. Raising her hand to his mouth, he kissed
the palm wetly, then brought her hand to his erection. "Better,"
he murmured when she'd taken him tightly in her grip. "Much
better!"

*Be patient,* Hawk thought, his legs flexed with the tension
he felt as he watched Samantha's small, tentative hands caressing him. She was inexperienced, he knew, but that did not
take away from his pleasure. *I'll teach her to be the perfect
lover.*

As that thought brought a fresh burst of desire charging
through his system, Hawk again took Samantha by the wrist
and removed her hand from him.

"Did I do something wrong?" she asked worriedly.

"Nothing you do could be wrong, Little Flower," Hawk said
with a roguish smile, the endearment spoken without conscious
thought. "Just the opposite." He knelt beside her and, still
holding on to her wrist, kissed her palm slowly, paying attention to each finger. His racing pulse slowed and his passion
cooled enough to restore his confidence that he was in control
of his desire. "Everything about you fascinates me." He began
kissing Samantha's wrist, then her forearm, his tongue leaving
a thin, moist trail where his kisses had traveled. "I could kiss
you for a thousand seasons and never tire of it."

They were the words Samantha most wanted to hear, though

she couldn't consider anything so nebulous as *forever* with him. Samantha closed her eyes and leaned back on her elbows as Hawk, kneeling near her hip, nipped teasingly at her shoulder and neck.

Her eyes closed, Samantha sighed with pleasure as Hawk's lips closed over her tingling breast at the exact moment his fingertips brushed lightly against the glistening, honeyed lips of her womanhood. She felt him search briefly to find her most sensitive bud, that tiny nub of pure sensation from which all feeling emanated.

A choked cry of ecstasy sounded in Samantha's throat, and she arched upward, raising her hips so that only her hands and feet were still on the ground. When she felt the pressure of Hawk's hands guiding her, followed by the prickly sensation of the grass against her buttocks, she realized he had coaxed her into sitting once more.

"I can't believe how you make me feel." Samantha's face tilted toward the sun as Hawk's rasping tongue flicked over her left nipple. Down low, she felt slippery, empty, neglected. Then, at last, Hawk eased a single finger into her, and she emitted a long, low, warbling sigh.

"There is much more," Hawk whispered. "So much more . . . and I will be your teacher."

Once again, Samantha wasn't entirely certain she approved of the possessiveness in Hawk's tone. He sometimes sounded as if there were no justifiable opinions that differed from his own. How had Hawk, who in so many ways was an outsider among the Sioux, developed such an aura of superiority? Samantha intended to pose this question to Hawk later . . . when her skin didn't feel as if it was going to burn in all the delightful places that she was being touched by Hawk, and when her bones weren't melting from pleasure.

"Lie back, Samantha," Hawk instructed, kneeling between her legs, leaning over her with one hand on her shoulder, pushing down. "Just lie back, relax, and let yourself feel."

For Samantha, relaxing was, quite simply, out of the question. Even *thinking* about relaxing was a bit ludicrous with Hawk touching and kissing her so intimately, and his fingers probing in just such a way to make Samantha feel as though she was expanding endlessly, opening for him. But whether she wanted to or not, Hawk was infinitely stronger and decidedly more persistent, and when he put more pressure against Samantha's shoulder she had no choice but to topple backward until she was stretched out in the fresh green grass.

Curious about Hawk's latest lesson, Samantha raised her head and shoulders enough to peer through the valley of her breasts at the warrior, who was occupied in leisurely kissing the inside of her left knee. When he caught her looking at him, he smiled, then dragged the tip of his tongue along her inner thigh, moving slowly upward, his gaze never once leaving Samantha's.

*He's going to kiss me there.*

This singular, inchoate thought was something even Samantha's erotic fantasies had not concocted. She'd thought her inner, hidden self—the one that created the sinfully pleasing dreams of passion while she slept—had in one dream or another run through all the possibilities of passion, yet this wasn't one she'd envisioned.

*I shouldn't let him.*

Samantha had no idea whatsoever why she should deny Hawk anything when clearly his competence in these matters was without parallel.

And then he kissed her. Kissed her there, down low, deeply, his tongue darting out to probe, and the sensation it drew from Samantha was nothing she could ever have expected. Once again she flinched as her body reacted to this newly discovered pleasure, her hips shooting upward. As before, Hawk was willing to resort to his greater strength to get what he wanted and, despite Samantha's rather frantic maneuverings, this time her legs ended up tossed over Hawk's broad shoulders, her heels thumping against his back as the tantalizing kisses continued.

Samantha's breathing grew labored, especially when she felt

strands of hair against her lips and in her mouth, eventually realizing that she was rolling her head from side to side, her own hair in wild disarray all over her face. Frantically, she pushed the hair away from her face, gulping in air, trying to keep herself from becoming more excited, still having no notion at all of why she should hide what she was really feeling.

A woman was whispering then, and it took a second or two before Samantha realized that she was the woman speaking the impassioned words. What embarrassing words—words of instruction to Hawk, asking, demanding, and sometimes even begging that the kisses continue unabated because she sensed that she was close . . . close to what, exactly, she wasn't at all certain, but whatever it was, it was awfully powerful. And close. Very close.

*Slow down* a tiny voice whispered inside her head, just loud enough to be heard above the ringing in her ears.

Samantha felt Hawk release one leg from his powerful grasp, and for a moment she worried that he would stop kissing her. Had she done something wrong in her uninhibited response to his wicked, wanton kisses? Then his hand was on her again, this time crushing her breast against her ribs, his long, forceful fingers grasping the firm, tender flesh.

Though she hadn't known it, this caress to her breast was exactly what she had wanted. Hawk had known, and her body had known, though *she* had not. With the pressure building tighter and tighter within her as she was pushed closer to the chasm by pleasure, what Samantha needed wasn't gentle, subtle caresses, but strong, forceful ones.

It took a moment before Samantha was able to calm herself enough to notice what Hawk was doing now, and how it made her feel. She opened her eyes for a moment, but the sun was blinding and she closed them again quickly.

The world didn't matter to her. Nothing external mattered. The only thing that was important was what she felt, what was going on within her own body.

"It's . . . so . . ." Samantha whispered.

She had tried to tell Hawk how magnificent he made her feel, but words failed her. However, she suspected he didn't have to be told to know. With her eyes still closed and her face warmed by the sun, Samantha moistened her lips with the tip of her tongue and tried briefly to slow her ragged breathing. It was impossible; she might as well have been on a runaway train. Nothing she could do would prevent the train from racing faster and faster until, eventually, inevitably, it ran out of track.

The tightening within her intensified, and suddenly Samantha's breath stopped altogether. It hurt now. She felt pain inside. Her stomach knotted and she curled inward, doubling forward, the pressure too great to withstand.

*Stop! Stop, stop, stop!* Samantha thought, but she could not speak, though she desperately wanted Hawk to cease his pleasure-giving, which was now eliciting such intense emotions and sensations that they were painful.

And then, when Samantha was certain she would die of happiness, that she simply could not withstand such ecstasy even a second longer, she shuddered through a series of contractions, like tiny explosions inside, one cataclysmic convulsion after another.

Trembling and weak, her body had been turned inside out and her breath came in quick, uneven gulps. As a gentle breeze played over her nudity, she suddenly felt cool. But rather than search for something to cover herself for warmth or modesty, her most overwhelming urge was to laugh.

"What . . . was . . . that?" she asked softly when her breathing had returned to nearly normal.

Hawk kissed her thigh, then her stomach, moving slowly upward, pushing Samantha's legs off his shoulders. There was a pleased smile on his lips. Samantha's surprised reaction to her own climax confirmed every suspicion he'd had about her romantic past. Though before he'd always avoided inexperienced women—their emotions tended to create complications—he was astonishingly pleased that he was the first man to ever please her so thoroughly.

He stretched out over Samantha, his chest resting lightly on the plush cushion of her breasts, most of his weight on his elbows.

"You want to know what that was?" Hawk teased, kissing Samantha's chin and then the tip of her nose. "That was just the beginning."

Samantha laughed softly, joyously, amazed at what she had felt and the way her body had responded to everything Hawk had done.

"I don't think I could live through anything like that again," she whispered, feeling the heat of Hawk's arousal burning her inner thigh, solid and pulsing with virility.

"Trust me." Hawk's lips brushed Samantha's as he spoke. "You won't die. In fact, you'll never be quite so alive."

"You *are* an arrogant man," Samantha said.

Some part of her needed to respond to Hawk's insolence. He was so confident about everything, so absolutely certain that he would always be triumphant, no matter what. But she kissed him, and when she did she could taste the nectar of her own passion upon his lips. Perhaps another time she would stand her ground. It was enough now to just enjoy his extraordinary skill and learn what it was he could teach her.

As they kissed, Hawk raised his hips sufficiently to guide the inflamed crown of his manhood to Samantha's entrance. With little pressure, he entered her slowly, only a little at a time, pressing deeper and deeper with each smooth, measured thrust.

Samantha had not thought herself capable of feeling anything again, but, as had been the case so often on matters regarding the limits of pleasure, Hawk was right and she was wrong. Each sweet thrust of his hips pushed Samantha back toward the edge of a chasm so frightening and beguiling.

She wrapped her arms tightly around Hawk's neck, holding him closely, kissing him continuously until at last she was certain that she'd taken the full length of him into herself. Only then did she break the kiss, and whisper "Hawk" softly, the name delicious on her tongue.

Making love to Hawk was different this time. She felt his great power thrusting deep into her, joining her to him. There was nothing but pleasure, not even the residual pain that had afflicted her earlier remaining to dampen even the most subtle sensation.

His hands explored her everywhere, knowing exactly where to touch her, toying with her breasts, tugging and rolling her nipples lightly, kissing her mouth, cheeks, neck, and ears, running his hands lightly up the backs of her thighs, squeezing her buttocks and pulling her up so that she met his downward thrust.

For Samantha, the accumulation of stimulations, each one unique in its own way, added to the mixture of feelings sending her careening toward another powerful orgasm.

She felt it approaching again—that great, cataclysmic eruption of sensation. Closing her eyes against the pressure, she concentrated on what she felt, what her body was going through, and how astonishing it was that the most unlikely man in the world had set her body free to experience all that was possible.

The spasms weren't quite as powerful the second time, but in the midst of them Samantha heard Hawk's low growl of ecstasy and realized that he, too, had reached the chasm. Though the pressure had not been as powerful this time, there was in its place a much more satisfying sense of oneness with Hawk, of being joined with him spiritually this time, as well as physically.

# Fourteen

Returning to camp was about the last thing in the world Samantha wanted to do. Actually, it was the second to the last thing Samantha wanted—what she really dreaded was returning to the ranch outside Deadwood.

*Don't think about that now!* was the ceaseless refrain going through Samantha's mind. There were so many things to worry about later, when she and Hawk were no longer together, when there was no longer the pleasure of reaching out and touching him, when there was no longer the happiness of looking into his rich, brown eyes and seeing the humor there.

Hawk *did* have a wonderful sense of humor, Samantha was discovering. Usually hidden, he kept it buried beneath him self-imposed discipline and duty. Samantha was discovering all sorts of wonderful things about Hawk . . . and that was why she felt the poignant loss of time so acutely.

Soon—either today or tomorrow at the latest—the alarm would sound at the Circle S Ranch. Her return would be too late to be on schedule, and Sonny would cause one hell of a commotion, as Samantha well knew, because he'd done it once before when she'd dallied too long without letting anyone know where she was.

How long would it take Hawk and her to reach the Circle S? At least a day and a half, she figured, provided they rode hard. Maybe two days. If the latter was the case, then there would surely be hell to pay by the time she rode through the ranch gates.

Hawk was standing by his stallion, waiting for Samantha, motioning for her to get up into the saddle. He would ride behind her, with his arms around her.

"No, you get on," Samantha countered with a hint of sadness in her voice. "I'll ride behind you."

Agreeably, Hawk swung up into the saddle, then reached down for Samantha and helped her onto the rump of the stallion. Slipping her arms around Hawk's middle, she laced her fingers together at his stomach and leaned forward to place her cheek lightly against his back. When she sighed he patted her hands; then he tapped his heels against the stallion's ribs to get the animal started down into the valley.

The descent would be slow. Neither Hawk nor Samantha was in any hurry to return to the camp. The sun had fallen and now almost total darkness covered the hillside, making the ride a more cautious one.

"How do you feel?" Hawk asked. They'd gone some distance from the clearing, leaving the memories of their hours of loving behind them.

"Wonderful . . . and sad," Samantha replied. She hadn't intended to be entirely honest, but now it seemed the best approach. Why hide her feelings from Hawk now? "You're right about me having to leave. I do. My brother's going to be furious with me, and I wouldn't be at all surprised if he doesn't . . . well, let's just say that I have to get back home."

"Yes," Hawk replied softly.

Samantha kept her eyes closed. It bothered her more, hearing Hawk say she had to leave, then hearing herself say it. She wished there was something she could do to make time stand still.

She and Hawk couldn't stay together always—for many reasons. They were too much alike in too many ways: both stubborn, each wanting to lead and neither willing to follow. They couldn't stay together forever, and Samantha accepted this. She just didn't want their time together to end *now*.

*I'm not going to cry,* Samantha decided when she felt hot tears burning at the backs of her eyes.

And she didn't cry, but the ache she felt inside was terrible. She probably would feel better if she did cry—if she'd just let loose all the emotions pent up within her—but Samantha had spent too long fighting such "womanly" emotions and responses to allow the tears to flow now.

"We'll leave at sunrise," Hawk announced.

Samantha nodded, her head against his shoulder and her arms around his waist, but she didn't speak as the big stallion carried them back to the tribe.

The bile rose in his throat, and Red Wolf had to close his eyes for a moment to compose his thoughts.

She was beautiful beyond words or measure, and when she looked at him the revulsion she felt showed in her expression, in the blue light that shone in her eyes.

Red Wolf hated with all his heart and soul the golden-haired woman who had arrived in the camp with Hawk. He loathed her because she saw him instantly for what he was . . . and for that she had to be punished. She was like the other women who felt themselves superior to a warrior like Red Wolf, though not too superior for Hawk.

But was his first impression accurate? In the past Red Wolf had held similar thoughts about other women, only to discover that they were not repulsed by him at all. During his sojourns to Fairmont, where he had gone alone three times, he'd felt that the white prostitutes had looked on him scornfully, though he'd discovered later that their passion could be purchased easily. Perhaps the golden-haired woman with Hawk would be no different from the others. How much gold would it take to buy her passion? he wondered.

Red Wolf thought about this for several minutes. Was the woman with Hawk truly scornful of him, or was that just her way of getting his attention? Her skin was flawless, Red Wolf had noted, pale and smooth, and her figure was curved despite her youth. Such beauty was wasted on a man like Hawk Two Feather! Hawk had known the pleasures of too many willing women for him to appreciate any one woman in particular.

The anger boiled once more in Red Wolf's stomach, this time because of Hawk and everything the half-breed warrior represented. The squaws and maidens flocked to Hawk, while only a few would give Red Wolf the passion he required. Surely the injustice of this was a sign of some evil power that Hawks exerted to keep Red Wolf from ever truly being happy.

What else could explain the way women reacted to Red Wolf, and the way they responded to Hawk?

What if the young woman's apparent disgust was just a ruse, a trick to get Red Wolf interested in her? She wouldn't be the first maiden to use such a trick on him, he believed. Twice before Red Wolf had needed to use force to get what he wanted from women, and though they cried, he knew that he hadn't done anything wrong.

A smile settled on Red Wolf's face as he realized why the beautiful golden-haired woman had dismissed him so quickly from her attention—because she had wanted him to pursue her with the cunning and determination of a mighty Sioux warrior!


They'd been unable to leave the camp as quickly as Samantha and Hawk had planned. Red Wolf had tossed out some accusations about their trip that Hawk needed to address, and even though almost everyone knew that Hawk was a proud warrior who would never abandon his tribe, he still needed to explain to the elders why it was necessary for him to ride with Samantha back to Deadwood.

Once on their way, as luck would have it, they nearly rode into a small band of Cheyenne braves. Hawk couldn't be sure, but he thought they might be renegades, like those who had attacked Samantha. They avoided the braves, but it had cost them several hours, forcing Hawk and Samantha to make camp for the night.

Samantha slept in Hawk's arms that night, but they didn't make love. She'd expected him to want to, and if his desires had moved in that direction, she would have submitted to him. There was an underlying and painful realization that if she made love with him again she would be doing so for the last time.

The next morning they rose early and, without much talk, saddled Daisy and Hawk's enormous stallion and headed off for Deadwood.

As they approached town, Samantha began to grow nervous. For all the things she had shared about herself, she'd never told Hawk her last name. Had he assumed she was some impoverished tomboy? Would he feel betrayed if she told him now that she came from one of the wealthiest families in the territory?

"Can we stop a minute?" Samantha asked. "There's an artesian well just west of here. We can let the horses drink there."

Hawk nodded, pushing a strand of ebony hair off his forehead. Once more wearing his buckskin trousers, cotton shirt, and leather vest and jacket, he appeared as handsome to Samantha as he had the first time she'd set eyes on him.

"How far are we from Deadwood?" Hawk asked. He was now farther north than he usually traveled. His rule had been to avoid the white man's towns as one would avoid a rattlesnake.

"About three hours." Samantha felt a strange tingling sensation in her stomach. She didn't like concealing the truth from Hawk. Withholding information carried with it an undercurrent of treachery that she didn't like.

"And your home is in Deadwood?"

"It's outside of town a ways. We'll be there in a little over three hours, I guess."

Hawk's eyes narrowed as he looked at Samantha. He could tell that there was something she wasn't telling him, though he couldn't guess exactly what it was. Was she ashamed to be seen with a half-breed Sioux? That wouldn't surprise him in the least.

"When we get close to your home I'll turn back," Hawk offered. He saw immediately the look of disappointment in Samantha's eyes, but he raised his hand to stop her protests before they started. "It'll be best. I know the way some people think. You and I traveling together . . . some in my tribe didn't like it, and your people won't either. It's just the way things are."

"It doesn't have to be that way," Samantha said softly.

"But it is."

Samantha squared her shoulders, taking a step closer to Hawk. "No," she said firmly. "After all we've been through, after all we've shared, after all the miles we've ridden together, you can't abandon me now. Not when we're so close to my ranch."

"But Samantha—"

"The least you can let me do is introduce you to my family, and show you a little of my hospitality. Can't you grant me that much?"

Hawk gave her a naughty grin, prompting a blush from Samantha that made him want to kiss her, though he resisted the urge.

"There are other types of hospitality, you know!" Samantha felt her cheeks turning pink and warm. Whenever Hawk looked at her that way the memories of the thrilling moments she'd known in his embrace came flooding back.

Hawk smiled, and it made something inside Samantha soften, made her want to take him into her arms, made her want to lead him someplace where the differences between them wouldn't matter. As it was—with the Sioux and her own people—more energy was spent making sure people of different cultures and races *weren't* happy together.

Now she wanted to kiss him, or in the very least hold him close, but if she did, she would also want to make love to him, and that part of their life together was over. With a sigh of resignation, and wondering, then, if perhaps Hawk's cynicism wasn't closer to reality than her own optimism, she fitted her boot into Daisy's stirrup and got up into the saddle.

It would be good to be home again, to have the creature comforts that had been denied her for so long. She would have to calm the fires of anger that were no doubt flaming within Sonny first, but then she would be able to relax.

Samantha smiled at Hawk as they headed into the final stretch toward her ranch. She hadn't said a word about herself, about the vast fortune that was hers . . . about anything that really mattered.

*He has to come to the ranch to get his reward for saving my life,* Samantha thought. *And if he thinks that I've deceived him by not telling him who I am, that's something I'll just have to live with.*

Sonny's first thought on seeing Hawk was, *This is a dangerous man.*

Not only was Hawk a Sioux warrior, but he carried himself with his head a little too high, and he dared to look straight into a man's eyes, instantly sizing him up.

Sonny had made his fair share of enemies in his day—no truly successful man could ever accomplish lofty goals without leaving lesser individuals feeling cheated. Sonny Sanders didn't back down from fights, though he chose his battles carefully . . . so what bothered him most was that Hawk was very much like himself.

"Now, Sonny, don't you dare be angry," Samantha warned him, stepping close so that she stood between her brother and her lover. "It wasn't my fault I was late, and it wasn't Hawk's fault, either. If Hawk hadn't come to my rescue"—she stabbed a finger into her brother's chest to emphasize her next words—"at considerable risk to himself, then I'd be dead right now."

Her voice dropped low as she shamelessly played on her brother's protective instincts. "Dead . . . or worse."

Sonny looked over Samantha's head at Hawk. Sonny was more heavily muscled, but Hawk stood a bit taller. In hand-to-hand combat, the violence between them would be horrific.

Sonny didn't want to hate this handsome stranger who had brought Samantha home, but he couldn't forget that Samantha should have been home at least three or four days earlier. What had they done together during those days?

"Sonny, please . . ." Samantha whispered, begging for understanding.

Sonny looked down into his little sister's face and smiled for the first time. "I never could stay angry with you."

Samantha threw her arms around Sonny, hugging him tightly. Then, at last certain that violence had been avoided, she turned toward Hawk, her face animated, alive with joyous emotions.

"Come on; I want to show you the house," Samantha said, as she took Hawk's hand. She tried to pull him across the threshold, but Hawk resisted. She couldn't budge him. "Please, Hawk . . . you showed me where you live, and I just want to do the same."

Hawk wasn't fooled for a minute by Sonny's smile. The man was furious that Samantha had disappeared for so long, and in Hawk's company. If the situations had been reversed—if it had been Aja who had disappeared for days without word and then showed up, appearing none the worse for wear despite telling a tale of multiple attacks by roving gangs of men, Hawk would have found it difficult to believe. If she returned with this man Sonny, Hawk wouldn't have believed the tale at all.

"No," Hawk said quietly but firmly. He had no intention of stepping into the house of a man who would probably kill him if the fact that Samantha was no longer a virgin should become known.

Samantha felt a nervous flush go through her. Just a few moments earlier she'd been overjoyed because her brother had put his anger aside. Now she was being confronted with an equally stubborn man who, for reasons Samantha couldn't even guess, had suddenly decided to rob her of her happiness.

Samantha glanced at Sonny. After a brief communication with their eyes only, Sonny said, "I'll go into the library and have a good stiff shot of rye. You coming home to roost seems a good enough reason to celebrate with a drink, I'd say." He took a step, stopped, and then said, "If you need anything, just holler and I'll come running." Then he walked away, leaving Samantha alone in the great archway of the huge ranch house.

Alone with Hawk, Samantha frowned, her hands on her hips. "You can't leave," she declared, quietly and forcefully. "Your camp is much too far away, and it makes no sense at all to sleep outside on your bedroll when we have a dozen perfectly comfortable rooms here for you to choose from."

"A dozen bedrooms unused?" Hawk cocked a brow, mocking her.

"I'm sorry if I wasn't completely honest with you before. It wasn't that I didn't want to be. I was afraid at first that if you knew of my family's status, you'd hold me for ransom." Samantha flinched inwardly at the look Hawk gave her. She'd hurt him with her comment, and she felt guilty about it. "It was my own suspicions, Hawk. Foolish, unfounded suspicions. It had nothing to do with you at all."

Hawk looked over Samantha's head into the entryway and, beyond that, into the foyer. The library, with its gleaming, polished double doors, was to the left. Hawk had noticed from the very beginning that Sonny had left the library doors open several inches. He might not be able to overhear a whispered conversation, but should Samantha raise her voice, Sonny could reappear in the hallway in an instant, probably with a blazing six-shooter in each hand.

The polished wood, cut-crystal doorknobs, thick rugs . . . all spoke of extraordinary wealth. Hawk didn't belong here. His mother had been borne into wealth and privilege, but she had turned herself into a travesty, sleeping with every Indian brave she could just to prove to her father that she was nothing like him. In the process, she'd become just as bigoted as he, hating herself and everything she had been. Eventually, when her self-hatred had reached its height, when there was no man, white or Indian, left who had a shred of respect or desire for her, she had chosen self-destruction. Hawk had always seen her as a coward, and the fact that her blood flowed through his veins frightened him.

"No, I can't go in there," Hawk said sternly, the old memories insinuating themselves once more into his thoughts. He stepped away from the threshold and onto the wide porch, as though afraid unseen powers would reach out and drag him bodily into the ranch house.

"What's wrong, Hawk? It's obviously something more than just my not telling you I'm a Sanders."

Hawk looked at her and smiled. She was wearing the soft leather shirt that Aja had given her, to replace the cotton one that had been destroyed in the attack, and her Levi's. A Sioux maiden's shirt and a man's trousers: Was it any wonder Hawk had never guessed that she was worth a fortune? Had Hawk been a man who laughed aloud easily, he would have then, at the absurdity of it all.

"You can't leave," Samantha said again, encouraged by Hawk's smile. "There's something my brother and I have to give you: a small reward for saving my life."

Hawk shook his head quickly. "I didn't do it for money Samantha. You know that."

"Yes, I know. That's exactly why I'm going to be so stubborn about this now. If you'd done it for money, I'd have paid you, but you wouldn't have had my respect. By being such a gentleman"—Samantha was stopped dead for a moment as she wondered whether a Sioux warrior could ever, in fact, be considered a gentleman, or would even want to be thought of as such—"you have earned my respect and my reward, and I will not allow you to deprive me of the privilege of being kind in return for all that you have done for me."

Hawk's expression softened as his opinion changed. Samantha wasn't trying to buy him off, or insult him. Not in any way . . . but Hawk still wouldn't accept money from her. He had no intention of being any wealthy white woman's bought-and-paid-for chattel.

Samantha saw that Hawk was determined to hold his ground, but she had spent plenty of time horse-trading with men much older and more experienced than herself. She wasn't easily mollified, and she wasn't above arguing on a purely emotional basis to get what she wanted.

"If you won't take the money for yourself, at least take it for your people. They'll think you're a hero for it."

"I don't want to be a hero," Hawk replied.

"It's too late; you already are," Samantha replied, her voice dipping as images of Hawk's extraordinary courage, intelligence, and resourcefulness flashed through her mind. "You can't change what and who you are any more than I can," Samantha continued softly. "Please, Hawk, take the money. You can buy many things with it, things that will make life easier for the women and children of the tribe. Think of them. You don't have to spend a single cent of it on yourself if you don't want to."

She had him there. Samantha had skillfully maneuvered Hawk until his position of refusal appeared—even in his own eyes—as proud, foolish, and, in a bizarre way, selfish and cruel to the women and children he was supposed to protect.

"You can be a very persuasive woman," Hawk said quietly. Absolute respect filled his eyes, even though he had been out-maneuvered by Samantha. His estimation of her went up slightly with his own defeat. "But there's got to be room for compromise."

Samantha's smile was bright enough to light up a midnight sky. "Compromise is my middle name," she said, guiltily remembering all the times she'd said that to horse-traders and eventually ended up getting pretty much everything she wanted without taking so much as a single step backward from her original position. "However, I see no reason in the world that we should . . ." she paused, searching for the right word before deciding upon ". . . *negotiate* the terms of our agreement out here. There are some very comfortable rooms inside, and I'd love a cool drink. If you would like one, I'd be only too happy to oblige."

Beneath the surface of her words was a romantic implication that Hawk didn't miss, but no matter how much he wanted to be in Samantha's arms once more before he returned to his tribe, he wouldn't enter her house.

"I plan to ride into town tonight, and tomorrow we can discuss what needs to be done," Hawk said. It had been quite a while since he'd been in Deadwood. Perhaps it wouldn't be as bad as he remembered it being.

"Why ride all the way to Deadwood and pay for a room?" Samantha glanced quickly over her shoulder toward the library doors. She didn't want Sonny to hear her. There was no mistaking that she wanted to be with Hawk, that she wanted to hold him in her arms and taste his breathtaking kisses once again.

"I just have to," Hawk replied cryptically. "Can we leave it at that?"

For once, Hawk had requested that a subject be dropped rather than simply clamming up and shutting Samantha out, and for that she was grateful. Not quite grateful enough to give up easily, but grateful just the same.

"Why spend your money?" she persisted with a coquettish lilt to her voice. "Do you have enough to get a suite?"

"No, I don't have enough for a suite," Hawk replied, an edge to his voice, "but then, I don't need a suite. My needs are very simple."

Samantha smiled, not at all put off by the sharpness in Hawk's voice. "Your needs may be simple but they can be . . . *voracious*"—she drawled the word sensually—"nevertheless. And don't try to deny it, because I know you, Hawk Two Feather. I know you better than you think."

Though stunned at Samantha's words, Hawk never allowed it to show in his face. Yes, Samantha did know him better, to be sure, than any of the other women who had traipsed lightly and quickly through the romantic and sensual quarters of his life.

"Tomorrow," he said, smiling now with some difficulty. Alone tonight, he could think about Samantha and figure out why he had allowed her, and no one else, into the previously unreachable regions of his heart and soul.

He turned then and headed for his stallion, not wanting to allow Samantha to say more. She was infinitely more intelligent than he had initially assumed, and that would cause him problems. Rather than blithely assuming that he could convince her of the rightness of his needs, he was discovering that she could, in all likelihood, convince him that her position was the correct one.

"But Hawk . . ." she whispered softly.

"Tomorrow," he said over his shoulder, using his long-legged stride to make his way to the stallion that had carried him through countless battles.

# Fifteen

The manager at the Deadwood Hotel saw Hawk coming, and he didn't like what he saw. His hotel was a respectable one. He didn't allow riffraff, footpads, or Indians into it. Yes, an occasional Indian prostitute plied her trade at the hotel, but the manager never considered that a violation of his code. Prostitutes, after all, weren't the same as customers. Never once had he allowed an Indian brave to procure a white prostitute in his hotel. Standards, after all, had to be maintained.

"I'd like a room for the night," Hawk said, using a tone of voice that was neither aggressive nor insulting. He looked straight into the hotel manager's eyes, sensing the animosity lurking behind the man's oily smile. "I'd appreciate it if you'd hurry. I've been riding a long time, and I'd like to get some sleep."

The manager was taken aback by Hawk's forceful and confident request. Usually braves realized that they had no business being in his hotel, and should they dare ask for a room, they spoke in begging tones. This particular Indian didn't speak that way at all, and the hotel manager wasn't at all pleased because of it.

"There's no room here for you," the manager said steadily, hatefully. He resented the fact that he even had to speak to an Indian, much less actually have to explain to him what his true place in society was. "I'm sorry. You'll have to go somewhere else."

Hawk looked past the hotel manager at the wall, where a

row of small, square boxes holding room keys was attached. Messages for the guests were also saved there. Even at a glance from a man who'd spent few nights in hotels, it was clear to Hawk that there were rooms to be had.

"I have money," Hawk said, resenting the fact that such a statement had to be spoken.

"Yes, I'm sure you do, but the fact remains that there are no rooms for you. Now if you'll please leave immediately, everyone will be happier for it."

The last little dig set Hawk off, making it impossible for him to walk away from this one. He was, after all, just as much white as he was Indian; why couldn't he rent a room for the night, providing he had the money to pay for it?

"No, I will not leave. If you need your money for the room in advance, I can do that."

Hawk watched as the man made a little move with his hand. In other circumstances it wouldn't have been a threatening gesture, but Hawk realized from the very beginning that trouble was on the way.

"Problems, sir?" a big, bearded man asked, his eyes cold and steady on Hawk. He'd stepped out from a back room. "I can get rid of this trash any time you want."

Hawk looked at the man who had entered the scene. Though he had bathed recently and was wearing reasonably new, fashionable clothes, Hawk pegged him instantly for hired muscle, several steps below a hired gun. The man was as big as an ox and powerful, though at least fifty pounds heavier than Hawk.

"I'm sure he'll leave now," the hotel manager said, a vicious, satisfied smile curling his lips as he looked at Hawk.

"That's where you're wrong," Hawk replied, his voice hinting at the violence and hatred that had been brewing for decades within him. "You see, I'm going to be treated just the same as anyone who comes here looking for a room and has the money to pay for it."

The hired muscle just couldn't resist opening his mouth. "You'll get treated just the same as all the other two-legged manure that walks in here, thinking they's just as good as white folk."

That was his first mistake. He hadn't been content with merely insulting Hawk; he had insisted on touching him as well.

That was when it began.

Precisely one second after the man's hand touched Hawk's shoulder, Hawk decided that he'd been pushed around as far as he was going to allow. He lashed out with his right hand, aiming not for the nose or chin but for the forehead. The heel of his right palm made solid contact, snapping the big man's head back on his neck in the blink of an eye. The large man fell to his knees, a stunned expression on his face, his eyes unable to focus. The entire force of the blow had been absorbed by the man's brain. Shortly after he dropped to his knees, Hawk swung far back and delivered a roundhouse punch to the man's chin, which sent him flat onto his back and into unconsciousness.

After checking to see that the heavy-set man would eventually recover from his injuries, Hawk wheeled on the hotel manager, blood in his eyes, his hands clenched into fists. Hawk wanted, at this point, to beat the man to a pulp. He reached over the counter and grabbed the lapel of the manager's coat.

"There are no rooms for you," the hotel manager repeated. Though he was maintaining his self-righteous indignation, the undercurrent of fear, the unspoken awareness that he wasn't in control and hadn't been for some time, could be seen.

Hawk shook the manager, feeling the lapel tear in his hand. "Do I get the room or not?" Hawk asked.

"Y-y-yes, sir," the hotel manager finally stammered, not having a clue as to what was expected of him now that his chief security man was lying unconscious on the floor. "Any room you want is yours for the asking. If there's someone in there now, I'll have him thrown in the street before you know it."

Hawk smiled. The hotel manager believed in nothing other

than strength. Like a spear of wheat, he stood straight and true only so long as there wasn't a wind blowing.

There weren't any lavish suites at the hotel, despite the man's words, but Hawk was happy with the simple, clean room. He tested the mattress and was pleased with its newness and quality. It would feel good to sleep in a bed again. How long had it been since he'd felt a mattress beneath him?

Samantha looked at the array of nightgowns in her closet and decided on the high-necked, simple white one. It had been a gift from Sonny, for either her birthday or Christmas. Samantha couldn't remember the occasion because her brother was absurdly generous with her and Vanessa, always buying them gifts, trying to do little things to make their lives easier, happier.

With slippers on her feet and clad in a nightgown and robe, Samantha went downstairs to the library, where Sonny was waiting for her.

"Now **tell** me everything, from the very beginning," Sonny said, sitting on one side of the couch with a whiskey glass in his hand. Samantha held a small glass of white wine. "If I'm going to pay this Hawk fellow a king's ransom for your return, at least I should get the details of his heroism."

Samantha smiled, took a sip of wine, and then began relaying the events immediately following her departure from the horse auctions at Fort Keough. She had been mentally rehearsing what she would tell Sonny since she'd returned home, and the facts now rolled effortlessly off her tongue. The deletion of certain details—like the way her body felt all jittery inside whenever Hawk was near, and the way she couldn't catch her breath whenever he kissed her—was an easy matter, though she'd never before had any reason not to tell her brother everything.

This time was different. This time there was a special man in her life, and even though he would soon be riding away, never to be seen again, Samantha knew that she'd keep memories of him in her heart forever. She wouldn't share them with anyone. Not ever. By keeping the memories to herself, by never speaking of them to anyone, she would keep them fresh and alive and infinitely precious.

"What was the vision quest like?" Sonny asked quietly, his eyes narrowing with concern. Not a particularly religious man, he thoroughly distrusted Sioux spirituality.

"It's wasn't very successful, I'm afraid, though I did see a doe briefly. Aja says the doe is my spirit guide, but that might not be the case. She said that in a vision quest the visions should last longer than mine did. I might have just made it up because I wanted to see something."

Samantha sipped her wine, knowing she couldn't tell Sonny that she very much wanted to go on another vision quest. Sonny was much too provincial in his outlook on life to view kindly such activities as vision quests.

They spoke then of Hawk, and Sonny was polite enough not to ask directly if the alleged hero was also a gentleman. Through omission, Samantha let Sonny believe nothing romantic had transpired between them. Then he busied herself with discussing the inferior quality of the horses she'd seen at Fort Keough, and that none of the mares or stallions had bloodlines worthy of the Sanders' herd.

By ten o'clock Samantha had pretty much told her brother everything she'd done. After a second glass of wine, fatigue came over Samantha, and she excused herself. Sliding between the sheets of her bed, she sighed, closed her eyes, and within seconds was asleep . . . and dreaming of Hawk.


A few minutes after ten o'clock, Hawk heard angry male voices coming from the dusty street. They could have been discussing anything, but Hawk had been an outsider long enough to assume he could well be the target of such aggressive language. Sitting on the edge of the bed, he picked up his revolver and holster and quickly strapped the belt around his lean waist. The moment his moccasins were back on, he heard the same angry male voices in the hallway.

Under his breath, Hawk cursed himself. Why had he ever assumed he could come to the white man's town and not suffer the consequences?

He stepped into the hallway just as the men—four of them, led by the bruised security guard—approached his room. Spotting Hawk, they spread out shoulder-to-shoulder, completely blocking the hallway. All armed and angry that an Indian had gotten the best of one of them, they were looking for swift vigilante justice.

"Are you going to let me pass?" Hawk asked, surprising the men by speaking first. He stood in the center of the hallway, his feet spread to shoulder's width and, his hands loose at his sides but ready to go for his gun in an instant. By Hawk's calculation, he could shoot one, maybe two of them, before they got him.

"Maybe," the hired muscle said. There was an ugly purple mark on his forehead, matched by an ugly look in his eyes. He wanted Hawk's blood. "Maybe we'll just stomp on you right here."

As vicious and violent as the men were, they were also experienced in such matters. All they had to do was look at Hawk to realize that they didn't want a one-on-one fight with either fists or guns.

Hawk stood his ground. He couldn't get past the men if they didn't want him to, and trying to walk between them to get to the stairway would be suicidal. The moment they had their hands on him, Hawk knew he was as good as dead, though these men probably wouldn't be in any hurry to kill him. He recognized the type who would prolong the agony before the inevitable murder.

Three doors in the hallway opened, then quickly closed. Nobody wanted to get involved.

"Walk away from this one," Hawk said quietly, his voice

even and measured. "I'll leave town on my own tonight. Just walk away from this one."

The smallest of the four men grinned broadly. "The red-skin's yellow! He's just a yellow bastard!"

Hawk gritted his teeth against the insult, not bothered much at being called a redskin, or a coward. What hurt was being called a bastard and knowing that, in truth, he was.

"Hey, redskin, what you got to say about that? Are you a coward, or ain't you?" the little man taunted. He jeered at Hawk from behind the big security guard, confident in the protection of his three friends. "Cat got yer tongue, redskin?"

"If you were man-sized," Hawk said slowly, "I'd take offense to such words. When you grow to be a man we'll talk."

The little man made up for his lack of size with sheer savagery. He had killed before when insulted, and he intended to kill again. He went for his revolver, thinking that Hawk, being outnumbered, would be too frightened to draw his own weapon.

But Hawk drew and fired. In the enclosed hallway, the revolver's report was a deafening explosion. He struck the little man in the thigh, dropping him to the floor as the fellow's gun sent a bullet into the floor between Hawk's moccasins. Hawk thumbed back the hammer quickly, seeing that his other three foes were drawing their weapons.

"Kill him!" the little man screamed in agony.

The big security guard was slow, so Hawk dismissed him as a pressing threat. But the man to his left wasn't. He was just raising his revolver from its holster when Hawk fired, his aim deadly accurate this time. The man fell onto his back and didn't move again.

The huge hired muscle was in a hurry to kill, which proved to be fatal for his little friend on the floor. Firing too quickly, his bullet struck the wounded man squarely between the shoulder blades. The guard was still staring in shock, appalled at his mistake, when Hawk's bullet found its mark, sending him toppling backward like a gigantic redwood that had been felled.

The one remaining man wanted no part of the fight with Hawk now. Three of his friends had been killed in seconds, and he'd never seen anyone move more quickly than Hawk. He tossed his gun to the floor and raised his hands over his bead.

"Don't shoot! Don't shoot me!" he shrieked, his eyes wild with fear.

Hawk wanted to pull the trigger but he didn't. He wouldn't be a cold-blooded killer; it wasn't in him.

"Get the hell out of here," Hawk said through clenched teeth.

The last man ran as though he'd been granted a reprieve from God Himself. Hawk holstered his weapon, wrinkling his nose at the smell of burned gunpowder and the stench of instant death.

What had made him think he could come into Deadwood and not find trouble?

"Don't move, Injin!"

Hawk looked first into the twin barrels of the shotgun, then into the face of the man who'd spoken—Sheriff Darren Richards. There on his vest was pinned the silver badge of authority in the courts of the white man.

"You're under arrest, Injin, for the murder of these men here," the sheriff said, keeping his shotgun trained on Hawk's chest. "Real careful and slow, you jus' drop that holster and lay down on the floor. You so much as breathe funny an' I'll cut you clean in half with this scattergun."

Hawk knew the sheriff was looking for an excuse to kill him, so he did as he was ordered, then felt the cold steel manacles being locked around his wrists.

"Do I get a trial before you lynch me?" Hawk asked when he'd been hoisted to his feet and pushed toward the stairway. He had to step over the corpses.

"We do things legal in Deadwood," Sheriff Richards replied.

"We're going to give you a trial, then hang you, all nice and legal."

Hawk was escorted out of the hotel and down the dusty street to the jail. Sheriff Richards opened the jail cell door wide and turned to Hawk with a smile on his face.

"Injin, you killed men who ain't much better than coyotes," the sheriff said. "Just the same, they was white men, an' it always looks bad havin' an Injin do something like that. If I don't do somethin' about it, the townfolk would have no respect for me at all."

With his hands manacled behind his back, Hawk was defenseless against the barrage of fists that followed. The sheriff began to beat his ribs and stomach, and when Hawk finally fell to the floor he kicked him several times. Only then, with Hawk writhing on the jail floor, his breath beaten from his lungs, did the sheriff grab him by an ankle, drag him into the cell, and lock the heavy iron door behind him.

"You sleep good now, you hear?" The sheriff smiled as he walked away.

Sheriff Darren Richards headed for the nearest saloon. He could hardly wait to taste the whiskey the men would buy him in congratulations for the beating he'd given Hawk. This was the kind of evening that had made Darren want to become sheriff in the first place.

# Sixteen

Samantha rode into town wearing new Levi's and a new blue cotton shirt beneath a jacket of lightweight brown linen. She'd polished her boots that morning so that they shone as though they were fresh from the cobbler.

This was the fourth outfit she'd tried on that morning. Her first three attempts had been dresses, which she'd rejected after looking at her reflection in the mirror. Though she wanted to look nice for Hawk, she didn't want him to guess the trouble she'd gone through for him.

She went to the bank first to withdraw two thousand dollars. The bank president, always alert when such large sums of money were withdrawn, smiled at Samantha and suggested that it must be a very beautiful horse the Sanderses were planning to buy. Not wanting to explain that the money would soon be in the possession of the most handsome Sioux warrior in the world, Samantha merely returned the smile, letting the banker think what he wanted.

There were only two hotels in town. Since the clerk at the first one Samantha tried hadn't seen Hawk, she was confident, on reaching the second, that she'd find him. Would she stir gossip if she went to Hawk's room without an escort? And once there, would she be able to control her romantic urges? Just thinking about Hawk's embrace brought a smile to her lips and a gleam to her blue eyes.

The morning clerk at the Deadwood Hotel, a Mr. Jamison, developed a troubled expression when Samantha began asking him questions. Though it was early—just a few minutes past nine—Mr. Jamison appeared to have been awake for many hours, and to have had insufficient sleep.

"These are not really difficult questions." Samantha was finding it impossible to remain polite to this evasive man. "Is Hawk Two Feather staying at this hotel?"

"He was," Mr. Jamison finally replied in as calm a voice as he could manage. He didn't like trouble, especially from someone as rich as Samantha.

"Then he's checked out?" Samantha was just about ready to vault over the counter, take Mr. Jamison by the throat, and choke straight answers out of him.

"Not exactly. You see, there was a disturbance last night, and I'm afraid Mr. Feather was in the middle of it." Mr. Jamison still couldn't believe that the night manager had been foolish enough to rent a room to an Indian. Everyone knew they caused nothing but trouble. Hadn't the events of last night proved as much?

Samantha had never been one to use the weight of her name carelessly. Nevertheless, she looked Mr. Jamison straight in the eye and warned, "Unless you tell me everything that happened last night, everything from the very beginning, I'm going to buy this hotel, and then I'll be your boss. Imagine what your life will be like with me telling you what to do every minute of the day."

Mr. Jamison could imagine such a horrendous thing. Consequently, he quickly summoned the night manager from his room, making him suffer the indignity of answering Samantha's endless, piercing questions.

By the time the night manager had explained his version of what had happened, Samantha was mad enough to burn every building in Deadwood to the ground, then chase every person in the city out of the territory. When she left the hotel, headed for the jail, she was already making plans to destroy the careers—and maybe even the lives, if her temper held—of certain people in town, most notably Sheriff Darren Richards.

The sheriff was nursing a wicked hangover when Samantha burst into the jail office. Darren Richards was sitting on the cot in the office, holding his head in his hands. The deputy, Foster Samuelson, had just cussed him out severely for beating Hawk.

Samantha pointed a finger in the sheriff's face and hissed, "You pathetic dog! You let Hawk out of jail or so help me God I'll destroy you!"

"You watch your tongue, little lady, or I'll arrest you, too!" the sheriff shot back, the ravages of his hangover temporarily obscuring the clout Samantha and her kin had in Deadwood, never mind how much trouble her lawyer sister could make for a man.

"Go ahead and try it, but you'd better think about your own long stretch in prison if you do, because if you put one finger on me, that's where you'll go!"

Although Samantha was furious, she was very aware that Vanessa had left Deadwood. If Vanessa's services were needed, it would take a couple of days for her to return. Unfortunately, Darren Richards represented legal authority in Deadwood, and even the territorial judge would consider his word as credible.

Deputy Foster Samuelson came walking into the office. "Now hold your horses for a minute, Samantha," the deputy said, placing his hands lightly on her shoulders. Samantha knew him to be an honest and dedicated man, and one who believed in making Deadwood a decent place for everyone to live. "I know what you're thinking, but we just can't let that fellow out of jail. There are three dead men over at the undertaker's, and that's something we can't pretend isn't so."

"It was self-defense, Deputy, and you know it!" Samantha pushed the deputy's hands from her shoulders. She knew he meant well, but she wouldn't be mollified by words or gestures—no matter how reasonable they were—unless they were followed up with the immediate action of freeing Hawk from his jail cell.

"Go talk to some of the hotel guests," Samantha suddenly

ordered the deputy. "If you say you can't let Hawk out of jail without evidence of his innocence, get busy and find some!"

Looking somewhat irritated and holding back a retort, the deputy left, issuing a quiet suggestion—which sounded more like a warning—to Sheriff Richards that he was to stay in the office and out of trouble until the deputy returned. Samantha's demand that she be allowed to see Hawk was rejected, and she suspected the sheriff refused only because she'd already made him so angry.

Two hours later the deputy returned. In that time, Samantha had devised no less than a dozen can't-fail plans to make Sheriff Darren Richards wish he'd never heard the name Samantha Sanders.

"Several people heard what was said in the hallway before the shooting started," Deputy Samuelson informed Samantha as he went to the large ring of keys that hung from a peg in the wall behind his desk. "It seems the Indian was trying to walk away from the fight."

"His name is Hawk," Samantha said testily, following close at the deputy's heels.

"What is he to you, anyway? You seem awful worked up about an Indian."

Now Samantha realized gossip would flow, but she didn't care a whit what anyone thought of her in Deadwood. Just the same she flirted with the truth when she replied, "He's a friend of the family."

When she saw Hawk sitting on the small bed in the jail cell, she wanted to rush to him and take him into her arms. She wanted to apologize not only for all of the citizens of Deadwood, but for everything the whites had ever done to the Indians. With Deputy Samuelson there, already highly inquisitive about the relationship between her and Hawk, Samantha kept her feelings to herself.

The instant Samantha saw Hawk move off the bed she knew that he'd been beaten. He tried to keep the pain from showing, but Samantha remembered too well his usual effortless grace,

like that of a mountain lion. His stiffness wasn't the result of
a bad night's sleep on an uncomfortable bed. As he bent over
slightly and approached the cell door, the light shining in his
eyes was fueled by pain and hatred.

"We're setting you free," Deputy Samuelson said, fitting the
long, heavy key into the iron lock. "If any family members
of the boys you killed cause a fuss, you may have to tell your
story to the judge."

Hawk didn't reply, merely looking on the deputy with total
loathing. The door finally opened and Hawk stepped out,
avoiding eye contact with Samantha, holding his head as high
and his shoulders as squarely as his battered ribs would allow.

"I'm going to make everything right," Samantha said to
Hawk, her tone and concern informing the deputy that she was
motivated by something more than mere friendship. A lifetime
of wealth made Samantha's declaration a credible one, though
a testimony to her youth as much as to her financial power.
"We'll get back to the ranch and send for the doctor."

"No," Hawk said, limping to the office of the jail.

The air seemed fresher to him now that he was no longer
locked in a cell, but when he tried to inhale deeply, his battered
ribs screamed in protest. He knew that some of his ribs were
probably cracked or broken.

"But Hawk . . ." Samantha began; then she stopped herself.
She wouldn't say anything else in front of the deputy. He
sensed too much about her and Hawk as it was.

When Sheriff Richards learned Hawk was being released
and given back his holster and his gun he decided it was safer
to anger his deputy than to face the armed wrath of the freed
and furious Hawk Two Feather. By the time Hawk had his
holster fastened around his hips again the sheriff had saddled
his horse and headed out of town for the day, intent on spending time at a little creek where the fishing was occasionally
good and enemies were nonexistent.

Standing on the boardwalk outside the jail, Deputy Samuelson turned to Hawk and said, "I know them boys didn't give

you a choice in the fighting, and I know what the sheriff did to you was wrong, but I'm going to give you some free advice right now, and if you're a smart man, you'll listen up. You just ride straight out of town and don't look back. Don't go looking for revenge, because that won't change any of the wrongs that have been done to you. Just ride out and put it all behind you. Deadwood isn't any place for you, I'm sorry to say."

"I'll *bet* you're sorry," Samantha shot back sarcastically. "But you're not nearly as sorry as some other people in Deadwood are going to be! I can promise you that!"

"Just in case you haven't figured it out by yourself," Samuelson retorted, not cowed by her anger, "I'm not your enemy. You'll have plenty of enemies—trust me on that—but I'm not one of them, so don't talk to me as if I am."

As difficult as it was for Samantha to admit when she was wrong, she looked directly at the man and said, "I'm sorry, Deputy. This whole affair has got me confused. It makes me say things I shouldn't."

Foster Samuelson replied, "Already forgotten. Now get out of town, both of you. And don't worry about the sheriff. I'll keep him in line."

Though Hawk was able to pull himself into the saddle, he couldn't hide the pain that ripped through his body like a lightning bolt. The cracked ribs caused him incredible pain. He could still feel where each boot tip had connected with his body, where each of the sheriff's well-placed kicks had hit him as he writhed, manacled and defenseless, on the ground.

Once in the saddle, his stallion ready to run, Hawk instead kept the great beast in check. His sides hurt too much for him even to think about riding out of Deadwood at a gallop. After a moment he swung down from the saddle. The stallion was more inclined to maintain an easy walk without Hawk sitting on his back.

"Are you all right?" Samantha asked softly, standing beside the horse and watching Hawk try to hide the pain.

"I'm fine."

"You don't look it."

"I never asked you for your opinion."

"No, you didn't," Samantha replied, too concerned for Hawk's welfare to allow his moodiness and prideful temper to deter her. "You seldom ask for my opinion, though I give it to you often enough."

"I've noticed," Hawk said, turning the stallion around and walking out of the corral of the livery stable.

Samantha, on foot, moved to block the stallion's path. The animal, highly trained and attuned to his master's wants, was skittish.

"Don't be a fool," Samantha hissed, disgusted with Hawk's display of stubbornness. "You can hardly walk. You couldn't ride fast if your life depended on it—and it just might, if I'm any judge of the vindictiveness of some of the folks in this town. What would you do if you got in a fight on your way back to your tribe? Will dying prove just how independent you are?"

For Hawk, this attack from Samantha was unprecedented. Women simply didn't talk to him that way. He turned away from her, needing distance from her sharp tongue, knowing that everything she said was true but not wanting to hear a word of it.

Samantha, not to be put off, maneuvered around so that she was once more blocking his path.

"You can't get away from me that easily!" Samantha reached out with her hands, intent on pushing Hawk so that he couldn't walk out into the street. The instant her hands got close to his ribs Hawk grabbed her by the wrists, his hands flashing out so quickly that she'd hardly seen them move. Samantha's horrified expression reflected just how badly the sheriff had hurt Hawk's ribs.

"You're afraid of me touching your stomach because you

hurt so much. Do you think your enemies would be more gentle with you?"

"You talk too much," Hawk said, pushing Samantha aside.

He stepped into the street, walking with long strides even though the motion caused his ribs to hurt like hell. He was doing everything he could to pretend that there wasn't a thing wrong with him. Up and down the street, people were looking at him, some of them openly gawking, others being more discreet about their curiosity. Even though he wore buckskins and not the traditional leggings and loincloth of a Sioux warrior, and even though anything more than a cursory glance at his gaunt, handsome features established that he had as much Caucasian blood in him as Sioux, the townspeople considered him an outsider, an Indian brave through and through.

*Now the townspeople will never stop talking about me,* Samantha thought as she stood there beside Hawk.

Hawk turned away from Samantha and checked his harness. The livery owner had saddled the stallion for him, and he didn't trust the man's work. He groaned slightly when he had to tighten the rear saddle surcingle.

"Just look at you," Samantha said, very quietly this time, more sympathy than anger in her tone. "You can hardly saddle your own horse, and you think you're healthy enough to ride out of Deadwood as though you hadn't made any enemies while you were here."

Hawk kept his back to Samantha as she spoke. He didn't want to believe that he was incapable of defending himself against his enemies. He'd lived by his strength and cunning for too many years to think that he was anything other than a capable warrior. But even pride and courage couldn't mend ribs bruised and broken by the toes of the sheriff's boots. When Hawk pulled himself up into the saddle again the pain seemed to shoot straight up from his ribs, exploding inside his skull like dynamite.

"The least you can do is take me to my horse," Samantha said, making it sound as though she was giving up the argument, though she had no intention of doing that. "I've got something in my saddlebag for you." She'd left a small fortune in cash in her saddlebag, completely unprotected, and was only now thinking about it.

Hawk looked down at Samantha after squirming in the saddle for a moment, trying to get comfortable. Never before had he been anything less than comfortable in the saddle. He'd always felt himself to be a man virtually born on horseback, but it didn't seem that way now.

"I'll walk," Samantha said, though she very much wanted to get onto the stallion behind Hawk.

She wanted to touch him, to hold him in her arms; not in a sexual way, but to give him comfort. She wanted to soothe his pain and ease his troubled mind. It infuriated her to know that he'd never allow her to do that because it would offend his preposterous notions of manly behavior. Most frustrating of all, Samantha had never before felt such tenderness in her bosom. She wanted to give Hawk comfort, protect and nurture him. Now that she was finally experiencing these feelings—feelings that were so *feminine*—she was denied the chance to express them.

Making their way back down the street, Hawk was fully aware of Samantha's compromised position. Walking beside an Indian brave on horseback simply had to make her look subservient, and yet she was voluntarily doing just that, with many of the townspeople of Deadwood looking on.

Though Hawk didn't want to look into the men's faces, it was in their eyes that he would discover his enemies. Expecting to see one or two men with enough hatred in their hearts to want to kill him, he instead saw half a dozen or more. Word of how he had killed several men in the hotel and then been released from jail obviously had spread quickly through Deadwood.

A grizzled man spit a stream of tobacco juice into the street, wiped his mouth with the back of his hand, and then muttered, "Somebody oughta string that redskin up."

Although Samantha wanted to scream at the man, she kept on walking. Telling the man who'd threatened Hawk what she thought of him would only make a spectacle of her, and the man would likely remain immune to her insults. As much as his words pained her, her words couldn't hurt a man like that.

Before she reached the hitching post where Daisy was waiting patiently for her to return, Samantha lost any respect that might have remained in her heart for Deadwood.

Untying the reins, she climbed into Daisy's saddle; it was easier talking to Hawk when she didn't have to look up so far.

"I've got two thousand dollars in my saddlebag for you," she said. "Don't even think about trying to refuse it because I'm not going to let you."

Three men had stepped into the street, fanning out just enough to obstruct Hawk and Samantha's exit from town. Samantha shook her head slowly in disgust. "They'll be waiting for you sooner or later. You know that."

"Yes, I know that." Hawk also knew that he couldn't take the pain of riding a galloping horse. No amount of willpower would help him to endure a speedy escape and still leave him the strength to fight.

"Come back to the ranch with me," Samantha said. She was actually pleased that the three toughs had decided to be intimidating, validating her concerns. "Give yourself a day or two to recover. Then, when you return to your tribe, you'll be stronger, and you can leave without all of Deadwood knowing about it."

"You know something, Samantha? You're about the smartest woman I've ever met."

Samantha couldn't tell whether he was being mildly sarcastic or purely complimentary. She smiled and replied, "That's what I've been trying to tell you for some time, only you wouldn't listen."

# Seventeen

Hawk's present environment made him uneasy. Surrounded by books, their smell filling his nostrils, he truly regretted not getting the education that he had wanted.

"The knowledge of the whole world is in this room," Hawk said quietly, a brandy snifter in his hand.

On his second brandy he noticed that the pain in his ribs was considerably duller now. The doctor had examined him, and once he'd bandaged the ribs tightly, Hawk had begun to feel better. The doctor had left a packet of powder behind, should sleep prove impossible, but Hawk was leery of using it, having heard stories of permanent imprisonment by white men's medicine.

"Not quite," Sonny replied, relaxing on the long leather sofa. "But we're trying. My sisters and I spend a lot of time here. I like being surrounded by books."

"So do I," Hawk said, "though I confess it makes me feel unlearned."

"Pick out whatever you want and consider it yours," Sonny said. His initial suspicions of Hawk having been put aside, he now felt a certain comradeship with the man.

Hawk ran his fingertip along the spines of some handsome leatherbound volumes. He'd always been thankful that the missionary priest, Father Lafevre, had insisted he learn to read. He selected a translation of Balzac.

"Thank you," he said, "but just for tonight. I'll leave the book here when I go."

"You don't have to. Please, I want you to have it." Sonny felt a bit guilty for the rude treatment he'd shown Hawk earlier, and he was trying to make up for it now by being overly generous.

When Hawk finished his second brandy he excused himself and went to the guest bedroom on the second floor of the ranch house. Samantha had gone to bed an hour earlier, leaving the men alone in the library to talk.

The bed was huge and unimaginably comfortable; the sheets brilliantly white, crisply laundered; the entire room casually and comfortably appointed. But Hawk couldn't envision himself staying here. Not for very long, anyway. He had the strange sense of being a thief, half-expecting someone to rush into the bedroom, exclaiming that there had been a terrible mistake and that this Indian didn't belong here and would have to leave immediately or the sheriff would be summoned.

Hawk stripped out of his clothes and tried on the nightshirt that had been provided for him but decided against wearing it. The nightshirt seemed to bind beneath his arms. Besides, he'd never worn clothes to bed before and saw no reason to start now.

He stretched out on the bed, his head and shoulders propped up by several pillows. After angling the reflecting mirror on the lantern so that it slanted light down across his book Hawk waited a moment for the pain from his ribs to diminish; then he opened the book and began to read. Balzac was the French writer the priest who'd taught Hawk to read had insisted was nothing more than a pornographer. From that time on Hawk, naturally, hadn't been able to get enough of Balzac, though it had been several years since he'd read one of the French writer's bawdy tales.

In her bedroom, Samantha considered the nightgowns she owned. Four of them were displayed on her bed; three more still hung in the closet. Choosing one was difficult since she'd

never before paid much attention to what she wore to bed.
Previously, her considerations centered on winter warmth and
summer coolness. Some nights, when it was terribly hot,
Samantha would sleep in the nude, though she seldom felt
entirely comfortable doing so. Even though no one, not even
her brother or sister, knew she'd slept naked, *she* knew, and
she felt positively wicked doing it.

She was naked now, though, her weight shifting from one
foot to the other as she tried to decide which gown she would
wear. And should she even bother? She highly doubted that
her courage would last long enough to get her to the guest
bedroom where Hawk was probably sleeping right now. Most
likely he didn't want to be disturbed, needing his rest so that
he could recover his strength.

Samantha picked up two of the nightgowns from the bed
and brought them back to hang them in the closet. Winter-
weight gowns of flannel, warm and cozy, they were not right
for this occasion. That left Samantha with two to choose from.

One, cream-colored, had a neckline that was positively scandalous, plunging deeply in a *V,* with lace along the bodice.
High-waisted, the skirt molded to her legs when she walked.
This gown had been a gift from a friend who'd had it made
especially for herself, with the intention of pleasing her new
husband. Unfortunately, the husband had transformed himself
into an entirely different man from almost the first moment
of marriage—the kind of man Samantha's friend no longer
wanted to please, in bed or out of it. This nightgown had been
given together with the warning that it might just be best to
stay away from men altogether, rather than risk making the
same mistake she had.

The other gown was also a gift—from Vanessa. Exactly the
kind of nightgown an older sister would give, it was plain,
simple, and comfortable as can be, and about as wholesome
as anyone could ask for. Samantha brought that one to the
closet also. Wholesome wasn't what she was after tonight.

She picked up her friend's gown, took a deep breath for

courage, and pulled it over her head. She'd never even tried it on before, having been somewhat embarrassed by any clothing blatantly intended to attract a man's eye. The sleeveless garment, made of light silk, shimmied down Samantha's body. After making some adjustments with the bodice—she had looked down at herself, shocked at the fullness of her bosom in the décolletage—she was ready to study her appearance in the full-length mirror in the corner of her bedroom.

The sight took her breath away. Was this what a man wanted a woman to look like?

The cream-colored silk was probably not the right color for her pale complexion. Perhaps a dark green or navy blue would have gone better with her honey-blond hair and her pale skin. But the gown itself—its fine silk defining the curves of her hips and breasts, the décolletage with its edge of fine, delicate lace presenting the inner swells of her bosom—all combined to give her an incredible appearance of femininity. And that, she knew, was what men wanted.

Looking at her reflection in the mirror, Samantha could scarcely picture herself in her usual attire of Levi's and man-cut shirt.

She turned right, then left, to look at her reflection in profile, and as she did so, she realized how fast her heart was beating. When she held out her hands, she saw they were trembling. Not with fear; at least, not entirely. Anticipation and sensual tension also played havoc with her peace of mind.

What if he didn't want her in his room? Hawk was so angry with the people of Deadwood that she wouldn't blame him if he didn't want anything to do with her. And even worse than being rejected by Hawk, what if she were discovered by Sonny? That thought sent a cool shiver racing down Samantha's spine. Peering into the mirror, she looked into her eyes. Was there really a passionate woman lurking there, ready to visit Hawk's bedroom wearing this unbelievable gown?

Yes. Yes, there *was* a passionate woman behind those eyes, and she was feeling the desire to touch once more the man who'd taught her what sensual excitement was all about, what heights of ecstasy were possible with a skilled and considerate lover.

Samantha adjusted the bodice of her nightgown once more, trying to conceal more of her bosom than the material would allow, then walked slowly on bare feet to the bedroom door, opened it, and, hardly breathing, searched the darkened hallway.

Her brother's room was right next to her own. The guest bedroom assigned to Hawk was down the hall and to the left. Taking a half step into the hallway, Samantha saw a thin beam of light beneath Hawk's door. At least he was awake.

She stepped into the hallway, pleased that Sonny's door was closed, and that no light emanated from within. She decided he was either in bed and fast asleep, as she hoped, or he hadn't gone to bed yet. Samantha wasn't dressed to search the quiet house for her brother and wouldn't know what to say should she come upon him. Rooted in place, she knew that if she thought too long on her fears, they would paralyze her.

*Go on, Samantha! If you don't see Hawk now, you'll regret it for the rest of your life!* she thought rather angrily. *Where has all your courage gone?*

She went to the far side of the hallway, as far away from Sonny's bedroom door as possible as she went past it, her bare feet soundless against the carpeted floor. When she reached Hawk's door she heard a sound from inside, and her heart nearly seized up. Waiting a moment, she realized it was just Hawk inside, yawning. Very, very lightly, she rapped her knuckles against the door, not even sure the sound would carry inside.

Samantha heard the mattress moving beneath Hawk.

"Yes?"

Rather than doing the polite thing—waiting for him to open the door for her—she opened the door herself and stepped inside, quickly closing the door behind her. Hawk was sitting up in bed, a white sheet tossed across his lap, his bandaged chest and ribs a reminder of the brutality that had been visited on him.

"I just thought I'd stop in to see if there was anything you needed," Samantha improvised in a whisper. She didn't know where to hold her hands. The urge to cross them over her breasts to hide the revealing décolletage was strong, but that would defeat her intention in wearing the nightgown in the first place. She left her hands at her sides and tried to appear more at ease than she felt. "Can I get you anything?"

Pushing himself a little higher in the bed as he leaned back against the pillows, Hawk stared at Samantha. She looked stunning in the cream-colored silk nightgown. Unimaginably beautiful. What had happened to the tough young woman who wore men's clothes? he wondered with a certain amusement.

He patted the bed, and Samantha crossed the room to sit on the edge of the mattress. Turning slightly away from Hawk, she nervously twirled with her forefinger a long strand of golden blond hair that had fallen free from the loose coiffure she'd fixed for the occasion.

"I have *almost* everything I need to make me comfortable," Hawk said quietly, the timbre of his voice deep. "Everything . . . now that you're here."

Samantha blushed. She was being terribly forward and she knew it. Sonny would never forgive her if he discovered her in Hawk's bed. But she couldn't think about that now, not when every second she had with Hawk was fleeting.

Samantha's pale cheeks glowed a soft pink. She could feel the heat of Hawk's gaze on her, warming her, touching her with invisible caresses.

"I'm sorry for what happened to you in town," Samantha apologized quietly. "You should have stayed here. Then it wouldn't have happened."

Bitter memories, much too recent for Hawk to shove them easily into the dark corners of his mind, came to the fore. His hatred for Deadwood and everything the city represented simmered within him.

"It wasn't your fault," Hawk offered after a moment. "And thank you for getting me out of jail. I'd still be in there now, if not for you. In jail . . . or dangling from a rope outside of town."

Samantha turned to look at Hawk, unintentionally showing herself in profile, the lines and curves of her body highlighted enticingly. "Let's not think about that now. You're here, and you're going to stay here until you get better."

Hawk quickly calculated how much pain his ribs could cause him, and how much noise the guest bed would make if he and Samantha made love on it. Though he was not a man given to denying his own passionate needs, he concluded that the pain would be too great and the noise too loud. Besides, with Sonny not far away, the intelligent thing to do was to postpone any romantic encounter.

"I don't know how long I can stay, but it can't be very long," Hawk said.

Samantha turned toward him and slid over on the mattress. She placed her hand lightly on his thigh, covered with the white cotton sheet. His words reinforced her fear that time, more than ever, was all too fleeting.

"How badly do you hurt?"

Samantha looked into the ebony darkness of Hawk's eyes and saw there that he *wanted* to make love to her but doubted that he could. His expression shocked Samantha with his vulnerability. She'd been the one to see him as invincible, a man who would be victorious under any circumstances and against any adversary. He was a man, ultimately, the same as any other man, and Samantha felt guilty for concerning herself with her own needs when he was in such pain.

"I'm sorry, Hawk," Samantha said suddenly, starting to rise from the bed. How selfish and foolish she had been! Why had she let herself even think about doing anything as silly as sneaking into Hawk's bedroom?

"Don't leave," Hawk replied, quickly reaching out, his large hand wrapping itself securely around her wrist. "I want you here with me."

Samantha instinctively tried to pull out of his grasp. She'd already made one mistake by coming to his bedroom; she didn't intend to make another one by forcing him to do something that would tax his battered body beyond what it could withstand.

"No, Hawk, don't," Samantha whispered, still attempting to free her wrist.

Injured or not, he was still incredibly strong, and she didn't have a chance of getting away until he decided to release her. He pulled her closer, his other arm looping around her waist.

"You didn't come here just to talk," Hawk said.

Samantha flinched. Somehow hearing him say that—even though it was patently true—seemed a little insulting, as though she were no different than the soiled doves who worked in the saloons in Deadwood.

"You're right; I didn't come here to talk," Samantha said, struggling a little as Hawk pulled her even closer to him. "But I also didn't come in here to hurt you."

She tried to pull away, and when she did she inadvertently pushed against his abdomen. He grit his teeth against the pain, and Samantha promised herself that she would rather walk across burning coals than ever hurt him like that again.

"I'm sorry! I'm so sorry!"

Hawk's smile was strained. He released his hold on Samantha, all thought of lovemaking abandoned. It was one more reason to hate Deadwood, and Sheriff Richards, with every drop of blood in his body. Making it impossible for him to make love with Samantha was an offense for which there could be no forgiveness.

"Remember . . . remember the night I asked you to hold me?" Samantha inquired softly. When Hawk nodded she said, "I can't stay the whole night with you, though you know I'd love to. But for just a little while, perhaps I could hold you instead. There wouldn't be anything wrong with that, would there?"

But Hawk, still set in his ways, insisted on holding Samantha. Placing her head lightly on his shoulder, he curled his right arm around her.

"Closer," he urged, aware that Samantha was doing everything she could to keep her weight off him. Though she didn't move any closer, she did toss her leg over his, transmitting the warmth of her body through the silk nightgown and the sheet. "There; that's better."

But Samantha still regretted having hurt Hawk. She wished now that she'd stayed in her own bedroom, where she belonged. How painful it must have been for Hawk to accept that he was incapable of making love. Because of her impetuosity, she'd forced him to do just that.

"Maybe I'd better go," Samantha whispered.

"In a minute," Hawk replied.

He kissed the top of her head, inhaling deeply, filling his senses with her scent. No woman in the world had hair as silky as Samantha's, he decided. Though she wasn't entirely curled up beside him, he could feel the slight pressure of her breasts against his side, and the weight of her leg over his. Idly, he stroked her shoulders and back. And then, much to his surprise, he felt himself responding to Samantha's presence, despite the pain still pulsing through his body.

Samantha's eyes were closed, her cheek against Hawk's shoulder, her hand resting very lightly on his stomach. As nice as this was, it wasn't what she wanted, and she knew that if she stayed in the room with Hawk much longer, it would only fuel the frustration now gripping her.

"I should leave," she whispered again, rolling away from Hawk.

She felt his hand on her back and wanted very much to feel him touching her elsewhere, with the consummate skill she'd learned to appreciate. But she also knew that this wasn't the night for such activities. Hawk was in no condition to satisfy her needs. She kicked her legs over the edge of the bed, then looked over her shoulder at Hawk, about to apologize once more before leaving.

And that's when she saw the condition of the bed sheet and realized pain wasn't the only sensation going through the Sioux warrior. The sheet was tented prominently, and there was a vaguely guilty, slightly impish expression in Hawk's eyes.

"I can't help it," he said softly, though there wasn't an ounce of regret in his tone. "You were so close, and that nightgown is so beautiful on you and . . . well . . . I'm incapable of being near you without . . . rising to the occasion."

For the dozenth time that evening, Samantha saw herself as a very passionate, very wicked woman. Rather than leaving Hawk, she curled her knees beneath her on the bed and leaned down to kiss him lightly on the mouth.

"Hawk, you must stay very quiet," she whispered, looking into his eyes even as her right hand slipped beneath the sheet. Her fingertips trailed over the crisp, curly hair that grew down low; then she gripped the throbbing shaft of his manhood tightly in her fist.

When Hawk groaned Samantha purred with contentment.

# Eighteen

Hawk's groan of pure contentment was one that Samantha had heard before; at least, she'd heard the female equivalent of it, coming from herself whenever Hawk touched her, caressed her with his libertine hands that drew such responses. His eyes were closed now, and Samantha could study his face, his subtly changing expression, as she moved her hand over him.

"Do you like that?" she asked, only half-facetiously.

She was too inexperienced in her sensuality to have confidence ingrained in her personality. A smile tugged at the right corner of Hawk's mouth as he nodded his head, not opening his eyes.

Samantha leaned back. Sitting on her folded legs, she pulled the sheet down, needing to see what she was caressing. Hawk, now leaning back against the headboard, was at ease with his nudity, enjoying Samantha's gaze moving slowly over him. He neither flaunted nor tried to hide himself.

"It must be a sin to commit violence to a body as beautiful as this," Samantha whispered.

The sheet had been moved down to Hawk's calves, where he kicked it off completely so that his bronzed body was displayed for Samantha's benefit. With the exception of the area from just beneath his pectorals to down just above his hips, which was concealed by the tightly wrapped bandage protecting his ribs, Hawk was magnificently naked.

Samantha placed her right hand on Hawk's thigh. Even at rest, the strength in his muscled legs was incredible. She ran her hand slowly up his thigh until she encircled his manhood with her slender fingers once again, whereon Hawk moaned softly in approval. This time she suspected the moan was for her benefit. In so many ways, he seemed to understand exactly when her confidence needed bolstering, and was ready to give it to her.

Samantha moved a little closer to him, still keeping her legs curled beneath her. She bent over to kiss his mouth lightly, quickly. "Lie down," she whispered, her face very close to Hawk's.

He slipped his arm around her, his broad-palmed hand cupping her buttocks. "Only if you lie with me." He smiled.

Samantha shook her head and kissed him again, slowly this time, letting the tip of her tongue touch his lips. When his mouth opened she languorously explored his mouth with her tongue, kissing him deeply.

She felt the simmering sensuality of her awakening body go through her, a sensation heated and tantalizing, making her feel moist and heated inside. Still kneeling, she pressed her knees together tightly, trying to stop the sensation from spreading. But the action merely increased the slowly building sense of emptiness and heightened the smoldering passion that had taken flame within her.

*He's wounded,* Samantha reminded herself. *He can't satisfy you.*

This was a disquieting thought, and she wished the real world, the world of cruel men and deadly guns, would stop intruding on the happiness she sought to share with Hawk.

She experienced so much at that moment, each individual sensation, each perception, with such crystal clarity that she wondered how she could have been unaware of all the separate feelings before. She tasted brandy on his mouth, and, when she kissed his neck, the unmistakable flavor of Hawk himself. She let her teeth nip lightly at his flesh and caught the fresh scent of soap from the bath he'd taken after arriving at the ranch. She was aware of the intense heat of his passion and his pulsing manhood. And most of all, she was aware of the solid arousal that signified his great need for her. The feel of his warm, powerful hand touching her buttocks through the silk nightgown made Samantha writhe as she kissed him on the mouth again, as deeply and passionately as before.

Samantha sat back suddenly, looking carefully into Hawk's face. Again, she'd almost forgotten that he was a wounded man who only minutes earlier she'd promised to leave so he could get the rest he needed to recover. But there was little pain in his dark eyes now.

A sense of relief washed over Samantha. She looked away from Hawk, out the window at the starry sky, her hands now folded in her lap.

*Stop now, before you go too far.*

She wished Hawk hadn't taught her to crave the feelings he could provoke.

"Come here," Hawk whispered. He hooked his arm lightly around the back of Samantha's neck.

She knew what that tone of voice meant, and she would have none of it. Careful to keep her hands on his chest, well above his damaged ribs, she prevented Hawk from pulling her into his intimate embrace.

"Don't!" Her hands, still resisting, felt his smooth flesh beneath her fingertips, the sensation of suppressed strength and power just beneath the skin. "You're a wounded man, and I'm a wicked woman for coming here. Tomorrow, when you're better, we'll sneak off together. I promise."

Hawk shook his head slowly, his ebony hair stark against the white pillows behind his shoulders. His face, always gaunt, appeared stark in the light of the lantern on the bedside table.

"I'm not *that* wounded," he whispered. He took Samantha's right hand from his shoulder, kissed the palm briefly, let the tip of his tongue moisten her fingertips, then brought her hand down to his arousal. Samantha held him gently, and Hawk moaned his approval. "As you can see, I'm not too wounded for you."

Such tempting words for Samantha to hear, particularly in
her state of heightened passion! He *did* seem hale and hearty.

*Don't be selfish! You're only thinking of yourself!* Samantha
thought. Why was leaving Hawk such an impossibility?

"Later, my darling," Samantha whispered, her tone tight and
strained, her needs escalating at an alarming rate. "I promise
you . . . later."

Hawk didn't say anything. Instead, he brought his right hand
to Samantha's bodice and gently cupped her breast through the
cream-colored silk. He brushed his thumb over the rigid tip,
displaying Samantha's nipple even more prominently.

"Don't leave," Hawk said, his words as much a command
as a request.

His touch, sure and skilled, tugged at Samantha's nipple
through the silk, destroying the willpower of the passionate
young woman who only moments before had been determined
to walk out of the room.

Samantha closed her eyes, allowing herself to concentrate
on what she felt and to forget for a few seconds what she
thought. She loved it all! The strength and skill of Hawk's
powerful hand touching her through the sheer silk added a new
and tantalizing aspect to the delicious moment.

Only when she heard Hawk sigh did she realize that she
had reached for him again, her fingers curled around him,
moving slowly, unconsciously, over the length of him. She
opened her eyes and looked first into Hawk's dark eyes and
then down to his waist.

"Didn't you get a nightshirt?" Samantha asked, knowing it
to be a silly question to ask a man whose throbbing erection
filled her hand.

"Yes. I tried to sleep in it, but it was too uncomfortable, so
I took it off. I guess I'm not very civilized."

"No," Samantha replied, her breath coming in tiny, rapid
gasps. "You're not a civilized man at all. In fact, you're the
most uncivilized man I've ever met." She let her eyes caress
Hawk's body, for once making no effort to hide her apprecia-

tion. His phallus was a living, rather dangerous animal filling her hand. "There's nothing about you that's in the least bit civilized," she said appreciatively.

With her free hand, Samantha took Hawk's wrist and pushed his hand from her. She couldn't think clearly when he touched her so provocatively. Hawk wasn't so easily dissuaded from his passionate quest. Not of a mind to lie passively when she was so close, wearing silk of the finest quality, he looked ready to continue.

"Stop it now," Samantha said, as sternly as she could manage. "You've got to preserve your strength." She took her hand from him, as though at last realizing her words had to be followed with appropriate action. "I promise you, tomorrow night we'll go somewhere together, and then I'll be the lover you want me to be."

Hawk looked at the tempting cleavage displayed by the silk nightgown, then into Samantha's eyes. His ribs still hurt, but his blood was racing, and any thought of waiting a minute, much less an entire night, seemed like a cruel torture to Hawk.

"Be patient," Samantha whispered, speaking as much to herself as to Hawk. "Besides, my brother is nearby."

*I'll kiss him, then I'll leave,* Samantha thought. *I've left him before when he's aroused, and he forgave me. He'll forgive me again.*

She leaned down, fully intent on giving Hawk a light kiss on the lips—one that whispered of passion delayed and the promise of later fulfillment. But the instant her mouth touched his, her lips parted to receive his tongue. The passion that Samantha had fought so hard to deny—Hawk's desires, as well as her own—flared up like a volatile substance. She kissed him fiercely, forcing her mouth even tighter against his, mindful of his damaged ribs as she reached once more for that ardent symbol of his passion for her.

"You mustn't make a sound," Samantha whispered when the kiss had finally ended. She wouldn't disappoint Hawk again. But Hawk couldn't remember a time in his life when he'd felt more frustrated. Blessed by nature with an extraordinary physique, strengthened daily by the physical demands he placed on himself and nightly by passionate pursuits, he found it intolerable to be at less than his best.

"My brother . . . he's very close," Samantha warned, her face close to Hawk's.

For the first time Hawk gave serious consideration to asking Samantha to leave his room. Perhaps she had been right from the beginning about waiting until tomorrow, allowing his ribs a day to heal and his strength a day to recover. It would be frustrating to have her leave . . . but what could be worse than having her so near when he couldn't move or even inhale deeply without discomfort? Even the slightest exertion brought teeth-clenching pain.

"Listen, Samantha—" Hawk said, but before he could say more she silenced him with a kiss.

When she finally pulled her face away from his there was a mysterious light in her blue eyes. "I've always hated sentences that start with 'listen.' Whatever comes next is something I don't want to hear."

Hawk placed his hand lightly upon her cheek, and Samantha turned her face to kiss his palm.

Was there another man quite like Hawk in the whole world? she wondered. Could there possibly be another man so strong and yet so gentle?

She moved her knees more securely beneath her, turning to rest on her hip near Hawk's waist. Her long blond hair spilled over her shoulders and onto his naked stomach, gold caressing bronze. Half leaning over him, ever mindful of his bandaged midsection, she looked at his legs, the thighs thick with muscle. A tremor went through her, an instinctive, primal response to the raw force of his beauty.

Slowly, with more determination than ever, she took him in her hand, squeezing and stroking, feeling his body tense as she pleasured this one incredible part of him.

*Is he watching me?* she thought, suddenly self-conscious of

what she was doing. She didn't dare look to see whether there
was passionate happiness shining in his eyes. She shifted her
position, turning so that even if Hawk was looking at her, all
he would see was her back and shoulders.

Slowly, tentatively, Samantha leaned down, lightly kissing
the flaring crown of Hawk's scepter.

*Is this what he wants me to do? Is this what others have
done for him?*

Putting her questions aside, she kissed him with greater ar-
dor. No longer was she concerned whether what she was doing
was right or wrong, or if other women had more experience
in such matters. She was simply determined to please him.

Hawk felt it all: the quick, wet, darting tongue; the soft,
moist lips; the warm breath passing over sensitive flesh. He
placed his hand lightly on Samantha's shoulder, his long,
curled lashes tapping against his cheeks before he finally simply closed his eyes and gave himself over to pleasure.

He caught strands of her silken hair and wound them slowly
around his forefinger. When she kissed him it seemed as
though all his senses were heightened, all his perceptions infinitely sharper than ever before. And then he felt his excitement escalating at an alarming pace. No pain caused by any
demented sheriff's beating could diminish the ecstasy that
Samantha was providing.

"Samantha . . ." Hawk whispered, leaning back against the
pillows piled at the headboard. Could he gently coax Samantha
from her passionate task? She resisted him, and it wasn't until
he grabbed her shoulder and forced her to sit up that she finally
acceded to his unspoken wishes.

Samantha's initial reaction was fear. Had she done something wrong? But all it took was a single look into Hawk's
dark eyes to know that she hadn't been stopped for that reason.
In fact, just the opposite was true. She quickly sensed that the
only thing bothering Hawk was that he wasn't in control.

"Don't you try to stop me, Hawk," she whispered, her glistening lips curled into a confident smile. At that moment, see-

ing Hawk's unwilling and yet total surrender to her charms,
Samantha felt like the most confident, sensual woman in the
world. "No matter what you say, you don't want me to stop."

She rose up onto her knees to kiss Hawk's mouth, then
smiled at him as she casually tucked his long, ebony hair behind his ear. Then, with her confidence soaring, Samantha set
out to please Hawk more thoroughly than he'd ever dreamed
was possible.


"There's enough food here for three people," Hawk observed, looking at the tray that Samantha had brought him.

"You need it to get back your strength," Samantha replied.
A telling glance from her blue eyes informed Hawk of precisely why she wanted him to return to his former physical
perfection.

"I'm feeling fine," Hawk said. To prove his point, he patted
his bandaged midsection to show he was in no pain. The gesture was a bit of a bluff, however, since his ribs did hurt when
he touched them. The sheriff's boots wouldn't be easily forgotten by Hawk's mind or body.

"That's good, but you're still staying in bed until at least
after the noon meal." Samantha unfolded a large white napkin
and spread it out on Hawk's lap. "Even Sonny insisted on that.
Apparently you made quite a favorable impression on him last
night." She gave him a puzzled look. "Truth is, my brother
doesn't really like most people."

Hawk was only half listening to Samantha. Though concerned with Sonny Sanders's opinion of him, Hawk was more
interested in the food under the covered plates on the tray on
his lap. Sitting upright in the bed, he removed the silver covers.
One plate held scrambled eggs, covering the plate in a golden
mound, with crisp strips of thick bacon piled on top. Another
plate held nothing but toast, liberally slathered with fresh but-
ter. A small bowl contained slices of dried apple mixed with

nuts. Finally, there was a large mug of steaming coffee, next to a glass of cow's milk.

When Samantha picked up a spoon Hawk quickly snatched it from her. "I appreciate everything you've done," he said a bit sternly, thankful for the abundance, but uncomfortable with being doted over by a woman. "However, I absolutely refuse to be spoon-fed like a child."

"You never let me have any fun," Samantha pouted, looking pretty as she sat at the foot of the bed, her feet tucked beneath her.

As usual, she was dressed in Levi's and a cotton shirt, appropriate for her early-morning task of supervising the new foals' feedings in the barn, then watching over the cooking of Hawk's breakfast. Now she watched him intently as he devoured the bacon, eggs, and toast with gusto. She plucked the pottery coffee mug from the tray and took a sip.

Hawk felt uneasy at first, eating under Samantha's watchful gaze. It was still strange for him to be in a large, comfortable bed, between clean sheets, and it was especially odd to be in bed when others had been up and about, doing their work for hours. Having worked virtually every day of his life, the habits of industriousness was deeply ingrained in Hawk, and he felt more than guilty that Samantha had been working that morning while he had slept on.

The food was delicious, especially the eggs. Hawk hadn't had chicken eggs in a year or two, so he chewed them slowly, savoring the taste and texture. Wasn't this the decadence Father Lafevre had warned against when Hawk, Aja, and Crow were young? Hawk didn't really care. If this was decadence, he wanted more of it.

"I figured you'd eat and nap a little, and then you might be interested in seeing the Circle S," Samantha said cheerfully, pleased that the breakfast she had prepared was disappearing rapidly.

Hawk glanced up at Samantha, his gaunt cheek bulging slightly as he chewed. There was mischief in his eyes.

"I know what you're thinking," Samantha said quickly, her tone hushed. "But that absolutely *must* wait until later, after the sun has gone down and the ranch hands have settled in the bunkhouse for the night. Last night was dangerous enough." She patted his leg through the blanket as embarrassing, though pleasing, memories of the previous evening's conduct pinkened her pale cheeks. "Just keep those thoughts to yourself until tonight. I'm proud of the Circle S, and I want to show it off. That's not so bad, is it?"

Hawk smiled, thinking that Samantha was remarkably unsullied by her wealth. Last night she had come daringly to his room wearing a revealing silk nightgown. And once there she had been more daring still, satisfying him with newfound skills that left him gasping for breath. When she'd left his room he was already half asleep, a grin on his lips.

Now Samantha was adamant that Hawk finish all the food she'd brought him. He couldn't, but she didn't protest for long, choosing instead to let Hawk rest, even though he wanted to get out of bed.

"Even if you don't sleep the rest will do you good," Samantha said, taking the tray with her as she left the room.

Hawk picked up the Balzac novel, but before he got more than five pages into the book his eyes grew heavy, and he fell asleep once more, this time with the novel open, facedown on his chest.

Suspicious looks from the white ranch hands notwithstanding, Hawk was enormously impressed with the Circle S ranch. He could only imagine the wealth such a ranch could generate. And though some of the men narrowed their eyes when they saw the buckskin-clad half-breed Sioux inspecting the grounds at Samantha's side, others had heard that it was Hawk who had come to Samantha's rescue on her recent adventure. Those men, who didn't care whether Hawk was half- or all-Indian or not-at-all Indian, only that he had been there for Samantha when she needed help, came forward with a smile and a hand extended.

"I'd say you've won over my brother and about half the ranch hands," Samantha said. She and Hawk had paused to look into a corral where undersized calves were kept with their mothers to give them more of a chance to grow. "By this evening you'll have three-quarters of the men." Samantha sighed wearily, letting her shoulders sag for a moment. "Of course, some of the men will never accept you because of your Indian blood. There's nothing you could do to make them like you."

Hawk couldn't take that personally. He'd faced bigotry virtually every day of his life, in one form or another. Long ago he figured he had two choices: either live his life, perpetually furious at the way he was treated because of his mixed-blood heritage and because he was born a bastard; or do all he could not to think too long or hard about the people to whom those things meant so much.

Hawk chose the latter.

"And where did you say your other sister was?" Hawk asked, paying minor interest to the small pen where yearling calves were kept.

Would it ever be possible for the Sioux to raise their food as the white man did? Hawk asked himself, studying the pen. It seemed unlikely, but Hawk realized that something had to change. The Sioux couldn't go on the way they had in the past.

"Vanessa's in Fargo right now," Samantha answered, oblivious to Hawk's distraction.

Some of the ranch hands had been clearly disrespectful of Hawk, but most of them hadn't, and for that she was thankful. And she was enjoying showing off the Circle S, with its various areas of interest. Though she never would have admitted it to Hawk or even to herself, she very much wanted to impress him with the ranch.

"Really?" Hawk asked, honestly curious.

"She's often there in court." Samantha looked around, saw that they were alone, and quickly took Hawk's hand in her own. She smiled up at him. "I'm glad you're here. I'm not pleased with the circumstances, but I'm glad you're here."

"So am I," Hawk replied, but it was only a half-truth.

Actually, he didn't feel comfortable at the Circle S. He couldn't feel at ease as Samantha's lover while her brother was so nearby. Hawk knew that though he had earned some of Sonny's respect, he wouldn't be able to keep it if the elder Sanders ever discovered how passionate Samantha had become because of an Indian.

Outside the building the sound of two men talking interrupted Samantha's reply, and she quickly dropped Hawk's hand. She might flout convention in many ways, but open impropriety was beyond even her standards.

"There's something else I want to show you," Samantha said, her blue eyes bright and alive as she quickly stepped out of the building. Hawk followed her, wishing they were somewhere else, not surrounded by people. "It's our new colts. They're the pride and joy of the Circle S."

In a small barn, immaculately clean and orderly, Samantha showed Hawk the six young colts, each in its own pen.

"They're the future of the Circle S," Samantha said as she reached into a small pail for a carrot. She gave the carrot to a foal, who munched contentedly as she stroked its neck and mane. "This is Mamie," she explained proudly. "Her mother was the fastest, her father the strongest. . . . Mamie will run for a couple of years; then we'll put her together with just the right stallion, and she'll have magnificent babies."

Hawk, a capable judge of horseflesh, needed only a cursory glance at Mamie to see that the animal did, indeed, have all the markings of a horse of distinction. But it wasn't the young horse that kept keeping Hawk's attention: Samantha and the love she had for her horses seemed to vibrate an enthusiasm for life out of her pores, and its energy touched Hawk.

"This is your favorite place in all the Circle S, isn't it?" he asked. He didn't need to ask the question to know the answer.

Samantha nodded, smiling, still petting Mamie. "It shows, I suppose, but I'm proud of this barn."

Overhead was the hayloft, and as romantic notions began filtering through Hawk's mind, he felt a sudden surge of hunger. He needed Samantha. He needed her here, now, in this place that was so special to her. In her own personal *Hocoka*.

"Up here," he said, beginning to climb the ladder leading up to the loft. He was careful of his ribs; though they weren't as tender as they had been the previous evening, they still gave him pain, especially when he moved too quickly.

"That's just the hayloft up there," Samantha said.

Hawk paused halfway up the ladder. He looked at Samantha, a half smile of sensuality tugging at the right corner of his mouth. "I know," he replied, then continued the climb.

Samantha watched him disappear up the ladder. She stood frozen in place, knowing full well what Hawk's smile had meant, and knowing with just as much certainty that she shouldn't follow him up to the hayloft. To do that was pure foolishness. Passionate foolishness, to be sure, but still foolishness. And it was dangerous. She could do irreparable damage to her reputation should the ranch hands ever discover she'd been in the hayloft with Hawk.

But thinking about Hawk's kisses, his sweet, stimulating touch, put a fire in Samantha's blood, and she started for the hayloft ladder.

*I'm weak,* she thought without censure, a smile similar to Hawk's playing with her lips.

# Nineteen

By the time Samantha got up to the loft, Hawk had already spread out a new horse blanket over a mound of hay.

"How fortunate to have new blankets up here," she said quietly, a bit nervously.

"If I didn't know better, I'd wonder if you'd planned it," Hawk teased as he sat down on the blanket and began unlacing his moccasins.

Samantha looked at him, then looked away. Hawk Two Feather was too bold, she decided; much too bold and daring and fearless for her own good. Though part of her wanted to rush over to him, there was another reaction—the one that said her brother would never forgive her if she was caught making love with Hawk in the hayloft in the middle of the afternoon— that kept her from going to him immediately.

She went to the large bay doors on the south side of the loft and opened one of them just an inch. She peered out cautiously. Outside, ranch hands were doing their chores; none of the men seemed to be paying any attention to the foal barn. Were any of the men aware that she was in the barn with Hawk?

"You're wasting our precious time," Hawk said softly, his voice deep, melodic, rich with expectation that touched Samantha like a caress.

Samantha's back was to Hawk when he spoke. She paused for a moment, wondering if this was really what she wanted to do. There was no future with Hawk; she knew that and accepted it. Soon—in a day or two, or, if she were lucky, three—Hawk would leave her to return to his tribe, where he belonged.

Why had nature conspired so against her? Samantha thought it tragic that the most she could hope for was another three days of stolen bliss with Hawk.

*If I only have three days, then I'm going to make the most of every minute,* she decided with angry determination.

Samantha turned slowly to look at Hawk. He had removed his moccasins and his buckskin shirt. He was stretched out, wearing only his leather trousers, bare-footed and bare-chested, the bandage still wrapped tightly around his midsection. With his fingers he combed back his long, ebony hair off his forehead. He was effortlessly casual, confident, sensual.

Twenty feet separated them, and Samantha took her time walking to him through the carpet of hay, wanting to remember him always as he was at that moment.

"It's really not fair of you to be so sure of yourself," Samantha teased, approaching the blanket.

Hawk was on his side, propped up on his elbow. He was gorgeous and he knew it, she decided. He understood all too well what happened to a woman's resolve when she looked at him. Samantha couldn't resent that in Hawk, even if she wanted to.

"You should be more confident," Hawk replied ironically, his gaze hot, his tone cool. Samantha had started to kneel on the edge of the blanket, but Hawk stopped her with a hand. "Not yet," he said in a whisper. "There's something I want you to do for me."

Samantha's brows furrowed in confusion. Only moments earlier he had been complaining that she was dallying when time was precious, and now he was suggesting just the opposite. She looked down at him, saying nothing, her eyes asking the questions her lips were afraid to speak.

"Take off your clothes for me." Hawk looked straight into Samantha's eyes as he spoke, daring her to look away, to defy him. "I want to look at you . . . all of you. It's risky, I know, with your hired men all about . . . but that's part of the excitement, isn't it? Everything off! I don't want you holding back."

Several thoughts came to Samantha, but she bit her tongue to keep from speaking. This wasn't the first time she had felt the heat of Hawk's seduction, and she knew that passion could explode without any clothes being removed. How well he had taught her that!

"Your boots first, I think," Hawk said quietly, a glittering quality in his dark eyes.

Samantha noticed that Hawk wasn't nearly as nonchalant as he was trying to appear. His mouth looked strained, but his eyes glittered—a pleasing reaction to her beauty.

"I don't know if I should follow your commands," she said softly, standing with her feet spread, her hands on her hips. "I've never been very good at taking orders."

"Not even from me?" He raised an eyebrow.

*"Especially* not from you."

"How do I rate special consideration?"

"Because you've had too many women following your orders already, that's why," Samantha answered, and the edge in her tone said that she knew this to be true. How she wished it didn't bother her!

"They don't matter. You're the only woman who counts."

Samantha would have resisted Hawk . . . but she was certain that, if she went along with him once again, allowing him to once again write all the rules of their passionate games, she wouldn't be sorry.

Samantha balanced on one foot, tugging off first one boot and then the other. Next, she removed her thick white cotton socks. Beneath her feet, the wooden floor was strewn with prickly hay, and she wished that she could stand on the blanket on which Hawk lay. But that proximity would spoil her presentation . . . and Samantha was determined to make her disrobing a performance that would leave Hawk gasping for breath.

She waited a moment for Hawk's next instruction. When it didn't come she unbuckled her belt, then slowly unfastened the brass buttons of her Levi's. Despite Hawk's calm demeanor Samantha saw a telltale glint in his midnight black eyes.

She hooked her thumbs into the waistband of her Levi's, pulling them down past the curve of her hips and wiggling her hips slightly to assist in the descent. She was well aware of Hawk's greedy gaze devouring her every move. She bent forward to remove her Levi's, and when she did, she took her time, allowing Hawk to look down the front of her shirt.

*He's seen me from head to toe,* Samantha thought as she straightened again. *But this time is different somehow, like we've never touched.*

Samantha paused for a moment, putting her hands back on her hips, covered by her new pantalets and topped with a new matching chemise. All for Hawk. She had planned on stealing away with Hawk after supper, perhaps to the guest house north of the snow fence. But Hawk, as usual, had plans of his own . . . and now she'd decided to follow them.

"Continue," Hawk ordered after several seconds.

The tightness in his voice was unmistakable. He cleared his throat, still pretending casual nonchalance. How his anxiousness pleased Samantha, enormously fueling her confidence and courage.

Slowly, teasingly, Samantha unbuttoned her shirt; then, with a shrug, she let it slide down her arms. Standing only in her chemise and pantalets, she waited for Hawk's next command. Her eyes enjoyed the naked expanse of his chest, exposed above the bandage, and letting her gaze trail lower, the long and bulging line of his erection, still trapped inside his buckskin trousers.

"More? Or do you want to remove the rest yourself?" Samantha challenged, her fingertips toying with the silk shoulder strap of her chemise.

Hawk experienced the pleasure of the subtle shift in the atmosphere between them. At first he had been in control, setting the tone and tempo of the encounter. Now Samantha held the power in her hands. Was she completely aware of it? Did she understand her own personal power? Unable to concentrate for long on the subject because of Samantha's close proximity in only her soft white pantalets and chemise, Hawk's own need for physical connection with her was escalating at an alarming rate.

"Continue, if you please," Hawk said.

Samantha grinned. "I please." She pulled the chemise quickly over her head and dropped it onto the pile of clothes discarded in the hay.

Standing there with her breasts bare, Samantha was distinctly aware of feeling on display. She battled momentarily against the negative feelings, telling herself not to feel embarrassed about her body, but this attitude was easier thought than wholeheartedly embraced. Without waiting for instruction, Samantha pulled free the knotted drawstring of her pantalets and shimmied them down her legs, stepping out of them to at last stand completely naked before her lover.

"Come to me, Samantha," Hawk whispered tensely. "Come to me now."

Samantha walked forward until she stood at the edge of the blanket near Hawk's feet. He reached for her, his long fingers curling around her ankle to pull her down. Though at first Samantha began to sink to the blanket and the welcoming embrace of his arms, she suddenly resisted Hawk.

"No," she said firmly.

Hawk still held on to Samantha's ankle, looking almost straight up at her. Her hands, folded one over the other at the juncture of her thighs, covered herself in the last vestiges of modesty. But then she removed them, placing them defiantly on her hips. This was too much for Hawk; he tried to touch her intimately but she slapped his hand away.

"No," she said again, even more firmly than before.

"Why not?" Hawk frowned, reaching for Samantha once

more. He wasn't accustomed to having women deny him much of anything, most certainly not at a time like this.

"Because it isn't what I want . . . *yet.*"

Samantha positioned herself on the blanket, looking down to see Hawk stretched from head to toe. Even from there she felt the heat of his passion, sensed the excitement sizzling through his veins. Suddenly all embarrassment she'd felt vanished. She felt wet, heated, needful, but she was determined to suppress these cravings for at least a few more moments.

"This isn't fair," Samantha said in a stern, commanding voice that pleased her because of its authoritative quality. "You see all that I am, but you're covered where you are . . . most interesting." Not wanting to conjure up unpleasant memories, Samantha conveniently neglected to mention the long, heavy bandage wrapped around Hawk's ribs.

"Then take them off for me," Hawk suggested, reaching up for Samantha's hand, intending to pull her down to his side.

Samantha shook her head slowly. Her long blond hair cascaded down her body, partially obscuring her breasts. Teasingly, she pushed the golden strands aside to expose her left breast, its areola pink with passion, surrounding a nipple that was hard and tight with excitement.

He reached for Samantha, and again she nimbly slipped out of his reach, which meant stepping off the blanket and onto the hay-strewn floor.

"You do it for me," Samantha said, easing forward so she was once more on the blanket, near Hawk's feet. "But not all the way off. I want them just low enough for me to . . . see how interested you are in me."

For several seconds Hawk assessed Samantha. Could it be this was all a dream? Was she really talking to him this way, teasing him and firing his passion with a skill that suggested Samantha Sanders was more experienced in sensuality than Hawk knew she really was? He pulled loose the long leather thong closing the front of his buckskins, then pushed them down to his thighs, just far enough to allow his erection to spring free. Samantha's gasp suggested that her passion was burning as hotly as his own.

Samantha moved deftly to straddle Hawk's body, her feet stationed on either side of his hips. Their gazes locked, each wanting, by this time, for the other to put the teasing aside so the real loving could begin.

"My . . ." Samantha said in a breathy whisper, looking at his bounty. "My, my, my!" And then, after a moment, with absolute possessiveness, she whispered, "Mine!"

Slowly, drawing out the first touch as long as possible, Samantha bent her knees until, at long last, their bodies touched. Already heated and passionately ready for Hawk, she dropped onto him, impaling herself. The consummation, unexpected in its haste and force, ripped through her in a torrent of emotion that left her shuddering and shaken.

Samantha was breathing deeply, blinking her eyes to clear her vision. The climax had hit her harder and faster than she had expected. She was lying on Hawk, her knees curled up near but not touching his injured ribs, her breasts pressed against his chest, her cheek touching his as she gulped in air.

Hawk pushed his fingers through her hair, smoothing the golden strands away from her face. Then she pulled away from him, far enough to look into his eyes, seeking confirmation there that what she'd done wasn't wrong.

"Remember me?" he asked, smiling, delaying his own passion while Samantha recovered.

Experience in such matters had taught him that she might need a few moments to fully understand what she had just experienced.

Samantha cradled his face in her hands as her breathing slowly returned to normal. She could feel him inside her, solid as stone. His control, she thought, was Herculean.

"Remember you?" she asked, still breathing somewhat deeply. "Not in ten thousand years could I ever forget you!"

After the words were out of her mouth, Samantha realized

there might be a second meaning to Hawk's inquiry. Did he feel forgotten, left out somehow?"

"My darling Hawk," Samantha said, putting her hands on his shoulders, high enough so that she was in no danger of damaging his painful ribs, "you've been occupying a majority of my thoughts from the first moment I saw you."

Samantha got her knees solidly beneath her, keeping them away from Hawk's ribs, and began to raise and lower her hips. She smiled down at Hawk, her eyes glittering like priceless blue diamonds.

"Trust me, my darling; I'm always thinking of you," she whispered, dropping down on him and giving her hips a forward-and-back shake to add emphasis to her words. "And now I'm going to do everything I can think of to show you exactly *what* I think of you."

And that was precisely what Samantha did.


A hot bath was a luxury not afforded to any Sioux. Hawk was settled into the deep tub, having twice washed himself from head to toe with soap that quickly developed a thick lather. Now he was contemplating just exactly how guilty he would feel if he lathered himself up once more, for good measure. There was no telling when he would have this luxury again: a large tub, plenty of hot water, and expensive soap.

The tub, in particular, struck him as almost absurdly extravagant. Who had commissioned the blacksmith to make it? Samantha? Or more likely Vanessa? The sides were twice as high as any tub Hawk had ever seen, and the back sloped gently to enable even a large man like himself to recline comfortably in the warm water.

He really did wonder if it was something Samantha would insist on having. She had seemed to enjoy herself while she was with the Sioux, but she was a wealthy woman who, he suspected, would sooner or later begin to miss all the comforts of her life here at the Circle S. How could she manage very long with Hawk's tribe without feeling terribly deprived?

A bitter smile crossed his lips. How had a warrior such as himself, the child of a wealthy white woman he despised, become involved with a wealthy white woman? Was he, like his mother before him, his own worst enemy?

Hawk took the enormous sponge that had been provided for him, filled it with water, and then squeezed it over his head so the soapy water cascaded down. Hot baths with wonderful soap were dangerously addictive, Hawk decided.

He heard the door to his bedroom open and was mildly surprised that Cookie, the cook and all-around helper at the Circle S, who had supervised the filling of the bath and brought the soap and towels to Hawk, hadn't knocked before entering. Hawk's initial thought was that if he had been a white guest instead of a half-breed Sioux brave, Cookie wouldn't have entered until being asked, but he quickly pushed these angry thoughts away. They would do him no good anyway, and nothing he thought would change the way Cookie felt.

"How is it?"

At the sound of Samantha's voice, Hawk grinned and shook his head slowly, wiping water out of his eyes. His long ebony hair was plastered to his skull.

"You're not supposed to be in here," Hawk said softly, mindful of the fact that the bedroom door had been opened but never closed. "And your brother would want blood revenge if he caught you here."

Samantha grinned as she slowly strolled across the room, a slightly exaggerated sway to her hips. She was mildly disappointed that she couldn't see through the soapy water and the thick white blanket of bubbles that floated on the surface. All that was visible of Hawk was his head, shoulders, and knees. She sat on the edge of the steel tub, making no effort to hide the appreciation she felt as she looked at Hawk.

"Samantha, I don't know if this is such a good idea," Hawk

said. He knew full well what the light in Samantha's blue eyes signified.

Samantha just grinned. "For an intelligent man, you make some really silly mistakes. You see, I think this is an absolutely magnificent idea." She swirled the water around with her hand, working the lather up, careful not to touch Hawk's leg. Delayed gratification, she was discovering, had a way of heightening the reward a hundredfold.

"But Samantha . . ."

Hawk was passionate, yes; suicidal, no. He wanted Samantha, but he didn't want to die because only that afternoon she'd discovered she could experience ecstasy repeatedly. No matter how skilled a warrior Hawk knew himself to be, he couldn't fight his way out of a ranch where he was outnumbered more than thirty to one.

"By now," Samantha said, speaking slowly, the tips of her fingers trailing in the warm, soapy water near Hawk's thigh, "my protective brother Sonny is nearly to Deadwood, where he's going to meet a woman. I don't know who she is, though I could make several guesses. Either way, I don't really care, so long as she keeps my brother happy. But you see, my brother is gone, and so is Vanessa."

"What about that bearded fellow?"

"Cookie?" Samantha smiled wickedly. "Cookie was just given, not ten minutes ago, a twenty-dollar gold piece and the night off. Cookie is headed for the bunkhouse, where there is always a card game going among the men. Cookie is going to stay there until he recovers from his excesses of gambling and drinking."

"Twenty dollars of gambling is excessive?"

"Cookie's a conservative card player but an unrestrained drinker. We pay him once a month, and he's broke three days after he's paid, but he has a good time in those three days, and the rest of the time he's fine."

"You think of everything, don't you?"

"Not true," Samantha said as she began to disrobe. "I've

learned to count on your imagination. It's one of the things I love about you."

The instant the word *love* was out of her mouth, Samantha wished she'd chosen her words more carefully. It wasn't that she *didn't* love Hawk's imagination—she did, with all her heart and soul. It was just that she didn't want to use the word, with all the emotions that went with it.

She was quickly naked, her clothes strewn carelessly around the room. "I've always thought this tub was large enough for two," she said, getting into the water. "I never dreamed I'd find out."

Hawk smiled and replied, "I like to be of service."

# Twenty

A smile spread across Samantha's lips as she sat in the rocking chair, watching Hawk nibbling at slices of cheese. He had, she now realized, a voracious appetite. Or at least he had the ability for voraciousness when the opportunity and abundance were there for him. She'd also seen him go for a long time without eating and not complain about it.

"In some ways you're like a wild animal," Samantha observed in the darkened guest bedroom. When Hawk looked up at her she laughed softly, realizing how her words could be misconstrued. "I don't mean that as an insult. It's just that you're like the mountain lion who can eat a great deal when there's plenty of food, then fast if there's nothing to be had. I suspect you're that way when it comes to making love, too. I wonder why that is?"

As though to remind herself of her excesses of late, she felt a twinge of discomfort between her legs. She was a little sore, but not in the least bit unhappy about her own voraciousness of late.

Resting on his side, a sheet tossed across his waist as he picked at the plate of cheese and sliced sausage, Hawk gave Samantha's question serious consideration before answering.

"It's because I come from a world where nothing is guaranteed; nothing is certain. In your world, you know that there will be plenty to eat for breakfast and when you're done with breakfast you know you'll be eating another meal in just a few hours. And another one just after the sun goes down, and maybe even a little something more if you decide to get up in the middle of the night. This allows you to eat only as much as you want, whenever you want. The Sioux developed the ability for 'voraciousness,' as you put it, because we've had to. Our next meal is often in doubt."

Though Hawk had spoken the words without any rancor, Samantha wondered if he was hiding his bitterness. Did he blame white people for the difficult life of his people? Did he blame *her?* She could hardly imagine a life of such uncertainty; even thinking about it filled her with dread.

"You don't have to go back, you know." Samantha spoke the words impulsively, without considering the full extent of their meaning. She was speaking from the heart, as she so often did, not knowing where her emotions would take her.

"Yes, I do," Hawk replied wearily, dismissing Samantha's comment with a simple shrug of his naked shoulders. He continued nibbling on cheese. "The tribe counts on me. I have to hunt to provide food."

"No you don't. I mean, the tribe could survive just fine without you, especially if you gave them the reward I'm giving you." Samantha smiled a bit sheepishly, aware that she was asking quite a lot of Hawk but feeling bold because they had shared so much in the time they'd spent together. "Money will buy anything the tribe needs."

Hawk cocked his head slightly at Samantha. This unconscious gesture surfaced whenever he was uncertain of what was happening. Samantha, having single-handedly confused Hawk enough times to be acquainted with the look, pushed on happily—though a bit nervously—with her proposition.

"I'm serious, Hawk. There's no reason for you to live in such desperation when there's more than enough at the Circle S. You know how many rooms we have here. More than enough! Would that be so bad?"

Samantha couldn't have known that she spoke the same words Hawk's mother had. She couldn't know that her proposal was everything Hawk found repellent in the world of the wealthy whites. Buy whatever and whomever you want, the message went, and if that means abdicating responsibility to one's family and friends, so be it! Toss around enough gold to assuage the guilt feelings produced by whatever action was expedient, then forget everyone else and simply have a good time.

"Yes, Samantha, it *would* be that bad," Hawk explained quietly, doing his best to control his temper. He told himself that Samantha was very young, and that she was prone to say things she'd not entirely thought through. "I'm not like you. I can't simply buy my way out of whatever trouble I get myself into. My responsibilities can't just be cast aside the moment they're inconvenient. It doesn't work that way with the Sioux."

He watched Samantha reacting to his words. He had hurt her and he knew it, but he couldn't leave his people, no matter how easy a life Samantha promised him. He gave her a smile, hoping it would soften the impact of his words.

"There might be another way," he said.

"Another way?" Her tone held a skeptical hopefulness.

Even though Hawk had believed earlier that Samantha wouldn't give up her wealthy life, he tried anyway. "You could come to the tribe." He touched his bandaged ribs and grinned. "Since it's clear that I can't live with your people without paying a terrible price for the effort, maybe you could come to the Sioux. You've got to admit that you were treated much better by my people than I was by yours."

"I . . . I just couldn't," Samantha replied. She ran her fingers through her disheveled blond hair, still tassled from the energetic lovemaking she'd just experienced. She wished now that she'd never gotten into this conversation with Hawk. "I've got too much to do here. My sister and brother count too much on my managing the horses for me to just leave the Circle S. Besides, this is my home, my inheritance. . . . There's a lot of money tied up in this ranch. It's been in the family for generations."

Hawk, a practical man by both nature and necessity, sighed.

As was so often the case, he'd known the answer before asking the question. He said, "Then there is a third option. One that, under the circumstances, might be the only one we can agree upon."

Samantha wasn't certain she liked Hawk's tone of voice. She asked softly, "And what might that option be?"

"Since you can't leave your home and your people, and I can't leave my home and my people . . . and since it is obvious that we are *so* good together . . . why not come to me? I'm not saying all the time. I know you have a life here that you can't leave behind. But once in a while . . . just for a few days, if that's all you can spare from the ranch . . ."

Samantha balled her hand into a fist and pressed it against her stomach. She could hardly breathe. He wanted her to come to his tepee and be his whore whenever she could no longer do without his kisses and his sweet lovemaking. Though it sounded possible at first consideration . . . the underlying message was that Hawk thought of Samantha as a whore. Perhaps a valued and desired whore, but a whore nevertheless. A part-time lover to be shown kindness, consideration, and endless passion . . . but only so long as it was convenient and didn't interfere with other, more important obligations to his tribe and himself.

"I can't . . ." Emotion choked off Samantha's words momentarily. "I can't believe you'd actually ask that of me, Hawk. It makes what we have together sound so tawdry. It makes me sound so cheap."

"I didn't mean for it to," Hawk protested, seeing Samantha's disdain for what he'd said but refusing to back down from his position. A compromise was necessary if they were ever to see each other, and though he was willing to compromise, he would not subjugate his will entirely just to satisfy Samantha's whims, no matter how attractive she was, no matter how exciting to make love with, no matter how clever and entertaining her conversations could be. "I'm not trying to be insulting.

I'm just looking at what choices are available to us . . . and they seem limited."

Samantha had feared she might have been asking a great deal from Hawk, but his response, she felt, was entirely unwarranted. More than that, it was vicious in its own way . . . and she couldn't tolerate viciousness from Hawk when her body was still warm and tingling with the afterglow of the lovemaking they had shared.

"What are you saying?" she asked softly. Then, "What *exactly* are you saying? Because if it's what I think it is . . . then . . . then I don't think you know me at all. Not even a little bit, Hawk."

Hawk's face remained expressionless as he looked at Samantha. "I'm saying that I cannot just leave my people. I do not give my loyalty lightly, and once given, I do not abandon it. Not under any circumstances, or for any reason. I don't expect you to understand that. I'm just trying to explain to you the type of man I am."

Samantha felt the warm flush moving up from her chest to color her neck and cheeks. Each time Hawk spoke, even if he was only trying to be conciliatory, he heightened Samantha's sense of indignation.

"I know what kind of man you are," Samantha said softly, leaning toward him, her body suddenly becoming tense. "At least I *thought* I knew the kind of man you are." She spoke the words in such a way that they couldn't help but convey a sense of distrust, an aura of profound disappointment. "But now that I listen to what you've offered me, I'm not so sure anymore. Exactly what is it you think of me?"

Samantha watched the invisible walls coming up to surround Hawk. She saw them as clearly as if they were made out of brick and mortar. How she hated them with everything that she held dear, knowing that from that point forward she would not get another substantive response out of him.

"Damn you," she whispered, rocking agitatedly in the chair,

furious that Hawk could sit so calmly. "Don't you try to pretend that you're not angry!"

But a change finally came over him, the spontaneous dropping of the veil of implacable logic. "You think your money
can buy you everything," Hawk accused softly. "Perhaps it can
buy studs for your mares, but . . ."

He said no more, leaving the sentence unfinished. But by
not finishing the sentence, he allowed Samantha to finish it
herself . . . and she didn't do herself any favors.

"Damn you straight to hell, Hawk Two Feather," she whispered. "You're not my stud for hire! Damn you!" In an instant
the faces of too many men who had looked at her with lust in
their eyes flashed through her mind. And because Samantha
had been insulted and wasn't above seeking revenge, she spat,
"I buy all the studs for the Circle S, Hawk. If you knew me as
well as you think you do, you'd know that I'm a *careful* buyer.
If I'd put more thought in it, do you really think I'd chosen
you?"

They were vicious words and Samantha knew it, though
they were no worse than those Hawk had spoken, and she was
still angry enough to lash at, to want to inflict pain on the
person who had *caused* her pain. She waited to see Hawk's
pain. After what she'd just said, he'd most certainly feel pain.
But he didn't react by being outwardly furious with her—as
she'd expected. He simply looked at her as though she'd said
nothing at all. And that aloofness, that calm detachment from
the reality of the moment, made Samantha hate him in some
ways.

"Damn you, Hawk!" She shook her head slowly, not entirely
sure of the appropriate response for the feelings going through
her. She was now uncomfortably naked, when only moments
earlier she'd luxuriated in her nudity in Hawk's presence. "You
think you're strong when you act this way, when you square
your shoulders and pretend that nothing I or anyone else can
say or do can hurt you. But all you're proving is that you are
as vulnerable as the rest of us."

Hawk didn't speak for a moment. "I am at least as vulnerable as other Sioux. When the sheriff's boots struck me I felt pain. I simply saw no value in complaining about it during the time I shared with you." He, too, shook his head, as mystified by Samantha and her behavior as she was by him and his. "You turn strength into weakness, virtue into vice. Is it any wonder your people—the wealthiest among you—never have enough, while the poorest of your kind have nothing to eat?"

Samantha felt her face growing hot. "Are you saying that I treat the hired hands badly?"

Hawk looked around the guest bedroom. "Do they live like this?"

"You go straight to hell!"

Samantha bolted to her feet and, in the darkness and confusion, tried to find her clothes. Tears of rage burned her eyes, but she wouldn't give Hawk the satisfaction of seeing her cry. Undoubtedly he was mean enough to *want* to see her cry, she thought.

How could a man who only minutes earlier had been making love to her suddenly turn so vicious? Even if she had suggested something he couldn't agree with, why had he made her feel as though she'd purchased his passion? Should she assume that everything he'd said and done to her was simply a response to money well spent?

Hawk was angry enough to kill. But whom could he kill? He'd left the Circle S ranch at sun-up and he hadn't seen a soul since. It was now nearing noon, and if he kept up this pace, he figured he'd reach his tribe by early the following morning.

*Damn Samantha.*

Hawk had tried to keep the thought of her from entering his head, but his anger was greater than his self-discipline. She had said things to him that were unforgivable. And after she'd

said everything that had come into her head, she'd left without
giving him even the chance for rebuttal.

In the morning, as he was getting ready to leave, he'd expected a teary apology, and perhaps a sentimental and romantic
goodbye. He'd received neither. In fact, when Samantha finally
showed up, she seemed distracted, as though the time she was
spending with him would be better spent dealing with matters
concerning the ranch.

*She was just doing that to get even with me.* Hawk enjoyed
this thought because it absolved him of any responsibility for
the rancor that now existed between himself and Samantha.
*Stop thinking about her. She's in your past.*

Once he was able to clear his mind, he sensed that something was wrong. Dangerously wrong.

Hawk twisted in the saddle to look through the trees to the
east and west on the sloping hill he was descending. He
couldn't see anyone . . . but he felt a presence, someone out
there somewhere.

His stallion, now sensing his unease, pranced a sidestep.
Hawk patted the animal's neck soothingly, turning the horse
for a better view of the territory he'd just crossed.

Allowing himself a minute to search for his followers, he
finally turned the stallion and continued on his way. Though
he appeared at ease, he mentally cursed himself for allowing
his thoughts to dwell on Samantha. Daydreaming was a luxury
only old men who had long ago given up their warrior ways
could afford, Hawk believed.

An hour passed, and though Hawk pushed his stallion into
a fast walk, he continued to pretend that he wasn't at all anxious, that he had no suspicions there was a man—or men—
trailing him.

He ran through a list of the enemies he'd made in the recent
past, and then throughout his life. The first list was fairly short,
the latter much longer. He could think of many people who
would like to hear of his demise. All in all, there were many

men, red and white, who would gladly pull the trigger or let fly arrows to see him die.

But who was it *this* time?

He very casually eased the thong from the hammer of his revolver. The thong, attached to his holster, prevented the weapon from bouncing out of the holster during a hard gallop, but it also prevented him from drawing the revolver quickly in a time of crisis.

"Our lazy days are over, boy," Hawk said quietly to his stallion, patting the animal's neck fondly.

He felt the transformation—his being becoming once again the warrior, the fighter. The days and nights with Samantha at the Circle S—eating well, relaxing often, loving regularly— were all behind him now. An attack could happen at any time.

A tight half smile pulled up the right corner of Hawk's mouth. He'd been docile long enough. His instincts, the whispered voice of warning that had sounded, had saved him once again. His time at the Circle S hadn't made him soft after all, it seemed.

Deputy Foster Samuelson could smell death, and he believed that the big Indian who'd been railroaded out of town was behind it. He didn't have so much as a shred of evidence to link Hawk Two Feather to the missing men, but Deputy Samuelson was certain he was involved.

Four horses had meandered into Deadwood, their saddles intact, their weapons still in the scabbards. They straggled into town at different times, searching for food and water; domesticated animals uncertain of their fate now that they were without riders.

Where were the riders?

So wondered the citizens of Deadwood. Many thought that bandits of one stripe or another had done the men in. Deputy Samuelson was skeptical of this. Bandits tended to steal everything possible, and yet four usable saddles, two Winchester rifles, and two shotguns had been left with the horses.

Nothing pointed to the Sioux warrior Hawk Two Feather until the deputy learned that one of the missing men was Sheriff Darren Richards's brother.

The sheriff, on learning that his brother's horse had walked into town, immediately began arranging a posse to "Kill that bastard!" When the deputy asked him who "that bastard" was, the sheriff tried unsuccessfully to pretend he didn't know. Though Deputy Samuelson never got a name from the sheriff, he suspected that the four men had ridden out intending to waylay Hawk on his way home from the Circle S ranch.

Sheriff Richards, his brother, and all their friends, were essentially a rotten crowd, the deputy believed. Poorly educated, hard-drinking, unnecessarily violent, these men thought nothing of hurting others, yet felt themselves to be unjustly put upon whenever they were shown anything less than full courtesy from everyone crossing their path.

More deaths in Deadwood. Even worse, unanswered-for deaths. Though the deputy had no facts or clues to indicate the men from Deadwood had been left dead, he believed they had. He also believed that Sheriff Richards knew who had caused the deaths and intended to get his revenge.

The deputy felt a dull, empty ache in the pit of his stomach. From the first moment Hawk Two Feather had ridden into town trouble had followed him. And now, even though he was long gone, the cloud of conflict still surrounded his invisible presence.

Sighing heavily, and not liking the violence undoubtedly heading his way, Deputy Foster Samuelson walked slowly back to his office. This would be a good time to clean and oil his double-barrel shotgun. He'd been deputy long enough to know that very soon he'd need all his weapons to be in working order.

\* \* \*

Hawk sensed a change in the mood of the camp even before he had reached it. Were the children looking strangely at him? He couldn't say.

Twisting just a little in the saddle, he tested his ribs. They still bothered him, but the serious pain, the kind that had made him clench his teeth when he moved, was gone now. He was thankful for that. He sensed a fight ahead and wanted to be at his best. Though the battered ribs could prevent him from being the warrior he was capable of being, he was confident there were few men, if any, who could challenge him and survive.

He'd gotten off his horse near his tepee and was tending to his stallion when a young boy approached with the message that Dull Knife wished to see him. It wasn't an unusual request. Any brave who was away from the tribe for more than a day or two would be expected to speak with the elderly Sioux chieftain. The difference this time was that it had been more than a request. Never before had Hawk been *summoned* to the tribal elders, and he didn't care for it now.

He took the leather saddlebag filled with two thousand dollars in paper currency. Hawk preferred gold coin, but since he had received the money as a gift, and not a payment, he hadn't felt he could complain.

Dull Knife was seated in the large tepee, his face devoid of expression. As he looked at Hawk, his eyes were unreadable. Behind the elderly Sioux leader sat two lesser chiefs, silent and unmoving. Hawk felt instantly on the defensive and knew in his heart that, during his absence, the men had been discussing him and his way of life.

"Sit." Dull Knife nodded toward a folded blanket on the ground.

Hawk noticed that there were no bowl of berries or other Sioux treats to welcome him home from his journey. He folded his legs beneath him, wishing that he'd taken the time to change out of the buckskin trousers, which were so much like the white man's clothes, and into his loincloth and leggings.

He was enough of an outsider without dressing differently as well.

"Your journey went well?" Dull Knife asked.

Hawk nodded, not liking the old man's cryptic comment, suspecting there was something more behind it. Though he reminded himself that Dull Knife was a good and decent man, an honorable man and one whose judgment the tribe counted on, Hawk's sense of unease did not abate.

"Yes," Hawk answered. "But it is good to be here. It is always good to be back with my people."

"The yellow-haired girl was returned to her family safely?"

"Yes."

For several seconds Dull Knife simply looked at Hawk. He made no move, nor did he make any expression suggesting doubt about Hawk's answer . . . yet in his eyes *something* undefinable whispered to Hawk that Dull Knife didn't believe what he had heard.

What else might the elderly chieftain not believe? Hawk didn't want to think of that now, though it was all but impossible to keep his mind from drifting in such directions. He felt as though he was fighting an enemy now, one just as dangerous as the sheriff in Deadwood, or the men who'd so foolishly set the ambush for him as he'd ridden away from the Circle S ranch.

*No,* Hawk thought next, *the enemy here is much more dangerous. The enemy here pretends to be something other than an enemy.*

"Then you are back with us now?" This time there was no mistaking Dull Knife's implication that Hawk had been away from his people too long and some of them weren't at all pleased with his absence.

"Yes, Dull Knife, I am back." Hawk looked the old man directly in the eye. "And I have brought back with me a bounty. The family of the yellow-haired girl has given me something for protecting her." Hawk was pleased when he saw the glint in the elder's eyes. Dull Knife might not want to show his emotions, but when it came to money for the tribe he couldn't contain his enthusiasm. "Her family was grateful to the Sioux for saving her life." Hawk was careful to credit all the Sioux, not just himself, for saving Samantha. He handed Dull Knife the thick stack of paper money, fresh from the bank in Deadwood. "There is two thousand dollars here."

Dull Knife took the money in his hands and stared at it for several seconds, as though he wasn't at all certain it was real. Then his face clouded over as he pulled the veil over his emotions once again. When he again regarded Hawk no thoughts or feelings could be discerned in the depths of his dark eyes.

"It is good that you have brought to your people such bounty," Dull Knife acknowledged quietly. "But you should know that there are many among us who have questioned your loyalty. They say that you ride away from your people, and when you return you have precious things that you have not hunted for. That makes many of us curious. You go hunting to faraway lands, searching for game, and what do you return with? Cheyenne horses. We are always thankful for Cheyenne horses . . . but we wonder how you came on them when you were searching for elk and buffalo. And then you ride away to bring the yellow-haired girl back to her people, and when you return you have a bounty that can hardly be believed. Is that not strange, Hawk Two Feather?"

Hawk wondered which answer he could give to maintain the slender thread of modesty he'd kept with his people. He'd actually shown himself to be an extraordinary hunter, often bringing game back to the tribe when the other hunters had failed. And though Hawk wanted greatly to point this out to Dull Knife, he knew he couldn't without sounding arrogant and disrespectful.

He looked at Dull Knife. He decided not to speak, suspecting that any answer he might give would likely become twisted somehow. Quite suddenly, Hawk felt as though he was a stranger to his own people, an outsider who might just as well be an enemy.

"But we must not speak too long on what might be," Dull Knife said then. "You have brought food to your people in the past, and I know you will in the future. You are back with us now . . . and you shall stay with us."

"Yes, Dull Knife, I am pleased to hear you say that, because staying with my people is what I want to do now," Hawk said, sensing that these were the sentiments that the old man most wanted to hear expressed, hoping they would assuage whatever fears and doubts were still in the elder's heart. "I have traveled far, and now I can once again know the peace of sleeping in my own tepee."

Dull Knife actually smiled at the comment, and even nodded slightly in Hawk's direction. Hawk didn't need to be told that he had chosen the right words to say, or that his time with Dull Knife was now over. He rose and left the tepee, a growing sense of being at war with himself and his people slowly and inexorably getting stronger within his breast.

*I mustn't seek out Red Wolf.*

The words rang out like a spirit's warning in Hawk's head. Stories had been told of him—lies, all of them!—and they'd put his name, his reputation, his loyalty . . . they'd put all of it in doubt. And there was only one man whom Hawk felt was capable of spreading such lies, and doing it in such a way as to make himself appear concerned only with the welfare of the tribe. That man simply had to be Red Wolf. Only Red Wolf's hatred burned hot enough, went deep enough, to do such a thing to him.

Even as Hawk walked away from the camp, he knew that he would have to find Red Wolf. How else could he put an end to the fury in his heart if he didn't confront the man who had caused it initially?

With some effort, Hawk forced himself to think logically, objectively; to see himself and his situation dispassionately. Wasn't it possible that he was blaming Red Wolf when, in fact, the person he was really angry with was Samantha Sanders? Wasn't it possible that he was blaming Red Wolf for being conniving and deceitful when it was Samantha who had been conniving and deceitful, who had, through her charms and her seductive ways, besmirched Hawk's reputation and put his name and loyalty in doubt among the chieftains of the Sioux tribe?

That was possible, Hawk consented . . . but it was unlikely. It was entirely true that he was furious with Samantha for the things she had said to him, the things she'd kept hidden from him when they were together and he thought she was a penniless waif. But that didn't make her responsible for his tattered reputation here among his own people.

Hawk knew he needed time alone—time to withdraw within himself, time to look into his own heart to discover the truth waiting there for him. Only then would he truly have the wisdom he needed to make the necessary decisions. At this moment his mind was too muddied, too chaotic and distracted, to have full command of his abilities.

The sweat lodge would strip his body of impurities, Hawk decided, and after that a vision quest was in order. Many moons had passed since he'd sought a vision, since he'd searched so deeply within and outside himself.

But there was always Red Wolf to think about—

*Don't think of him now!*

Leaving camp, Hawk walked quickly, purposefully, toward what he hoped would be the return of the serenity he'd lost the moment Samantha had entered his life.

He was almost out of camp when Red Wolf approached him, riding one of the Cheyenne horses Hawk had brought to the tribe.

"You are back," Red Wolf said, a sneer on his lips. "I am surprised. I had thought the yellow-haired woman would keep you away longer than this."

"Not every warrior thinks with what is between his legs," Hawk replied, painfully aware of the hypocrisy of his statement. All too often in his life he had responded to the demands of his passionate instincts.

"True. True," Red Wolf replied. "But you are not one of those warriors with a dead spear between his legs, are you? Not you, Hawk. There is not a warrior nor a maiden in this tribe who has not heard of your prowess!"

Red Wolf spit out the words hatefully, viciously. He had intended them to be something of a distorted compliment to his enemy, Hawk Two Feather, but his true emotions had come to the fore, revealing his utter contempt for the half-breed who had bested him—in women, in competition, in hunting—continuously since they were children.

Hawk turned on his enemy, understanding with knowledge acquired through his instincts and his spirit guides that listening to Red Wolf was a mistake. Allowing Red Wolf's words to create anger was folly, yet he couldn't help himself. He managed to stifle the urge to take Red Wolf by the throat, but only because out of the corner of his eye he saw a gathering of women and children. It wouldn't do to make the entire tribe aware of his inability to maintain his self-control and temper.

"You lowest of maggots," Hawk hissed, using the vilest insult in the Sioux culture to describe his enemy. "Every word you utter is a defilement!"

In response, Red Wolf smiled, his smile suggesting that he would be pleased should Hawk attack him when others in the tribe could see.

But Hawk turned and walked away, determined to put as much distance between himself and his people as possible.

The vision quest: only there would he find the answers to the questions that plagued him.

# Twenty-one

In the sweat lodge Hawk felt perspiration running down his naked body and, as time passed, he sweated out the impurities and defilement of the past weeks. Soon, very soon, he would be whole and complete again, free of the influences of a culture that wasn't his own, free of a woman he could never call his own.

He was punishing himself. The heat of the sweat lodge was greater than it should be, Hawk realized, but still he stoked the fire, heating the rocks on which he poured the cool water from the hollowed-out gourd, creating the steam. Moment by moment, fresh rivers of perspiration ran down Hawk's naked chest and back.

The white woman wasn't worth it.

Samantha Sanders simply wasn't worth the torture that he was putting himself through . . . and he was doing everything he possibly could to make himself believe that.

The trouble was, no matter how often he told himself a lie, he was aware of it. And lying was something that Hawk had disliked no matter what the circumstances, had avoided with all he held sacred.

Stretching out on the buffalo mat, Hawk closed his eyes and tried to imagine what wonders would be his to experience during his vision quest. It had been quite some time since last he'd dared look so deeply within himself, and he was frankly curious about what treasures would be his to experience . . .

and what horrors would be revealed. True knowledge was a two-edged sword.

Hawk wasn't a man who frightened easily, but at this moment he felt anxious. Would he even be capable of having a vision, after all the time he had spent living in the white man's world, speaking the white man's language, eating the white man's food?

*The white man is not my enemy,* he reminded himself.

Had being so closely involved with the Caucasian culture infected his soul?

What most disturbed Hawk, sweat pouring from his body, was that he continued to think about Samantha, even when he was doing everything he could to forget her. In the past, women who occupied his time and shared his passion had only been on his mind and in his thoughts when they were physically with him. With astonishing speed, Hawk had forgotten virtually every incident he'd shared with a woman once they were no longer lovers. It wasn't that the women meant nothing to Hawk, or that he was scornful of them once they were no longer sharing passion. They were simply no longer of *immediate* concern and, since they weren't, no longer occupied his thoughts.

He stretched his muscles, inhaling the moist air, enjoying the burning of the steam as it filled his lungs and expanded his chest. He felt the sweat running out of his body. In his heart, Hawk was convinced that when he was finished with the sweat lodge his soul would be purer. The anger he felt toward Samantha and Red Wolf, along with the anger he felt toward himself for having allowed his weakness for women to distort his judgment, would be gone. He should have known from the very beginning that Samantha would bring nothing but trouble to his life.

But how could he have known she'd bring a passion that burned more brightly than he'd thought possible?

The instant the memories of their lovemaking began to fill

his head, Hawk sighed and forced himself to begin thinking about his duties to the tribe, and where next he would hunt.

Night Flower stood alone in the shadows, searching inside herself to find the courage to finish what she had started. Her knees were trembling, and her heart was racing with fear and anticipation. This was her sixteenth summer, and she felt it was time to find a warrior for herself. Other Sioux women her age were no longer maidens. They had accepted invitations to a courageous and proud warrior's tepee, and some of them were already mothers, raising the next generation of the tribe.

Night Flower was attractive, and her beauty and spirit had drawn the attention of several warriors in the tribe, though she'd kept her distance from all of them so far. None had measured up to the standards she'd set for herself. None of the braves who had smiled at her and wished to dance with her during the ceremonies was what she envisioned for herself.

But there *was* one brave in the tribe who measure up to Night Flower's standards of manhood—Hawk Two Feather. He alone was able to make Night Flower's heart accelerate by just smiling at her. When he was near Night Flower felt safe and secure, as though he alone was capable of defending the tribe from all its enemies.

Twice she had tried to let Hawk know that she was interested in him, and twice Hawk had simply smiled at her, treating her kindly but giving no indication that he realized the depths of her desire for him. Tonight, Night Flower intended to make her intentions toward Hawk clear. There would be no possible misunderstanding . . . not when she walked into the sweat lodge, when she knew Hawk was inside, alone and naked.

She looked around one more time, her mouth dry with nervousness as she searched for spying eyes to witness her entrance into the sweat lodge. Seeing no one looking at her, she made her move quickly. Stepping out from her hiding place, she dashed across the small clearing and then through the buffalo-hide flap of the sweat lodge.

He was spread out on his back, arms and legs outstretched, his glorious body completely naked and glistening from head to toe with perspiration. Night Flower, one step into the tepee, was transfixed in place, her eyes wide, her mouth slightly open as she looked down at the man who had been the object of her fantasies since she'd begun to have them.

He raised his head after a moment, blinking his eyes, clearly annoyed at having been disturbed from whatever thoughts had occupied his mind. Then, after blinking his eyes several times, he focused his gaze on Night Flower. He raised his right knee just enough to block his manhood from her view, but other than that he didn't move.

A small eternity of time passed with neither of them speaking a word. Finally Hawk spoke, with a gentleness and understanding that surprised Night Flower.

"You have honored me, Night Flower," Hawk said softly, "but you should not have come here."

Night Flower tried to speak, but though she moved her lips, no words came forth. She cleared her throat, moistened her lips, and tried once more, determined to succeed now that she had come this far.

"I *had* to come here," she said, her voice a whisper of uncertainty. "I have tried to let you know that I want to be with you in your tepee. But when I have tried you have cast me aside like an old moccasin. Now I am here, alone with you in the sweat lodge, and you cannot cast me aside."

"No, I cannot," Hawk replied. "But you still should not have come here."

"I had to. You left me no choice."

Night Flower bent at the waist, reaching for the bottom of her buckskin dress, about to lift it up and over her head. But Hawk moved quickly, catching her wrist with his huge hand to stop her. Their eyes met, and after a moment Hawk shook his head.

"This is not the way it is to be for you," he said quietly, releasing Night Flower's wrist from his grasp.

Still standing, Night Flower looked down at Hawk, hating herself at that moment for having been foolish enough to intrude on a proud warrior's private sweat lodge ceremony. She had, she realized, made a terrible mistake, and she hoped that the rest of the tribe would never find out about what she had done. But she wasn't yet willing to give up on the plan; Hawk's reputation as an insatiable lover had been spread throughout the tribe, and Night Flower had received too many compliments in her young life for her to not know that she was a beautiful Sioux maiden.

"You are a mighty warrior, Hawk Two Feather," Night Flower said at last, thankful that she had finally found her voice, "but you do not know my future. This *is* the way it should be for me . . . and for you. I believe in my heart—" to emphasize the point, she placed her hand over her breast, and was pleased that Hawk's eyes followed her every move— "that you and I were meant to be together. I am the maiden the spirits wish you to mate with. The spirits have told me so."

Night Flower looked away for only a moment. Guilt caused her to look away, because the spirits had told her no such thing. But in her desperation she was willing to go to any length to get the man she desired—Hawk, to be hers, from this night forward.

"There are other braves who look at me, and I can feel their hunger," Night Flower continued. "But you look on me differently. I know that you desire me. I have seen that desire in your eyes. But you do not look at me the way others do . . . and because you do not my desire for you has grown."

Night Flower took a step closer to Hawk, then got down on her knees at his hip. She could tell that he was very anxious in her presence, but she'd already gone too far with her plan to back away from it now. "Touch my breast, Hawk," she said softly, "and feel how I can feed the child we will create."

Hawk finally pulled up to a sitting position, folding his legs beneath him, casually placing the corner of the buffalo mat across his lap. He had known that Night Flower was interested in him. He would have had to be blind not to have noticed, and Hawk had a notable ability to perceive interest from any woman instantly. Night Flower was a maiden, he knew, and much sought-after by the other braves in the tribe . . . and though she would surely make a magnificent wife, Hawk also knew that he must not touch her. She wasn't the woman for him, no matter how much his body desired the release that she clearly was willing to give him.

"Can you feel how nurturing a mother I would be?" Night Flower asked, taking Hawk's hand and placing it on her breast.

Involuntarily, Hawk's fingers closed over Night Flower's breast, squeezing her through her dress. But rather than the instant burst of passionate interest he had expected to experience, he thought how she was neither as large nor as firm as Samantha, and the comparison immediately destroyed whatever sensuality the moment might have possessed.

"Night Flower is beautiful and rare as her name suggests," Hawk said, easing his hand away from her, "but she is wrong to think that I am the only brave for her. Night Flower is very young and very kind . . . and she must find for herself a warrior who is both strong and kind. But that warrior . . . that warrior cannot be Hawk Two Feather."

It astonished Hawk to say such words. Could it really be that he, a man given to profligate excesses where women were concerned, was turning his back on a virgin? A young maiden not needing to be seduced, but rather needing only the attention she'd already shown she was desirous of?

For a moment Hawk closed his eyes, trying desperately to make some sense of his behavior. Was it Samantha who had caused him to be unreceptive to Night Flower's offer? Had Samantha somehow taken possession of his soul, causing him to behave so uncharacteristically?

"Tell me what you desire," Night Flower pressed, her voice

a frightened whisper. "I will do anything you want. Teach me . . . and I will be yours forever."

Hawk took Night Flower's hands into his own and kissed them. He felt guilty that she desired him, as though he had encouraged her, though he could not say how. He looked into her eyes and saw the longing and the fear buried there.

"Night Flower is beautiful, but Night Flower must wait," Hawk replied. "There will be another forever for you. There will be a warrior who will teach you all that it is you do not know, but that warrior will not be Hawk Two Feather. Trust me. This is the truth that the visions have given me."

Though Hawk had never even thought of Night Flower in his vision, that lie didn't matter. What mattered was that he refuse her request without making her feel belittled. When he looked into Night Flower's eyes he saw a mixture of relief and sadness. She wanted him—or at least she thought she did—but she was mortally afraid of the reality of actually having a sexual relationship with him.

"There will come a time, in a year or two, when Night Flower will find the brave who will be her companion for life," Hawk continued, "but that time is not this time. Go, now, and be thankful that we both have listened to what the spirits have spoken."

Night Flower kissed Hawk on the forehead, then left the sweat lodge, loving Hawk more than she had when she entered, though she no longer saw him in her mind's eye as the only brave who was worthy of her uncritical praise. Her footsteps were light and sure as she made her way through the darkness, taking a parallel course to the tribe, wanting to be by herself for a while so that she could think about everything Hawk had just said to her.

# Twenty-two

The mare was responding exactly as Samantha had hoped she would. Though new to the saddle and bridle, the mare was quick to learn the movements necessary to be a good cutting horse. Samantha's legs grasped tightly around the mare's ribs, her entire body ready for the animal to move in any direction. Ahead of her, the year-old steer was trying to decide whether to run to the right or to the left, his frustration growing as the mare cut off his escape every time.

When the steer bolted to the left the mare moved in unison, and an instant later the steer was herded through the corral gate into the pen, where Samantha had wanted him.

"Good girl," Samantha purred, patting the mare's sleek, well-muscled neck. "You were perfect today. Every day you keep getting better and better."

Billy, sitting on the top rail of the corral, had been watching Samantha through the training. Impressed with the young mare's ability to respond to the steers, Billy was even more impressed with Samantha's ability as a horse-trainer.

"You've got yourself one fine horse there, Miss Samantha," Billy said as Samantha came closer.

"She is a good one," Samantha replied. "I don't think I've ever had a horse take to cutting quite as quickly as this one has."

"What's her name?" Billy asked.

Samantha shifted her weight in the saddle, uneasy with the question. Why didn't the mare have a name? Such a magnifi-

cent animal *should* have a name, she reasoned . . . but was it
possible that she hadn't named the mare because of something
Hawk had told her? He said the Sioux didn't believe in giving
their horses names, only in giving their horses respect.

"Miss Samantha?" Billy asked, a bit more softly this time.
Samantha looked Billy straight in the eye and did her best
to smile. "Billy, I'd be pleased if you'd name her for me,"
Samantha said. "She doesn't have a name because everything
I think of just doesn't seem to fit. Maybe you can do better."

Billy's face broke into a broad smile. "I'd be right proud to
do that for you, Miss Samantha! Right proud, indeed!"

Samantha swung down from the saddle and handed Billy
the mare's reins. He would take care of the animal, seeing that
she was brushed down, watered, and properly fed.

As Samantha started on the long walk from the training
corral to the ranch house, she groaned softly. Her muscles felt
stiff and sore from all the hours she'd put in lately, working
to train the new cutting horses that would be sold in a month
or two. The strain of the days had settled in her neck and
shoulders. In fact, the muscles in the back of her neck were
always tense and tight these days, always knotted painfully.
Even when she massaged her neck, the muscles relaxed only
briefly before tightening up once again.

The hot bath she'd take would relieve her aching body temporarily. Her nightly baths in the large tub, the steaming water
laced with scented soap, was the only extravagance she allowed
herself—and they were something she began looking forward
to earlier and earlier each day, it seemed.

Samantha knew why she was pushing herself so hard: Hawk,
and the way he made her feel. No man had made her feel
more precious . . . and no man had made her feel more cheap
and tawdry. He'd brought her to the heights of ecstasy and the
depths of abject humiliation. Samantha would drive his memory out of her mind with endless hours of hard labor.

Even most of the ranch hands, men not known for sophisticated perceptions, noticed something other than training the

cutting horses was driving her on. They'd worked with her long enough to realize the difference in her behavior, though none of the men suspected the real reason for her abrupt change in work habits. No one would ever have connected the Indian's stay with their mistress's new mood.

How many times since Hawk had ridden away had she snapped at one of the ranch hands, castigating the poor man much more harshly than he deserved for an offense either real or imagined? Just off the top of her head Samantha could think of three such incidents in which she had later apologized to a hired hand. And those were only the times when she had gone completely overboard in her response to an offense. Samantha was certain there were plenty of other things she'd said recently that she should have apologized for but was too emotionally distracted to be aware of.

Samantha sighed, hoping she hadn't caused any long-lasting hard feelings. She had always had a fine working relationship with the hands at the Circle S ranch, and she wanted it to stay that way.


The dress had arrived that morning. Now, as Samantha looked at her reflection in her bedroom's full-length mirror, she wondered once again whether it was such a good idea to wear it for Travis Newton.

*He deserves to have you dressed like a lady, not a saddle bum.* Samantha felt angry with herself as she stared into the reflection of her own eyes. *Maybe if you'd dressed like a lady for Hawk, he would have considered you a woman instead of a tramp.*

"I've got to stop thinking about him," Samantha whispered aloud, hoping that the sound of her own voice would somehow add emphasis to the order.

The eggshell white gown was modest and attractive, and the dressmaker's craftsmanship was beyond reproach. It was one of five gowns Samantha had ordered, impulsively deciding that if she made her wardrobe more feminine, her life might not feel so empty and barren without Hawk.

There was a soft knock on the door. "Samantha, Travis is here," Sonny called out.

Samantha inhaled deeply, closing her eyes. A silent, hopeful prayer passed through her mind that the evening would be entertaining, and that Travis would be the man to take her thoughts away from a Sioux warrior whose opinion of her was sorrowfully low.

Travis was waiting for her in the library, and the instant he saw Samantha in her new evening gown his jaw dropped. A handsome man several years older than Samantha, he came from a good family whom Samantha had known for several years. Even so, she'd never really considered allowing Travis to come courting before.

"Miss Samantha, you have never looked lovelier," Travis said, rushing forward, his face beaming with happiness. "Never, *ever* have you been more beautiful!"

"It's just a dress, Travis," Samantha replied, suddenly unsure of what it was she wanted. She had chosen the dress so that Travis would be pleased with it, yet now that she had gotten exactly the response from him that she'd wanted, his pleasure rather annoyed her.

"But what a dress! I truly have never seen you look so much like . . . like—"

"Like a lady?" Samantha cut in.

"No, Samantha, that wasn't what I was going to say," Travis replied quickly, sensing that his enthusiasm had placed him in an unfavorable light. "That wasn't what I was going to say at all."

Samantha merely smiled at Travis. "You needn't be afraid, Travis. I'm fully aware that my usual attire is less than feminine. In fact, it's rather mannish, I should say."

"You would be lovely no matter what clothes you wore," Travis said, clearly relieved that Samantha wasn't really angry with him. Impulsively, innocently, he added, "I'll bet you'd be the prettiest girl in the whole territory even if you didn't have a stitch on!"

The instant the words were out of his mouth, Travis Newton blushed crimson red with embarrassment. Samantha laughed openly at the comment, realizing that Travis hadn't meant to insult her, and that his embarrassment was a thousand times worse than her own.

"Travis, why don't we step outside onto the porch?" Samantha suggested. "We can sit on the swing. I'm sure you could use a whiskey, and I'd like a glass of wine."

Travis nodded, and then his eyes widened in surprise. "Miss Samantha, I didn't know you drank spirits!"

"I'm only going to have a glass of wine, Travis. It isn't as if I'm breaking the law or anything."

"But do you think you should have it outside, where the workers might see you? They might not have such a high opinion of you if they found out you touch alcohol."

Samantha managed to keep her anger in check, though only because Travis was so genuinely concerned with what other people thought of her. "Why don't you let me worry about my own reputation? I'm sure we'll get along better that way."

"Whatever you want, Miss Samantha. My only concern is for you."

They sat on the front porch swing and discussed horses. Samantha was grateful for the topic, one that she could discuss at great length without having to feign interest. Even better, it was one Travis knew quite a bit about, though Samantha disagreed with him when it came to the best methods of training cutting horses and the use of spurs.

"I'm working with a mare that looks like she's got all the right instincts to be a first-class cutter," Samantha explained. In the back of her mind she wondered whether Billy had come up with a name for the mare.

"Will you be keeping her, or selling?"

"I think this one will have to stay at the Circle S," Samantha answered. "She's exactly the kind of horse that this ranch needs to rejuvenate its bloodlines."

Travis chuckled softly. "Doesn't seem to me the Circle S needs much rejuvenating, Miss Samantha. It's already the envy of every horseman for three hundred miles around."

Samantha playfully glanced sideways at Travis. "Just three hundred miles? I'd have thought our reputation goes farther than that."

"If you say it does, then it does, Miss Samantha," Travis replied agreeably.

Samantha knew that Travis was only trying to ingratiate himself with her, but she wished he could have stuck to his guns about the three hundred miles. Or, at least, that he could have teased her a little about her own boastfulness. Instead, he continued to go along with everything she said, subjugating his own honest feelings in an effort to have her like him. In the process, she lost some of her respect for him.

Travis bridged the narrow space that separated them on the swing, cautiously taking her hand in his. "It would give me the greatest pleasure if you could see it in your heart to let me hold your hand, Miss Samantha," Travis said softly, solemnly. "And when I leave here later tonight I want you to know that I'm not one of those men who'd go looking for a kiss good night. I respect you too much to ask that of you. You see, I'm a gentleman, and you're a lady, and that's the way I'll always treat you, Miss Samantha . . . like a real lady, and nothing less."

"That's kind of you, Travis," Samantha said softly.

She didn't know what else to say. What would his opinion of her be if he knew the things that she'd done with Hawk? Would he think her so fragile if he knew the uninhibited behavior she'd exhibited in the arms of a half-breed Sioux warrior?

There was a certain comic quality to Travis being satisfied with simply holding Samantha's hand that not only touched her in a way, but also embarrassed her. Hawk wouldn't be satisfied with just holding her hand. Travis was too polite to even expect a kiss good night. And Hawk? Hawk's kisses were hotter than fire, touching her in ways she'd never imagined, kissing her in places she'd never dreamed of. There was simply no similarity between Hawk Two Feather and Travis Newton.

Finally the sun went down and Travis rose slowly from the swing. Still holding Samantha's hand, he gently pulled her to a standing position.

"Miss Samantha, it has been an honor to have this time with you," Travis said quietly, looking into Samantha's eyes. "I never thought I'd get the chance to be with you without other fellas around."

"You've been very sweet," Samantha replied honestly.

Travis Newton *was* a sweet man, kind and considerate, and he would make some woman a wonderful husband . . . but that woman wouldn't be Samantha. It wasn't that she didn't think he was suitable to be her husband. He was a wonderful man . . . but she knew that in time she would learn to hate him because she could control him, make him bend to her greater willpower. She needed a man who was as strong, as determined, as solid in his views as she was herself. She needed a man *like* Hawk, but not *Hawk.*

"Then you'll see me again?" he asked.

*So filled with hope,* Samantha thought sadly. She replied, "Someday. We'll see. You've been very kind, Travis. You're a perfect gentleman."

He left then, and Samantha watched him ride out through the arched gateway of the Circle S ranch. How could any man be so happy just to have held her hand? A gentleman could and would be happy just to hold the hand of a woman he was courting, Samantha thought.

She wasn't pleased with her thoughts. Travis was a kind and decent man, but she felt more protective than passionate toward him. Though he was older than her by several years, she felt herself to be the more worldly, the more experienced in life.

When she stepped into the house she saw a light glowing in the library. Sonny, casually dressed in a green robe, was reading a newspaper and having a whiskey.

"I'm going to bed now," Samantha said, standing in the doorway. "I've had a long day, and I've got a lot to do tomorrow."

Sonny looked up from his book and smiled. "Why don't you sleep late tomorrow? The ranch can survive one day without you getting up at sunrise."

"No. There's too much to do for me to start getting lazy now."

"Lazy? Samantha, you're the hardest-working woman I've ever known in my life! Go ahead and take a morning off. It'll probably do you a world of good. You really have been pushing yourself too hard lately."

"Good night, Sonny," Samantha replied, turning away from her brother with a smile. "I'll see you in the morning."

"How was Travis?" Sonny called out.

"Fine. Just fine," Samantha replied, already heading down the hall.

She could hardly wait to get out of the gown, out of the corselet, out of the garters and stockings and all the other accoutrements of sophistication that she was unaccustomed to wearing. She wanted to crawl between the sheets of her bed and forget about every man in the world until morning. She hoped that with a good night's sleep her world wouldn't look quite so bleak and colorless.


*He's more beautiful than ever.*

This reaction didn't surprise Samantha, though it was disconcerting, coming so soon after promising herself to never become either physically or emotionally affected by Hawk's looks again. But here he came toward her, and while she knew she shouldn't be attracted to the man—his opinion of her was a matter of record and the hours she had spent crying because of his words had *not* been forgotten—her body wasn't listening. In fact, her body had grown all jittery just at the sight of Hawk Two Feather.

He wore the leather loincloth she'd seen him in earlier, only now he was bare-chested and without the leggings. Only the loincloth and moccasins kept him from being completely naked. His broad, bronze-hued chest drew Samantha's eyes like a magnet, a magnet that wouldn't let go. She couldn't look away—not when the sheer perfection of his physique was there for her inspection. To make matters worse, there was an ebony fire in his eyes that told Samantha that his calm exterior hid an inferno in his soul.

"Say something," Samantha said. Her voice sounded odd in her ears, trailing an echo, as if she were talking while standing inside a large empty grain bin. "Why have you come here?"

It occurred to Samantha that she didn't know where *here* was, though that hardly seemed to matter when Hawk was so near . . . and wearing so little.

"What do you want from me, Hawk?" Her anger was surfacing now that he had chosen to re-enter her life, yet remain his typically silent, aloof self. "You can't keep doing this to me! It isn't fair! You know it isn't!"

Hawk still said nothing, standing there like a statue, his feet spread to shoulders' width, his hands on his lean hips. She knew how fully aware he was of the impact his physical beauty had on women, that he counted on that impact to make up for whatever frazzled nervous and frayed tempers his idiosyncrasies elicited.

"Damn you, Hawk Two Feather," Samantha said, hating him then because he expected her to go to him. But she was just as furious with herself for being willing to do just that.

As she approached him slowly, everything seemed ethereal and disconnected to Samantha. His eyes were black as midnight, tempting as sin. He neither moved nor spoke, yet Samantha felt as though his thoughts and desires were somehow being transmitted directly into her being.

And then the strangest thing happened. Hawk's hands were on her, touching her in exactly the way he had taught her to enjoy, brushing the pads of his fingers lightly over her enflamed nipples before pinching them firmly. She heard herself sigh, a long, soft, warbling moan of contentment and passion, a sleepy sound of delight in the joy of living.

*Yes, my darling,* Samantha thought, rolling her head from side to side.

Then she suddenly realized that she was no longer standing but was instead in a bed with Hawk. Her eyes were closed and the room was engulfed in darkness. And even though Hawk had yet to speak even a single word, Samantha felt his presence with her in the bed, recognized the familiarity of his touch, the surety and confidence of his skilled hands as his exquisite caresses sent her senses soaring.

"Yes, oh, my darling, yes-s-s!" Samantha sighed, giving herself over completely to the feeling of the moment.

It didn't matter to her, then, whether or not Hawk respected her. It didn't matter that he had said cruel, vicious things to her the last time they were together. Nothing truly mattered but Hawk's touch, and the way she felt when he touched her.

*I shouldn't let him,* Samantha thought as she parted her knees.

It was a silly thought because she knew that she could deny Hawk nothing. Not this night. She had been denied the sweetness of his passion for too long. How had she become addicted to the ecstasy of his lovemaking with such frightening speed? She would give him everything, deny him nothing. When it was all over she might feel guilty—or maybe she wouldn't. Either way, she wouldn't stop now. There would be no barriers between them tonight.

Samantha arched her back with the slowly building tension and knew from experience what that meant. Soon Hawk would take her to that magical place where the pleasure was so intense that she had no choice but to explode, her body turning inside-out as her ecstasy reached its pinnacle. Closer and closer she felt herself being drawn.

"Yes, Hawk," Samantha purred, no longer hiding her pleasure.

She wanted to let Hawk know that she was willing to do anything, endure anything, provided he no longer deprive her of these feelings that she had become addicted to.

The moment of truth, that cataclysmic moment when the pleasure of Hawk's caresses couldn't become any more intense, was only seconds away. Samantha welcomed that approaching moment, knowing in her heart that afterward she would experience a blissful lassitude of mind and body that couldn't be achieved any other way.

At that moment, when she was teetering at the edge of the chasm, about to fall into ecstasy and experience once more the glorious freefall of orgasmic culmination . . . she awoke.

For several seconds Samantha refused to believe that it had all been a dream, that Hawk hadn't really returned to her, and that the pleasures of the flesh that she'd experienced were a result of a dream-based imagination.

"What is happening to me?" she murmured aloud in the dark bedroom. She rubbed her eyes and blinked.

Suddenly, she was embarrassed at her state of arousal. Her body had responded to the fantasy of Hawk just as readily as it would have responded to the reality of his seduction. But now she lay alone in her own bed, trembling softly, her heart fluttering as she sought to calm the chaos within her.

She kicked off the light blankets and got out of bed. On the stand nearby stood a water pitcher and a basin. She poured cool water into the basin, cupped her hands in the water, then washed her face. The water felt refreshing. She wished she could as easily wash away the stimulating dream.

More than anything, Samantha was shocked by the realization that there was now a face on the fantasy man of her dreams. Now, when erotic fantasies gripped her sleep, the faceless man of limitless seduction would have an identity and a name.

Was this knowledge a plague or a blessing?

Perhaps she would rest easier if she hadn't discovered that Hawk had become her dream lover.

Samantha went to the open window and breathed in the Dakota night air, unnaturally cool against her skin. She realized then how heated her body had become because of the erotic dream of Hawk.

"He's out of my life forever," Samantha determined softly.

She walked slowly back to the bed and crawled between the sheets. With some trepidation, she closed her eyes, hoping that sleep would bring her nothing but rest until she awoke in the morning.


Walter Morrison was more than just a decent fellow, and Samantha knew it. Not yet forty, he owned the largest bank in Deadwood, and was partner in another bank somewhere in Minnesota. He had one child, who was in a private school in the East. His wife had died in a tragic carriage accident. Wealthy, rather handsome, profitably engaged in business matters, Walter Morrison was a man whom many of the young and not-so-young women in and around Deadwood hoped to "hook" as a husband.

As Samantha rode in the carriage beside Walter, she wondered what kind of husband he would make. By all accounts he was a man who loved women, and that was good to know. Samantha had discovered that there were some men who coveted women sexually yet despised them in every other way. She couldn't tolerate the thought of living with a man who wanted her sexually, yet considered her inferior in every other way.

"This has been a wonderful evening, Samantha," Walter said as he guided his fine carriage through the arched gateway leading into the grounds of the Circle S ranch. "Do you feel the same way?"

Samantha almost said that she did; but then she wondered whether Walter had meant something more, so she simply nodded her head. When Walter repeated the question she made herself speak: "It was a fine evening. I've enjoyed myself."

"As have I. We should do this again sometime soon."

Out of the corner of her eye, Samantha looked at Walter and wondered why she didn't feel blessed. She could think of at least three women her age who would do anything to have spent an evening with Walter Morrison. He had behaved like a perfect gentleman, naturally, but Samantha knew that his experience with women was considerable. Since the death of his wife, and after a suitable period of mourning, Walter had been seen in the company of many of the more fashionable ladies of Deadwood, as well as Fargo. And, rumor had it, even St. Paul.

Samantha was impressed, but she simply wasn't interested. She had accepted Walter's offer of a carriage ride and dinner at a fashionable restaurant in Deadwood because she'd hoped that it would take her mind off Hawk. But instead, when Walter arrived in his carriage with the two matching horses, Samantha's first thought was about Hawk. Hawk Two Feather could never afford such a carriage, and even if he could, he would be so concerned with the needs of the tribe that he wouldn't spend the money on himself. No, thinking about Hawk was not the way Samantha had intended to spend her evening with Walter Morrison . . . but he played on her thoughts just the same.

From a distance Samantha saw that the lights from the bunkhouses had dimmed. Samantha guessed there might be a card game still going, but not much more than that. As the carriage approached the ranch house, she noticed the windows were still illuminated from the lamps within. This didn't surprise her at all; her brother wouldn't go to bed until she was home.

When the carriage came to a stop Walter quickly climbed

down and rushed around the carriage to help Samantha out. His hands felt firm and confident as he placed them on her waist, even though Samantha had put out her hands, hoping he would take them instead.

Still, his touch on her was oddly disconcerting, and at first Samantha couldn't say why this was so. Clearly Walter hadn't been brutishly forward or even inappropriate in his attentions. Rather, he had touched her in a socially prescribed manner, in a way that Samantha had been touched before by prospective suitors. The touch was suggestive, but nothing more than that. The unspoken message was that if she responded to his touch unfavorably, he wouldn't touch her again; if she didn't respond at all, he might touch her again; if she responded favorably, he would feel emboldened to touch her more intimately.

Samantha realized all of this in the second or two that separated the time that Walter's hands touched her waist to the time her slippered feet touched the graveled drive.

The instant her feet reached the ground, Samantha stepped straight back away from Walter, though she didn't instantly turn away from him. She'd done that before with Hawk, and when she had her move unintentionally placed her breast into his hand. And that little mistake, however unintended, had led to caresses that were *not* unintentional . . . and led to love-making that was most certainly intentional, and satisfying to the *nth* degree.

"I'd like to thank you for this evening," Samantha said, unaware that she sounded exactly as if she was talking to a horse trader interested in something more than just selling horses to her. "I've had a very entertaining time."

"Just entertaining?" Walter asked, following Samantha as she walked backward toward the front porch.

"Isn't entertaining enough?"

"It's good . . . but it isn't enough," Walter replied.

Samantha didn't like the tone he used. She couldn't say that he had been ungentlemanly, but it was clear that he was hoping

for something more from her than just a *thank you* for time
and money spent.

Was that so much different than Hawk? Samantha asked
herself. Hadn't Hawk, with his unshakable confidence, assumed that Samantha would fall prey to his seductive charms?
Had Samantha thought negatively of him for his romantic as-
sumptions? *No.*

*Yes,* Samantha amended a moment later. Perhaps she hadn't
thought negatively at the time he was seducing her, but she
did think nasty things of Hawk now that she was no longer
under the influence of his erotic charm.

"What are you thinking of, Samantha?" Walter asked, in
step with Samantha as she turned around to reach the front
porch.

"Nothing."

"Nothing?"

Samantha blushed slightly, wondering whether all men who
had slept with several women had developed the ability to read
the female mind. But she was making a terrible mistake by
thinking about Hawk and Walter at the same time, by making
any comparison of one to the other.

*Give Walter a chance!* Samantha decided. *He's a good man,
and he's certain to treat you more respectfully than a certain
Sioux warrior had.*

Samantha walked straight to the double front doors of the
ranch house, then turned so that she faced Walter. She smiled
up at him, a friendly smile that wasn't at all a come-on.

"Good evening, Walter," she said quietly, confidently, secure
at last that she was going to put Hawk and his memory behind
her. "I do want to thank you for this evening. I really have
enjoyed myself."

"You have? I wouldn't have guessed," Walter said with a
grin, placing his hands on Samantha's shoulders as he bent
down to kiss her.

Samantha saw the kiss coming, and though her first instinct
was to avoid it, her hope was that Walter—with his experience

with women—would help her forget the Sioux warrior who'd been too much in her thoughts for too long. Walter wasn't a pathetically naive young man like Travis. Walter knew what he wanted from women, and if Samantha's guess was correct, he'd been successful often enough in his amorous quests to have acquired at least some skill and finesse in such matters.

She closed her eyes. When Walter's lips touched hers Samantha waited for the quickening of her heart, for the rush of blood through her veins, for the heightened sensitivity to touch, to smell, to taste. She waited for all the things that had overwhelmed her with Hawk's kisses.

She waited . . . and waited . . . and waited.

Nothing happened.

The experience hadn't left her with a sense of revulsion, but though kissing Walter wasn't repulsive at all, it wasn't thrilling, either.

He pulled away finally and looked down into Samantha's eyes. She didn't know what to say or do. She didn't want him to kiss her again, but she didn't want to shatter his hopes. More than anything, she wanted to get to her bedroom, get out of her dress and into her nightgown, and climb into her big, comfortable bed—the same bed she had wanted to share with Hawk, but hadn't because of circumstances that had been beyond her control.

"Samantha . . ." Walter began, but the words wouldn't come. He had kissed enough women to know when a woman wasn't responding.

"Good night, Walter," Samantha said a bit apologetically, taking another step away from him.

Walter looked for a moment as though he were going to say something, then went to his carriage. He didn't look back.

# Twenty-three

Riding into Deadwood, Samantha got an eerie feeling, though she tried hard to dismiss it. This foreboding, she was convinced, could be attributed to the fact that the last time she'd come to Deadwood, she'd discovered Hawk jailed, beaten, and utterly contemptuous of anyone who didn't have Sioux blood flowing in his veins.

For a moment she wondered whether Walter might have said anything bad about her after their evening together, but she dismissed this thought instantly. Walter was too much a gentleman to speak badly of a woman, and besides, even though the single kiss they'd shared hadn't start a fire, it wasn't as though Samantha had castigated him afterward for being a cur, either.

She did, however, feel the eyes of some of the people gathered along the boardwalk following her. Why were they watching her? This fear, as those before it, was put aside as Samantha realized people were gawking at what she was wearing: Levi's, a man-cut cotton shirt, and a Colt strapped in a holster riding low around her hips. That was why the people were looking at her—for the same reason they had for several years now.

Samantha rode more easily in the saddle after that. She'd long been the subject of discussion among the polite society of Deadwood because of her attire. Usually they spoke of her with some degree of pity, wondering why an attractive young woman, coming from a good family and with plenty of money behind her, would choose to dress and behave like a tomboy when she could wear the finest gowns that money could buy.

By the time Samantha reached the sheriff's office she was feeling pretty good about herself. She might not be appreciated by most of the citizens of Deadwood, but at least she was noticed by them. To Samantha's way of thinking, being scorned was infinitely better than being ignored.

She strolled through the front door of the sheriff's office and was surprised to see Darren Richards sitting behind his desk. His boots were up on the scarred desktop, and a cigarette dangled from his lips. He barely opened his eyes when Samantha first entered the room, though his lips did curl into a smile that made Samantha wary.

"You got my message." There was no courtesy in the sheriff's tone. "I like it when young gals do what they're told."

Samantha instantly felt her anger rising. "I got the message that the *deputy* wanted to see me. You may be the sheriff, but everybody knows the deputy is the only real law in this town," Samantha said. Then, when her gaze met the sheriff's, and she recalled Hawk's experience with him, she couldn't resist adding, "And now that I look real close, I see you aren't really much of a lawman, or even much of a man. Sheriff, I do believe you're not much of anything at all."

The insult wasn't lost on Sheriff Richards. He kicked his feet off the desk, hoping to make such a display of masculine anger that she would cower with fear. Samantha Sanders didn't take even a single step backward when Sheriff Richards bolted to his feet.

"You're in more trouble than you think," the sheriff warned.

He stepped closer and caught the faint aroma of Samantha's clean skin and fragrant hair. His blood boiled, and he wondered how many people had seen her step into the office.

"Trouble? I haven't done anything."

"So you say, but I've got a brother what's missing. He up and disappeared, and I've got a feeling that that Injin I had locked up had something to do with it."

Samantha finally did step away from the sheriff. Would Hawk murder a man for no reason? She shook her head. "I don't know what your brother was doing, but if he picked a fight with Hawk, he made a big mistake. I've seen Hawk fight, Sheriff, and he isn't a man who loses."

"No stinkin' Injin could whip my brother and his drinkin' buddies in a fair fight!" Sheriff Richards spat, not wanting to hear what Samantha was saying, fearful of the truth in her words.

Samantha's brows were raised. "How many of his friends did he bring along, Sheriff? Fair fight? Not likely. I'd say there wasn't anything fair about it at all, and still your brother ended up dead."

"Ain't nobody said he was dead! I said he was missing, that's all! Don't you go spreadin' rumors about my brother bein' dead!"

Samantha heard the desperation and fear in Sheriff Richards's voice, but she could afford him no sympathy. *Fair fight?* He was the man who had beaten and kicked Hawk when his hands were cuffed behind his back. *That* was the kind of fair fight Sheriff Richards liked, and his brother was probably no different.

"I'm surprised you didn't go along with your brother." Samantha's lips curled with derision. "I've seen the way you fight, seen how brave you are when a man's hands are manacled behind his back. Were you afraid Hawk would come back for you? Did you *send* your brother after Hawk?"

Sheriff Richards's eyes became angry slits. He had never had a woman speak so contemptuously to him before, and if Samantha hadn't come from such a wealthy and powerful family, he would have slapped her to the floor for the way she spoke. Instead, he asked bitterly, "How well do you know that Injin? Sounds to me like you and he got yourselves *real* acquainted. That's what it sounds like, if you ask me."

"Well, I didn't ask you, Sheriff, and if you know what's

good for you, you'll keep your damned opinions to yourself!
If you start telling people lies about me, I swear I'll—"

"You'll what?" Sheriff Richards cut in, stepping forward so
that he glared down at Samantha. With his right hand already
on the butt of his revolver, it wasn't easy for him to control
his urge to draw the weapon and hit Samantha with it. "You're
in big trouble, little lady! You had a criminal staying with you,
and a judge might think you was aiding and abetting! That's
against the law! Judge might even put you away for a couple
of years for it."

Samantha's hand was also on her revolver. What angered
her most was that the sheriff's insinuations—his insults—were
absolutely true. Samantha *was* closer to Hawk—or at least *had*
been closer—than anyone knew, or that she would admit to.

"I think maybe you'd better start telling me everything you
know about that redskin," Sheriff Richards said, his insolent
gaze crawling over Samantha's ample bosom. "Maybe you're
one of them girlies that likes the dark-skinned ones." He
chuckled, then wiped saliva from his lips with the back of his
hand. "Is that why you've always shied away from men at the
dances and church socials? 'Cause they weren't the right color
of skin?"

"You worthless pig!" Samantha hissed. She tried to make
herself turn and walk out of the deputy's office. Why should
she stand motionless and take the vicious man's insults? Still,
inexplicably, she couldn't make her feet move. "You think the
worst of everyone only because the worst is in you!"

The sheriff laughed then, openly and scornfully. "Now I
know you was spreadin' yourself for that Injin! Only a bitch
that's spreadin' would—"

Samantha slapped him. Her right hand lashed out, as though
it had a will of its own. When her palm connected solidly with
Sheriff Richards's cheek his head snapped around. When he
looked at Samantha again his gun was in his hand and pointed
at her chest.

"Assaulting an officer of the law's gonna put you in jail," he growled, slowly thumbing back the hammer of his gun.

"Officer of the law? Hardly! You're just a criminal with a badge," Samantha replied.

But despite the brave front that she was showing the sheriff, there was fear in her heart. Whether he was a cretin or not, he was a duly appointed sheriff, whom she had assaulted. Samantha didn't doubt that her family connections could get her out of whatever trouble her temper had gotten her into, but she didn't need the trouble anyway.

"Git your hands up in the air!" Sheriff Richards's eyes were bright with lust and hatred. "Git 'em up high 'cause I gotta search you for weapons before I lock you up."

The thought of Sheriff Darren Richards's hands on her body, touching and defiling her, jolted Samantha's senses. She turned on her heel and walked to the front door of the sheriff's office. Only after she had the door open, and she was standing where people out in the dusty street could see her, did she turn back toward the sheriff. She looked down the barrel of his revolver, knowing he wanted to shoot her, and that only the prospect of witnesses was stopping him.

"You want to arrest me, Sheriff? Go ahead and try. But if you ever touch me, if you ever lay a finger on me, I swear I'll kill you."

Samantha was trembling with fear and rage as she climbed up into the saddle and turned Daisy back toward home. The threats that the sheriff had spoken rang in her mind, and though she tried to think of other things, she couldn't. The hatred, the foul lust, the twisted masculinity that Sheriff Darren Richards represented made her want to rush to her bedroom, close and lock the door, and never come out.

Sonny—damn him straight to hell—was with his woman, whoever that happened to be. Samantha was furious that her

brother was with another woman on the night when she needed
desperately to speak to him.

Several things were absolutely clear to Samantha at that moment. One was that all men were unworthy of her total trust.
Another was that even a woman's brother, no matter how much
he said he promised to be there for his sister, might be with
his lover when his sister needed him. The third was that a
horse was infinitely less likely than a man to disappoint a
woman.

Even Samantha realized her line of thinking was convoluted.

Samantha paced through the long hallways of the ranch
house, feeling restless, furious, and frustrated beyond anything
she'd ever believed possible. The sheriff had enraged her. Most
frightening of all was that Samantha realized that if she hadn't
had the Sanders name to back her up, if she hadn't the financial clout and a brother named Sonny who was willing to kill
to protect her, she would have had to suffer through the des-
picable sheriff's mauling.

Suddenly Hawk's words, spoken long ago, came back to
Samantha. Was it *really* so self-evident that her culture was
vastly superior to his? Even though Hawk had the tendency
to eat and love and live to excess when the opportunity was
there, did that mean that his Sioux culture was vastly inferior
to her own?

All that she'd been certain of was now subject to question.

The peace and contentment that Samantha had known while
she was living among the Sioux was something she had never
forgotten. In the brief time that she had been together with
Aja, she had learned many things. But more than anything
else, she had discovered that it wasn't the hours or minutes a
person spent with another person that was important, but
rather, it was the sense of *oneness* that was experienced.
Samantha had many friends whom she'd known longer than
she'd known Aja, yet she couldn't think of a single one she
truly felt closer to. In the brief time that they'd known each
other, Samantha had spoken more words to Aja straight from

the heart than she'd ever said to any of the friends she had grown up with.

Remembering her vision quest, Samantha went to her bedroom and, after pulling off her boots—what a hideous reminder of the constrictive society in which she lived—she sat in the middle of the bed, crossed her legs beneath her, and closed her eyes. Then she did something that she had never really done before.

Samantha let her thoughts travel aimlessly.

She simply thought, letting her mind move in whatever direction it wanted. Nothing more than that; no action taken whatsoever. All she did was sit alone in a perfectly dark room, close her eyes . . . and look inside herself for the answer to a question she didn't entirely understand and which she didn't completely comprehend.

*Go to him.*

The thought was so startling, was such a revelation, that Samantha's eyes snapped open.

Was she really to go to Hawk after all the things he had said to her, all the things she had said to him?

*Go to him now.*

For a moment Samantha wondered whether or not she was simply experiencing some aftereffect of her vision quest, the one which had been only partially successful. Then Samantha realized that the direct influence of the quest had long since passed. Whatever thoughts going through her head now were a result of her own imagination.

*Go to him, Samantha.*

The voice sounded more clearly in her mind this time. What preparations would be necessary to go to Hawk? Two horses for riding, along with a packhorse. That would be the fastest method of getting to the Sioux camp.

She sat on the edge of her bed, tapping her toes lightly, nervously, against the floor. She wanted to go to Hawk. She knew that now, and accepted the reality of her desire. But did she dare go to him?

Sonny would be furious. Sonny liked Hawk, but not so much that he would turn a blind eye to an open affair. He would be more angry with her than with any of the other things that she'd done that had disappointed him in the past. And Vanessa would give her a lecture as well. Vanessa would tell Samantha how she was a Sanders, and consequently was held up to standards that other people weren't, so she had to always bear that in mind before she acted impulsively.

If Samantha went to Hawk, she would disappoint her family; if she stayed at the Circle S, she would disappoint herself. Which was more important?

As Samantha began changing her clothes, she decided that Daisy would be her primary riding horse. She'd leave the new cutting horse behind. Maybe Billy would have a name for her by the time she returned. And food . . . what food was on hand that she could take with her? The larder was always fully stocked.

Rushing around her room, gathering up some necessary travel items, Samantha wondered: If she rode as hard as possible, how long would it take her to reach the camp?

"You looked tired," Aja said, standing close to Samantha, a hand placed protectively on her shoulder.

"I am. Where's Hawk?" The words were out of Samantha's mouth without her thinking them through very carefully. She took a breath and said to Aja quietly, "I'm sorry. I don't mean to be abrupt. It's just that—"

"That you've ridden hard and fast from wherever you came to see Hawk, not me." Aja patted Samantha's cheek lightly, a gesture more fitting coming from a grandmother than a girl still in her teens. "I understand. I'm just happy to see you again." Aja glanced away for a moment before looking back at Samantha. "Hawk's not here now. Since he came back from your home he's had a difficult time. There have been accusations of disloyalty." Aja closed her eyes, clearly distressed with the lies that

had been spoken about her brother. "It's all wrong, but the false-
hoods hurt anyway. He's fasting now. Or perhaps he's already
on his vision quest. He won't be back with us for a few days."

Aja watched Samantha's shoulders suddenly sag at the news
she'd received. Understanding the news to be deflating, Aja's
heart went out to Samantha.

"He'll be back. I promise he will. Just give him a few days.
And until he does, you'll have time to rest, get into clean
clothes, make yourself pretty for him." Aja eased off Samantha's felt hat, giving her friend a smile of sympathy. "You love
him, don't you? Only love could make a woman push herself
as hard as you have."

In all the time Samantha had spent since leaving the Circle
S in the dead of night, she'd never honestly asked herself that
question. Now that Hawk's sister had put the question into
words, she couldn't avoid it any longer . . . even if the answer
frightened her.

"I don't really know," Samantha answered finally. "Sometimes I think I love him, but at other times I know for certain
that I hate him. I know that doesn't make any sense but—"

"It makes perfect sense. Every woman hates the man she
loves . . . at least a little bit, and at least some of the time."

Samantha's eyes narrowed as she looked at Aja. After a long
silence she said softly, "How did such a young woman become
so wise?"

Aja shrugged her slender shoulders, her smile wide and
guileless. "Would you like to try another vision quest?" she
asked quietly, realizing how close Samantha had come last
time. "You have far to go before you can completely understand the majesty of them."

Samantha nodded. "After I rest it would be good." Though
the prospect of a vision quest was tantalizing, that wasn't the
reason she'd ridden so hard to the Sioux camp. "How long
until Hawk returns?"

# Twenty-four

"Are you ready?" Aja asked.

Samantha looked down into the valley. She could see the camp, see the children running and playing, see the women working. If she could see them, could they see her? *Ida Maka,* Mother Earth, wasn't ashamed of her nudity, Samantha reminded herself. Besides, from this distance she was little more than a pale speck against the foliage.

"If you don't want to go through with this, you don't have to," Aja said, kneeling on the buffalo hide where Samantha sat. She placed a protective hand on Samantha's shoulder. "A vision quest can be a frightening experience. The truth is not always pleasant."

Samantha shook her head as she patted the back of Aja's hand. "No, I'm not afraid of the vision. I just wish it wouldn't take so long."

Aja smiled. "Impatience is not a Sioux trait. Cross your legs now. Sit as I've told you. Close your eyes and then I will leave. I'll be back for you tomorrow."

Samantha angled her face toward the morning sun, closing her eyes. She crossed her legs and sighed, enjoying the warmth of the sun on her naked body. It didn't matter to her that neither Sonny nor Vanessa would ever understand what she was going through, or why. She hoped that the letter she'd written to Sonny before leaving the Circle S would give him some understanding of why it had been necessary for her to ride out

in the dead of night to return to a people who were not her
own.

She had not heard Aja walk away, but that didn't surprise
her; Aja was very nearly as silent in her movements as Hawk
was. Samantha wondered if she could ever learn to be so
stealthy, and just how many traits of the Sioux she could
adopt . . . and then she remembered that she wasn't supposed
to be thinking at all, because conscious thoughts kept the visions from coming.

She inhaled deeply, feeling a sense of serenity pervading
every pore in her body, touching and surrounding her with
such bliss that her mouth curled into a smile. Blond hair and
pale skin be damned. She was becoming more and more of a
Sioux all the time!


Red Wolf felt his anger rising. His hatred was so intense,
he was on the verge of being nauseated. Despite the afternoon
heat, he was alone in his tepee, his fists clenched into impotent
weapons that lacked an object to strike out at, to beat down
and punish.

Perspiration ran down from his forehead, stinging his eyes.
He cursed, using foul, savage words, hating all gods and mor-
tals alike. Surely everyone, even the gods, deserved to be punished for the cruel treatment that Red Wolf had received from
Night Flower.

Two nights earlier, feeling his need for a woman continuously growing stronger, Red Wolf had sought out Night
Flower. She was of an age now where she should choose a
warrior, and her beauty made her a desirable Sioux maiden.
Red Wolf knew in his heart that he alone was man enough to
tame Night Flower's restless spirit.

On that night he had spotted her walking between several
tepees, heading toward the perimeter of the camp. Sensing a
vulnerability on her part, Red Wolf followed her immediately.
He asked himself how far he would go to convince the young

woman to accept him, and even Red Wolf realized the answer
depended upon whether anyone had witnessed him with Night
Flower. If he got her alone in the darkness, far enough from
camp so her screams would not be heard, then he would not
have to stop, no matter how desperately she begged. And when
he was finished, when his pent-up lust had poured forth, he
would silence her forever. If the spirits were generous with
him, the Cheyenne would be blamed for her death, or maybe
the white man.

Night Flower had been walking purposefully. But when Red
Wolf noticed her checking frequently behind herself, he realized she was doing something she shouldn't. His heart began
to pound against his ribs in restless anticipation because he
knew that if he caught the young woman doing something the
tribal elders would not approve of, then he could demand the
satisfaction from her that he otherwise might have to take forc-
ibly from her.

He'd been getting closer to Night Flower, moving farther
away from the tribe's center of activity. Just seconds before
Red Wolf was about to make his move, intending to rush forward and pounce upon her from behind, clamp a hand over
her mouth, and then carry her into the darkness . . . the worst
possible thing happened. Night Flower stopped, looked around,
and then dashed into the sweat lodge. Red Wolf remembered
Hawk was in the sweat lodge and so was certain that Night
Flower knew that the sweat lodge was occupied, and by whom.

Standing alone in the darkness, his jaws clamped in rage,
Red Wolf had stared at the sweat lodge, hatred blinding him
to everything else. Why did Night Flower go to Hawk, when
he already had so many other women wanting him?

Red Wolf's hand was clenched tightly around the handle of
the long, deadly knife in the sheath at his hip. He thought of
rushing into the sweat lodge and killing them both, but he
worried that he might not be victorious even against an unarmed Hawk. Besides, he needed to disguise his crime of murder, not wanting to face the wrath of the elders.

He determined it would be best to wait until Night Flower left the sweat lodge. He would force himself upon her, then kill her. He concocted a vague plan of blaming the girl's murder on Hawk. But as this general plan was forming in his mind, two braves walked by, pausing to look at him, their eyes questioning. At that point, Red Wolf knew that should anything bad happen to either Night Flower or Hawk as they came out of the sweat lodge, he would be suspected immediately.

Frustrated in both his desire for revenge and for brutal passion, he'd walked off into the night, vowing that the day would soon come when all his desires would be fulfilled . . . no matter how many people had to die.

Rising from his sitting position, shaking away thoughts of the recent past, Red Wolf now knew he had to leave his tepee. It was dreadfully hot, especially with the flap closed. His body glistened with sweat. When he stepped outside he squinted because of the brilliant sunlight. He waited several seconds for his eyes to adjust, then looked around at the camp.

To his left, working near their tepee, were two of Walking Elk's wives. When they saw him they snickered between themselves, making Red Wolf's anger grow just a little hotter, his desire for violence just a little more deadly.

What did they find so funny?

About to confront the women, Red Wolf felt a hand on his arm. He twisted sharply, shocked that anyone could walk up on him without being heard. Anger had blurred the sharp edge of his perceptions.

"Red Wolf acts like a guilty man," Dull Knife said, taking a step back so that he could scrutinize the young warrior. "Why is that? What have you done that makes you behave like a man whose guilt weighs heavily upon his shoulders?"

*You pathetic old man,* Red Wolf thought. And though he tried to keep his feelings from showing on his face, he wasn't entirely successful.

"I think Dull Knife is mistaken," Red Wolf said finally,

aware that the Sioux chieftain wouldn't leave until he'd received an answer.

"Perhaps. And perhaps Red Wolf knows that he has told lies about another warrior," Dull Knife countered, almost completely without emotion. "I have believed some of the tales you have told, and my belief is not to my honor. You spoke with such conviction! Such concern for your people rang in every word you spoke! But now I am wiser, and I see that you are perhaps more clever than I thought you to be. Are you a clever man, Red Wolf? Are you clever enough to destroy a man you hate with words when you cannot destroy him in battle?"

Red Wolf now was completely ill. Looking at Dull Knife, he saw the old man harbored more suspicions about him than just those he was willing to discuss. All of Red Wolf's lies, all the tawdry tales and veiled innuendo regarding Hawk's conduct and character, were now coming back to haunt him. He saw in Dull Knife's face the unraveling of his plan to destroy Hawk, which would have provided the opportunity for his own ascension in the tribe.

"Red Wolf is cunning to say nothing," the Sioux chieftain said. "It is words that have put his name in disfavor among the elders. Perhaps it will be silence that will make Red Wolf's name no longer sound like a curse."

Dull Knife walked away, having spoken his piece. Red Wolf stood frozen in place. How had the old man figured out that the stories he had told about Hawk weren't true? At first, when Red Wolf began telling them, the elders had listened carefully to everything he had said, and they had seemed to believe him. And now—this!

A brittle smile of contempt contorted Red Wolf's mouth. He knew that his desire to completely destroy Hawk's reputation beyond salvage had caused him to tell stories that were beyond believability.

How long would it be before his own reputation was in rags? Red Wolf shuddered at the thought of no longer being feared by the young braves, no longer looked up to by the more gullible of the maidens. Everything he had lived for was suddenly coming apart . . . and it was all because of Hawk— Hawk and that golden-haired woman who had ridden into camp again just that morning, the one who looked at Red Wolf with such open scorn. If *she* had only given Red Wolf the passion due him, he wouldn't have had to destroy Hawk's reputation with lies.

Red Wolf walked without seeing where he was going. He was thinking about every insult, every scornful look he had ever received from a woman. All women are evil, he realized then. Every woman, white or Indian, was vile because she had the power to make a man crave her, then refuse to quench the desire she'd stoked.

They should all be punished, every one . . . but the golden-haired woman and Night Flower would be the first to feel his wrath, would receive the punishment they deserved for being women. And when Red Wolf was finished with them he'd move on to Aja.

She deserved punishment as well, though Red Wolf could not say exactly why.

When Samantha was aware that she was no longer hungry or thirsty she felt certain her desire for a successful vision quest would be realized this time. As she lay naked on the buffalo mat beneath the stars, a sense of peace, of inner calm, came over her so slowly and completely that she wasn't at first aware of it.

*It's happening,* she heard, recognizing the words spoken inside her head, as clearly as if she'd spoken them aloud.

*Yes, it is happening . . . welcome,* an answering voice replied.

At first the sound of the voice startled Samantha, but she instantly saw the lovely doe of the earlier quest. There was little in her background that could prepare her for such an occurrence, but communicating with the doe now seemed as natural as eating or sleeping.

*I did not know if I would see you again,* Samantha thought.

*There is much you have to learn, much I have yet to teach you.* The doe sent a sensation of love that filled Samantha's soul.

*Will I ever learn everything?*

The doe paused, her ears twitched, and her tail flicked. Samantha sensed that the animal was considering her answer. *No,* the doe finally answered. *You will not learn everything, but no one ever does. When we have learned everything there is to learn then we will no longer have any need to be.*

*What can you teach me?* Samantha asked. The silence was intolerable now that she had finally made contact with the doe.

*Patience is one thing I will teach you,* the doe replied. *You must learn that before you can learn anything else.*

Samantha understood that she had been told that her impatience wasn't a good thing. She had promised herself a dozen times that she would learn to be more patient, though she'd never really meant to keep the promise. This time she suspected it would be different.

*What else must I learn?* Samantha inquired.

The doe raised her head swiftly, looking away. Samantha saw that the doe was always cautious—aware of her surroundings and the dangers that might be lurking just out of sight—yet she didn't seem continually edgy. How could she exhibit a perpetual awareness of the dangerous world she lived in but no intrinsic fear of that world? This, too, Samantha realized, was a lesson she would do well to learn.

*As important as learning is un-learning. You know in your heart what is right for you. Listen to your heart. That is where you will find the truth. But your truth will be tested often. Love will help you through those tests. Believe in yourself. Listen to your heart. But if you seek the truth, you must know that there is a cost.*

Instantly, all of Samantha's fears came to the fore. She'd

long believed that everything had a price, that nothing was truly free. She was profoundly disappointed to discover that this encounter, this vision quest, also had a price that she must pay.

*What must I pay?*

*You will learn that in time,* the doe instructed. *Listen to your heart. It is in your heart that you live, and it is a voice from the heart that will keep your love alive.*

There was a rustle in the bushes, and Samantha looked but couldn't see what had caused the noise. When she turned her mind's eye back to the doe all she saw was the animal's white tail as she leaped lightly between two trees and disappeared into the woods.

Samantha came out of her meditation and sat up, crossing her arms over herself, instantly self-conscious of her nudity. But when she looked around the hillside she affirmed that she was alone and had been undisturbed throughout the night.

To the east, the first rays of morning sunlight were just showing pink and yellow on the horizon. Samantha pushed fingers through her hair, smoothing it away from her forehead. She rose slowly to her feet and stretched her arms over her head, working the tightness out of her muscles.

She had thought that if her vision quest had been successful, she would feel overjoyed, as though she wanted to celebrate. But now that she'd had her vision, she didn't feel overjoyed. That was too much of a surface emotion to truly express her feelings. Even now, as she looked far down into the valley at the Sioux encampment, she could remember everything that the doe had said to her, each little morsel of wisdom, along with the puzzle that she'd left with Samantha.

*A voice from the heart will keep your love alive.*

That could mean any number of things, Samantha realized. But she wasn't afraid. She refused to feel fear. Furthermore, the doe had given her words of wisdom that she would be foolish not to follow. She walked around slowly, enjoying the feeling of the grass beneath her bare feet. She didn't go without her boots often enough, she decided. Looking back at the camp, she saw several thin spirals of smoke coming from the morning campfires. The people moving about were just specks in the distance, but Samantha felt a little uneasy looking at them while she was naked.

*I am with Ida Maka,* she remembered, as all uneasiness vanished completely. She wiggled her bare toes into the grass and rolled her head slowly around her shoulders, turning to warm herself in the morning's pleasing sunlight. *There is no reason for me to hide or be ashamed when I am alone and at one with Mother Earth.*

Her clothes were hanging from a limb of a tree nearby, but Samantha felt no need to go to them. For a moment she considered returning to the camp instead of waiting for Aja, but she dismissed this as impatience. She would wait for Aja, and together they would return to the camp . . . Samantha would consider that her first lesson in patience.

When Hawk stumbled it took several steps before he completely regained his balance. His legs were weak, and exhaustion weighed upon him as though he carried a boulder on his shoulders.

He'd gone three days and two nights without food or water. After purging his soul in the sweat lodge he'd gone to speak with Dull Knife, who had suggested a vision quest. Hawk had walked alone into the hills, where he'd danced and chanted until he dropped exhausted to the ground. The visions came to him, one after another, each one more powerful and cryptic, more mysterious and enlightening, than the one before it.

He'd never before had visions so powerful, nor had he pushed himself so hard to receive them. His mouth was hideously dry, and even when he ran his tongue around his lips he couldn't moisten them. There was simply no more saliva left in him. And though he had always tended to be gaunt, his leanness was heightened greatly from his fasting; his ribs displayed the muscles in his stomach, shoulders, and chest in stark relief. Only the inherited darkness of his skin kept the remainder of the bruises from being visible.

Hawk had hoped that the visions would bring him peace, would return to him the clarity of thought he'd known prior to Samantha's entrance into his life. But the visions hadn't brought him peace of mind, though they had given him understanding. For that reason, he was enormously grateful for Dull Knife's firm insistence that he go on a quest.

The understanding Hawk found was to put the memory of his mother, and the bitterness she had brought to them both, behind him. He had to bury the bitterness as a man would bury a deceased love one and, once buried, never speak of it again. Only then, by burying his anger, would he be able to look forward to the future with unclouded eyes. If he continued to cling to his anger, he'd never see the beauty of *Ida Maka* surrounding him, nor would he see the beauty in the people who populated his world. His past, he realized, was still painfully with him.

The visions had taught him something else: that Samantha wasn't to be blamed for what his mother had done. Samantha was white, wealthy, and rebellious, just as Hawk's mother had been . . . but that was where the similarities ended. For Hawk to blame Samantha for his mother's transgressions would be as irrational as Samantha blaming Hawk for her father's absence in her life.

Hawk made his way back to the tribe. So engrossed was he that he didn't notice Red Wolf striding purposefully to intercept him at the outer edge of the encampment.

"Why have you not run away like your coward friend Crow?" Red Wolf taunted aggressively.

Looking up, Hawk said nothing at first. It was obvious his old enemy was spoiling for a fight, and though Hawk might have welcomed the opportunity to give Red Wolf the beating he so richly deserved, he knew that he was now too weakened by hunger, thirst, and sleep-deprivation to successfully battle Red Wolf.

"I am no coward, Red Wolf, and you know it," Hawk replied.

He spoke much more softly than his enemy. There were several young maidens and squaws nearby, and Hawk knew how impressionable they could be. He had no desire to make himself look weak in front of them, nor did he want to do anything that would make Red Wolf appear strong and manly.

"I am tired," Hawk continued. "Go away now. If you must talk to me, speak when I am not recently arrived from a vision quest."

Hawk started walking again, but Red Wolf moved to cut off his path. A dull ache began in Hawk's stomach, and he felt as he had when his hands had been manacled behind his back and Sheriff Darren Richards had been about to beat him.

"You have called me a liar," Red Wolf said, speaking louder than before.

The youngest of the maidens in camp, he had learned, were the most likely to be easily impressed with overt displays of strength. Hawk was a most formidable warrior, as everyone in the tribe knew, and to defeat him in front of young maidens would make Red Wolf appear virile, superior, manly.

"That is an offense that you must answer for. What have you to say for yourself?" Red Wolf demanded.

When Hawk looked into Red Wolf's eyes what he saw there frightened him. He'd always thought that Red Wolf was an evil man, but a man nevertheless. Now, when he looked into Red Wolf's eyes, he saw nothing at all, not even the slightest spark of humanity.

"You are an evil thing," Hawk whispered, shocked that he had not truly understood before how vile the man was.

Red Wolf nodded subtly so that only Hawk saw the movement. The slight curl to his lips was identical to that of a rabid hound who had taken to killing for pleasure. Though Red

Wolf's one hand lay on the haft of his knife, the other hand ever so slightly motioned Hawk closer, daring him to try to return to the tribe.

"You are a very brave man," Hawk whispered sarcastically, calculating his odds of winning in a fight against Red Wolf.

He did not like his chances. He wore only a loincloth and moccasins, and he did not even have his knife with him. And, of course, he had been badly weakened by the vision quest. Red Wolf had none of these disadvantages. Even under the best of circumstances, Red Wolf was a formidable foe. Hawk doubted he had any chance at all of surviving a fight, especially not a knife fight.

"But you are only brave," Hawk noted, "when I am very weak. Isn't that so, you spawn of a maggot?"

Red Wolf chucked hatefully. He knew who his parents were, even though he did not respect them. "Brave talk for a bastard," he replied, keeping his voice down now because he did not want the maidens watching and listening to hear what he was saying. "Do you even know who your father is? Your mother spread her legs with every warrior whose path she crossed."

The words bit into Hawk's heart, and their truth burned inside him. He glanced quickly at the young maidens standing nearby, wondering whether or not they thought Red Wolf was somehow heroic for what he was doing now. He wanted to lash out at Red Wolf, seeing him for the menace he represented to the tribe as a whole and to the young maidens nearby who did not understand the extent of his immorality.

"Be a warrior," Hawk challenged, looking Red Wolf straight in the eyes. "Meet me in one day. Just the two of us. We'll settle our hatred with fists or with knives, whatever you choose."

Red Wolf shook his head slowly, and he took a step closer to Hawk. "What did you call me, bastard of a white whore?" he shouted, making sure that the maidens could hear.

A wave of revulsion swept over Hawk. Though he realized

that Red Wolf required all his attention, he could not resist glancing over at the young maidens tanning elk and deer hides. All they had heard was Red Wolf's incensed declaration that he had been insulted, and even though Red Wolf's reputation had already been besmirched throughout the tribe, the young women now regarded him as a brave man willing to stand up to a hero of the tribe to defend his own name and honor.

"Death would be too merciful for the likes of you," Hawk said under his breath.

Red Wolf attacked without warning, lashing out with his right fist and then his left, striking Hawk rapidly in the jaw and cheek. Hawk staggered backward but did not drop to his knees, as he was certain Red Wolf had wanted. He braced himself for Red Wolf's next attack, but it did not come. Though hatred and rage begged for Hawk to rush his enemy, logic told him that he was too weak to fight effectively.

"You are a smart man," Red Wolf said loudly, turning and grinning triumphantly at the young maidens who were watching in rapt attention. "You know when you are not man enough, and you shrink away like a gopher to his hole. Run away now, little man, or I will step on you!"

"You vile maggot!" Hawk hissed. He no longer cared if he was defeated in battle. He could not listen to such insults without responding.

"You two disgrace the ground you walk on!" Dull Knife interrupted, stepping forward, and even though he did not raise his voice, his words had the impact of gunshots.

Red Wolf walked away immediately. Hawk stood there, all but quivering with rage, forced to face the angry Sioux elder.

"Did you think he was worth your anger? Was Red Wolf sufficient to make you want to disgrace yourself?" Dull Knife asked, shaking his head slowly. "Do not allow such a warrior to force you into behaving as badly as he," the elder continued, his tone softening. "If you had fought and won, you would not have impressed anyone but those young maidens, and they are too young to truly know anything at all. That is why we as elders do not allow them into a warrior's tepee."

"Yes, Dull Knife." Hawk's voice cracked with his disgrace. He was not angry with the elder, only with himself for allowing himself to be manipulated into precisely the disadvantageous position Red Wolf had wanted.

"The golden-haired maiden has returned," Dull Knife announced. When Hawk took a step toward camp the elder placed a firm hand on the young warrior's shoulder to stop his progress. "You are weak, hungry, thirsty. If you saw her now, you would impress her as little as you impressed Red Wolf. Think through your actions before you make them, Hawk, and you will be a leader among your people rather than just a lone hunter the squaws long to hold."

Hawk was shocked at the candor with which Dull Knife spoke. Did the old man know all of his secrets?

"Go now, and do not see the golden-haired maiden," the elder said sternly. "She has traveled far and fast to see you. Do you want her to see you as you are now?"

Hawk almost began to thank Dull Knife but then silenced himself. He knew that the older man didn't want to receive any compliments.

"I accept your wisdom, old one," Hawk replied finally, each word ringing with respect. "In time, if the spirits look kindly upon me, I will see *Ida Maka* our people, and myself, as clearly as you do."

Though he wanted greatly to rush to Samantha, Hawk walked away, believing Dull Knife's wisdom was worth following.

Moving slowly toward his tepee, Hawk rubbed the side of his face, testing the swelling that Red Wolf's fists had caused. But despite this, a smile creased his mouth. Samantha had returned to him, and though Red Wolf had undoubtedly impressed several very young maidens, he had embarrassed himself in front of Dull Knife. The maidens would soon forget the incident; Dull Knife never would . . . and neither would Hawk.

There would come a day when he would seek his revenge, and when that time came he would be as merciless as Red Wolf had shown himself to be.

the baby bear, but supposedly it ... and nothing ... would leave.

... there would ... but ... he realized and then ... that he would die quickly, since he had been ... snow shoes.

# Twenty-five

Samantha slowly dressed in her Levi's and cotton shirt. She wished she had Aja's old dress, even though it was too small for her. Now that she was among the Sioux again, she wanted to be dressed like them.

Samantha was putting on her boots when she felt something in the breast pocket of her shirt. Her brows pushed together in confusion. Straightening, she reached inside, and even before she saw what the pocket held she began to smile. Extracting an oblong quartz crystal, she turned it over slowly in her hand, watching the way it reflected the early morning sunlight.

"My power stone." She closed her fingers gratefully around the crystal.

Closing her eyes, she uttered a small thanks to whatever powers had given her the stone. She still didn't know exactly what to believe about Sioux spirituality, but her mind had opened now. Nothing limited her thoughts, feelings, or perceptions.

"Good morning!" Aja called, walking into the clearing, leading Daisy and another horse with her.

Beaming, Samantha waved at Aja, who returned a knowing smile.

"You had a vision!" Aja cried. Samantha triumphantly held up the crystal between her forefinger and thumb. Suddenly, sunlight reflected through the crystal, causing a rainbow to form across her chest. "And there is your natural name," Aja said confidently. "Rainbow Heart is what you will be called among the Sioux."

"I like it," Samantha replied. She rolled the name over in her mind, listening to the music of the words. Rainbow Heart. Sonny would never understand it, and neither would Vanessa . . . but the truth of the name was so clear to Samantha that she wanted to sing it out to all the world.

"You'll be happy to know that Hawk has returned to camp from his own vision quest," Aja said. She saw a light come into Samantha's eyes and knew exactly what it meant. "He's sleeping now. Or maybe he's still eating. It was a very difficult quest for him. He's lost a great deal of weight. It will take some time for him to recover completely."

Samantha managed to contain her joy at the news. She was disturbed to hear that the vision quest had been so much more arduous for Hawk than for herself. "But he'll be all right soon?"

Aja nodded. "Better than ever, I should think. I didn't have much time to talk with him, but I could tell that he had learned much in the quest. He was going to speak with Dull Knife about it."

"Am I expected to speak with the elder?"

Aja shook her head. When women went on vision quests, then sought advice or clarification regarding what they had seen, they went to elderly women of the tribe.

"I'm famished." Samantha walked toward Daisy. "Will there be anything to eat when we return to camp?"

"Yes. And your belongings have been put into my tepee," Aja said. "Hawk will have to sleep elsewhere." Even as Aja spoke the words, she suspected that the affection between Hawk and Samantha was such that they would not be separated for long, no matter what obstacles the tribe elders put between them.

Hawk brought the gourd to his lips and drank deeply. He felt strong and clean, inside and out. After sleeping for several hours he'd filled his stomach with venison stew. Each mouthful made him feel stronger.

The memory of what Red Wolf had said continued to haunt Hawk, though he was trying to push the incident aside. Since Red Wolf was more of an animal than a man, Hawk now realized, it was absurd for him to worry about anything the man said. Logic told him this, but his masculinity which had always sought to defend his name and honor, wanted to seek out Red Wolf and give him a well-deserved thrashing.

Night Flower approached him. When Hawk's gaze met hers she smiled softly at him. "Did you enjoy the stew?" she inquired as, shyly, she knelt beside him. "I made it myself."

"You will make a proud brave fat if he is not careful," Hawk joked, and Night Flower's smile brightened.

"Someday," the young girl replied quietly. "But I will wait until I am certain that I am ready to be a brave's wife." She took the empty bowl and gourd from Hawk, and though her fingers lingered briefly against his during the exchange, she was no longer trying to seduce him. "You are a kind man," she whispered, aware that there were many people near as she spoke. "What I did—"

"Sh-h-h!" Hawk replied. "You must not be embarrassed at what you did. I was flattered then, and I am flattered now . . . but you were not ready for a warrior then, and you are not now. When you are ready you will know it in your heart, and you will look into the eyes of a good and decent brave who will hunt often to see that you are never without food. He will teach your male children to be good braves."

"That will happen?" Night Flower wanted, with the simplicity of heart of only the very young, to believe every word Hawk said.

Hawk nodded, and Night Flower walked away with the empty wooden plate and gourd. As he watched her go, he felt pleased with the way he'd handled her intrusion into his sweat lodge. He'd done the proper and manly thing, yet had not tarnished Night Flower's self-esteem as he denied her passionate request.

Hawk rose slowly to his feet. It felt good to wear nothing but Sioux clothing, he decided. The moccasins, loincloth, and elk-hide vest did not constrict his movements. There would be no buckskin trousers for him while he was in camp, he decided, and no revolver in the holster, either. He would still carry the prized revolver with him only when he left the safety of the tribe.

Out of the corner of his eye he noticed Night Flower talking to Kahlia and Shining Lake. Shining Lake was a shy maiden a year older than Night Flower, and Kahlia, her older sister, was a widow. Hawk noticed Kahlia and Shining Lake look in his direction, then confer quietly between themselves. Hawk knew they were talking about him, and he wondered what it would be like to accept both sisters as wives. Neither woman was terribly attractive, though not hideous to look at, both would make wonderful mothers, and neither would cause disgrace to a warrior, or to his family.

A grin tugged at Hawk's sensual mouth as he considered the irony of going so long without taking a wife, and then taking two of them at the same time. He heard soft laughter coming from the trio of women. Now he was certain they were talking about him.

Perhaps Night Flower had even confessed to her friends what she had done, and how Hawk had responded. Kahlia, whose husband had died in battle the previous winter, was experienced enough to give the younger women advice about warriors, and what a squaw should expect from a brave. Where Shining Lake looked away the instant Hawk's gaze touched her, Kahlia looked back at him boldly, and the smile that touched her lips was a subtle invitation.

Hawk was happy to be thinking of a woman other than Samantha, and especially pleased to be thinking of women in the plural again. After Samantha had intruded into his life she'd taken over all his thoughts, been the center of all the romantic and libidinous urges that were so much a part of his nature.

As Hawk walked on, he fantasized about Kahlia and Shining Lake and the kind of life he could expect to have with them. The smile that had tickled his lips suddenly vanished. He couldn't make up for Samantha's loss with two women, or even three or four.

"Damn her," Hawk whispered, unconsciously slipping back into English when he thought of the blue-eyed vixen who had turned his thoughts, his life, even his identity upside down.

After his vision quest, Hawk had determined that it was foolish to hold Samantha responsible for the life his own mother had led. This epiphany had made her seem less threatening. Nevertheless, he also had decided that only a Sioux woman should be his wife. A golden-haired woman bearing his children would carry the blame for seducing him from his lifelong goal: a tepee filled with Sioux children, who would bear Sioux grandchildren, with the stain of white blood eventually eradicated. To deviate from that goal now would be to allow his passions to control his life. Hawk wouldn't allow that to happen.

Though Samantha had been in camp for a day and a half, Hawk had not seen or talked to her. Now he was looking for her, though only a moment earlier he hadn't been completely aware of it. He walked purposefully, his head high, his shoulders squared, the confusion and doubt that had plagued him completely gone. He knew exactly what he expected of himself, and what the tribe expected of him. This certainty of purpose gave him confidence, and allowed him to seek out Samantha without fear that her physical attractiveness would melt his resolve.

First he would deal with the reason she'd returned to the tribe. He would handle her as gently and painlessly as he had Night Flower. He would explain why he and Samantha could never see each other again.

Once he'd finished with Samantha, he'd search out Red Wolf

and beat him into unconsciousness. Hawk would suffer the punishment the tribe elders deemed necessary and appropriate for the aggressive offense, but Red Wolf *had* to answer for his insults. Hawk was strong and rested and had eaten well; now he demanded justice.

At last his mind and his body were in an accord he hadn't known since the first time he'd kissed Samantha.

There was no vacillating possible; Hawk had no doubt that his decision was not only best for him, but also for Samantha and the tribe.

He spotted Samantha standing beside Aja outside his tepee. She was wearing a Sioux dress that fit her perfectly. Her hair was a golden spray of color cascading over her shoulders, in beautiful disarray. Her legs were long and lovely, bare to above the knee, her feet encased in moccasins.

When she noticed Hawk stopped dead in his tracks at the sight of her, she smiled at him. She did not rush into his arms, as he'd expected her to. Any woman riding that far to see a man ought to at least run to him when she finally saw him, Hawk thought. The trouble was, Samantha wasn't just any woman. In fact, as he was continually surprised to discover, she wasn't like any woman he'd ever known in his life.

To Hawk's frustration she was, at that moment, more appealing than she'd ever been before. Her poise, combined with her own distinct beauty and enhanced by Sioux clothing, distorted his thoughts and conspired in the blink of an eye to make him forget his carefully planned speech—the one that would send Samantha on her way back home.

A thousand different things struck Hawk about Samantha at that moment, but most of all it was her serene smile and the blue of her eyes, brighter, more beguiling, than he had remembered. The sight of her took his breath away, and even though he was a warrior too experienced in matters of the flesh to be rendered mute and breathless by the sight of a woman, that was precisely what had happened.

*Damn,* he thought. *Damn.*

"You're here," he said, glancing at his sister. Aja knew that the look meant she was to leave, but she refused to go.

"Yes, I've come to see you," Samantha replied, looking up into Hawk's face with an expression unfamiliar to him.

She had changed, Hawk could tell, though he couldn't say how.

"Are you feeling better? I understand your vision quest was rather arduous," Samantha said. "You pushed yourself very hard . . . but then, you always do, don't you?"

Hawk didn't recognize Samantha's tone of voice, either; calm, confident, unusually mature and poised. He would much rather have had her giddy with excitement at seeing him. He tried to remember the vicious things she'd said to him at her ranch, but he couldn't think of a single cruel remark she'd ever made. Only the sound of her soft, passionate sighs as they made love came to mind. Then he remembered the scent of her hair as he held her head lightly on his shoulder, and that intoxicating look she would give him when she was eager to put an end to their loveplay—when nothing would satisfy her but Hawk's thrusting passion.

"Samantha went on a vision quest," Aja announced, injecting herself into a conversation that really didn't include her. She'd never seen her brother so thoroughly flustered by a woman. "You can tell it was successful just by looking at her, can't you?"

"I can tell," Hawk agreed. Then, as a flicker of memory reminded him of his original resolve, he added, "Please, Aja, leave Samantha and me alone now. There's much that we must discuss."

Aja pouted, looking to Samantha for support. When she saw none forthcoming, she turned and walked slowly away.

"She's a lovely girl," Samantha said once Aja had gone. "It surprises me how mature she is, how much of life she understands at such an early age. I wish I could say as much for myself at that age."

Hawk still felt disoriented standing alone before Samantha.

He couldn't think of a single thing he'd intended to tell her. Again he was aware of being watched by the women, young and old, who were paying close attention now that Samantha had returned to the tribe.

"Yes, Aja is lovely, but she's also impulsive." Hawk searched for an appropriately stern tone. "She shouldn't have taught you about vision quests. Whose clothes are you wearing? They are not Aja's."

"No, they're not. I don't know who they belong to. Someone kind, I'm sure. I've met so many very kind people since I've been here."

"You must leave." Hawk forced the cold words out of his mouth. Samantha's calm implacability had become a threat to him, particularly since he felt anything but calm. "I'm sorry if you've ridden all the way here from your ranch, but you've got to go, Samantha. You can't stay."

"And why is that?" When she looked him straight in the eye Hawk looked away.

"Samantha, I must take a Sioux wife. I must. Just as you must find some rich white rancher to marry."

Samantha shook her head slowly, her eyes on Hawk. "No, I don't have to do that. In fact, I don't have to do anything I don't want to do. That's more than you can say, isn't it, Hawk?"

"Don't try to make me angry, Samantha. My mind's made up. There are . . . there are forces stronger than either of us that are at work here. We can't fight those forces and hope to win."

"You may be without hope, but I am not, Hawk. I've never given up on anything. Not on myself. Not on you . . . and not on us." She smiled, as though she knew something that Hawk could never truly understand. "You're afraid, Hawk. That's why you're saying these things. You're letting your fears make you behave stupidly."

Hawk's lips twisted into a scowl. No Sioux warrior who had joined repeatedly in battle could listen to such words from a woman without reacting negatively. "Afraid? Was I afraid when I returned to the Cheyenne and stole their horses? Was I afraid when I went back to them a second time to take back your saddle from them?"

"You are brave and strong when your enemy is a man who wants to kill you, but when you are confronted by a woman who only wants to love you, then you *are* afraid, my darling. There is no other word for it."

Hawk looked skyward and muttered, "Aja never should have taken this blue eyes to my *Hocoka*. It has twisted her mind."

Samantha swallowed her anger, though Hawk's continued refusal to listen to reason was wearing her patience thin. *"Hocoka?* That's a sacred space, Hawk. You thought I didn't know, but I do. Aja taught me. I even had my vision quest—the first one, anyway—where you had your first one. I've got a natural name now, and there's nothing you can say that will change that. I've been to your *Hocoka*. I've experienced it as my own sacred space, and even your stubbornness cannot take that away from me."

Samantha stepped closer to Hawk, concentrating on his every move, his every gesture. She was oblivious to the women who now surrounded them.

"I will learn your language, Hawk," she said, "just as you have learned mine. And I will learn the ways of the Sioux, just as you have learned the ways of the white man."

"Perhaps," Hawk said, his eyes hard and cold as pieces of ice, "but I *am* both Sioux and white. The blood of both flows in my veins. You cannot say the same."

"You hate and dishonor the blood that flows in your veins, Hawk Two Feather," Samantha replied, sensing Hawk's growing frustration. "You dishonor it by wishing the white blood was not a part of you. Isn't that true, Hawk? How can a man have peace in his heart when he hates what is a part of himself?"

"I don't have to listen to this," Hawk hissed, furious now that Samantha wasn't flustered.

He'd spent much of his adolescent and all of his adult life

able to charm women, able to control conversations with them so that the discussions went wherever he wanted them to go, centered on the topics that he desired. With Samantha he could do neither.

"Such a *brave* man," Samantha whispered, drawing out the damning word for all it was worth.

"If you were a warrior . . ." Hawk countered, his huge hands balled into fists that would have frightened anyone but Samantha.

"If I were a warrior," Samantha replied, an incendiary emotion flaring in her blue eyes, "you wouldn't be so helplessly in love with me."

# Twenty-six

Hawk was walking, and walking fast. He'd begun moving away from Samantha when he didn't know what to reply to her utterly infuriating statement.

He couldn't really love her, could he? What madness that she'd spoken such words!

His eyes were cast down as he walked, and he did not respond when he heard a brave call his name. He did not want to speak to anyone until he could determine whether Samantha was the most tempting liar ever to walk *Ida Maka,* or whether she spoke a truth that he could not bear to hear.

Hawk wanted to talk with Crow. His trusted friend was well versed in the ways of women and, in addition, was very wise. But Crow was still in Fargo. Hawk's mental agitation couldn't wait until Crow returned to the camp. He needed to discuss his problems with someone else; only the venerable Dull Knife was available to provide wisdom and guidance.

He found the Sioux chieftain sitting with several other elders, nibbling on sweet berries, sharing stories of better times for the tribe, when the buffalo herds were vast and roamed far.

"May I speak with you, Dull Knife?" Hawk asked. "I seek your wisdom."

The elder's wizened face creased into a proud, knowing smile. "You do not seek my wisdom; you seek your own. What you want is for me to make wisdom easy for you to find."

Though Hawk grinned, he was still not in a good mood.

"As usual, you are more than correct," he said. He knew that if he did not tell the whole truth to Dull Knife, he would be lying to himself as much as to the elder. The two men walked far enough to find privacy for their discussion. Then Hawk said, "The golden-haired woman is troubling me, and I cannot say exactly why. When I went on my vision quest I saw many things, had many questions answered. I saw in my visions that I must stop troubling myself with thoughts of Samantha, that I must forget her."

"*Forget* her, or stop *troubling* yourself with her?"

"I do not understand."

The old man smiled. "That is why you are here. Now think about my question; think about your vision. Are you to stop troubling yourself with her, or to forget her?"

"The two would be the same . . . wouldn't they?"

"Hawk, I know that your life has been a difficult one. You have searched for a people you could call your own, and I do not know if you have completely accepted the Sioux as your people."

When Hawk started to defend his loyalty to the tribe he was silenced by an upraised hand.

"In some ways our people have been as unkind to you as the blue-eyes have," Dull Knife continued. "You think you can become of pure blood if you have a wife whose skin is dark, and who will give you children who are darker than yourself." The old man smiled at Hawk's expression. "Do not look so surprised. We have talked of you often at the council of elders. We have seen you grow into a worthy warrior, and we know when you are invited into a squaw's tepee. The council of elders has not always been proud of you, Hawk. You are strong and handsome, and the words you say please the maidens . . . but you have not taken a wife, have you?"

Hawk looked away for a moment, wondering if he'd made a mistake by speaking with the Sioux leader. He had not really been seeking advice, he now realized. Rather, he'd hoped Dull

Knife would agree with him when he said that any lingering involvement with Samantha would be a mistake.

"No, I have not taken a wife," Hawk admitted. "I have not found the right squaw, I suppose."

The old man rarely smiled, but his lips curled forgivingly at the corners. "If that is true, it is not because you have not *tried*. How many squaws *have* you . . ."

Hawk gave Dull Knife a look of incredulity. He would not answer this question, and he was shocked that he was even asked it. Then he saw the expression on the old man's face, and discovered, much to his surprise, that the elderly man possessed a sense of humor and was enjoying himself at Hawk's expense. Then even Hawk couldn't resist smiling, actually enjoying being on the receiving end of a friendly joke.

"When a man searches and searches and cannot find, then he is either not searching honestly, or he is searching where what he seeks cannot be found." Putting his hand on Hawk's shoulder, Dull Knife looked up into the young warrior's eyes with a mixture of sincerity and sympathy. "You have not had an easy life, young one, seldom choosing the easy path to follow. Perhaps the spirits have chosen a difficult path for you; perhaps you have chosen that difficult path yourself. It matters not . . . what matters is that you live in harmony with *Ida Maka* and with yourself.

"The golden-haired girl, you think, will bring disgrace to you because her skin is white. But her blood is red, the same as yours and mine," Dull Knife explained. "From what I have heard, the vision quest she experienced was almost as though the blood of the Sioux flowed in her veins. Do not, yourself, be so much like the white man that you blind yourself. Will hating her make you a more powerful warrior? Answer that question for yourself, and then you will know the path that you must follow."

"Yes, Dull Knife, I will do as you suggest," Hawk said.

But he was not content, his heart and soul not at ease. The words that he'd heard were ones he hadn't wished to hear. He had expected Dull Knife, who had fought many wars against the white man, to warn that Samantha was tempting but dangerous, both for himself and for the tribe. Instead, the wise elder had suggested that Hawk let his heart guide him, rather than his lifelong prejudice.

Confused, yet wanting desperately to be considered an honorable Sioux warrior, Hawk thanked Dull Knife once again for his time and his wisdom and walked away. Never was a proud and noble warrior so adrift between two cultures, neither of which accepted him completely. For once in his life, not only was Hawk Two Feather unsure of what was expected of him by his tribe, he no longer had a clue what he expected of himself.


Hawk sat alone, leaning back against the base of a tree, looking at the tepees in the valley below. He chewed on a piece of pemmican and sipped from a skin of cool water. Though his eyes were open, he saw nothing at all. His mind had traveled back to the recent vision quest, and to the strange and tantalizing scenes that had unfolded before him.

What had they meant? There had been an eagle in a hawk's nest, and he'd seen the eagle and hawk together in other places several times during the course of his visions. But what did it mean?

Hawk considered how angry he'd become when Dull Knife had chosen to be cryptic rather than enlightening. Or perhaps Dull Knife was just trying to be annoying by not giving Hawk the answers he sought.

*No,* Hawk thought, *Dull Knife is not cruel just to be cruel. He speaks, and when he speaks, he teaches. Whether I learn from his teaching is up to me. I must find the answer that cannot be given to me.*

Since Dull Knife's intention had not been to make Hawk angry, it had to have been to teach him something . . . but what?

Never before in his life had Hawk felt as though he was being attacked from all sides by an enemy he couldn't see or understand. Red Wolf had challenged and insulted him in front of the squaws when Hawk had been physically incapable of defending himself. Then he had been thoroughly prepared to tell Samantha that he had no room in his life for her. Rather than the histrionics for which Hawk had prepared himself, Samantha had calmly and confidently called him a coward and said he didn't know what he was talking about. And lastly, when he sought out sage advice from Dull Knife, certain that the Sioux chieftain would proclaim that only a Sioux maiden would truly be worthy of a warrior . . . Hawk had been given a totally different view of the problem.

An eagle in a hawk's nest. But there was something else . . . what was it? During the vision something that had seemed perfectly natural at the time had appeared to Hawk, but now he realized it as something with much to teach him. But what had it been?

After he'd relaxed for awhile the image came back to him, and, as it unfolded, struck him as being profoundly odd. Was his memory of it accurate? An eagle in a hawk's nest . . . and there, just peeking up over the rim of the nest, was a young dove. . . .

What did it mean?

Instinctively, Hawk began moving away from the base of the tree, twisting sharply on his knees, all his senses knife-blade keen even before he realized why he had moved at all.

Red Wolf, who had been approaching him from the high side of the hill, stopped short.

"Attacking from behind!" Hawk spat the words. "I expected no less from you!"

Having already risen to his feet, Hawk wished he had his revolver with him. How he wanted to shoot Red Wolf down like a rabid animal! Hawk flexed his arms and legs, testing his strength, hoping he had regained enough to withstand this formidable foe. Without even a knife, he felt naked.

Red Wolf approached slowly, his eyes judging Hawk, gauging how much strength had actually returned to the warrior who'd been his enemy for too many summers, too many winters.

"I came here to be with *Ida Maka*." Hawk watched Red Wolf's every movement. "Why are you here?"

"You scurried away from me before, when I could not follow you," Red Wolf taunted, inching forward.

As he walked, he put his hand on the haft of his long, deadly knife. He did not intend to kill Hawk; to do that wouldn't accomplish what Red Wolf desired. He wanted to crush Hawk, to batter his beautiful face with his fists until it was no longer beautiful, then show the squaws his ugliness. They had for so long thought that Hawk was handsome and strong, but Red Wolf would see to it that he was no longer appealing to them. When he was finished he would prove his supremacy, to the squaws and to the rest of the tribe.

"Do you expect me to run?" Hawk asked.

Red Wolf wanted to continue to taunt Hawk, but the truth was that he did not expect him to run. He'd known his nemesis long enough to hold no illusions about the cowardice of which he'd accused Hawk earlier. He watched Hawk move, a little surprised at his nimbleness. Hawk had recovered from his fasting and his vision quest quickly.

"No, Hawk," Red Wolf finally answered. "I expect you to bleed."

Hawk had known that Red Wolf would attack and wasn't surprised by his brutality. With a rabid-sounding growl, Red Wolf rushed forward, flaying wildly with his fists. Hawk easily blocked the initial blows intended for his head and, pivoting on the toes of his right foot, he aimed a short, chopping punch to Red Wolf's kidneys.

The blow never landed. Red Wolf's attack, blunt and crude, had been a ruse, nearly working to perfection. As Hawk almost landed a crushing strike to his body, Red Wolf spun sharply, swinging in a wide arc with a huge right fist. Targeted for

Hawk's temple, if the blow had connected it would have sent Hawk into unconsciousness instantly. Instead, Red Wolf's knuckles slammed into the side of Hawk's jaw, snapping his head around, causing his knees to buckle momentarily. Brilliant lights exploded in his head, and Hawk very nearly went down, but a voice warned him that if he did, Red Wolf would show him no mercy. So he rose up again, adopting a defensive posture to protect himself against the onslaught that he was certain would follow immediately.

Once he'd hurt Hawk, Red Wolf became impatient. He rushed forward, hands outstretched, going for Hawk's throat. He was certain that if he got a stranglehold on the warrior, he could choke the life out of his enemy. He sought to kill now, no longer satisfied with maiming.

But Hawk ducked as Red Wolf attacked. He brought his left fist sharply sideways, batting aside Red Wolf's clutching hands. Stepping close, Hawk threw a short, chopping punch to Red Wolf's stomach. The breath gushed from his lungs, and before he had a chance to inhale, Hawk followed up the first strike with a left fist to the solar plexus.

Hawk stepped back. Still dazed from the blow to his jaw, Hawk could see that Red Wolf was also badly hurt, perhaps even more than he was himself.

"When the elders say that you must be killed I will ask to kill you myself." Hawk blinked his eyes, hoping his vision would clear soon; hoping, too, that Red Wolf would not realize how dazed he was. "You are like a dog who eats the poison berries. You attack those who would defend you, so it will be an act of mercy to put you out of your misery."

Hawk had seen what happened to any animal who'd eaten the purple, poisonous berries that grew in the Badlands. The animal first went mad, attacking whatever was near him. In a day or two, after the poison had worked thoroughly through its system, the animal writhed in hideous pain, dying a slow, painful death.

In his heart Hawk felt that Red Wolf, the vile warrior who

loved to kill, was afflicted with a similar poison. Hawk wanted to believe that *something* was responsible for Red Wolf being the way he was, rather than him simply being evil from birth.

"The elders . . . are weak . . . old men," Red Wolf gasped, slightly bent over, pretending not to be hurt. His expression was strained with hatred and pain. "They . . . would not dare . . . banish me! None have the courage to . . . give the order to send me to the spirits! They hate me, but they fear me . . . and it's their fear I've wanted all along!"

The two combatants began circling each other slowly. Red Wolf searched Hawk's face, wanting to see signs of fear. Instead, he saw a slight swelling where his knuckles had struck, but no fear. Hawk had recovered much more quickly and thoroughly than he had anticipated.

"I had intended to beat you down . . . then spit on you," Red Wolf said, circling slowly. "You have become strong again. . . ." He pulled out the long, deadly knife from the sheath at his hip. Never without the knife, now he was prepared to not only kill but torture and brutalize as well. "And because you are not weak, I will have to kill you here and now. The coyotes will have eaten your carcass before anyone finds you."

Hawk's mind raced as he watched Red Wolf slowly twisting the knife in his hand. Without a weapon of his own, Hawk realized that he was in grave danger. But even as he stared at the knife, he still found it hard to believe that he actually needed to raise a weapon against a member of his own tribe.

As he circled Hawk, Red Wolf's confidence grew. He had made a mistake in his fight against his lifelong enemy, but the error had cost him nothing more than a little breath and some pain. In the process, he had learned much about Hawk and what it was he must do now. He *did* want to beat Hawk. Ruining his face for the fawning squaws would bring only half the satisfaction.

This scenario could be played out only provided Hawk posed no serious threat to Red Wolf in personal combat. Red Wolf had come to realize that Hawk was a legitimate threat,

which reinforced the course of action that would satisfy Red
Wolf: He would kill Hawk, and hope the coyotes and wolves
ate the corpse, here on the hills, before it was found.

Hawk had made enough enemies during his lifetime; no
individual would automatically be assumed to be the culprit.

Red Wolf watched Hawk, looking for a defensive weakness,
but found nothing.

"How was it with Night Flower?" Red Wolf decided on a
new tactic. "Did she bleed when you took her?"

Hawk tried to block the words from his mind, understanding
that if Red Wolf made him lose his temper, he would become
a less formidable foe. Warfare was best waged with cool detachment, not with anger. Just the same, Hawk couldn't help
wondering how Red Wolf knew that Night Flower had come
to him seeking passion.

"Was she good, Hawk? Or did she lay there like dead
flesh?"

Hawk clenched his teeth. Red Wolf wasn't worthy of speaking the name of such a gentle and loving maiden.

"You speak the words of a fool," Hawk said, balancing
lightly on the balls of his feet. He kept himself ready to spring
upon his enemy if the opportunity presented itself, or leap
away if Red Wolf attacked with the knife.

"Do I? I saw her go into the sweat lodge." Red Wolf's dark
eyes glittered with hatred. He wanted to make sure his deadly
blade found flesh and spilled blood on his next attack. "Everyone knows you'll lay with any squaw."

Hawk felt a small sense of relief at Red Wolf's answer. All
Red Wolf had seen was Night Flower going into the sweat
lodge. Everything beyond that was speculation from him, and
faulty speculation at that.

"Tell me about the golden-haired girl." Red Wolf decided
to escalate his psychological attack. His eyes were on Hawk's
hands. Though he held a knife and Hawk did not, Red Wolf
had experienced Hawk's lightning reflexes. It would be particularly ignominious to die by one's own knife. "Is she like

so many of the blue-eyes? I've had many of them, and they are all alike."

Red Wolf noticed with pleasure the tightening of the muscles in Hawk's forearms. Mentioning Night Flower had gotten only a slight response from Hawk, but mention of the white woman had provoked a much stronger reaction, despite Hawk's efforts to hide it.

"Have you turned her into a cow yet?"

"You maggot!"

It took all of Hawk's willpower to keep from rushing Red Wolf. Only the big, deadly knife in Red Wolf's hand kept Hawk back. Some of the Sioux men had adopted the white man's language in ways that were insulting to the white man. They spoke, thus, of white women in terms of cattle, with "heifers" being white women who had not yet borne a child, and "cows" those who had. It was a vile insult used mostly by braves who visited brothels filled with white women.

"What does she like? Tell me, Hawk. Does the golden-haired whore drop to her knees for you?"

Hawk couldn't listen to Red Wolf demeaning Samantha any longer.

In the end, the fight between them had little to do with experience in warfare; rather, reflexes and strength would determine the outcome, despite Hawk's disadvantage at being unarmed.

Rushing forward just as Red Wolf lashed out with his knife, Hawk dodged, enabling him to catch Red Wolf's wrist. They wrestled to the ground, and Hawk grabbed Red Wolf by the throat. Instantly he began pummeling his foe, smashing his fist time after time into Red Wolf's mouth, nose, and chin until his enemy dropped his knife. Once the knife was out of the contest, Hawk used both fists against his foe. Though Red Wolf delivered a few bruising punches, the early damage he had received could not be overcome. Then, when Hawk suddenly landed a bone-crushing punch to Red Wolf's nose, his head snapped to the side, his eyes rolled back in his head, and the brave lapsed into unconsciousness.

Gasping for breath, Hawk stood up on shaky legs and looked down at his vanquished, unconscious foe.

*I should kill him.* Hawk believed with absolute certainty that, had Red Wolf won, he would have cut Hawk's throat. *Sooner or later, he'll cause great pain and suffering for the tribe. It would be better for everyone if I killed him now. Then the women will be safe.*

Hawk looked on the ground at the knife, which would have been used to kill him had he not been just a little quicker, a little stronger, than Red Wolf. Hawk picked it up, slowly turning over the weapon in his hands, wondering how many times Red Wolf had used it against a helpless enemy. How many women had died from this knife? The question itself sent a shudder through Hawk. He looked down at Red Wolf and saw the blood flowing from both nostrils. Hawk had broken his nose, smashing its broad bridge. Red Wolf would never again be thought of by any squaw as a handsome brave. He would always carry the smashed and flattened nose as a reminder of the fight he'd had with Hawk.

*I should kill him now,* Hawk thought again. *Now, while I have the chance. I'll regret it if I don't.*

But he couldn't do it—not like this, anyway. Red Wolf's life had been an insult to all the Sioux, but Hawk could not make the decision to end it. That decree, should it be made, would come from the Council of Elders.

Turning, Hawk tossed the knife deep into the trees, then slowly headed back toward the encampment. He had to speak with Samantha. He did not know exactly what he would say once he found her, but he knew he had to speak to her.

# Twenty-seven

The great, body-wrenching sobs had finally ended. Samantha sat with her legs folded beneath her, her face in her hands, trying to even her breathing. She had no more tears left to shed.

She had never truly considered the possibility that Hawk wouldn't want her back, that he wouldn't be happy to see her . . . that he wouldn't see the world as she saw it. It was so logical: They were *meant* to be together. Why couldn't Hawk accept that simple, unalterable truth?

She looked around the tepee, which suddenly seemed so foreign to her. *Of course it looks foreign,* she thought angrily. *You don't belong here!*

Samantha wiped the tears from her eyes, determined to get her spirits back and her thoughts in order. The question she had to ask herself next was one she didn't want to answer: What to do now?

Samantha had to think about it. She had, after all, ridden away from the Circle S ranch in the dead of night. The note she'd left probably prompted more questions than answers. Next, she rode hell-bent-for-leather through the countryside to the Sioux encampment, where she'd recently discovered she was not welcome. At least not welcome by the man who'd made her act so foolishly.

But when exactly did this foolishness begin? Clearly, when Hawk entered her life, her rock-solid willpower became a negotiable thing. Ironically, after Hawk had rescued her, he himself had ensnared her, showing Samantha Sanders that she wasn't as impervious to the charms of men as she'd always believed.

She stopped her pacing for a moment and looked herself over. The dress she wore, made of leather (she could not say with any confidence whether elkhide or deerskin), fit her perfectly. She'd truly enjoyed wearing it until only moments earlier, when she decided that she was in unfriendly territory.

"To hell with him!" The tone of her voice in the tepee sounded in her ears. For hours now the only sound to reach her ears was that caused from her own weeping. Now, a second time, more forcefully than the first, she said, "To *hell* with him!"

Samantha felt better saying the words. How unfair that Hawk should have such power over her life, that he could—with a simple wave of his hand—dismiss her completely, relegating her to nothing more than a passing memory! He might *think* that he had the power to simply snap his fingers and make her leave, but that was just . . .

"Just what?" Samantha asked herself aloud.

She didn't have any rights in the tribe, and she knew it. She would be allowed to stay, but only as long as they wanted her to. All her wealth, the social connections that the Sanders name provided, meant nothing at all. Here she had to stand, wearing a borrowed leather dress unadorned with even a single strand of beadwork anywhere on it, upon her own merits. But her own merits, which she'd thought sufficient for Hawk were, quite simply and bluntly, insufficient. At least he felt they were.

For an instant Samantha thought the tears would return, but she held them back. Tears were for weak women, and she wasn't weak. A huge, empty, aching hole had been cut into her heart by the man she'd been silly enough to fall in love with . . . but that didn't mean she was weak. Foolish? To be sure. Unwise? Undoubtedly. Naive? Naturally. Weak? Not in ten thousand years.

Samantha felt her confidence returning, which was a good sign, she decided. Just a moment earlier it had seemed as

though everything she had ever accomplished had been rendered worthless because Hawk Two Feather had said she
couldn't stay in camp, that he didn't want her to be a part of
his life. Embracing her anger, she clenched her fists and
pounded them against her thighs as she paced back and forth
in Aja's tepee.

"To hell with Hawk Two Feather!" Samantha's voice grew
louder still. "He's a damn fool if he doesn't know a good
woman when he sees one!"

Samantha paced faster and faster, as if marching into the
future, refusing to let any man—even Hawk Two Feather—
dominate her life, her thoughts, her emotions. She had problems, she knew, but she could overcome them.

*What would the people of Deadwood think?*

She sighed, knowing her reputation in Deadwood was ruined. They would never forgive her for the behavior she had
exhibited the last time she and Hawk were in town. Though
she didn't much care what the people thought, she was concerned that her behavior might reflect badly on her family.
However far outside the boundaries of decency she had
stepped, Samantha didn't want her brother and sister to suffer.

"To hell with the people of Deadwood!" Samantha longed
to tell the fine people of Deadwood exactly what they could
do with their opinions. Now she had the perfect excuse to
write them all off forever.

From outside the tepee came a voice. Samantha stopped her
pacing and asked, "Yes?"

"Samantha, Hawk's here." The nervous tension in Aja's
voice could not be missed. "I think you'd better come out
here."

"No!" Hawk said loudly, forcefully. "I'll go in there!"

Samantha's heart stopped in her chest.


Hawk put a hand on his sister's shoulder and pushed her
aside. Still charged with the adrenaline that had been produced

by his fight with Red Wolf, he was behaving rashly, and he knew it.

"I don't want to be disturbed," Hawk told Aja.

"Don't send her away." Aja implored. She'd never seen her brother in such a state, and she was frightened.

"Silence," Hawk said, without raising his voice. He stepped into the tepee, pausing at the sight of Samantha, and announced, "I have come to talk."

"Good. Just be prepared to listen."

Her reply took him back, and he moved no more deeply into the tepee. Looking into Samantha's eyes, he saw not only that anger glittered in their blue depths, but that they were also slightly red-rimmed from crying.

"Perhaps . . . perhaps you would like to talk first," he offered.

Putting her hands on her hips, Samantha glared at him. She no longer trusted anything Hawk said, and her distrust showed. Finally she shook her head.

"You've come to me." The tone of her voice indicated that she'd backed down all she could, cried as many tears as her eyes held. "You talk first. When you're finished I'll talk . . . and when I'm finished we'll be finished talking. That seems fair enough, doesn't it?"

Hawk opened his mouth, but no sound came out. Fair? Indian braves never negotiated with women. It was clear that she already had her mind made up, and that nothing he could say or do would change the way she felt.

"I fought Red Wolf." The words were hardly out of his mouth when he realized they had nothing to do with what he wanted to say.

"Why? Not to impress me, I hope," Samantha replied. "I've always found violence abhorrent."

"Actually, it did have something to do with you, in a way," Hawk replied. "He was talking about you, saying things about you."

Samantha looked at Hawk, impressed with how he looked,

unimpressed with what he was saying. There had been a time, when the renegade Cheyenne braves were surrounding her, that she had needed violent behavior from Hawk. But that time had come and gone.

Hawk felt his anger growing and didn't have a clue as to whom he was really angry with. Himself? He accepted that. He'd made enough mistakes in the last weeks to fill a lifetime.

"You shouldn't have come here," he said. Once again, the instant the words were out of his mouth he wished he hadn't said them.

"You've already told me that."

Hawk looked at her, half-expecting her to say something more, perhaps toss out an insult or try once more to make him see that he should keep her in his life. She didn't do any of those things, and because she didn't, he felt disoriented.

"Yes, I have," he said finally, not knowing what else to say. He rubbed his jaw, which was slightly swollen from the fight.

"Yes, you have. So what else have you got to say for yourself? It's clear by looking at you that you've got yourself in a state. It's safe to assume that there's a reason for it. Perhaps you'd be kind enough . . . for a change . . . to let me in on it?"

"I didn't come here to listen to your sarcastic comments."

"I'm sure you didn't."

"Are you going to keep them up?"

"Only as long as you haven't got anything worthwhile to tell me."

Hawk looked Samantha in the eye and for the first time wondered if she was worth all the trouble she'd caused him. From the first moment she'd entered his life, when he'd ridden into the clearing to save her life from the white outlaws, she had been nothing but trouble to him.

The problem was, she was also something more. She was the epitome of excitement. She was the only woman who had ever captivated his mind as well as his body. He thought about

her even when he wasn't with her, and that was something
that just didn't happen to Hawk Two Feather.

And she wasn't a Sioux. Worse than that, she was white.
Samantha Sanders was what the tribe had always thought of
as the enemy, what Hawk had both publicly and privately considered a demon. She was everything he found tempting,
everything he despised . . . and he loved her anyway.

"I suppose you'll have to leave," Hawk said.

Samantha continued to look straight into his eyes, but again
Hawk broke the connection.

"Marry me." Hawk's eyes opened wide, and for a moment
he looked around, wondering who had spoken such nonsense.
A second later he understood he was the only person talking.

Samantha looked at him quizzically, wondering if she'd
heard him correctly. "What did you say?" she asked finally.

Hawk closed his eyes for a moment. *Is that what I want?*

"Marry me."

He looked into Samantha's beautiful blue eyes, taking her
small hands into his. Suddenly the enormity of his words
struck him. But as he looked deep into her eyes, he knew that
if he didn't make her his wife, he would regret it for the rest
of his life. She had vexed, tantalized, and tormented him . . .
but she had made him feel more alive and joyous than anyone
else. He couldn't let her ride out of his life a second time.
He'd left her once before, and he'd never again let that happen.

"Marry me, Samantha. I don't care how or where, just
marry me. I want you to be my wife."

So shocked was Samantha that she wondered if Hawk was
under a spell of some sort, a trance, or perhaps the influence
of his vision quest. Maybe he'd been struck in the head in his
fight with Red Wolf and it had addled his brains.

"What did you say?" she asked, a slight tremulous quality
to her voice.

"I said I want you to be my wife." Hawk squeezed her
hands tighter. He hadn't expected to ask Samantha to marry

him, but now that he had, her hesitancy in giving him an answer was most unsettling.

"You want me to be your wife. That isn't exactly the same as wanting to be a husband." Samantha tried to pull her hands out of Hawk's but he held them too tightly. She wanted to step away from him to think clearly; the influence of his handsome features made logical thought so difficult.

"Of course it is."

"No, it's not. Some men want wives, but they don't want to be husbands." Samantha was all too aware of Hawk's profligate past, of his reputation with women, women of all colors. She wouldn't sit idly by while her husband shared his passion indiscriminately.

"I want you to be my wife, Samantha. I want to be your husband." Hawk, suddenly aware that in his nervous tension he was squeezing Samantha's hands too tightly, relaxed his grip. He raised his hands slowly to gently cup her face, his palms and fingertips lightly touching her. "Say you will marry me, Samantha. Make me the happiest man in the world."

"In a church?" Samantha ears were ringing, and she felt as though she was in a daze. This was what she had always wanted, she now realized, yet now that the moment was here she could hardly make her mouth form the words.

"In any church you want," Hawk replied.

And that was all that Samantha really needed to know. As long as she could have a church wedding, then surely his sentiments had to be sincere. She stepped closer to Hawk, twisting her arms around his middle, pressing her cheek against his chest. "I don't care about the differences between us," she said softly. "I know our life together is going to be difficult, and that many people won't approve of what we're doing . . . but I don't care. I want to be with you, Hawk. Not just for a little while, but for always . . . and that's all that matters to me."

Feeling his hand stroking her hair, hearing the soft murmur of his love words, Samantha knew she had made the right decision. She had chosen love. She had fought that love, and so had Hawk, and still the love remained.

Whatever anyone else thought of her marriage to a Sioux warrior was immaterial; she had followed the guidance of her heart, and her heart wouldn't lead her astray.

## Twenty-eight

Throughout the ride from the Sioux encampment to the Circle S Ranch, Hawk had been planning what it was he would say to Sonny. Once Samantha realized that Hawk intended to ask Sonny's permission to marry her, Samantha's fury began to boil. She believed her marriage was nobody's business but her own. But Hawk, distinctly aware of the many transgressions he was committing by simply *wanting* Samantha to marry him, insisted that at least some semblance of protocol and decorum should be maintained.

Now that the two men were sitting face to face, brandy snifters in hand, Hawk had serious doubts about whether Samantha's brother could be made to see reason. The cold look in Sonny's eyes suggested he could not.

"Once more?" Sonny asked. He sipped his brandy, not believing his ears had betrayed him so completely.

"I said, I would like to marry your sister, and I'd like your blessing."

"And if I say no?" Sonny asked, shocked by the idea of having a Sioux warrior for a brother-in-law.

"Then Samantha and I will get married anyway." Hawk's tone was like granite. Polite enough to ask Sonny for his blessings, he would not be so polite as to allow for an unwanted answer. "Don't be mistaken, Sonny; I'm not really *asking*. I'm actually warning you. Samantha and I *are* going to be married. Nothing and no one can change that. I'm just trying to be as polite as I can about this . . . under the circumstances."

Sonny looked at Hawk critically, carefully. Had it been another man, he might have taken him by the jacket collar, hoisted him out of the chair, dragged him out of the library and down the hall, and then tossed him out of the ranch house. *Nobody* talked to Sonny Sanders that way . . . except Hawk Two Feather.

"You're determined to marry her, aren't you?"

Hawk nodded his head, his gaze never leaving Sonny's. Though his posture appeared casual, his nerves were taut, ready for action should the need arise.

"Do you know what I'd do to anyone who came in here and talked to me that way?" Sonny asked.

"I can make a pretty good guess what you would try to do," Hawk replied, letting Sonny know that he didn't back down from threats.

"I suppose that's got to make you a pretty brave man . . . but then, a man would have to be brave to want to marry Samantha." Suddenly Sonny realized the unintended double entendre, and a twinkle came to his eyes. He sipped his brandy and tried to decide what his father would say in his place. Nothing in all of Sonny's life had prepared him for this moment. Part of him wanted to lock Samantha in her bedroom and keep her there; another part realized that she'd never find anyone who was even half the man that Hawk was. "Does Samantha want to marry you?"

"You can ask her that for yourself," Hawk answered, seeing the new brightness in Sonny's eyes and sensing his acceptance, but not willing to believe it entirely until he heard the words. "But I think she does. She says she does. I know she can be impulsive, and sometimes she says things that she doesn't completely mean, but she loves me and I love her, and that's what is most important."

Sonny sighed. A long, weary sigh. Though his shoulders sagged, there was a smile on his lips and a brightness in his eyes. He had been protecting Samantha for so long, it was difficult for him to relinquish his hold. But if ever there was a man who could keep Samantha safe from harm, it was Hawk.

"It's a strange world we live in, isn't it, Hawk?"

"Yes." Hawk wanted to smile, but he wouldn't allow himself to do so until he received Sonny's answer.

"I don't suppose there's a damn thing I can say or do that will stop the two of you from getting married."

Hawk shook his head slowly, his lips curled downward at the corners. He'd been concerned that Sonny might try to bribe him into leaving Samantha. And though he didn't seem about to do that, Hawk still couldn't be sure.

"Then as long as there isn't a damn thing I can do about it anyway, I don't suppose I have any choice but to give my blessing," Sonny said. Now that the words were finally out of his mouth he smiled broadly. "You know, I'm going to have a hell of a time finding a priest who'll marry the two of you." Sonny rose from his chair and crossed the room to where the brandy decanter sat on the liquor cart. Unstopping the bottle, he brought it over to Hawk and poured a hefty measure into his snifter. Then, filling his own snifter, he said, "What the hell! I've never had a drink with a future brother-in-law before. Why don't we have a few too many drinks and a couple of good cigars, and find out what we're both made of, eh?"

Hawk looked at the brandy in the snifter. It was a lot of liquor, and though he suspected that Sonny might just be trying to get him drunk so he'd let his defenses down, he decided to meet the challenge.

The cigar was as good as Sonny had promised, and by the time Sonny had refilled Hawk's snifter again, the two men were talking and laughing like lifelong friends.

Samantha was mad enough to kill. Maybe not kill, exactly, but certainly mad enough to knock her brother's and her lover's heads together.

Standing outside the closed library door, she heard the raucous laughter coming from inside. The telltale signs of alcohol consumption were unmistakable, as was the smell of cigar smoke. An hour earlier, when Samantha had knocked on the door, she had been told that she wasn't allowed in. Her brother had broken into a peal of laughter, accompanied by, if Samantha was not mistaken, Hawk's muffled laugh. Samantha had returned to her bedroom to fume about the situation.

In the first place, she'd told Hawk not to ask for Sonny's blessing for their wedding. Samantha felt she was old enough to make her own decisions. But instead of following her wishes, Hawk had barricaded himself with Sonny in the library, where they had been for almost three hours now.

Able to contain her fury no longer, she returned to the library and pounded on the door. "Damn it all, open the door this instant!" When there was no response Samantha impulsively kicked the door. Since she was barefooted, her agonized gasp created more noise than her toe had on the door. Sonny opened the door, his eyes a bit glassy from brandy, a smirk on his lips as Samantha danced around on one foot, holding her throbbing toe in her hands.

"I hope you're satisfied," she snapped, her fury now reaching a fevered pitch.

"Why blame me? I'm not the one who kicked the door."

"You're the one who locked it!" Samantha growled. As she limped past her brother into the library, she delivered a sharp elbow to his ribs.

Hawk was seated on the sofa, his long legs stretched out and crossed at the ankle. He wore his buckskin trousers and leather-fringed shirt. For an instant, Samantha was stunned at how perfectly natural he looked in the library, with a brandy snifter in one hand and a cigar in the other.

"I suppose you think this is all very funny, don't you?" she asked, still limping up to the sofa, looming over Hawk.

"I confess, there are elements of humor that have not completely missed me," Hawk replied quietly, a smile curling the edges of his mouth.

Samantha had never before seen Hawk having had too much to drink, but she could tell from the look in his eyes that the brandy was affecting him . . . and that he was feeling romantic. This observation did absolutely nothing to lessen Samantha's combative mood.

"I'd like to talk privately with you." Samantha's teeth were clenched in rage. That the men weren't taking her anger seriously only fueled her fury.

Sonny wobbled somewhat as he crossed the room and set his snifter down on the liquor cart. "You're on your own, my friend." His words were a little slurred. "You might just as well get used to this now. My sister has a hellish temper when she gets her feathers ruffled."

A deadly look from Samantha hastened Sonny's retreat from the library. When she turned back to Hawk he was getting to his feet. The penetrating look in his ebony eyes suggested familiar pleasures . . . which Samantha, this time, had no intention of experiencing.

"You think it's funny to sit here with my brother, the two of you men discussing my life, deciding what it is you will and won't let me do!" Samantha waggled a finger under Hawk's nose. "Well, I've got some news for you, Hawk—news you're not going to want to hear."

"Then let it wait until later." The smooth texture of Hawk's tone made Samantha wonder exactly how powerful her conviction was. "Why waste the remainder of this perfectly fine evening discussing that which, as you've already pointed out, I do not want to hear?"

Casually, he reached for Samantha, but she slipped away. She knew her own weaknesses, how difficult and sometimes impossible it was for her to remain angry whenever Hawk touched her. But this time would be different.

"No more loving, mister!" Samantha warned. She glanced away from Hawk to the door, and noticed that her brother had closed it behind him. She didn't want her brother to hear what she was about to say.

"What?" Hawk looked at Samantha skeptically. How well he knew her passionate nature, the desires she was capable of feeling! Wasn't it a little late for her to be taking a vow of celibacy?

"I said no more loving. Not one little bit. Not until we're husband and wife."

Hawk stopped his slow advance. His brows pushed together and he turned his face slightly to the side, peering suspiciously at Samantha.

"You can't mean that."

How long could it take to arrange a church wedding? He didn't want to be deprived of Samantha's charms until then.

"I *can,* and I *do!*" Samantha answered, and now she was the one who was smiling. "Want to make my decisions for me? Fine! Go ahead! You and Sonny can sit in here and decide my whole life for me if you want to, and drink until your eyeballs fall out for all I care! But here's a little something for you to think about . . . you're not touching me, not kissing me, not even being alone in the same room with me until you and I are legally wed."

Samantha turned then, striding purposefully to the door. She couldn't let Hawk talk to her for long because if she did, she knew that soon he would be touching her, and then there would be kisses and more, and then her speech will have meant nothing at all.

"You can't mean that," Hawk said again when Samantha had reached the library door.

"Oh, lover, I most certainly do." She smiled triumphantly—and a bit wickedly—at him, sensing that she had won an enormous victory, and that from this point forward he would pay closer attention to her wishes. "Sleep well. I'll see you in the morning." She tossed her head back, laughed heartily, and left the library.

As Hawk made his way to his bedroom, he pondered the possible problems caused by his being a Sioux warrior wanting to marry a white woman. A priest had taught Hawk how to

read and write. Would another priest be open-minded enough
to officiate at a wedding ceremony? And just exactly how determined *was* Samantha to keep Hawk at arm's length until
they were married?


Red Wolf eyed the council, unintimidated by the suspicions
of the elders who thought him a troublemaker. For every elder
who disliked him and refused to believe his words, there was
one on his side, listening carefully to everything Red Wolf
said, nodding occasionally in agreement.

"We mustn't allow ourselves to become weak, dull, diluted."
Red Wolf, speaking slowly and clearly to the old men, looked
around the large tepee, feeling his confidence growing. "We
have suffered greatly in the past, suffered from the white man
and his ways. And what does Hawk do? He takes a white wife!
Is he here now, teaching her our ways so that she can act as
a squaw should? No, he is not. He is with the white man!
Does he hunt to feed his own people? He does not! He rides
in and out of camp without so much as a word to anyone!"

"That isn't true," Dull Knife interrupted. "Hawk talked with
me before he left camp with the golden-haired one. He explained that she has ways that he must follow."

"Yes, she has ways . . . but what of *our* ways? Does he
think of that? No, I think not. Does he care that there are
women and children here who must be cared for, who need
food in their bellies and tepees that are warm and safe?"

The effort to control his rising anger stiffened Dull Knife's
old, lined face. "He has given us much money," the elder reminded, a tightness in his words indicating his roiling emotions. "With that money blankets can be bought. Much good
can come of it."

Red Wolf sneered, as though the thought of accepting money
from the white man was, under any circumstance, abhorrent.
Only Dull Knife, who had long ago realized the avaricious

heart that beat in Red Wolf's chest, was fully cognizant of the warrior's hypocrisy.

"Why do you come here, Red Wolf? Why do you say these things about one of your own?" Dull Knife asked quietly. "What do you seek by saying such things to us?"

"I seek a stronger people," Red Wolf replied without a moment's hesitation. Prepared for the question, he was enormously pleased with the affirming response he saw on the faces of many of the elders. "I seek strength! Can you call a warrior who takes a white woman as his wife strong? We have been fighting the white man for years, and now Hawk sleeps in the bed of a white woman! What warrior can know this and not be ashamed for Hawk? What warrior can know his shame and not turn his eyes downward in disgust?"

The elders were nodding. Most of them were, anyway, and that was enough for Red Wolf to consider himself victorious.

"I do not doubt that you seek strength, Red Wolf. I do not doubt that you seek power." Dull Knife looked at the warrior as though seeing him for the first time. "I do not know for whom you seek the power—for your people . . . or for yourself?"

Spreading his hands, Red Wolf smiled and looked at the elders. No need to answer aloud, he knew; the looks he received from most of the elders told him they found his concerns about Hawk's loyalty valid.

An hour had passed since Red Wolf had spoken with the elders. In that time he'd felt the heat rising in his blood. He had discredited Hawk, at least partially, and soon his revenge would be complete. Hawk had bested him in combat, and for that offense he would suffer greatly. Hawk would be a man without friends, without a people, without a home. But even if all that happened, it still wouldn't be punishment enough for Red Wolf. There must be something more, a greater price still, that Hawk must pay.

Red Wolf hadn't really planned in advance how great a price he intended for Hawk to pay. It wasn't until he had noticed Aja heading away from camp, moving toward the hillside where the berries grew fat and sweet, that he fully understood the penalty Hawk must pay for besting him at every turn.

Now, from a safe distance, Red Wolf followed Aja. With each step he took, he could feel his heart beating just a little faster, feel the heat in his blood become just a little hotter. Aja's smooth flesh would be the perfect balm to satisfy Red Wolf's fury. She was young and beautiful, her mixed-blood heritage making her skin lighter than other maidens in the tribe. And now she was headed away from camp, walking in her usual carefree, exuberant stride.

As Red Wolf followed her, he glanced around, making certain that no one else was watching him. The spirits had at last chosen to be generous, for they were directing Aja to the hills, where she would be alone . . . where Red Wolf could feast upon her tender flesh and make her pay dearly for his misfortunes.

But once Aja was out of camp, and Red Wolf about to follow her, a voice called out to him. Startled, Red Wolf wheeled toward the voice, his hand instinctively moving to his hips, where his knife used to be. But his hand remained empty; he had been unable to find his knife after being knocked unconscious in his fight with Hawk. His heart was pounding fast with excitement and guilt, which he tried to keep from showing in his expression as the old man who had called out to him approached.

One of the elders was following him, seeking further explanation regarding Hawk's danger to the tribe. Though Red Wolf was not in a mood to continue the discussion, he had little choice in the matter, especially since the old man was clearly an ally against Hawk.

Though Red Wolf answered the old man's questions, it took all of his willpower not to glance in the direction in which Aja had gone. When the curious old man had finally heard as

much as he wanted, Red Wolf discovered that Aja had completely disappeared into the trees.

A cruel, feral smile curled his lips. So she had disappeared!
He would hunt her down as he would any other animal that
he intended to devour to sustain his life. He would prove his
superiority over Aja—and over her brother—by tracking her
down, by taking his pleasure with her, and then by silencing
her, once and for all!

Dull Knife could not say why he felt the need to follow
Red Wolf. The warrior had merely left camp to go to the hillside . . . but there was something different in Red Wolf's step,
in the way he moved and held his shoulders, that gave Dull
Knife a feeling of unease.

Red Wolf was far away, almost at the lower edge of the
treeline, before Dull Knife had gathered his horse and headed
out of camp. He was an old man but still nimble and sure
when riding a well-trained Sioux pony, and he covered the
distance to Red Wolf quickly.

The elder could not be sure that Red Wolf was up to no
good until, at the sound of a horse, he spun around quickly
to face the approaching rider. The expression on Red Wolf's
face clearly indicated guilt, though of what Dull Knife could
not say.

"What are you doing?" Dull Knife asked.

Red Wolf walked another dozen feet, moving deeper into
the trees so that he was completely hidden from the camp, in
case anyone was paying close attention. He was pleased when
Dull Knife walked his pinto into the trees.

"What do you think I am doing?" Red Wolf replied, looking
up at the old man, who remained astride his pinto.

Dull Knife was shocked at Red Wolf's undisguised lack of
respect. "A warrior does not answer a question with a question! He does not speak that way to an elder!"

Red Wolf stepped a little closer, looking up at the old man.

Suddenly it was as though a blindfold had been taken off Red
Wolf's eyes. He saw Dull Knife differently than he ever had
before. Instead of appearing as a feared and respected leader
whose opinion could either make a warrior's life easy or difficult, Dull Knife was just a frail old man, worn down by the
years and the battles of earlier days.

"Why have you come out here? Why have you followed
me?" Red Wolf asked. "What makes a tired old man do that?"

Not even Dull Knife's extraordinary discipline could keep
the revulsion he felt from showing in his expression. No warrior had ever spoken to him in such a manner, with such complete lack of respect.

"You have done all that you could to turn the council against
Hawk," Dull Knife said after a moment. "You have even succeeded . . . for now. But in the end you will not succeed. I
do not know what you plan, but I believe you will fail. You
are evil, and evil will always fail eventually. The spirits will
have it no other way. Now tell me . . . why have you come
out here?"

Red Wolf moved another step closer to Dull Knife. He
looked into the old man's eyes and said, "I've followed Aja
out here. She's somewhere around, picking berries. I don't
think anyone knows she's out here. I don't think anyone knows
you're out here either. I know that nobody knows I'm out
here."

The words, with their underlying meaning, made Dull Knife
feel ill. He had seen men who killed for pleasure, men who
were evil through and through, but he hadn't thought that any
brave of his tribe was one of them. Instinctively, even though
he had not actually fought in years, he reached for the knife
at his hip, his fingers gripping the handle of the weapon.

Red Wolf saw the move and smiled. It made him feel powerful to strike fear in the heart of a tribal elder.

"Where is your knife, Red Wolf?" the elder asked. No warrior would be without his knife, which was both a weapon and

a tool. Red Wolf had a reputation for being skilled in knife fighting.

It was that question that solidified whatever doubts might have been in Red Wolf's mind about the action he was about to take. Had Hawk spoken with Dull Knife, telling the old man about the fight, and that Hawk had taken Red Wolf's cherished weapon? Red Wolf could picture the two warriors, one old and frail and the other young and strong, laughing between themselves about Red Wolf's failure.

"Old man," Red Wolf said, taking one step closer, "you ask too many questions."

Red Wolf moved quickly, decisively. His reflexes were swift, his strength overwhelming. He leaped forward, catching Dull Knife's wrist with one hand, preventing the old man from drawing his knife. With his other hand he pulled Dull Knife off the pinto's back and tossed him to the ground.

Red Wolf did not taunt his victim. He did not toy with him as a cat does with a mouse before the final deadly defeat. Red Wolf used the elder's own knife against him, and when he was done, when he stood triumphant over the corpse of the old man, the laughter that bubbled up out of his chest revealed such sublime joy that tears welled up in his eyes and rolled down his cheeks.

Red Wolf felt the sweat running down his chest. He was gulping air, with a fury burning in his soul and making him clench his teeth so hard, his jaws ached from the strain.

After the ecstasy of killing Dull Knife, Red Wolf realized that he could not let the elder's pinto live. The animal would surely walk back to the camp, which would prompt an immediate search for Dull Knife. Red Wolf couldn't afford that; with the elder's own knife he dispatched the horse as well.

And then, on foot, he set out, searching for Aja. By his reasoning she could not be far away.

But that had been two hours earlier, and the sun was almost

down now. Within minutes he would be plunged into darkness. Somehow, some way, Aja had eluded him, even without trying. Her aimless wandering in search of berries had taken her to areas Red Wolf had not found. By now, with the sun nearly beneath the horizon, she was back at the camp, sharing with the tribe the berries she had gathered, eating and chatting with others before going to her tepee for the night.

Red Wolf cursed the spirits for allowing Aja to escape the punishment he felt she deserved. He wanted to scream at the heavens, but doing that would accomplish nothing. For several minutes he stood at the treeline and watched numerous campfires come to life in the valley below. Aja would be alone in her tepee, now that Hawk had left camp with the golden-haired woman.

Did he dare sneak inside the teepee in the dead of night? Could he get away with entering her tepee with so many others surrounding him? If she made even a single sound of alarm, Red Wolf would be overwhelmed by countless warriors who would swarm over him in defense of the maiden Aja.

How had it all gone so thoroughly wrong? If only he had found Aja in the woods, away from the prying eyes of the camp! Had he found her there, his revenge would have been at least partially satisfied. Aja's body would have been discovered by searchers, along with that of Dull Knife. As a member of the search party, Red Wolf's feigned shock and horror at "finding" the slain bodies of the tribal elder and the young maiden would have confirmed his innocence.

It would have been so perfectly easy, if only Aja had cooperated and allowed Red Wolf to catch her.

Though Red Wolf felt futile hatred welling up in him, he also felt the early stages of a slowly building panic. Dull Knife was no longer a young man who might somehow be excused if he was not in his tepee on a particular night without explaining his whereabouts. As a wise and respected tribal elder, Dull Knife was continually being sought out for advice on all sorts of subjects. His absence might already have been missed.

Red Wolf closed his eyes for a moment, giving himself time
to consider what he had done. It was not really such an offense,
he reasoned, to kill Dull Knife. The old man had lived a long
life—too long, with his continual open contempt for Red
Wolf's behavior. That had to be a serious enough offense for
which to die, wasn't it?

He started back toward the encampment, feeling a little more
confident about the future than he had. Dull Knife had paid
his penalty and in time Aja, too, would pay for her offenses
against Red Wolf. When that was done there would be the
golden-haired girl to think about. . . .


"Come on, Darren, don't let it spoil the whole night," Beth
Ann said as she sat on the bed behind the sheriff and began
rubbing his neck and shoulders.

Beth Ann was the sheriff's favorite prostitute at the Arone
Saloon. He saw her almost every other week, when he had the
money to spend. She knew that he had enough money in his
pocket right now for her, but his mood seemed more inclined
toward heavy drinking than toward sexual satisfaction. But
Beth Ann was confident that she could turn his attitude around.

"That lousy bitch," Darren Richards hissed, slurring his
words slightly. He brought the whiskey bottle to his lips and
took a swig, grimacing as the cheap liquor burned its way
down his throat. "She's gonna git herself hitched to that
stinkin', murderin' redskin!"

"Don't let that worry you none, darlin'," Beth Ann purred.
She leaned closer, pressing her breasts against the sheriff's
back. Her goal was to turn his thoughts away from Samantha
Sanders's upcoming wedding and toward herself, the willing
woman currently in bed with him. "What about you and me
just havin' ourselves a gay ol' time? One of those bounce-off-
the-walls great ol' times?"

Sheriff Richards mumbled something beneath his breath,
completely ignoring Beth Ann even as she played her hands

over his shoulders and chest. She leaned away from him, looking at him from behind, doubting now that she really wanted
to be with him.

Though the sheriff was one of her regulars, he was a brutish
man, often harshly physical to the point of being violent when
they were together in bed. On two occasions he'd demanded
her professional services, then refused to pay her. Since he
wore the town sheriff's badge on his chest, there wasn't much
she could do to stop him, and there was no one to complain
to, either.

If it hadn't been for her sister's pressing financial concern—
the second one this year—caused by Gerald, her improvident
husband, Beth Ann wouldn't have urged the sheriff on. But
she needed the money, and business had been slow for the
past couple of days.

Yes, Sheriff Richards was a repellant customer, but he was
one that Beth Ann knew and understood, and he generally presented no problems she couldn't tolerate.

"Forget about her. She's not worth it," Beth Ann purred.

"You talk too much." The sheriff took another swig.

Beth Ann recoiled from the comment. It wasn't that she was
insulted; in the past she'd been spoken to much more insult-
ingly by the sheriff and hadn't taken offense. What scared her
was that the last time the sheriff had said something like this,
he had followed it up with a backhand across the mouth that
sent her spinning to the floor. She'd been left with a fat, bloody
lip that curtailed business considerably for the better part of
a week.

Beth Ann almost spoke back to the sheriff. He carried a
badge and a gun, but that didn't mean he was better than she
was, she reasoned. Furthermore, it was her firm conviction
that she was no worse than the men who rented her passion
and they had no right to look down their sanctimonious noses
at her. Speaking out against the sheriff, however, was not an
idea that lasted long in Beth Ann's mind. She had learned that,

as often as not, it was best to let sleeping dogs lie, and the sheriff was a dog if ever there was one.

"You're right, as usual," Beth Ann said, with just the right amount of solicitous regard for Darren Richards's delicate sensibilities. "Instead of me doin' all the talkin', why don't you jus' tell me every little thing that's on your mind? Jus' unburden yourself to Beth Ann, an' let her share your troubles."

Sheriff Richards looked over his shoulder, confusion showing in his eyes. Beth Ann was good, but usually only in bed. Now she seemed to be displaying actual concern for him, and this was surprising, rather pleasing . . . and a little suspicious.

"Why is it you're such a curious little bug all a-sudden like?"

Beth Ann smiled, batted her lashes, glanced away briefly, and then back to the sheriff. "I just don't like to see you upset," she said, monumentally pleased with her performance. For the first time in her life she began to seriously wonder if she could make more money with her mind and her ability to manipulate men's emotions than she could using her body and satisfying their lusts.

"Is that a fact?" the sheriff asked, smiling. He couldn't remember anyone actually liking him for who he was. He pulled loose several buttons on his shirt and tried to relax as Beth Ann once again began kneading his back and shoulders. "It's that Sanders girl that's causin' all the trouble. She's gettin' married to a redskin. I know the fella. Stinkin' redskin is what he is!"

"They're all stinking if they're redskins, if you asks me," Beth Ann added, getting into the spirit of the conversation.

"Isn't that a fact!" the sheriff said, grinning now, enormously pleased with Beth Ann's attitude. "Anyway, I know for a fact that it was that redskin who kilt my brother."

"You do? Then why don't you go an' arrest him?"

"Well, I know I should, but I don't know what I can tell the judge. You see, when you're a sheriff and a sworn officer of the law, you gotta do things jus' so. It ain't jus' anybody that can do it, you know."

"Don't I know!" Beth Ann exclaimed, moving close enough to the sheriff once again so that he could feel her breasts against his back. "Tell me more. I want to know it all."

"It's the Injin that's got me all outta whack," Sheriff Richards continued. "I jus' know he kilt my brother, and now he's gonna marry himself all that money, and he's going to be a rich man. It jus' don't seem right to me that there should ever be such a thing as a rich redskin, 'specially not a *really* rich redskin!" The sheriff twisted suddenly, his eyes dark and dangerous. He grabbed Beth Ann's upper arm so hard that she knew instantly she'd have bruises. "You ain't never let a redskin touch you, have you? I jus' couldn't live if I knew I'd done it with a whore that done it with a redskin."

"No, of course not, Darren," Beth Ann said, managing to smile weakly. "What kind of lady do you think I am?"

After a moment the sheriff turned around, and only then did Beth Ann breathe a sigh of relief. She had, in fact, slept with several Indian men. Her priorities ran more toward the color of a man's money, rather than the color of his skin. But she knew that when Sheriff Richards said he couldn't live with himself, what he really meant was that he would kill her if he discovered she'd slept with an Indian.

The vitriol continued, with Sheriff Richards vowing an assortment of violent acts upon Samantha Sanders, the Indian she was about to marry, and several of the more respectable residents of Deadwood. Beth Ann listened carefully and talked little, only occasionally asking questions.

She carefully monitored the level of whiskey in the bottle from which the sheriff swigged. Shortly after it was completely empty, and just before the sheriff was snoring loudly in her bed—and thereby preventing her from bringing anyone else from the saloon up to her room—Beth Ann was told the real reason the sheriff was so furious about the upcoming wedding of Samantha Sanders and some Indian.

Apparently Sheriff Richards had beaten the man and now was concerned that the Indian, with the Sanders wealth behind him, would come looking for revenge. Yes, Sheriff Richards was concerned about the disappearance of his brother, and he held the Indian responsible, but the truth was that he'd never really thought that much of his brother, and the more the sheriff drank, the more the truth had spilled out.

Beth Ann sat in her corset and stockings on the window ledge looking out over the street below, smoking a cigarette and listening to the sheriff snore as she watched the men walking from saloon to saloon in Deadwood.

Tonight she had learned that Sheriff Richards had, for no reason at all, severely beaten an Indian. That Indian had, apparently, killed the sheriff's brother, though from the facts Beth Ann had been able to glean, it appeared that nobody other than the sheriff knew that the Indian had killed the men missing from Deadwood. She figured there had to be a way to make a profit from knowing what she had learned.

From the bodice of her corset Beth Ann pulled out four dollar bills. That was all the sheriff had on him. She'd expected him to have much more than that, and she'd been disappointed at the results of her theft. In the morning, when the sheriff discovered his money missing, Beth Ann would complain that he'd been such a stallion that she wouldn't be able to work for a week. After that comment Sheriff Richards would smile sheepishly, pretend he actually did remember the night-long sexual marathon to which Beth Ann alluded, then gingerly put his sweat-stained felt hat back on his throbbing head and leave her room.

Beth Ann sighed wearily as the sound of the sheriff's snoring became deeper, stronger, the alcohol settling into his system. She hoped that one of the other prostitutes would let her sleep in her room so she wouldn't have to listen to the sheriff all night.

As she tossed the remains of her cigarette out the window, Beth Ann wondered if she should tell Samantha Sanders that the sheriff of Deadwood was planning to kill her fiancé. By the time Beth Ann reached the door she decided that the best thing she could do was mind her own business.

# Twenty-nine

"You look so beautiful," Vanessa said, standing back so she could get a better look at her handiwork with Samantha's hair. The string of tiny pearls that Vanessa had carefully woven into Samantha's coiffure was the final touch. That accomplished, she was certain that Samantha was, beyond doubt, the most beautiful bride ever to walk the face of the earth. She'd been saying as much for the past twenty minutes.

"Do you really think so?" Samantha implored.

Had it been any woman other than Samantha, Vanessa would have been convinced that the question was an appeal for compliments. But Vanessa understood her sister and so did not casually dismiss the anxiety behind the question.

"Samantha, you are a very beautiful g—" Vanessa caught herself before uttering the word *girl,* briefly pretending to be choked with emotion, then continued. "Beautiful woman. There isn't going to be a man or woman in this church who won't realize that the instant they see you."

"I don't care what anyone else thinks," Samantha said, "so long as Hawk thinks I'm beautiful."

Vanessa kissed her younger sister on the cheek. "He will," she whispered. "Now I'm going to leave you alone for a bit, as the priest asked me to. He wants you to think about what you're about to do."

Samantha clutched her older sister's hand, not wanting to be left alone. Then, almost immediately, she released Vanessa. "Go," she insisted. "I'll be fine."

000

Samantha wasn't afraid of becoming Hawk Two Feather's wife. Actually, quite the opposite was true. She believed with all her heart that her marriage to Hawk was the perfect thing to do. Though Samantha had not yet completely inculcated the spirituality of the Sioux, she believed in her heart that her marriage to Hawk was preordained, decreed by the spirits.

It wasn't what *she* thought about the marriage that worried her; it was what everyone else thought about it, and how those feelings and prejudices would affect the running of the Circle S Ranch. Samantha herself was perfectly willing to face whatever excoriating hatred the people of Deadwood might feel toward her for falling in love with a Sioux warrior, but she didn't want her family to suffer for what she had done.

Alone in the back room of the church, Samantha sat in the high-backed, hard wooden chair and closed her eyes. She thought about the doe that had come to her in her vision quest, and about Hawk, and the kind of life they would have together. She thought about Aja, and how important it was to completely empty the mind of all thoughts and emotions so that only the truth remained, so that only the truth was left to enter the mind and heal the soul.

As Vanessa left Samantha's room, Sonny Sanders walked out of a small back room on the opposite side of the church, leaving Hawk Two Feather, resplendent in his wedding finery. Hawk was in no mood to contemplate the future, nor to ponder the possible reactions of others to his marriage. As much as anything else, he wondered how long he could stand to wear the infernal black shoes that Sonny had absolutely demanded be worn during the wedding ceremony.

With a conscious effort to control his rising anger, Hawk stopped pacing the small room, closed his eyes and forced himself to take several long, deep breaths.

Hawk had never set foot in a church until that morning, but from all he'd heard, there had never before been so many people in this church at one time—and the wedding was still an hour away!

With a rueful acceptance of a wealth Hawk could hardly imagine, he quickly had come to realize that between Sonny and Vanessa, absolutely no expense would be spared on the wedding. Everything that could be had to give comfort or happiness to Samantha Sanders had been purchased; any item that might, even many years down the road, be a cause for a happy memory had been snapped up by Sonny or Vanessa without a moment's hesitation.

Hawk had never seen so many cut flowers in one place. Sardonically, he concluded that if Samantha had wanted that many flowers near her when she got married, then she should have chosen a place near the flowers, rather than insisting that the flowers be cut and moved to her.

With no small effort, Hawk forced himself to sit in the only chair. Immediately feeling uncomfortable, he moved to the floor, crossed his legs beneath him and willed himself to forget the stiff new shoes and the necktie that threatened to choke off his breath at any moment. He asked himself a single question: Why was he so angry?

The answer came to him quickly: Every little thing was bothering him now because Samantha, more than a week ago, had vowed to deprive him of her sensual charms until they were legally husband and wife. As the week had worn on and Hawk found himself being rebuffed at every turn, he realized she wasn't simply mouthing empty threats. And worse, she hadn't merely deprived him of her sensuality, she hadn't even allowed him the pleasure of a kiss.

Celibacy had been avoided by Hawk for most of his life with approximately the same zeal that other men avoid small rabid animals.

It occurred to Hawk, as he sat with his eyes closed on the back room floor of a church that would never have accepted him into the fold if the Sanders fortune hadn't come along with him, that the clock was ticking. In less than an hour he would be able to caress Samantha's thigh, and it would not be against any law in the territory. No longer would he be able to steal a kiss and truly call it stealing.

In less than an hour the way of life Hawk had always known, would be gone forever. He would be—against all odds and earlier predictions—a married man.

He felt peculiar. It wasn't that he didn't want Samantha to be his bride, or that he didn't want all the world to know that he was her husband. What Hawk wanted at that moment was one last reckless, impulsive adventure before his days and nights as a single man were gone forever. When Samantha had entered his life he had discovered her to be his equal in adventurous spirit. Though she had lacked experience, she was an apt pupil, and on more than one occasion she had proven herself to be not merely a student in the art of sensuality, but a teacher as well.

Hawk was on his feet in a moment, positioning a chair beneath the attic grate in the ceiling. The grate lifted with little resistance, and not nearly enough noise to draw the attention of the men and women in the main area of the church.

His heart pounding and a grin on his lips, Hawk mentally prepared himself. Leaping high, he got a good handhold on the attic lumber, which creaked in protest at his weight. Always agile, Hawk soon pulled himself completely through the square opening in the ceiling to crouch in the dusty attic.

How much noise had he made?

He did not wait for his eyes to adjust to the darkness of the attic. He didn't have time for that. From his jacket pocket he extracted a small box of matches, removed one, and lit it. Hawk could see that the attic had at one time been used as a storage area but had not seen any use recently. A thick layer of dust covered the various boxes and packages jammed against the walls.

Before the match had burned to Hawk's fingers, he determined the direction to the room in which Samantha waited. He didn't bother with a second match. The low ceiling made it impossible for him to stand, so he duck-walked across the width of the church.

Part of him wondered what the priest would do if he heard noises overhead, and part of him wondered how long it would take Samantha to forgive him for what he was about to do.

Reaching the ceiling grate above her room, he looked down through it without alerting Samantha to his presence. Sitting in her lovely white gown she was nervously chewing on a knuckle.

For an instant Hawk was stopped by her extraordinary beauty. The woman he'd seen dressed so often in denim trousers and a flannel shirt wore a gown that had cost more than many ranchers earned in a year. Her long blond hair had been swept up in an intricate coiffure laced with a long strand of small pearls. Had Hawk not already witnessed the incredible polarity of her personality, he would not have believed that this angelic woman sitting nervously in a church back room was the rough-and-tumble Samantha Sanders he'd come to love.

When Hawk lifted the grate Samantha jumped so high and fast that she practically levitated out of her chair.

"Be quiet," he said, carefully lifting the grate and setting it aside. He placed his hands on either side of the opening, let his legs dangle down into the room, and then lowered himself as far as he possibly could before dropping to the floor.

Absolute incredulity filled Samantha's face. Looking as though she wanted to scream the church down, she seemed afraid of making even a single sound for fear that the priest would hear and come to investigate.

"I couldn't wait to see you," Hawk whispered. Now in a room that was filled with light, he could see how dusty his black suit had gotten in the attic. He dusted off his pants quickly and, as he batted away the dust on the elbows of his jacket, began advancing on Samantha.

"You shouldn't have come here," Samantha said a bit weakly, her head spinning and her thoughts in utter disarray.

Why was he walking toward her with a smile on his face? She knew only too well what that meant. "This is a mistake."

Hawk was still smiling as he advanced. He said, "I recall saying something very much the same to you not long ago when you had come to me. It turns out I was wrong to try to push you away, and you were right to come to me. If it was right then, it must be right now."

Samantha had backed up until she felt the wall against her shoulders. The days she'd spent without tasting Hawk's kisses had been difficult for her, but she hadn't backed down from her promise to refuse Hawk so much as a kiss in the days before their marriage.

The separation, however, had caused her passionate dreams to reappear nightly, and with a vengeance. Each morning Samantha awoke convinced she was even more exhausted than she had been when she'd gone to sleep. And the memory of her dreams—and it was always Hawk in her dreams, working his erotic magic on her—never failed to color her cheeks. This embarrassing condition delayed her appearance at breakfast with her sister and brother each morning.

To see Hawk standing before her now, looking deliciously sophisticated, yet earthy and wild, with his long ebony hair and his burnished skin, sent shivers of alarm racing through her. *Never* had Hawk looked so enticing to Samantha, not even when all he wore was his loincloth and moccasins.

"What are you doing here?" Samantha whispered, recognizing the gleam in Hawk's eyes. "Can't you wait just a few more hours?"

Hawk shook his head slowly, then reached for Samantha.

She twisted nimbly to the side, moving out of his reach. His grin broadened.

"I can't wait, Samantha, and I suspect you can't either."

Samantha put her hands on her hips and stamped her slippered foot. "I can control myself very well, thank you very much! That's why I'm *not* giving in to this foolish little whim of yours!"

"Trust me," Hawk said, moving so that he had Samantha trapped in a corner of the room. "This is neither foolish nor a whim."

He placed his hands lightly on the curve of her hips. Though her dress was beautiful, all the starch and stiff lace gave its texture a severity that Hawk found less than sensual.

Samantha wanted to be angry with him. Looking up into his eyes, she could see the humor bubbling from his soul, the seductive sense of mischievous adventure she found absolutely impossible to resist. She wished that she could have known Hawk as a boy, before the things that now made him angry had become ingrained in him, before he'd begun to learn about prejudice and injustice, hunger and unending hard work.

"Please, Hawk," she whispered, her thoughts spinning dizzily in every direction. "Everyone is just outside. Soon we'll be married. I promise, it won't change between us. I'll always want you."

"Then want me now."

Hawk's voice was husky with passion. He brought his hands up Samantha's sides, very nearly touching her breasts, and watched as she sucked in her breath. She put her hands on his chest, trying to push him away. But he'd seen this move before.

"Soon we'll be husband and wife," Hawk continued, bending so that his face was closer to Samantha's and looking deep into her blue eyes. "Just another married couple like so many other married couples."

Samantha laughed softly. "There's not going to be anything about us that's like anyone else, Hawk, I assure you." She didn't mention Hawk's mixed blood, or her own wealth, though those characteristics wouldn't be forgotten by anyone else who knew them.

"We weren't meant to be like the others," Hawk agreed, his fingers spreading, his hands sliding slightly higher up Samantha's sides, his thumbs now grazing the outermost curve of her breasts. She brought her hands from his chest down to his wrists, about to push his hands from her. "Remember when the Cheyenne were so close, and still I couldn't keep my hands off you? I couldn't keep from kissing you, touching you, even though we were in so much danger. The danger added to the excitement, Samantha."

Even through the material of her wedding gown, Samantha could feel the heat of Hawk's hands upon her. In her heart she knew that what he said was absolutely true; their passion *was* different. It blazed like a comet streaking across the sky, white hot against the ebony darkness. It had never been, and would never be, commonplace, for the faint of heart.

Samantha closed her eyes for an instant, inhaling deeply, needing to compose her thoughts. The scandal of marrying a Sioux warrior would be nothing compared to the stories that would circulate if she were to give in now to Hawk's passion—and if her weakness were discovered.

"Just wait," she whispered, her eyes still closed. The warmth of Hawk's hands was a temptation she was still capable of resisting. "I promise, just as soon as we're married and alone, I'll . . ."

Samantha's words were cut off, her breath sucked in, when Hawk's hands moved to brush the tips of her breasts with his thumbs. An instant later his lips touched her in a soft kiss promising further enticements. When Samantha tilted her head back the kiss became firmer. She felt dizzy, and rather than push Hawk away her fingers curled around the lapels of his jacket.

"I can't wait that long." Hawk's lips were moist and warm against Samantha's as he spoke. "And I don't think you can, either. This is our last chance to be truly wicked and scandalous."

Samantha turned her face away from Hawk. His thumbs, brushing lightly across her breasts, had brought her nipples to fierce arousal, making them hard and infinitely capable of feeling even the most gentle caress. She felt him kiss her cheek, her temple, and then trace the shell of her ear with the tip of his tongue, carefully avoiding the dangling diamond earbob.

His fingers spread, encompassing her breasts, squeezing them
firmly through the stiff, lacy bodice of her gown as he kissed
her temple.

"I don't want to be scandalous," Samantha whispered, the
quiver in her voice caused by suppressed excitement. "I just
want to be your wife."

"You can't have one without the other," Hawk replied.

She turned then and looked at him, knowing that he was
right, and that her marriage to Hawk was against every crite-
rion imposed upon her by white society. With a slight tug
against his lapels, Samantha closed her eyes and Hawk kissed
her once again, fiercely and deeply. His tongue invaded her
mouth, adding to the heated excitement that Samantha had
tried so hard to deny.

Very much aware of the people just outside the door, Hawk
moved Samantha's body sideways as he continued kissing her,
until her shoulders rested against the outside wall of the room.

He wanted to pull the pins from her hair to let the blond
tresses cascade down around her shoulders in the manner that
he found most attractive. He wanted to feel her hair's silken
extravagance against his palms as he feasted upon her mouth,
but he couldn't; in mere minutes she would be standing at the
altar in front of a priest and all her friends, and there would
be no way of explaining a disheveled coiffure. Besides, he
knew that she and Vanessa had tried countless variations on
the style in the past few days, and it would be a shame to
undo their handiwork before the guests had a chance to see
it.

He leaned into Samantha, feeling the voluptuous curves of
her body molding to his, hearing the soft intake of breath when
she became aware of the fierceness of his arousal, still trapped
inside his trousers. He kissed her hard, pressing her against
the paneled wall, reaching down to grab the skirt of her gown,
pulling it up her legs.

"Hurry, Hawk!" Samantha whispered, bringing her hands
up his chest, wishing she could feel his skin instead of the

crisp white shirt. She laced her fingers together behind his neck. Unsure of exactly how Hawk intended to consummate their passion, she felt certain that if she did not feel him thrusting deep inside her soon, she would surely lose her mind.

Inexperienced with formal gowns, Hawk was surprised at the number of fine petticoats obstructing him. When at last he'd reached the last one he ran his hand up her thigh. Enjoying the texture of her stocking against his fingertips, he felt Samantha's trembling readiness as he brought his hand up to cup her buttocks. He pulled her hips toward him, showing her the extent of his need for her.

"Hurry," Samantha gasped, clutching Hawk, her passion heightened by the danger of the moment.

His touch scorched her flesh when at last he brought his hand around to touch her through her pantalets. Samantha gasped and raised up on her tiptoes, her legs quivering with excitement.

As he fumbled with the drawstring of the pantalets, she couldn't help him, fearing she would fall to the floor if she didn't continue holding onto his powerful shoulders. She felt his fingers curl into the waistband, then heard the tear as her impatient husband-to-be ripped the satin undergarment from her.

"Hurry, my darling!" Samantha whispered, raising her right knee and sliding her leg along the outside of Hawk's as he opened his trousers to free himself.

She was balanced precariously on one foot, her right leg wrapped around Hawk's thigh. She wanted to tell Hawk how much he excited her, and that he always would. She wanted to tell him a thousand things, but just as she was about to speak Hawk bent his knees and entered her in a single breathtaking thrust. Samantha felt her hips strike the wall behind her, and heard the soft *thump!* of her head striking it as well, but she couldn't concern herself with what noises were made, or who might hear them. Not when Hawk was filling her so completely and she could feel every magnificent inch of him sliding deep inside her.

There was nothing gentle about their lovemaking. Hawk's hands cupped Samantha's buttocks and squeezed tightly, pulling her hips toward him as he thrust into her with such strength that he very nearly picked her completely off the floor. She wanted to kiss him, but he was too tall, and her breath was too labored.

"Yes, Hawk!" Samantha gasped, each fierce thrust slamming her against the wall, sending her soaring closer to the chasm of ecstasy. "Oh, yes-s-s!"

In an oddly distanced way, Samantha was aware of all that was happening to her, yet detached from it. Now she was two distinct people: one a woman of wealth and privilege, rational and sane; the other a daring sexual adventurer mad with desire for the man she loved. She heard the crackling sound of her dress, bunched up at her stomach and trapped between her body and Hawk's, being crushed by his thrashing movements, and wondered whether the fabric would be so wrinkled that everyone in church would realize instantly how the garment had been bruised. She was distinctly aware of the strength of Hawk's hands, pulling her toward him. She had no choice but to meet the forceful thrusts that sent her backward against the wall, and she wanted it no other way.

She was aware of the heat and strength of Hawk's manhood as it lanced into her, filled her, possessed her so thoroughly and completely that she knew with certainty that she would always want to make love with Hawk. The dichotomy of his nature had never been more apparent than at this moment, as they made wild, dangerous love.

Samantha felt the rapid tightening of the muscles in her stomach and knew she was going to reach the summit of ecstasy with frightening speed and force. She squeezed her eyes shut, her hands grasping frantically at Hawk's shoulders, holding on tightly as he thrust upward time and again. She felt utterly possessed by Hawk's extraordinary strength and virility, and completely protected by it.

Her mouth opened wide as she felt the scream of ecstasy

about to explode in her throat. To prevent a sound from escaping, she caught the lapel of Hawk's jacket between her teeth and bit down with all her might.

As the last of her spasms subsided, Samantha heard a mighty rumble erupt from Hawk's great chest; then he thrust into her harder and deeper than ever before, raising her to her tiptoes as his surging passion erupted.

Samantha was gulping in air as though she'd run a dozen miles. How long had it been since Hawk had first entered this room? Three minutes? Five at most? Was it possible that their passion could burn that hot, that fast?

The low hum of a voice caught Samantha's attention. She blinked her eyes, not yet fully back to earth from the heights to which her passion had taken her. Hawk was still within her, leaning into her, trapping her between himself and the wall. She put her right foot down on the floor but continued to hold onto Hawk because her legs were weak and wobbly.

"Someone's talking to you," Hawk whispered.

Samantha looked at Hawk, pleased that he looked nearly as disheveled as she felt. What difference could it possibly make if someone was talking to her? She was with Hawk, and that was all that counted.

"Samantha, are you all right in there?" Vanessa asked softly through the closed door.

Samantha's eyes opened wide, and the afterglow in which she had been reveling vanished instantly. She pushed against Hawk's chest, forcing him to take a step backward. She felt warm and wet inside, and disquietingly empty.

"Answer her or she'll come in," Hawk said, struggling to rearrange his own clothing.

"Samantha?" Vanessa asked.

As Samantha saw the knob turn, she made a dash for the door.

# Thirty

The door opened just an inch before Samantha hit it with her shoulder. She heard Vanessa gasp on the other side of the door, but she couldn't apologize, nor could she give any reason for her peculiar behavior.

"Samantha, are you all right?" Vanessa asked again, louder this time.

Samantha leaned against the door, frantically looking for a lock, horrified to discover that there wasn't one. She looked over her shoulder just in time to see Hawk step up onto the chair, then leap high to reach inside the attic grate. For a few seconds he seemed to dangle in midair in the center of the room, and then his brightly polished boots disappeared through the square opening in the ceiling. Only then did Samantha stop pushing hard against the door.

The moment she released her pressure on the door, Vanessa forced her way into the room. There was a worried look in her eyes as she took in Samantha's appearance.

"What happened? Your dress is all wrinkled, and look at your hair! Samantha, what on earth were you doing in here?" Vanessa asked, already attempting to tuck a lock of blond hair back where it belonged.

"I was just pacing, I guess," Samantha said, struggling desperately for a lie that might sound plausible. "I tripped and fell over, and I was cursing under my breath, I guess, when you knocked on the door."

Samantha studied Vanessa's face as her sister worked on her

hair. Vanessa was as preoccupied with the wedding as Samantha was, it seemed, because she didn't question the story which, even on the face of it, lacked a great deal of credibility.

"I was worried about you," Vanessa said, taking Samantha by the shoulders and turning her to work on the hair that had formerly been secured with pins near the back of Samantha's head. "I've been working on this wedding, day and night, and it's going to go off just as your brother and I have planned. That's all there is to it!"

"Don't worry, Vanessa, it'll be just as you planned," Samantha said comfortingly, a smile on her lips. This was one of the very few times in her life she'd seen her learned sister, the tough lawyer willing to fight anyone in a court of law, appear thoroughly nervous. "Shouldn't we put on my veil now?"

The instant the words were out of Samantha's mouth, something on the floor caught her attention. There, near the chair, were her pantalets, destroyed by Hawk's powerful hands when he'd ripped them from her body.

"Someone's at the door," Samantha said quickly, almost pushing Vanessa in that direction.

"I didn't hear anything."

"Check, won't you?"

While Vanessa opened the door a crack, Samantha moved to the chair so that her pantalets were hidden beneath her now-wrinkled gown.

"I guess I'm just a little nervous," Samantha explained when Vanessa returned to her with another questioning look in her eyes.

"I guess you've got a right to be nervous," Vanessa said as she picked up the white lace veil and began to pin it into place for her sister.


Father Patrick O'Rourke had his misgivings about this wedding. He wasn't the kind to look kindly on marriages between white women and Indians, but Sonny Sanders had made an enormous donation to the church, as well as a sizable offering to the priest's personal finances. Father O'Rourke told himself that he could do much good for his flock if he simply accepted the money and performed the ceremony.

He looked out over the congregation and thought that if he could draw this many people on a Sunday, he wouldn't have need of Sonny Sanders's bribe. This bitterness was short-lived, however. A pragmatic man, the priest realized that rules sometimes had to be bent if a greater good was to be realized. There were times when saving souls required money as well as faith.

He turned away from the congregation and went to the side room where the heathen, Hawk Two Feather, was waiting. An instant before the father's knuckles rapped on the door, he heard a *thump!* of boots striking the floor boards. Without bothering to knock, he opened the door wide and stepped inside.

"What was that noise?" the priest asked sternly.

Hawk spun quickly to face the intruder. The priest's face was suspicious. "I'll only ask you one more time; What were you were doing?"

"I'm not used to wearing shoes like these," Hawk explained. "They're pinching my feet. I can't wait to get out of them and back into my moccasins."

Father O'Rourke was about to scold the redskin, but then he saw the dust on the knees of Hawk's trousers. A slow smile spread across the priest's lips.

"Try to be calm," Father O'Rourke said, stepping forward to pat the tall Sioux warrior's shoulder comfortingly. "At a time like this everyone tends to be a little nervous, but there's really no need for it. Just listen to my instructions, and I'll guide you and Samantha through the service. Oh, and one more thing; brush the dust off your knees. They got dusty when you were kneeling to pray." His eyes held promise in them as he looked fondly at Hawk, believing wholeheartedly that he had found a convert.

* * *

The wedding celebration was the most lavish party anyone in Deadwood could remember, and nearly everyone was invited—everyone, except Sheriff Darren Richards, and the whole town knew why he had been excluded. By the time of the wedding the rumor mill had succeeded in informing all of Deadwood, and almost everyone in the territory, that the sheriff had beaten Hawk after arresting him on trumped-up charges. Later, Richards's brother and other men known more for working with guns than with their hands, had decided they would even the score with Hawk.

There were a dozen different explanations of what happened next—including two eyewitness reports bearing no similarity to each other—with only one common thread of truth: Some men had ridden out of Deadwood intending to do Hawk bodily harm, and that was the last anyone had seen of them.

To prove that he made his own decisions, Sheriff Richards had gone to the wedding. He stood at the outer ring of bonfire light, watching off in the distance as the line dancers moved in unison to the music of a six-piece band. The sheriff was thinking about the undetermined fate of his brother, and how unjust it was that Hawk should now be married to a beautiful and wealthy woman. A redskin shouldn't have that much luck working for him, plain and simple, and the sheriff figured he was just the man to right the wrong.

Hanging loose in his left hand was the bottle of whiskey he'd taken from one of the long tables set up just outside the Circle S ranch house. Some of the tables were laden with food, some with drink. There was enough for all the guests to immoderately partake in food and drink.

The ranch hand at the table had volunteered to pour a whiskey for Sheriff Richards, but the sheriff wanted the entire bottle. When the man said that wasn't the way the shindig was supposed to be, Darren Richards pointed to the badge pinned to his leather vest, then calmly withdrew his revolver and threatened to arrest the man. The sheriff got a full bottle of whiskey all for himself, no more questions asked.

This fine whiskey rattled the sheriff's nerves. All that good whiskey being given away? The cost of the shindig, complete with a steer on the spit and delicacies of every variety, was something the sheriff could hardly stand to think about. Why was it that he, a hard-working man, couldn't afford to throw such a party, and yet a redskin could? It wasn't right. Something had to be very wrong in the world for something like this to happen.

He took another swig from the bottle and felt the delicious burn of the liquor going down. The line dancers had stopped and the band had started a romantic ballad, sung by a fiddle-playing, sweet-voiced boy barely in his teens. Couples paired off quickly and began swaying under the stars to the slow, melodic music. Sheriff Richards saw this as the right time to show some of the unattached ladies of Deadwood just what they had passed up thus far.

Her name was Susan Quist—Suzie, to her friends, though she now believed that at seventeen she was too old for such a childish moniker—and she'd never looked twice at the sheriff. He decided, with a quarter of the contents of the whiskey bottle now in his stomach, that it was time to change her opinion of him.

"Evenin', Miss Quist," the sheriff said, finally coming closer to Suzie who was standing near the dancers. "Let's you an' me dance." He reached for her hand, but she pulled away from him as if he were poison. The sheriff grinned, but it was tight and forced. "I think it's time you and me got better acquainted. Now let's dance."

The three girls Suzie had been standing with looked as though they all wanted to run for their lives, though none was willing to abandon a friend. Huddling together, their eyes were wide and filled with both caution and contempt.

Ernest Quist, Suzie's father, stepped forward. "Walk away, Sheriff," Ernest said, his eyes hard as diamonds. His right hand held a mug of beer so tightly, his knuckles were turning white. His opinion of Sheriff Richards, evident in his expression, indicated that he wouldn't tolerate the sheriff even speaking to his daughter.

"Are you telling me what to do?" Sheriff Richards asked with a sneer. He still held the bottle in his left hand, but his right hand was free for his revolver.

"That's right, I am." Ernest had just enough beer in his belly for him to have no respect for Darren Richards, or his position. He had always loathed the sheriff, seeing him for the bully that he was.

"Maybe I oughta arrest you for that."

Darren Richards waited to see the fear in Ernest's eyes, but it never came. Looking around, the sheriff discovered nearly fifty men and women, their activities stopped, surrounding him. And even though none was armed, all looked ready to take up weapons against him.

"This ain't no place for you, Sheriff," Ernest said, staring down angrily at the smaller man. "Any place my daughter is ain't no place for you. In fact, any place *any* decent woman is ain't no place for you."

A smattering of laughter from the guests tore into Darren Richards's insides. Then someone from the crowd shouted, "That's telling him, Ernest! I wouldn't let the skunk near my daughter! No how, no way!" Someone else shouted, "He's just a bum with a badge, Ernest! We're on your side!"

It was bad enough to have the men laughing at him. Sheriff Richards had had that happen to him on several occasions. What he couldn't tolerate was looking over at Susie and finding the girl and her friends laughing at him.

Sheriff Richards wanted to gun them all down, every one of them. And he might have done just that if he hadn't been so certain that the most he could do was kill six of the people now laughing at him. The instant his revolver was empty they would pounce on him and hang him from the nearest tree.

He took a drink from his bottle and pulled his Colt half out of his holster as a threat. Then he let the weapon fall back into place. He'd seen an instant of fear in the eyes of some of the women when he'd feigned drawing his weapon, and that sign of fear was all he'd really wanted. He tossed his head back and laughed, then sauntered away, pretending not to care that the laughter he heard was at him, that the hatred directed toward him was so thick, he could practically taste it in the air.

Hawk sensed that something was wrong, though he couldn't say what. He'd seen several ranch hands glancing in his direction and then look away. They didn't seem angry with him for marrying Samantha. But something was wrong; the ranch hands were looking for leadership, and they weren't yet comfortable looking to him for it.

"What is it, Billy?" Hawk asked, approaching the young ranch hand whom he knew Samantha thought a great deal of.

Billy avoided Hawk's eyes for a moment. When Hawk placed a large hand on the boy's shoulder Billy's lips pursed into a thin line. "I'm really sorry to have to say this, but Sheriff Richards is here, an' it looks like he's fixin' for a fight."

Billy was surprised that Hawk's expression didn't change at all at the news. The young hand was beginning to understand how little emotion was revealed in Hawk's expression unless he wanted to make his feelings known.

"Thank you for telling me, Billy," Hawk said, squeezing the boy's shoulder and issuing the smallest of smiles, even though he was furious with the sheriff for disturbing his wedding reception. "You've done the right thing."

"The sheriff was over near where we're all dancin', last I heard."

"I want you to keep an eye on Samantha. I don't want this celebration disturbed for her. I don't want her made unhappy for any reason."

"I understand, sir," Billy replied.

Hawk turned away from the young man, searching for Darren Richards. Hawk believed in natural justice, the justice understood by the animals in the forest and on the grassy plains. He didn't have any faith, nor take any comfort, in the justice found in courts. Crow believed that wrongs could be righted working through the legal system, and that guilty men could be made both to see the error of their ways and to face an appropriate penalty for what they'd done.

Hawk believed men held justice in their own hands.

With each step Hawk took, his feet still uncomfortable in the stiff black shoes, Hawk felt his anger rising. His senses were becoming more sharp-edged as he realized that he should have sought out the sheriff long before this moment. Had he gone after Sheriff Richards earlier, when Samantha was safely tucked away at the Sioux encampment, the foul lawman wouldn't be here now, trying to spoil the party. Hawk held himself responsible for this lack of foresight, but he intended to make up for his mistake, once and for all.

Sheriff Richards had moved away from the musicians, realizing that there wasn't a female at the shindig who would dance with him. What bothered him most was the lack of respect in the eyes of the people who looked at him. Never before had the sheriff seen so little fear in the people he passed.

He'd long known that there were those men and women in Deadwood who didn't like him, and others who loathed him. But those people had always been careful to keep their feelings hidden from him as best they could. They didn't dare face his wrath, it had seemed.

But now all that had changed. Never before had the sheriff felt so isolated and outnumbered. And though his impulse was to leave, his pride refused to let him do so. If the rest of Deadwood was invited to the shindig, then he should have been, too. He was just as good as anyone in town, and better than most. There wasn't a man alive in any position to tell him what he could or couldn't do.

He passed a long table where a dozen fried chickens had been laid out for guests to feast upon at their leisure. As he drew nearer the table, the people who had been picking at the delicious chicken, chatting with each other as they ate and sipped beer, spotted the sheriff and moved away, wrinkling their noses as though they suddenly smelled something foul.

Contemptuously, Sheriff Richards ripped the leg off a chicken, took one bite from it, and then tossed the uneaten food to the ground. He wiped his fingers on the white linen tablecloth. A dozen people saw the disgusting gesture, and none of them hid their displeasure.

"You're leaving now!"

The commanding male voice came through the crowd, which parted quickly to make way for the tall man's angry, long-legged form. When Hawk, his tie pulled loose and his jacket and the top two buttons of his starched white shirt unfastened, stepped into the clearing, his hands were already bailed into huge fists.

"Are you talkin' to me, Injin?" Darren Richards flipped the half-empty whiskey bottle aside and placed his right hand on the butt of his gun. His eyes went over Hawk, taking instant notice of his lack of a weapon. The right side of his mouth pulled upward in a cruel smile. "You better watch your tongue, boy. I gave you one beatin', and if you're not real careful, I'll give you another."

"No, you won't." Hawk approached slowly. A hush had fallen over the crowd, and the musicians had stopped playing to watch the scene in the clearing. "The only thing you're going to do is leave. Leave now and never come back . . . if you know what's good for you."

The sheriff made a snorting sound of contempt, but he took a step backward just the same. He was aware of all the eyes upon him, and how the buzz of activity had stopped at Hawk's entrance. Though at first the sheriff might have felt fear, he had just enough whiskey in his blood to want to prove himself in front of all the people who had never truly given him the respect he'd always deserved.

"Boy, you'd better learn to watch your tongue!" Sheriff Richards took a big step toward Hawk. Now the sheriff's wicked grin became feral and cruel. "I suppose you think you're something special now that you married yourself into all this money, don't you? Well, I've got some news for you, redskin. As far as I'm concerned, you're just another murderin' Injin! That's all you'll ever be! An' right now I'm takin' you into town for questioning."

"No, you're not," Hawk replied, his voice a breath above a whisper.

Someone from the crowd said, "Good Lord, Sheriff, the man just got married! Can't your questioning wait until tomorrow?"

Darren Richards shook his head slowly, never taking his eyes off Hawk. The more he thought about it, the more he liked how it would look to take Hawk away from his own shindig. Once the sheriff had done that, nobody would ever again question his authority.

"I'm takin' you back to the jail, redskin, and while we're there I'm going to ask you a few questions about my brother. He's disappeared real sudden like, and I'll bet if I ask you in just the right way, you'll give me the answers I've been lookn' for."

Hawk looked at the sheriff and thought, *Your brother was as big a fool and a bushwacking coward as you are.*

He knew then that something permanent had to be done about Darren Richards, something to prevent him from hurting decent, honest people. Hawk suspected that he wasn't the only person to have been victimized by the badge-wearing monster. Undoubtedly, there had been many other people in Deadwood who had crossed paths with the sheriff, and suffered for the experience.

"Let's go, boy," the sheriff said, taking another step closer to Hawk. Barely five feet separated the men. "Don't make me have to hurt you."

Hawk wondered how many times the sheriff had made such a statement to innocent men, and how many times he had beaten them, simply for the pleasure of hurting another human being.

Hawk unclenched his fists, his hands hanging loose at his sides as the rigidity left his body. Hawk kept his weight on the balls of his feet, his stance slightly wider than normal, allowing him to spring forward or backward in the blink of an eye.

From the crowd, Hawk heard Billy say quietly, "Don't trust him, Mr. Hawk. The sheriff's got mean blood in him."

Sheriff Richards grinned, liking what he heard. "The boy knows the truth, redskin," he said, almost in a whisper, standing just outside arm's reach. "You bes' just come along or I'll put a bullet in you right here, right now . . . and there ain't a damn thing you can do about it."

Darren Richards had seen it before: the anger, the futile rage of a man not wanting to give ground, yet knowing in his heart that he had to. It was one of the things about the job that Darren Richards never failed to appreciate. The only thing that bothered him was the look in the tall Indian's eyes. There wasn't a shred of fear, not even the slightest glimmer. But that didn't completely disconcert the sheriff. He figured that after he'd tapped Hawk half a dozen times on the head with the butt of his revolver, then introduced his ribs to the toes of his boots once more, he'd see fear in the half-breed's eyes.

"Let's walk, boy," the sheriff said, slowly taking the gun from his holster.

The crowd gasped in unison at the sight of the weapon.

"Either you walk or I'm taking you back to Deadwood tossed over a saddle . . . and we'll see what answers the undertaker can get from you!"

The sheriff reached for Hawk, but his hand didn't quite go far enough. Something in Hawk's stance warned Sheriff Richards, and he stopped his hand, then took a step backward and thumbed back the hammer of his revolver.

"I told you to walk."

"You'll never get away with it. Not this time, Sheriff. To you I'm just another Indian, which means you think you can do to me whatever you like, and there's nothing that anyone else will do or say about it. But this time there's money behind the Indian. Money and power . . . and those are two things you don't have; isn't that so . . . boy?"

The notion of an Indian calling him *boy* was more than the sheriff could tolerate. He raised his gun, pointed it at Hawk's head, and squeezed the trigger.

Sheriff Richards had never seen a big man move that quickly. Even before he was able to pull the trigger and send a bullet smashing into Hawk's face, Hawk's hand lashed upward to grab the barrel of the gun and push it skyward. The sheriff's bullet went harmlessly into the night sky.

Sheriff Richards swung hard with his left fist, red-hot rage boiling in his veins. Though Hawk held the barrel of his revolver, Darren was still in control of the handle and trigger, and he fired again as he struggled with Hawk, this time sending a bullet ricocheting off the ground and hitting the leg of a table, splintering the wood and causing it to buckle under the weight of the feast.

Sheriff Richards again thumbed back the hammer, determined this time to put a bullet in the Indian's stomach and watch him die writhing on the ground. The sheriff had spent his life teaching men just like Hawk that they weren't worth the dirt beneath his feet, and he wasn't about to stop giving those lessons now—even if the redskin had managed to marry himself into the richest family in the territory. With a grin on his lips, Darren Richards squeezed the trigger of his revolver . . .

And felt the bullet slam into his own stomach because Hawk had twisted the weapon in his hand.

It was like being kicked by a mule, and the sheriff staggered backward three steps, releasing his hold on his revolver. A glazed, confused expression filled his eyes, followed by a ringing in his ears, and he couldn't seem to catch his breath.

"You stinkin' redskin. When we get back to jail I'm going to kick your guts out for this," Darren Richards said, falling to his knees.

The sheriff looked confused about why he could no longer keep his legs beneath him. And when he landed on his face in the dirt his last thought was that he was *really* going to make Hawk suffer this time.

Hawk wasn't surprised by the commotion that followed. However, the words of encouragement and support given to him by people whose names he didn't even know astonished him. "I saw the whole thing," one elderly woman was saying, tugging at Hawk's sleeve to get his attention. "The sheriff was mad! Mad in the head loco! He didn't give you no choice, and I'll tell the whole world in court, if you want me to." Another man was telling Hawk that he'd done Deadwood a favor by killing Sheriff Richards, and if Hawk hadn't done it, someone else would have sooner or later.

Sonny came rushing forward, pushing people aside, a grim look on his face. "I'll explain later," Hawk said, placing a hand on his brother-in-law's broad shoulder. "Right now, I just want to make sure Samantha doesn't see any of this. I don't want the evening ruined for her."

"I'm afraid that's already happened," Sonny commented sternly. "Go to the library. I'll meet you there, with Vanessa and Samantha. We'll discuss what must be done now."

Fifteen minutes later, Hawk was pacing the library while Sonny smoked furiously, and Vanessa comforted Samantha.

"I've got twenty people as witnesses," Hawk said. He took a sip of brandy, then set the glass aside. Circumstances had taken the flavor out of the liquor for him. "He wasn't invited, and everyone saw him spoiling for a fight."

"There's nothing for you to worry about," Sonny said, angry

that the celebration had been disturbed. He didn't care that Sheriff Richards had been killed. What bothered him was that Samantha's party hadn't turned out to be the enjoyable event he'd planned for her.

However, Vanessa, as a lawyer, saw the situation through eyes unclouded by hatred. "It's self-defense, to be sure, but it's also a situation where an Indian man killed a white sheriff. Times have changed. We can't just pretend this didn't happen, as so often happened in the old days. Hawk's going to spend time in jail until we can clear his name."

The word *jail* put an end to Hawk's pacing. He'd lived his life too free, too unencumbered, to ever consider spending another minute locked up like an animal. Holding his words in check, he looked at Vanessa. Maybe she had something else to tell him.

"Would you both mind leaving Deadwood for a while?" Vanessa asked, looking first at Hawk and then at Samantha. "I don't know for how long; at least a couple of weeks. Maybe through the winter, and then you can return in the summer. Would it be too much to stay with Hawk's people?"

Samantha shook her head vigorously. "Not at all!" she answered. Then, realizing she was speaking for Hawk when she probably shouldn't, she looked to him with a question in her eyes.

"We can leave tonight, if that would be best," Hawk said, relieved at Vanessa's solution. He stepped forward, reaching down for Samantha's hands. When he held them tenderly in his, he got down on one knee before her, kissing her fingers lightly. "I'm sorry, Samantha, that you won't have the comforts of your home—"

"Don't apologize," Samantha said quickly, her eyes glistening with tears at the sincerity in Hawk's eyes. "I'll be more than happy to live with your people. They're my people too, now, in a way. I don't care where I live, or how, so long as it's with you."

"Then we'll leave tonight."

Vanessa said, "We won't tell a soul where you've gone. By

spring, I'll have pulled enough strings with territory authorities and judges to make it a guarantee that Hawk won't even have to make a statement."

# *Thirty-one*

The trip to the Sioux encampment was leisurely. Hawk paid even more careful attention to Samantha than usual. He suspected that she was secretly disappointed at not being able to stay at the Circle S, to enjoy all the comforts of life that were there for her, but was hiding her innermost feelings from him. They rode slowly, stopping regularly, to frolic in a stream that they came across; to make love often, sometimes in the sunlight with only *Ida Maka* to witness their happiness, and sometimes under the moon and stars, sharing their bliss with the night.

Samantha's appetite seemed to have increased somewhat, Hawk noted. He hoped she was pregnant, now that he was her husband. Having been born a bastard, he understood all too well the almost insurmountable difficulties a child faced not having a father, not having a name. Once he teased Samantha, suggesting she might be pregnant, but she dismissed the joke quickly, insisting she'd be the first to know if she was going to become a mother.

Hawk was disappointed as they approached the camp. He hadn't had enough of Samantha yet, hadn't gotten tired of monopolizing her time and attention. Her bright and sunny smile was just as heartwarming to him now as it had been the first time they had touched. And when she opened her arms to hold him the fire burning within him was just as intense as it ever had been.

"Don't be surprised if the children touch your hair," Hawk

said as they walked their horses into camp. "Now that you're with me, they'll probably take a few liberties."

"Why would they want to touch my hair?" Samantha asked, thinking this very odd behavior.

"How many blonde Sioux have you seen? When you were a guest they kept their distance somewhat. They didn't want to be disrespectful. But now you're here with me, and they'll want to know if your skin feels different from theirs, your hair different."

Samantha looked to her left, where children had stopped playing and simply stared as she and Hawk rode into camp. "I think we're going to surprise a few people with our return."

It was Hawk who first sensed something was wrong. It wasn't just the children's behavior—he expected such bluntness from children—but squaws and braves also stared as they passed.

"What is it?" Samantha whispered, sensing Hawk's unease. She too studied the group and realized that she was no longer looked upon as a guest or stranger but now—and why?—a threat. Samantha didn't like the sick feeling growing inside her.

"Red Wolf," Hawk concluded, keeping his voice down so only Samantha could hear him.

"What's he done?"

"I don't know yet, but I'll find out."

Samantha shivered in the saddle. She could tell that Hawk had no real proof that Red Wolf was responsible. Hawk was simply going on his instincts, following the warnings of an inner voice. But Samantha had looked into Red Wolf's eyes, and she'd sensed from the very beginning that there was evil in the man's heart. She had no doubt, like Hawk, that Red Wolf was behind whatever troubles were about to descend upon them.

Crow approached them first, with Aja running to catch up with them all.

"We've got to talk," Crow said, taking the reins of Hawk's

stallion. He turned to Aja and said, "Will you take care of the horses?"

"No, I want to—"

"Aja!" Hawk spoke the single word sharply, and it silenced the girl. "Do as Crow says. There will be time later for you to learn what has been said."

Aja was clearly unhappy about being excluded, however temporarily, but she did as her brother instructed. Despite the unmistakable aura of trouble around the camp, Samantha felt pleased that Aja could be a girl acting her own age, rather than the wise-beyond-her-years young woman she usually appeared to be.

They went directly to Crow's tepee. If Hawk hadn't known better, he'd say that some of the braves in camp actually walked away from him to avoid acknowledging his return to camp. Though Hawk had been treated with disrespect as a child, once he'd reached his full height and learned to hunt and fight for himself and his tribe, few braves openly scorned his presence, and none directly to his face.

"What has happened here?" Hawk asked the instant the tepee flap fell back into place behind Crow.

"Dull Knife is dead."

Hawk grimaced in physical pain at the news. Crow placed his hand on Hawk's shoulder. Both men had liked the elder chieftain, but the loss was especially hard for Hawk, who had placed such value on the man's advice.

"He was murdered about the time that you and Samantha left for Deadwood. That's what people here are guessing, anyway."

"Who killed him?"

"We don't know. He was found up in the hills. The wolves have—" Crow stopped himself and glanced over at Samantha, not wanting to say anything that might offend her, even if it were the truth.

"You don't have to worry about me," Samantha said, accurately reading the look she'd been given. "I don't need to be coddled. I just want to know the truth."

"There are stories going around the campfires, Hawk," Crow continued. "Some braves have had their suspicions about you for a long time. Not everyone thinks you're as charming as the ladies do." Crow glanced at Samantha again. "And there's the missing money . . . almost half of the two thousand you gave to the elders is gone."

"Let me guess," Hawk said bitter. "The money disappeared about the same time that I left camp, right?"

"Naturally."

"What kind of logic does that make?" Hawk snapped. "Why would I give money to the tribe only to steal it back? That would be like stealing from myself! Isn't there anyone who understands that? And if I was in such need of money, why would I give it to the council in the first place? Nobody knew I had the money!"

"That's what I've been telling everyone who will listen. Unfortunately, not many on the council have been interested in what I had to say." Crow shrugged his shoulders in a gesture of futility. "It's not like in a white man's court, where I get to give my side of the story to the jury and they have to listen to me."

"I'm gone a little over two weeks and all this happens?" Hawk asked incredulously. "What more could they have against me?"

"Your wife, I should think," Samantha said, stepping forward.

"We're not that way," Hawk informed her.

"Yes, we are," Crow replied. "I'm sorry, but it's true. You marrying a white woman has not endeared you to many in the tribe. It's just one more thing that casts you in a suspicious light."

"And it has been Red Wolf who has spoken out most against me, hasn't it?"

Aja came inside the tepee then, doing the almost unthinkable by entering without being invited. She went straight to Hawk and put her arms around him. He stroked her hair lightly and said, "None of what you've heard is true. It's all lies."

"I knew they were lies," Aja said quietly. "But it's good to hear you say so."

Never before had Samantha felt quite so much like an outsider as she did now. She understood so little of what was expected of Sioux men and women. She watched as her husband, her sister-in-law, and her husband's best friend talked. But now the words flowed over Samantha, not really touching her, not registering in her brain. Though all three—with their dark hair, eyes, and skin—looked reasonably the same, she looked completely different. How it pained her that Hawk, under suspicion for a crime he did not commit, was more deeply incriminated because he'd fallen in love with a stranger and had taken her for his wife!

A single question kept going through her mind: How much would the man she loved suffer because he'd married her?

Hawk, Crow, and Aja were already sitting in a tight triangle, their knees touching. Samantha, on the outside, quietly stepped behind Hawk, then knelt and placed her hands lightly on his shoulders. She leaned forward to put her cheek against his back. Closing her eyes, she issued a silent prayer of hope, then listened to what was being said.

Crow said, "We've got to face our accusers. It's the only way we'll ever gain any credibility."

"It's not *our* accusers," Hawk said. "You're not the one they're blaming for the murder of Dull Knife."

"We're in this together," Crow said with quiet conviction.

Hawk placed his hand over Crow's, squeezed his friend's hand a moment, then nodded. They'd been through many battles together, and an attack upon one was an attack upon both.

"Then we'll face our accusers standing shoulder to shoulder," Hawk said, a glint of love in his eyes as he looked at his friend. "I say we find Red Wolf now and take him before the elders. Then we'll hear what he has to say when we are there to defend ourselves from his lies."

"But first there is something we must do," Crow said.

Hawk gave him a quizzical look. Hawk had always been the man of instant action, and Crow was the more thoughtful, methodical one.

"Samantha is the target of anger and suspicion," Crow continued. "Why not remove her from danger, at least until we can explain to the elders that we're not responsible for Dull Knife's death, or the missing money."

Samantha's immediate reaction was negative. She didn't want to be separated from Hawk. However, she held her tongue, keeping her fears to herself. Hawk had enough troubles, had to carry enough of a burden, without her adding to it, she reasoned.

"The cave? You haven't told anyone else about it?" Hawk asked.

Crow looked at him and smiled. "Never! We made a promise to each other!"

The cave was tucked away, completely isolated from the camp high in the hills. Crow and Hawk had discovered it as young men when they'd first begun to hunt on their own for food for the tribe. There they could sit quietly and talk without fear of being overheard. Both men were loners, and when the crowded camp became too cloying for them they'd often spent a day or two at the cave alone. Whenever the tribe was in the area, Hawk had visited the cave to enjoy some solitude.

"Aja can take Samantha there," Hawk continued, liking the idea more as time passed. "I've brought plenty of food here with me. We can give them enough to last three or four days. That should be all the time we need to remove the stain from our names."

"We're going to hear about that," Hawk commented quietly as he watched Samantha and Aja ride away from camp, leading a packhorse laden with supplies and food. "The elders are going to wonder why I've sent Samantha away so soon after arriving, and they'll want to know why Aja went with her. They'll be furious at not being consulted first."

"Don't worry about their questions," Crow replied, patting his friend on the back. "At least you know now that your wife and sister are safe."

When Hawk turned around, facing the inner circle of the camp, he could feel the eyes of braves and squaws upon him. How many of them believed that he was responsible for the murder of Dull Knife?

The sun was high overhead, and Hawk was thankful. He didn't want Samantha and Aja traveling at night. The rocky terrain surrounding the cave held countless natural dangers. Who could be sure that a horse wouldn't be spooked and stumble off the trail, sending horse and rider plummeting over a steep, craggy cliff?

Though the huge tepee loomed before them, Hawk was surprised at how little trepidation he felt. When he was younger a meeting with the elders had always troubled him. Now, with his wife and sister safely out of camp, he welcomed the chance to challenge his accuser. Face to face, he would confront Red Wolf before the elders, and when he was done he would not only have cleared the name of Hawk Two Feather, but he would have more credibility with the elders than ever before.

They had almost reached their destination when Red Wolf stepped out from behind a tepee, leading his horse by the bridle. He seemed shocked to suddenly find himself facing Hawk, though neither victory nor anger showed in his expression.

"Running away, Red Wolf?" Hawk asked, his lips twisted in a scowl. "Afraid to end what you have started?"

"Not at all," Red Wolf replied quickly. "I welcome the chance to teach you once and for all that a bastard is just a bastard." He turned away.

When Hawk moved toward Red Wolf, Crow intervened, stepping between the two braves.

"Don't start a fight; it's just what he wants you to do."
Crow was determined not to let Hawk's fiery nature work
against himself. "You'll only look bad before the council if
you attack him now."

Hawk grit his teeth, knowing in his heart that the words
Crow spoke were wise ones. But it was impossible to look at
Red Wolf's evil face and not want to attack him, not want to
strike out at him for being the foul man that he was.

"We'll see how you smile when the council hears what I
have to say," Hawk said, looking over Crow's shoulder at his
enemy. "Then we will see who has courage, won't we?"

"Run away, you fatherless maggot," Red Wolf replied, but
even as he spoke he was already moving away from Hawk and
Crow.

As Red Wolf retreated, Hawk at first felt he'd achieved some
kind of victory because he had stood his ground and his enemy
had retreated. Then he wasn't so sure. He didn't understand
Red Wolf's behavior—at first surprised to be confronted by
Hawk, then strangely unwilling to engage in a more forceful
confrontation.

"Ignore him." Crow nudged Hawk toward the giant tepee
once more. "Red Wolf has already built a funeral pyre for
himself. It's only a matter of time before he lights the flame
himself."

"You're right, of course." Hawk couldn't shake the feeling
that somehow, some way, he had once again been manipulated
by Red Wolf.

Crow spoke slowly, choosing his words carefully for the
emotional impact his information would have upon the stony-
faced tribal elders. He spoke for an hour, detailing the exploits
of Hawk Two Feather and the heroism and selflessness he'd
shown toward the tribe throughout his life. Crow chronicled
major events, including the time when, in the dead of winter,
Hawk had tracked a small herd of mule deer for several days.

With bow and arrow he had killed four of the deer. With the meat those deer provided for the tribe, Hawk had eased the hunger that had gripped the tribe for weeks.

And Crow spoke of the bravery Hawk had shown in battles against the Cheyenne and Blackfeet. Yes, Crow said, Hawk's ancestry was suspect. But to hold him accountable for the misdeeds of others? Hawk's loyalty to the Sioux was limitless and unwavering. Hawk should be judged by his actions, Crow argued, not by the words of a man who had, throughout his life, shown little interest in the welfare of the tribe.

Reaching this part of his speech, Crow glanced sideways at Hawk, as though to let his friend know that now he was going to change tactics. He had first established Hawk as an honorable warrior for the Sioux; now he was going to call into question the motives and honor of Red Wolf.

But Hawk was hardly listening. Looking into the faces of the old men judging him, he tried but failed to anticipate the verdict. Instead, his thoughts were distracted by the confrontation he'd had with Red Wolf. What was it about those brief moments that should mean something to him?

"I see that Red Wolf is not here." Crow's voice rose slightly. "That doesn't surprise me. Why should a liar stand before his elders and be proven to be just exactly that?"

"Red Wolf was told to be here," one of the elders said. It was the first time any of them had spoken since Crow had begun, and the sound of his voice caught Hawk by surprise.

"Red Wolf is supposed to be here?" Hawk repeated.

The eyes of the council turned to Hawk. Not having been asked to speak, he showed either a lack of understanding of the ways of the Sioux or a disrespect for their customs to do so. Crow turned to look at Hawk and, without words, warned Hawk with his eyes not to speak again unless asked.

Hawk couldn't be bothered with the customs he might be violating or the propriety he was offending. Instinctively, he knew that Red Wolf was up to something, that he had some devious plot in mind and perhaps was even now putting it into

motion. What could be so vital that Red Wolf would miss this?
He had, with his lies, turned Hawk's reputation into a sham-
bles. Now he could be finishing Hawk's destruction, before
the elders, by voicing his "concern" for the safety and integrity
of the tribe. Instead, he was allowing Hawk to clear his own
name without rebuttal. Why? What could be so compelling?

Reactions circulating through the group in the tepee flowed
over Hawk, and though the significance for his future could
not be overestimated, he didn't listen to a single word.

Hawk asked himself: What does Red Wolf want most in this
world? An answer came instantly to mind: to destroy me. Then
he asked himself: What would destroy me? At first he thought
of the obvious—murder. But then another thought came to
mind, and it was so blood-chilling that Hawk, though he was
a brave man who had faced mortal danger without blinking,
shivered. What would destroy him, sentence him to a living
hell, was not the loss of his own life . . . but the loss of
Samantha's.

"I have to leave!" Hawk jumped to his feet, addressing
Crow, who immediately caught Hawk's wrist to prevent him
from walking out of the tepee. "I have to leave," Hawk repeated, more quietly this time, though everyone in the tepee
could still hear him.

Crow's eyes were dark as midnight. Though he was a man
who took pride in never—not *ever*—losing his temper, his
words hissed between teeth clenched in absolute fury. "You
*will not leave!* Not now! If you leave now, you'll make yourself
look more guilty to these men by your actions than by anything
Red Wolf has said!"

Hawk looked around at the faces of the tribal elders. He
could not tell how many understood English well enough to
follow Crow's words. All Hawk was certain of was that he did
not care. He didn't care if the elders thought he was guilty of
every crime known to the Sioux, or even the white man. All
that mattered and motivated him was the fact that Red Wolf
wasn't in the tepee when he should have been.

Hawk shook his arm free from Crow's grip. "I'm sorry," he said, leaving his friend in a terrible position with the elders, yet seeing no other course of action open to him. "I'm sorry, but I *have* to go. I think Samantha's in danger."

"How?"

"Where's Red Wolf?" The instant Hawk's question was voiced, Crow saw the progression of his thoughts. "Keep the elders here as long as you can." Hawk garbled his speech just enough to make his words impossible to understand unless a listener spoke English fluently. "I'll look guilty by leaving, so you've got to convince them that I had to go get something and that I'll be back. Make up any story you think is convincing. I'm going after Samantha. I think that's where Red Wolf is headed right now."

"He's more than an hour ahead of you," Crow said.

In the next instant Hawk was out of the tepee, pausing only for a moment to hear the beginning of Crow's eloquent, though rambling, explanation of why Hawk Two Feather, esteemed hunter and loyal warrior for the Sioux, would leave the presence of the tribal elders without asking permission. Hawk smiled grimly to himself, wondering what kind of lie Crow was about to give, then began jogging to his tepee. First, he would get his weapons, then his stallion, and then, if he was lucky, he would ride to the cave where Samantha and Aja were hiding and discover that his fears were groundless.

But as a Sioux, for whom a feeling was as good as a fact, he knew in his soul that Samantha was in danger, and that Red Wolf was the cause of it.

# Thirty-two

"Someone's following us," Samantha said. The words had simply entered her head, and it was only later, after she'd heard what she'd said, that she felt fear.

Aja reined in her pinto, turning the animal around to align it with Samantha's Daisy. Aja looked back into the foothills they'd just ridden through and saw no evidence of horse or rider. "Where?" she asked, "My eyes do not see what yours do."

Samantha apologized. She had always been a woman who spoke first and decided later whether it might have been better to remain silent. She looked back into the foothills, searching for the source of her concern.

"I . . . I don't see anything either," Samantha concluded. She was about to turn Daisy around and continue on her way toward the cave, but Aja stopped her.

"Perhaps you are looking with your eyes instead of your mind," Aja said, still staring intently into the foothills. "Your mind and soul can see that which your eyes cannot."

Samantha tried to dismiss her worries as unfounded, but the sense of unease would not leave her. She wished that Hawk was with her. When he was near, even if the enemy was many and mighty, she felt confident, sure that Hawk would think of some brilliant strategy with which to either defeat or elude them.

"How far do you think we are from the cave?" Samantha

wasn't disguising her concern now, which was infectious enough to affect Aja.

Aja pulled the crudely drawn map from her parafleche and unfolded it. She looked up from the map to check the twin mountain peaks that were their destination. The trek would become progressively slower as the ascent grew steadily steeper. "At least two hours, provided . . ."

"Provided we don't get lost?"

Aja grinned nervously, trying hard to maintain the same brave front as Samantha.

"Don't worry, we won't get lost," Samantha assured her, tapping her heels to Daisy's ribs. "You shouldn't let imaginary worries play on your mind. Soon enough, you'll have a man in your life. That's when you'll *really* have something to worry about!"

Resisting every urge to look over her shoulder, Samantha forced herself to pretend that she felt no fear. It was bad enough that she was worried; she didn't want to incite Aja's fears as well. So, though she did not feel at all lighthearted, Samantha kept up a continuous stream of stories for Aja regarding the wedding, and how handsome a figure Hawk had cut in the immaculate suit he had complained about constantly.

"It didn't bother you that the ladies were all looking at him?" Aja's fears were abating now, with Samantha's storytelling. Adoring her half brother, she believed him to be the most handsome man in the world, and she loved hearing tales of what he was like away from the tribe.

"At first it did a little, I guess," Samantha admitted, "but then I realized that it didn't matter how many women were looking at Hawk so long as he was only looking at me."

Aja laughed softly. As Samantha twisted in the saddle to look back at her, a movement caught her eye, far off in the foothills. Studying the area where the motion had come from, she again saw nothing unusual. The movement could have been caused by anything from a mule deer or a coyote to dried brush tossed about by the wind.

"Was my brother really nervous before the wedding?" Aja asked, mischief in her voice.

She loved hearing how her warrior brother, who had ridden so often into battle without blinking an eye, had paced nervously back and forth with tension. Samantha had decided *that* version of how Hawk had dealt with his nervous tension was better for Aja to hear than what had actually transpired just prior to the wedding ceremony.

"Incredibly so," Samantha said as she repeated the fabrication of only a few minutes before.

Hawk's great stallion—lathered, with its enormous chest heaving and its nostrils flaring, as powerful muscles propelled horse and rider ever higher—had to be making ground on Red Wolf. Without any actual proof that the renegade Sioux warrior was after Samantha and Aja, Hawk knew it in his heart.

Around his hips hung his holstered revolver. The heavy-caliber Colt was the only weapon he had grabbed before rushing out of the camp. What weapons did Red Wolf have with him? Hawk clenched his teeth as he thought of Red Wolf's suspicious behavior and his unwillingness to fight just before the meeting with the elders.

As he was cursing himself for what he could not possibly have known, Hawk's stallion made an odd, sideways movement. Years of riding experience kept Hawk in the saddle, but the stallion's stride had changed just enough for Hawk to know that something was wrong.

"Come on, boy," Hawk urged, leaning low over the stallion's neck and imploring the spirits to banish the hitch in the animal's gait.

He waited five more strides, and when the slight hitch in the stallion's stride became a limp he could no longer pretend to not know what had happened. He reined the horse to a stop, though the stallion at first resisted him. The two had been together long enough for the stallion to sense his master's urgency, and the horse possessed the same restless spirit that his master did.

Hawk dismounted, then raised the stallion's front left hoof to look at the underside. There, near the soft inner circle, was the stone bruise, already beginning to swell and discolor. Hawk cursed, his eyes squeezing shut for only an instant as the consequences of the minor injury washed over him like a tidal wave.

Hawk was now on foot. Even if he had been cruel enough to continue riding the stallion, pushing the animal onward, it would have been only a matter of time—and very little time at that—before the hoof's swelling would cause the stallion to be in constant, increasing pain. Before long, not even the stallion's great will to run would be enough to keep him pushing onward. The only remedy for a stone bruise was time and rest.

"Go on, boy," Hawk ordered.

The stallion pranced a few steps to the side but did not go on. He turned huge brown eyes on his master, willing to push on despite the pain.

"Go on, I said!" Hawk slapped the animal's rump hard, and this time the stallion headed back toward camp.

Hawk turned uphill and tried to calculate how much time he had before sundown. Once the sun went down, his dangers—and the dangers for Samantha and Aja—would become increasingly ominous. Ahead was the woman he loved enough to make her his wife. Also ahead was the only man in the world Hawk wished he had killed when he'd the chance.


Red Wolf knelt to inspect the tracks more closely. The rocky ground made it difficult to trail riders, though the task was made slightly easier because Samantha's mare was shod. Horseshoes tended to leave marks on the rocks that unshod hooves would not.

How far ahead were Samantha and Aja? Where were the two women headed? Near the dry bluffs? That was a possibility to which Red Wolf didn't give much consideration. The dry bluffs weren't fit for man or beast. But there was . . . the high cave? Red Wolf had once tracked Crow to find out where he went when he left camp. Though he'd lost Crow several days later, Red Wolf had discovered a cave, looking as though it had held a recent occupant. If Crow knew about the cave, then so did Hawk, Red Wolf reasoned. Perhaps the women were going to the cave.

If that was the case, then Red Wolf knew a shortcut, making it possible for him to beat the women to their destination!

Red Wolf climbed back onto his pinto. A cruel smile tightened his lips. The lies he'd been telling about Hawk would soon come completely unraveled; Red Wolf knew and understood this, accepting it as fact. Once Crow got to talking, using skills he'd learned in the white man's schools and courts of law, the inconsistencies would become increasingly obvious until, at last, the old men would have no choice but to eventually come to the conclusion that Red Wolf was the liar, the threat to the tribe, the one worthy of being tossed out of the camp, naked, without weapons to defend himself, clothes to warm himself, a horse to carry him.

But the elders would come to this conclusion too late. By the time the old men had discussed his fate, after a long and painful deliberation, Red Wolf would already have ridden many, many miles to the south. He would abandon the tribe before the tribe cast him out . . . but he would leave them with something to remember him by. He would exact his revenge upon Hawk, and the rest of the tribe, by attacking Samantha and Aja.

Now the spirits were conspiring together with Red Wolf to make his vicious dreams come true, he thought. Though Samantha and Aja had a sizable lead on him, Red Wolf believed he knew where they were headed and his confidence was soaring. Now that they had ridden away from camp without either Hawk or Crow to escort them, the spirits were telling him that he was justified in taking his revenge upon Hawk's two women.

Red Wolf kicked his pony with his heels, urging the animal on. It was all perfectly fitting, he thought. He was riding a pony stolen by Hawk. In time, he would capture Hawk's sister and wife. And with them under his power, he would prove he was many times the warrior Hawk was. And once he'd convinced them of his superiority, he would kill.

That accomplished, he would ride south. He would ride hard and fast, with the thousand dollars he'd stolen from Dull Knife's tepee to help him forget that he was a warrior without a tribe, a man whose name was a curse, his existence a blight.

He pushed up the foothills, his eyes searching for the women. In a corner of his mind he pondered a single question: Would he force Samantha to satisfy his desires first, or would he first teach Aja a lesson in humiliation?


Samantha looked up at the rock formation and smiled. It was exactly as Hawk had described it: two large boulders standing with a flat boulder lying atop both, creating a natural archway.

"There it is," Samantha breathed softly, pointing to the archway. "Hawk's hiding place. We're safe at last." Trying to sound confident, she really only sounded relieved.

"I knew Hawk wouldn't let us down," Aja replied. She rushed forward to inspect the cave, part of her enormously pleased that her brother had discovered a place so secret and private, and part of her irked that he would have kept this wonderful spot from her all these years.

Samantha looked around, still not certain that the cave was such a secret. There was no source of water, and if the wind blew strong and cold from the north, the cave itself would be unbearable. But taking those factors into account and planning for them, one could use the cave as a safe haven of warmth and security.

She looked to the west and smiled. In only a few minutes the sun would settle beneath the horizon, and then the narrow arroyo where Hawk's cave was hidden would be plunged into darkness. Then she and Aja could pass the time sharing stories until Hawk at last put an end to all the damaging rumors that had been spread about him.

"Take the water in first," Samantha said, dismounting. "Once we take care of the horses for the night we can finally relax."

Samantha looked around the arroyo one more time before starting to remove Daisy's saddle. She still felt something . . . but what? She was confident that she hadn't allowed anyone to follow them.

She heard a sound from inside the cave, and Samantha's heart skipped a beat. Then she recognized the sound, and sighed. Aja had dropped the water pouch. Samantha wondered what problems the inaccessibility of water would cause, but dismissed the matter from her immediate concern. Whatever was necessary would have to wait until the morning.

"Aja, are you all right in there?" Samantha called out after a moment.

There was no answer. Samantha glanced into the black entrance of the cave, and frowned. Then she removed the saddle from Daisy.

"Aja?"

Still no answer. Samantha felt a coldness in her stomach and a tightness in her throat. She dropped the saddle to the ground and took a single step toward the cave. Then Aja stepped out, with Red Wolf directly behind her, his arm around her throat and a huge knife in his right hand, the point of the blade held against her ribs.

"Damn you!" Samantha hissed, frozen in midstride.

"He wanted me to tell you to come into the cave, but I wouldn't," Aja said, her eyes wild with fear.

Red Wolf shook Aja so that her entire body quivered, her

toes barely touching the ground. Both her hands clutched the forearm, thick with muscle, that pressed against her throat.

"Don't hurt her," Samantha said, her voice deceptively calm and quiet. She raised her hands toward Red Wolf, fingers spread to show that she held no weapons. "She's only a child!"

The grin Red Wolf showed Samantha was pure evil. "She is old enough for me," he said softly, malevolently, tightening his arm around Aja's throat. "When I am finished she will feel like an old woman!"

He laughed then, and Samantha knew deep in her heart that Red Wolf was mad. She had heard about men like him, men who possessed no sense of right and wrong, and standing face to face with such evil made her shiver.

"My horse is over that rise," Red Wolf said, nodding to the left, where more boulders had been piled by nature. "Get him and bring him to me. If you don't hurry, I will kill her. You know I will."

"Don't do it, Samantha," Aja warned. "Run while you have the chance."

Red Wolf shook Aja again, and pressed his knife more securely, causing her to gasp softly. Though she was trying to pretend the blade pressing against her ribs didn't hurt, she could not hide the pain.

"Hurry, I say!" Red Wolf hissed, his eyes brilliant, demonic. "She would not be the first squaw I have put my knife through!"

Samantha knew that Red Wolf was telling the truth. Looking into his eyes she saw a man who enjoyed inflicting pain, especially when there was no chance that he would be hurt himself. She ran to the rise and saw the horse. The animal was nervous, sensing danger, as Samantha brought it back to the entrance of the cave.

"I've done what you've asked." Samantha approached Red Wolf and Aja slowly. There was a rifle in a scabbard affixed to the horse's saddle, but she made no effort to remove it.

"Your rifle is still where you put it. I can't hurt you . . . so why don't you let her go?"

"Inside," Red Wolf said, his grin even more broad and wicked as his victory seemed imminent. "You will soon learn what it is to be with a real warrior!"

Samantha looked from Red Wolf to Aja. The girl was terrified, her young body rigid with fear. She looked to Samantha as though for salvation.

"Let her go," Samantha said with quiet authority. She knew there was a chance her tone would anger Red Wolf, but she had to risk it to save Aja. "She's not the one you want. It's me you want, because you hate Hawk. Isn't that so?"

Red Wolf was half hidden in the shadows at the mouth of the cave, and his teeth shone eerily white in the darkness as he smiled. "You are wise for a squaw."

"Yes, I am wise. I know how to please a man," Samantha replied, and the sound and meaning of her words made her sick to her stomach. Already she felt violated, even though she hadn't been touched. "Why waste your time with a girl who knows nothing when you can be with a woman who knows everything?"

"Hawk has taught you well?" Red Wolf asked, the tone of his voice curious, envious.

"Hawk has taught me *everything*," Samantha replied. She took several steps forward, letting the reins of Red Wolf's pinto fall from her fingertips. She exaggerated the sway of her hips as she walked, and hated herself just a little for the seductive way she gazed at Red Wolf and moistened her lips. "And I've liked what I've learned . . . and you will, too."

They were words no beautiful woman had ever spoken to Red Wolf. Not even the prostitutes he'd bought had been able to say such words so convincingly—even though he'd demanded it of them. With Samantha almost within arm's reach of him, he could hardly wait to touch her, to feel her voluptuous body crushed beneath his. He had dreamed that he would teach her what it was like to be with a real warrior, but now he wondered whether she would be the one to teach him what pleasures of the flesh were possible.

"Just let the girl go," Samantha said, her voice still a seductive whisper. "She means nothing to either of us. She'll only get in the way, don't you see?"

Red Wolf needed a free hand and he had none. He had chosen to use the knife because it was his favorite weapon, so deadly, so personal. And it was especially gratifying to know that it was Dull Knife's weapon that he now held in his hand. Though he felt the warmth of Aja's young body, her back against his chest, suddenly she was not as desirable as she had once seemed.

"Go inside," Red Wolf demanded of Samantha, his eyes wide with a feral light.

"Let her go first," Samantha replied in a sultry purr, keeping just out of arm's reach from Red Wolf. "She'll only get in the way of what we want to do."

She could see that the arm around Aja's throat wasn't as tight as it had been, and though Red Wolf continued to hold the large-bladed knife in his hand, the deadly point was no longer touching Aja's ribs.

Red Wolf almost released Aja then. He was almost willing to take his arm from her throat and set her free because Samantha's words had sounded so sensual, so enticing. But then it struck Red Wolf that she was just like all the prostitutes he'd ever been with, her words a sensual experience in themselves, her actions as beguiling as any man could desire . . . right up to the moment that money changed hands. Then she became just another prostitute in a hurry to satisfy her customer so that she could be done with him.

"I cannot be tricked by a white woman!" Red Wolf spat, his eyes glowing orange like the embers of a campfire. "Go into the cave!"

He reached for Samantha, attempting to hold the heavy knife in one hand as he tried to catch the sleeve of her shirt in the fingers of the other hand. Samantha didn't hesitate to make her move. She lashed out at Red Wolf's wrist, hitting it with all her might. The knife twirled out of his grasp.

"Run, Aja!" Samantha shouted, lunging at Red Wolf, her fingers curled as she clawed at his eyes.

Samantha felt the soft tissue of Red Wolf's face tear beneath her fingernails, then felt the warrior's fist slam into her stomach, knocking the breath from her lungs. Her knees buckled beneath her, but she still managed to shout for Aja to run one more time as she continued her struggle with the renegade Sioux.

She wasn't entirely certain what happened next because Red Wolf's fist struck a glancing blow against the top of her head. But an instant later it was she who had her back to Red Wolf, his forearm tight across her throat. He'd recovered his knife and was brandishing it against her cheek. Through blurred vision, she watched as Aja disappeared out of the cave.

"Run!" she cried triumphantly.

Red Wolf was hissing into Samantha's ear, words she didn't understand, although their meaning was clear: he was going to punish her for freeing Aja. Samantha had done what she had to do, what her sense of honor and her heart had dictated, and if she had to pay a price for her actions now, then so be it.

When Aja had almost disappeared into the darkness outside she stopped and looked back into the cave. Samantha could see the fear in her eyes. She didn't want to leave.

"Go!" Samantha shouted, and for her defiance, Red Wolf shook her hard, the arm around her throat tightening so that she could hardly breathe.

"Come back or I will cut her!" Red Wolf shouted.

Aja turned away and disappeared into the night, and Samantha felt an almost overpowering sense of accomplishment, of victory over evil. "You still have me," Samantha said after a moment, though Red Wolf continued cursing in Sioux. Now that Aja was safe, Samantha was already thinking of a way to free herself.

"She's gone," Samantha said quietly, feeling the razor-sharp blade against her cheek. "There's nothing you can do about that now. But you've still got me, Red Wolf."

"You will suffer. When I am done Hawk will hate the sight of you."

Samantha had no doubt that Red Wolf had made others suffer so. He pushed her toward his pinto, which had been spooked when Aja had bolted from the cave.

At that moment Hawk appeared out of the shadows, like the embodiment of vengeance. He held his revolver in his hand, though it was not pointed at Red Wolf.

Red Wolf spotted Hawk a moment after Samantha did. He flinched and bent his knees so that he was partially hidden behind Samantha's body. He brought the knife around, touching the point to her back.

"Let her go, Red Wolf," Hawk said, moving slowly, thirty feet still separating him from the man he now wished he'd killed when he'd had the chance not many days before. "Let her go now and I will not kill you."

Red Wolf moved his right hand just enough to show Hawk that he held a knife to Samantha's body. As she looked helplessly at Hawk, Red Wolf's chin was nearly touching her shoulder. His grin remained cruel.

"Drop the gun," Red Wolf said. As frightened as he was of Hawk, he was nearly giddy now that he had his rival in a position where he could finally be rid of him for good. He hadn't thought that he'd be able to defeat his greatest enemy before riding out of the territory forever. "Drop the gun or I'll cut her right now! You cannot stop me. Do as I command!"

Hawk didn't drop his gun, though he did holster the weapon. He saw that Red Wolf had Dull Knife's knife in his hand, and in an instant he realized who had killed the wise chieftain. Hawk felt his heart tighten at the thought of Dull Knife's senseless death.

"Toss the gun away!" Red Wolf snapped, bringing the

deadly edge of his blade once more to Samantha's cheek. "Do it or you'll watch her bleed!"

Hawk shook his head slowly. He had delayed long enough so that his breathing was now almost normal. His eyes locked with Red Wolf's, he slowly walked forward, his hands hanging limp at his sides, his posture indicating a man at ease, though Samantha knew that this wasn't the case.

"Let her go." Hawk spoke a little louder than he had before. "I'll kill you if you spill a single drop of her blood. You know that is true."

"She will die before your eyes if you take another step." Red Wolf spoke in a flat, level tone, equal to Hawk's. Each of the old, hated enemies knew exactly how far the other could be pushed. "Now take the gun from your holster and drop it. Do it before I cut her just to hear the sound of her screams in my ears."

Samantha expected Hawk to do as he had been commanded to. She knew he loved her, and that he would do anything to see to it that she was safe. But instead of tossing the Colt to the ground, Hawk simply stood there, shaking his head slowly, his eyes boring into Red Wolf's.

For an instant Samantha squeezed her eyes shut. Why wasn't Hawk doing as he'd been told? Did he want to see her hurt?

"Let her go," Hawk said, taking yet another step closer to Red Wolf and Samantha. "Do it now and I give you my word of honor that I will not harm you."

"Your word? What good is your word?"

"You know what it is!" Hawk shot back quickly, stepping closer to reduce the distance between them to less than twenty-five feet. "It is my life. You cannot say as much. Your honor is without value! You are no more trusted than a white man!"

Red Wolf's body tightened from head to toe at the insult. He had been called many things during his life, but never had a half-breed Sioux—one born a bastard, of all things—dared say that he was lower than a white man.

"Can you make it?" Red Wolf said after a moment, his

voice tight and strained, a twisted smile curling his lips. "Can you make the shot, Hawk? It is what you are thinking. Do not tell me you are not asking yourself whether your skill is enough to save your life and end mine."

At first Samantha didn't understand what the men were talking about. Make the shot? Hawk had no shot to make, she thought. Red Wolf was completely hidden behind her, with the exception of his head. He was using her as a shield, his cheek pressed against her ear . . . too close to her, surely, for Hawk to risk firing his revolver.

Samantha had become a pawn in a gigantic, all-too-real chess game, with life and death stakes. She wanted to close her eyes to shut out the horror, but she didn't dare. She wanted to scream, but her throat had tightened to make breathing difficult, and speech impossible.

Hawk was standing with his feet spread slightly apart, his hands held away from his hips, the handle of his revolver inches from his grasp.

"Are you that good, Hawk?" Red Wolf asked, then chuckled. "If you miss, you will shoot your wife. I have killed women before . . . have you?"

Samantha had heard enough. Red Wolf was beyond pure evil. If she allowed him to live, if she did anything that would make it possible for him to go on in his villainy she knew she could never forgive herself.

"Do it," she said to Hawk.

At that moment a doe sprinted out of the shadows. Red Wolf's attention was diverted for only an instant.

The move was so quick that Samantha hardly saw it. One second Red Wolf had his face pressed up tight against hers, his big, lethal knife ready to take her life with just a flick of his wrist. But Hawk moved so swiftly his action was just a blur, and then there was an enormous roar as his revolver fired a single deadly bullet. Red Wolf's head snapped back on his shoulders.

Samantha waited, afraid to turn around, fearful that some-

how Red Wolf would still be behind her, his deadly knife still
in his hand.

"It's over," Hawk assured her, holstering his weapon as he
rushed forward to take Samantha into his arms. "It's all over,
Samantha."

Samantha was too frightened and too relieved to cry. The
doe, as promised in the vision quest, had saved her life because
she'd trusted her love. She buried her face in Hawk's neck and
held on to him tightly, her arms encircling his waist. When
she could hear Aja to her right, crying softly, she reached out
a hand for the girl.

"We're together now," Samantha whispered, not taking her
face away from Hawk's neck even to speak. "Nobody can separate us again. Promise me that."

"I promise," Hawk whispered, his arms so tight around
Samantha that they nearly crushed her. "Together for always."

# Epilogue

It was the first snow of the winter, and Samantha was oddly pleased to watch the heavy white flakes drifting to the ground. When she had lived near Deadwood in her big, comfortable ranch house she had hated the coming of winter. The long, cold days with nothing much to keep her occupied had lay ahead. Boredom, more than the cold and the snow, was her enemy.

But it would be different this winter. She was at work stitching together a heavy elk hide cape that would keep her warm, and Aja had already made her a pair of oversized moccasins that, when properly insulated with prairie grass, would be considerably warmer than any boots Samantha had ever owned. Aja had promised it. The cape would keep her warm in the strongest winter winds, and was large enough to allow for her expanding waistline.

Samantha patted her belly, a faint smile curling her lips. Hawk's vision quest had come true, she realized. He'd had the vision of an eagle in a hawk's nest, with a small dove just peeking its head over the rim of the nest. Samantha believed that she represented the eagle in Hawk's nest, and the dove—the Dove of Peace—was the child now growing within her. That child, Samantha believed, would bring peace to the Sioux, would be a bridge between the two cultures that all too often had been at war with each other.

The sound of an approaching horse drew Samantha's attention, and she looked up to see Hawk approaching. A smile curved his lips, though concern darkened his eyes as he dismounted.

"You should put on something warmer," he said, taking long strides to where she was kneeling just outside the tepee they shared. "There is a chill in the air."

From inside the tepee Aja began to laugh. "You are sounding more like a father all the time!" she teased her half brother

Samantha made no effort to suppress her grin. "She's right you know. There's no need to worry so much about me."

Hawk got down on one knee beside his wife. He placed a hand gently upon her slightly rounded stomach. "I only worry because you have never spent a winter in a tepee. You don' know how difficult it can be, especially carrying a baby."

Samantha pressed her palm against her husband's cheek. Since he had discovered that he was going to be a father, he'c become very concerned with her happiness and comfort, anc for that she was eternally grateful.

"I keep telling you that I've never been so happy in my life I wish you'd believe me. In the spring, after the baby is born maybe we can return to the Circle S, if that's what you really want to do. But I'm perfectly content here. In fact, I've neve felt so happy." When she passed the pad of her thumb across Hawk's lips he kissed it. "Truly. I have never been so happy."

Hawk bent to kiss his wife, and Aja stepped out of the tepee

"Are you two kissing again?" she teased.

Hawk shot his sister a comically stern look and replied "There's going to come a day when I'll disturb you every time you try to kiss the person you love; then we'll see how funny you think it is!"

"Enough now, both of you!" Samantha interrupted, enjoying the almost continual banter between brother and sister. They were her family now, and soon there would be another addition a beautiful child who would bring peace to the land that hac known little peace in many years.

peak

# TODAY'S HOTTEST READS
# ARE TOMORROW'S SUPERSTARS

**VICTORY'S WOMAN**                                    (4484, $4.50)
by Gretchen Genet
Andrew—the carefree soldier who sought glory on the battlefield,
and returned a shattered man . . . Niall—the legandary frontiers-
man and a former Shawnee captive, tormented by his past . . .
Roger—the troubled youth, who would rise up to claim a shocking legacy . . . and Clarice—the passionate beauty bound by one
man, and hopelessly in love with another. Set against the back-
drop of the American revolution, three men fight for their
heritage—and one woman is destined to change all their lives forever!

**FORBIDDEN**                                          (4488, $4.99)
by Jo Beverley
While fleeing from her brothers, who are attempting to sell her
into a loveless marriage, Serena Riverton accepts a carriage ride
from a stranger—who is the handsomest man she has ever seen.
Lord Middlethorpe, himself, is actually contemplating marriage
to a dull daughter of the aristocracy, when he encounters the
breathtaking Serena. She arouses him as no woman ever has. And
after a night of thrilling intimacy—a forbidden liaison—Serena
must choose between a lady's place and a woman's passion!

**WINDS OF DESTINY**                                   (4489, $4.99)
by Victoria Thompson
Becky Tate is a half-breed outcast—branded by her Comanche
heritage. Then she meets a rugged stranger who awakens her
heart to the magic and mystery of passion. Hiding a desperate
past, Texas Ranger Clint Masterson has ridden into cattle country
to bring peace to a divided land. But a greater battle rages inside
him when he dares to desire the beautiful Becky!

**WILDEST HEART**                                      (4456, $4.99)
by Virginia Brown
Maggie Malone had come to cattle country to forge her future as
a healer. Now she was faced by Devon Conrad, an outlaw
wounded body and soul by his shadowy past . . . whose eyes
blazed with fury even as his burning caress sent her spiraling with
desire. They came together in a Texas town about to explode in sin
and scandal. Danger was their destiny—and there was nothing
they wouldn't dare for love!

*Available wherever paperbacks are sold, or order direct from the
Publisher. Send cover price plus 50¢ per copy for mailing and
handling to Penguin USA, P.O. Box 999, c/o Dept. 17109,
Bergenfield, NJ 07621. Residents of New York and Tennessee
must include sales tax. DO NOT SEND CASH.*